BOUND

The Silverton Chronicles

CARMEN FOX

Bound
Copyright © 2016 by Carmen Fox All rights reserved.
Website: www.carmen-fox.com
First Print Edition: 2016

Editors: Dylan Quinn and Monique Fischer

ISBN: 978-0-9931992-9-5

Genre: Urban Fantasy Romance

Cover design by Ana Grigoriu

Formatting: Streetlight Graphics

First published by Smart Heart Publishing 2016

To Nana

WYWH

CHAPTER ONE

I SUCKED IN A HUGE BREATH of helium from the tank.

"Why are we doing this again?" I asked in a high-pitched voice. My head spun, but it was totally worth it.

Ivy punched me in the arm. "If you could be serious for a second, you'd realize it's necessary. You can't just stomp into another pack and demand they join yours. They need to be schmoozed."

"Schmoozed?" Eyebrows raised, I wrinkled my nose.

"It's a word."

"Yes, but at this time in the morning, your sentences usually consist of grunting and the word 'coffee.'"

Ivy poked her tongue out at me. She was on the short side, but had the inner strength of a soldier. And the body of a goddess.

I might not be interested in her *that* way, but I wasn't blind to her attributes either.

Parker entered the multi-purpose hall and tilted his head up at the streamers. "Is this really necessary?"

Blue and yellow balloons lay scattered across the floor, while banners and pens cluttered the table.

"Her fault." I pointed at Ivy. "She made me."

Parker let out a low growl, and I scooted behind the helium tank.

"Come here." Ivy stood on her toes to demand a kiss from him.

He complied, and the kissing sounds forced my attention back to the balloons.

When they came up for air, Parker brushed his thumb over Ivy's chin. "The place looks good." He smiled.

Typical. Ivy got away with anything. And unless I seriously rethought my lifestyle choices, I'd have to suck it up.

Parker strode into the corner and stood, arms crossed, to survey the goings-on. Today he wore jeans, T-shirt, and a scowl—his idea of casualwear. Ten recessed lights illuminated the room, including the two picnic tables I'd pushed together last night as a makeshift bar.

Voices drifted in from the door. Around twelve *James Bond*

lookalikes crowded into the room, carrying an assortment of knives and other weapons. One waved at me with his dagger.

Ivy met my glance and shrugged.

After living with the werewolves for a while, we'd become a lot more accepting of their quirks.

I moved to Ali's side. His raven hair shrouded his ears and framed a face that always found a smile for me. The son of Indonesian immigrants, Ali grew up an orphan after his parents had been killed when he was six, yet his dark past never got him down.

"The guys are taking this party very seriously, don't you think?" I hopped and landed ass first on the sturdy windowsill next to him.

His shirt was a crisp white, his slacks wrinkle-free. The dude didn't own a single sloganed T-shirt. Most werewolves preferred the scruffy look, but Ali never let me down. He and I were the style police, sadly without any real-life powers.

He tied off a balloon then leaned toward me. "You're the one throwing the party. They're simply preparing for our guests' arrival."

"Right." I dangled my legs. "Do we know any more about the trespassers? One guy said they're camped out in the clearing on the far side of the river, but I'd like a bit more intel before going in."

"Not really. It's Rollo's old pack. You know, the one that kicked him out when he was young? I hear it's run by a woman now."

Ali's tone remained measured, but his inner turmoil spilled into me, making my skin itch with an energy that wasn't my own. Ever since an ancient werewolf commitment ritual had made me part of the pack, Ali had been hijacking my emotions, and I his.

Living in a large community surrounded by friends was perfect. Sharing my innermost neuroses with someone wasn't. I'd spent six months trying to figure out how to cut my and Ali's link without the approval from the pack's Elders—Studied ancient books, quizzed just about every werewolf, I even had Ivy use her contacts to dig into the secret. All it got me was a total brain freeze. No plan.

Sometimes magic wasn't as wonderful as *Disney* would have us believe.

"A woman leading a pack?" I rested my back against the cool windowpane. "I didn't know that was possible."

Ali nodded. "All we know for sure is she killed their old alpha. The rest is rumor and speculation."

"Has anyone talked to her?"

"That's. Your. Job." He poked my chest on every syllable.

"Oh and here I assumed you kept me around for my sparkling personality."

"Yup, that's the reason, all right." He flashed his teeth. "And I thought we were being subtle."

"You sound like you're making fun of me, but I think deep down you're serious." I glanced at the alpha in the corner. "Why does Parker want their pack to join ours anyway? This place is crowded enough already."

My room was basically a glorified broom closet.

"Many reasons. The more members a pack has, the higher its standing among werewolf society. Our scouts tell us they're a small pack, so they're probably here looking for protection anyway. Then there's the security issue. We are the largest and strongest pack out there, and letting outsiders occupy our territory sets a dangerous precedent." Ali looked at his fellow werewolves. "But a new pack also means new females, which is getting our guys very excited. You know how rare females are."

I jerked my head toward Zac and Freddy, the poor werewolves Ivy had roped into helping her. "So that's why everyone's rolling up their sleeves."

"Yeah."

"And the weapons?"

"Ceremonial. They're meant to impress, not to intimidate." Ali squinted and traced two fingers over his lips. "But listen. Even though I don't foresee any problems, uniting two packs is a delicate undertaking. So make sure to dot the I's and cross the T's."

"Are you coming?"

"No. Parker needs me here. Besides, this situation requires tact, and a certain amount of charm." Ali shot me a smile that made me shift nervously, because in it I read hope for a relationship that would never be.

"You should leave now." He looked at the assortment of wannabe spies.

"Yes, sir." I saluted, then slipped off my seat and shook out my legs. "Wish me luck."

With a last glance at Ivy and her life-or-death struggle with a stubborn balloon, I took off across the vast room.

Living among werewolves was a blast, but some behaviors still baffled me. A shindig was good for the soul, no question, but the knives seemed total overkill. To court the ladies, flowers and a few glasses of wine had a much better chance of success, at least in my experience.

That was my motto. Charm first, then the whip.

In a way, it was a miracle Ivy had convinced Parker to try the party, instead of going in guns blazing. Well, maybe not that much of a miracle. Any excuse to party, and werewolves were first in line at the kegger. But for Parker, dealing with the intruders was a priority. In fact, the whole pack buzzed with anxiety and anticipation.

I headed up the stone stairs to slip into a leather jacket that said casual, but authoritative—actually, it said *Ted Baker*—and left to complete my mission.

The sun's rays filtered through the foliage of the woods behind the pack's mansion, but they failed to warm my naturally cold skin to human temperature, even with the jacket.

Just one downside of being a vampire.

I wasn't the most obvious person to negotiate on behalf of, or with, werewolves. Too often, their kind took offense at my vampireness, but I could pull this off. After all, diplomacy was in my wheelhouse.

That's how packs worked. Everyone did their part.

As alpha, Parker pointed the way. In his spare time, he ran a multimillion-dollar business with enough assets to make our pack the envy of others. When Rollo wasn't enforcing pack law, he was in charge of electronics. Ali took care of the books. And I made parking tickets disappear and mediated confrontations.

Who would have guessed my association with the pack would become a long-term arrangement anyway? Ivy and I joined the pack in a ritual that transferred our magic powers to Parker. He'd needed the help after Ivy brought a statue into his house that turned out more dangerous than it looked.

The idea was simple. Do the ritual, destroy the object. Then we wait for the Elders' approval to disband our link.

Except that's not what happened.

Ivy and Parker maintained their new connection for obvious reasons. Hell, you couldn't separate those two with a crowbar. As for Ali and me... Maybe the paperwork hadn't cleared, or the Elders were on vacation, but for whatever reason, they had yet to consent.

"What are you doing here?" Rollo's voice startled me from my mental black hole.

He sat against the trunk of a tree, knees drawn to his chest. The toes of his sneakers burrowed into the ground, while he plucked at the grass. His impressive size was one of the reasons he'd become Parker's number one enforcer. The frayed shorts Rollo loved so much were his disguise. Even I had thought him no more than your typical blond-haired, beach-tanned surfer dude when I first met him.

But then, wasn't that what clothes were designed for? To make us into the person we wanted to be, not who we actually were?

"The question is what are *you* doing here?" I joined Rollo on the cold grass, which was still wet from morning dew.

"I have the mother of all hangovers." He rubbed a blood-shot eye. "You missed one hell of a party last night."

I frowned. "I was there."

"I meant after you went to bed. Piss-poor stamina, dude." He nudged me.

"Says the guy who, just last week, admitted defeat after his fourth round of shots. Seriously pathetic." I grinned. "Anyway, Ali told me about your problem. Family, man. Never easy. Have you spoken to your old pack?"

His shoulders jerked. "We're not supposed to."

I tugged on my jeans to unsquash my balls. "You didn't answer my question."

"You noticed that, huh?" Rollo cocked his chin to the right then winced. "My head hurts. Let's not talk about this."

And Ali says I'm the one who's emotionally unavailable?

"I'll take your non-answer as a yes." I flicked dirt off my pant leg. "So what happened? Why did they kick you out?"

Rollo tapped a finger on his knee, as if counting the bones in it. Leaned forward. Back. And let out a stream of air.

"Garland, the old alpha, was a tyrant. He only kept the males he could control." He looked off into the distance. "Teenagers like me, or anyone who didn't toe the line, had to leave. Bad enough for us dudes, but a female without a pack's protection?" He shook his head, gaze back on me. "They're little more than prey to rogue werewolves. And Garland made sure they had no money or education."

"And the females put up with that?"

"Had no choice. They played along, became part of his harem. Beats being out in the world alone. And it's not like there are shelters for females with the space to let them run in wolf form."

"And your sister?"

He whacked the back of his skull against the tree. "What do you think?"

"I'm so sorry."

Rollo's calm, welcoming attitude hid his demons well.

His leg kicked out. "Parker gave me a home and a family. I should have gone back to get her out too, but I wanted as much distance from that part of my life as possible."

"You were young, Rollo."

"Still."

I snapped off a blade of grass and crushed it between my fingers. "Have you considered joining them now the old alpha is gone?"

"My sister wants me to, but I've sworn my loyalty to Parker. So they're in a tight spot, because they have no males left. No adult males, at least. After the female alpha killed Garland, the other dudes thought they might be next, so they ran."

"Good."

"Yes, but about half the females are pregnant. That makes them vulnerable."

"It's going to be okay. You'll see." I nodded. "Once they're united with our pack, you and your sister will be together, and they'll all be safe."

"They're not joining us."

I tilted my head. "What? Why not?"

"Far as I can tell, it's a step they're not ready to take. My sister isn't too forthcoming about pack issues, so I don't know for sure." He waved me off. "Women."

"Ah, the voice of enlightened youth."

"Shut up." He grimaced.

I patted his shoulder. "Well, I'm on my way to speak to their alpha. I'll work something out."

"Don't get your hopes up." He scoffed.

I shook my head. "Aren't you a ray of sunshine? Listen. I'll tell them about the land Parker owns, what a nice guy he is, and how wonderful the rest of us are. If that doesn't clinch the deal, I'll mention the complete protection Parker tends to force on his people. You know, whether we need it or not."

Ivy and I often had to deal with Parker's interference when a situation got too tricky for his liking, even though she and I were the private investigators, and he—alpha-hood aside—was just a computer geek.

Rollo scrunched his nose, and a strand of blond hair fell into his face. "Go ahead. It's your funeral. The female alpha has a posh accent, but she's one tough bitch and not afraid to stand her ground."

"Good to know." I shifted around to catch his gaze. "I always wondered if calling a female werewolf a bitch is as much an insult as it is for everyone else."

"Seeing how females can disembowel you in seconds..." His teeth fake-snapped for me. "How eager are you to find out?"

"Gotcha." I hopped to my feet and brushed various types of plant material off my ass. "Anyway, I'll keep you in the loop. Don't do anything stupid in the meantime."

"Yeah, you either." Rollo's sudden grin transformed his face into that of any other carefree twenty-two-year-old. "Hey. If she kills you, can I have your stuff?"

"I doubt there's anything of mine you haven't already stashed away to your room, but sure."

"Well, nice knowing you." He gave a mock wave.

I waved back then strode off to find the ladies who had created all the fuss.

CHAPTER TWO

THE OVERGROWN PATH SNAKED THROUGH the woods, and splashes from the narrow river pointed the way to the trespassers' site. As Rollo said, werewolf women weren't like ordinary women. Giving the impression I was sneaking up on them could prove fatal, so I made as much noise as my soles would let me on the soft underground.

No dried-up branch scattered on the forest floor went uncrunched. No stone unkicked. More were-elephant than werewolf—or even graceful vampire—I stomped my way over the wooden bridge and into the grassy clearing.

Ten white canvas tents, each large enough to house two average families, circled a crackling fire. The camp seemed deserted, except for one woman. Her light-blonde hair, cut into a short bob to ear level, reflected the sunlight, yet her face was all thunder.

She didn't have the broad shoulders I'd expect in an enforcer, but she made one hell of a welcoming committee. My mouth dried, and I took a second to appreciate the wonders nature offered.

She'd poured her slender, yet shapely figure into a stained pair of jeans. With that small nose and perfect mouth, a smile would have guys lining up outside camp. Her breasts were on the generous side and perfectly round.

My chest hummed in appreciation.

If this *weren't* business, my conversation with this woman would run differently than the one I had planned. Half an hour with me, and she'd turn her frown into a satisfied post-coital smile.

But Ali hadn't sent me to get anyone under the sheets.

A child's head peeked out from behind a gazebo-sized tent, but was yanked back by an adult hand. Perhaps they were scared of newcomers, especially those that weren't werewolves.

I raised my hand. "Hi."

The woman's eyes widened, and I halted.

"Who are you?" Her voice was softer than her firm expression suggested.

The color of her skin was a deep tan, more golden than brown. Even from fifteen yards away, her lips beckoned.

"Florian." I took another couple of steps until her cherry soap's scent reached me. "I'm here to talk to your alpha."

Pronounced cheekbones gave her face the unblemished beauty of a blonde Snow White. Well, almost unblemished. Two scars crisscrossed high on her throat. Only a complete bastard would seek to ruin the satin perfection of her skin, but she wore it like a badge of honor.

She met my gaze with bright blue eyes and lifted her chin. "I'm the alpha."

I shifted my weight onto my back foot. "*You're* the alpha?"

Her quiet growl, inaudible to humans, blew down my spine, straight into my balls.

Jesus. Thank God Parker's alpha power had never done *that.*

"Is that so hard to believe?" She cocked her hip.

"No." I teetered on my heels. "Looks like you picked a good spot." I gestured around me.

"Indeed."

"Plenty of space." I squinted into the cloudless sky. "Airy."

She didn't laugh.

Epic fail, as Rollo would say. "Anyway. I'm here on behalf of Parker's pack, but you've probably already figured that out."

"If you're interested in open dialogue, you're most welcome." Her British accent, with each *T* receiving its dues, rumbled in my chest. "But if you're here to tell us to bugger off, save it."

So much for my charm.

Hang on. She should have recognized I wasn't a werewolf, yet she hadn't questioned my loyalty to Parker. Interesting.

Then again, I kind of did consider myself an honorary werewolf, even if my transition hadn't been easy. I'd stowed my bondage gear in the back of my closet, never quenched my hunger for blood in their presence. Even became celibate—since looking didn't count— to fulfill my role as Ali's *intended* according to werewolf customs. In everything but genes, I *was* a werewolf.

At any rate, the alpha's misconception might make my job easier. At least we could leave the typical anti-vamp propaganda out of the discussion.

"No. I'm not here to ask you to leave. Quite the opposite." I pulled my jacket straight. "We're throwing a party, and I would like to invite you and your pack to join us."

I beamed. The invitation was delivered in full, and with the right amount of ceremony. Check and check.

"Oh. Well, thank you, but no." She flicked her head back. "We have a lot to do here."

Time for plan B.

"Okay." I scratched behind my ear. Did I even have a plan B? "In that case, I would like to invite you to join our pack. It's the largest and richest in the country, and it would be our honor to make your lives in Silverton safe and enjoyable."

A subtle reminder of our strength couldn't hurt.

"Yes, I thought that's why you really came." She shook her head. "Once again, no, thank you. However, I would like to return the favor by inviting your pack to join ours."

She what?

I never assumed she'd become alpha through looks, but by God, the balls on her...

I dialed back my gawk to mild surprise. "We thought you came to Silverton to become part of our pack."

"Nope."

I exhaled sharply. Ali had made it sound like this was a done deal.

She narrowed her eyes. "You thought it would be so easy to get my females? Thought we're here for the taking?"

"What? No." *Well, kind of.* "I just don't understand why you're here then. Entering another pack's territory is risky and more than a little rude. Parker would be well within his rights to kick you out. Instead, he's offering to share what's ours with you."

"I appreciate that. But the reason we came was to see if any of your males would like to join our pack."

I scoffed. "Why would our guys join your pack? What are you smoking back there in your tents?"

"Why is that any more outrageous than expecting my females to join yours? Just because we're women?" Her eyes sparked. "Besides, don't rule out their interest just yet. We have our...attractions."

"Clearly." My gaze soaked up her curves, the few inches of silky skin inside the low-cut neckline of her top, and then roamed to her stoic face.

Yup. Still stoic.

Dammit. Usually one suggestive glance was enough to make the toughest chick squirm. My supernatural gifts picked the worst moment to desert me.

I flexed my shoulders. "Using womanly wiles is not exactly fair."

"Fair? Eh." She shrugged. "Necessary? Absolutely. Nothing is stronger than a wolf's instinct to bond. I wouldn't be surprised if we enticed more than a handful over to our side, and your pack is large enough to absorb the loss." Her tone was as stiff as her stance. Not a twitch or shift.

If it weren't for her moving lips forming a red bow against her skin, I'd have thought her a doll. And what fun games I could play with this doll, her long body draped across my bed. Hands bound. Eyes begging to be disciplined.

Okay, dickhead. Drop the dirty thoughts and stick to the plan.

I cleared my throat. "Let's start at the beginning. What's your name?"

Her cheeks took on a shade of pink. "Keely."

Keely. The two syllables tumbled through my mind. A good name. I should tell her that. Women love compliments. *Move, mouth. Move.*

"Anything else?" A coy smile spread across her features. "I'm all ears."

I tilted my head, not at all pleased with my performance so far, but I'd be damned if I'd show it. "You're a lot more than just ears."

Even though her smile disappeared behind a scowl, she couldn't hide the reddish patches on her cheekbones.

I swallowed and adjusted my clothes again. Maybe I should have opted for something more elegant than a leather jacket.

"Did you have anything of substance to add?" Keely's dismissive tone bugged me.

Who did she think she was?

My sire once told me it wasn't my easy charm that made me a good diplomat. It was the ruthlessness lurking beyond my empathy.

I'd just never been quite so reluctant to use it. Maybe that was a mistake.

I hooked both thumbs into my belt loops and lifted my head.

"Let me remind you, you're trespassing on private property. Not to mention, violating our territory. My alpha is willing to offer you shelter and protection. I don't see any reason for hostility."

Her carotid jigged the way a fly might to escape a spider's web, forcing the monster in me to stand at attention.

Great. A full-blown blood frenzy would totally derail my diplomacy train.

A breeze lifted a strand of her hair. The gaze of her eyes, bluer than the sky, traveled across my face.

"You know nothing about our pack, so let me give it to you in a nutshell: We will not be ruled by a male alpha. Asking us to submit to yours is a bloody insult. Other than that, I'm willing to negotiate."

Rollo warned me she was stubborn.

Good thing I was patient. "I know you had trouble with your old leader. But Parker isn't like that. If you join us—"

"Let me cut to the chase. As your neighbors, we're offering our physical strength for as long as we stay, should you need it. But we will not bow to you."

The subtle shift in her posture drew my gaze once more to the golden shimmer of her neck. Primal hunger coursed under my skin, like a greedy fire, itching to break free.

I used my two-inch advantage to look down at her. "For God's sake, be reasonable. The way I understand it, most of your females are pregnant and uneducated. And you live in tents. What kind of strength can you realistically provide?"

Her alpha energy slammed into me like a blast from an uncontrolled blaze, urging me to step back.

Instead of retreating, I gritted my teeth and stayed rooted to my spot. Her fragrance intensified and before I could stop myself, I inhaled, letting her scent flow into my lungs. My dick filled with blood, my teeth brimmed with the need to kiss her, consume her, and make her mine.

Squaring up to Parker never felt like this. So…intoxicating.

"How dare you call us weak?" She scoffed. "Did my lack of swoon at your cheap smiles offend you?"

The flames of her power licked the inside of my chest. A clever riposte would be good now. Hell, I'd settle for a single word, yet the only part of my body showing signs of life was south of my brain.

I was attention-starved. That had to be it. Too much time spent with the guys, and not enough around women.

Keely stepped into my personal space, so close her plump lips were but a finger's breadth away. "Please tell me the other werewolves aren't like you. I might have to rescind my invitation. We do have standards, you know."

The nerve of this woman.

Using the last reserves of self-discipline, I suppressed even the hint of a frown or squint.

"I don't mean any disrespect." My voice showed strain.

She raised her eyebrows and inched back again.

"I'm just being practical." I shifted briefly onto my toes. "We have more than thirty wolves. Not one of us is pregnant, and even our youngest member is a mean fighter. We're strong. And compared to us, you're not. Please don't make me out to be a jerk here."

She tucked a few stray hairs behind her ear. The alpha shield she clung to wavered, and for a second, I caught a glimpse of the girl inside.

The cold steel inside me warmed.

I gave her my best puppy dog eyes. "Truce?"

The hard line around her mouth relaxed into—hell, was that a smile? Even a hint of one was enough to make her eyes shine.

I took a deep breath. "I know Parker, and he's not going to give you a lot of latitude. He expects you to join, or come up with a convincing reason to explain your presence here."

Nope. The smile I'd imagined didn't appear. A silent plea flickered in her eyes, utterly distinct from her grade-A, werewolf-or-not bitchiness.

"I'm offering you our numbers to fortify your pack's strength." She lifted her arms to the sides to signal total honesty then interlaced her fingers in front of her. "We're tough and determined, and have made it this far without men. Believe me, we're not useless." Her tone lost its hard edge. "I'm giving you everything I can."

She'd started this negotiation from a position of weakness, and for the first time, the taste of victory soured on my tongue.

"It's not enough. I'm sorry." I kept my shoulders still so as not to give away my quickening breaths. "And I never meant to imply you were useless."

She crossed her arms and widened her stance. "I don't need your pity."

The sharpness was back in her voice.

"It's not pity. Jeez." Why did every step of mine end up right back in my mouth?

For a second, we stared past each other.

I licked my lips, but my mouth was dry. "You've argued well, and I understand your position, but it's time to accept reality. Can I tell my alpha you'll at least think about his invitation?"

Please say yes.

"No." She gripped her waist, narrowing her eyes. "You really don't hear well, do you? That's the one point I cannot and will not concede to."

Keely's glare struck harder than a kick in the nuts. No matter what kind of shit I threw at her, she kept coming back. Her features exuded a strength that was, quite simply, sexy as fuck.

My heart glowed inside my chest with unfamiliar warmth. I'd never met a woman like her. Part of me even rooted for her. If I had the power, I'd give her what she wanted. Recognition. Safety. A night she'd never forget. *Anything* she wanted.

"What else?" She kinked her head, bit her bottom lip. An expression determined to battle it out—not give in—yet fraught with vulnerability.

A pressure coiled inside my stomach, urging me to spread her on the ground before me, to bury my fangs in her and stake my Claim.

Whoa.

I shuffled back to get a Keely-free breath of air. *Stake my Claim? Christ.*

"What's wrong with you?" She squinted against the midday sun.

How did she have this power over me? This couldn't be real. I had already won. She was supposed to back down and do as she was told.

A bothersome werewolf chick would not derail my mission. *Not happening.* This wasn't about doing Parker a favor anymore—this was a matter of pride.

"You can't help yourself, can you? You must keep on poking and provoking." I shaped my mouth into a sneer.

"Aren't you having fun?"

Fun? What about this was fun? I had the moral and legal high ground, and for a minute there, she'd shown weakness. Yet somehow, she got back on top. How did I let that happen?

Damn her. She was the remote control to my body, speeding up my pulse with a look, drying my mouth with a gesture, and emptying my brain with her words.

Keely flared her nostrils and sniffed.

"Oh." She stepped back, the self-assurance wiped from her face. "You're bonded. To a male."

Way to douse a guy's passion.

"I'm not." I shook my head. "Ali and I did the *intention* ceremony, granted, but we're not bonded. No way."

Who cared if I was engaged or married? Perhaps I should have led with 'I'm not gay' or 'What difference does that make?'

I kept my gaze level, reining in my galloping lungs. "So it looks like we're at a stalemate, because you're not getting our wolves. Your only option is to join us."

Her eyelashes fluttered as if caressed by the wind, and she blinked fast.

Gotcha.

The softness in her expression, this chink in her armor, was not a figment of my imagination. If ever there had been a woman more in need of being held and loved—

Oh Christ. The L-word. Second in badness only to the C-Word. Claim. Another thought I needed to purge at once.

I was always up for sex, no questions asked. In fact, my mouth would have Keely begging for release at the drop of her panties. But the L-word? Talk about skipping a few hundred dates.

"Rollo."

Her gentle tone drew my focus. "Rollo? What about him?"

"Give me Rollo, and I'll move my people to another town. Final offer."

"Him? Really?"

What the fuck would she want with him? He was tougher than he looked, sure, but she needed a man to protect her. Not a boy.

"He used to be part of our pack," she said. "Let him come home, so he can be with his sister. You do that, and you won't see us again."

This might not be the worst solution. I'd hate to see the kid leave, but if Parker ordered him to join the women, Rollo wouldn't need to feel guilty, and Keely's pack would be on their merry way.

I tilted my head. "I might get Parker to sign off. Tell you what. You stay put, don't seduce anyone behind my back, or you know, behind Parker's back—" *Jesus.* "—and I'll do my best to swing that for you."

"Fine." She bowed her head slightly. "You may go now."

"Oh. I may, may I?"

Yet there was no denying our conversation had run its course. The same could be said for my restraint.

"Don't party yet. I'll be back." I turned on my heels and stalked off. "Soon."

Her wolf hearing was good enough to have caught my last mumbled word. And was it wishful thinking, or did she breathe a soft, "*Okay then?*"

CHAPTER THREE

THE CONVERSATION WITH THE FEMALE alpha hadn't gone as I'd pictured. She was supposed to succumb to my charisma, not disarm me with her indifference, or in any way, shape or form fight back.

I stomped through the woods, treading on branches and kicking stones. No sign of grace in my walk.

The whole party planning was for nothing. Well, not for nothing. Rollo's hangover notwithstanding, he and the guys would, no doubt, make good use of the preparations. Maybe I'd stop by for a drink or three. I needed them.

Shit. Figuring Keely out was going to drive me straight into the cuckoo's nest.

My cell beeped. *"Where are you?"* my sister wrote.

She'd slipped my mind. Not the first time this month.

"On my way." I pocketed the phone and picked up my pace.

Sometimes, my life sucked. A less than ideal situation, even for a vampire. Spending time with Julia had gone from dull to fucked up beyond all recognition over the last few months. She was always pissed at me, nagging me about my skewed loyalties.

I ran zigzag through the trees, past the pack's mansion, across the road to where my sister and brother still lived, and ripped open the door.

"Florian?" Julia's acute hearing didn't miss a beat.

"In a minute." I charged up the stairs and headed to my quarters.

Since moving into the tiny room in Parker's mansion, I had to limit my wardrobe choices. In fact, most of my clothes were still up here, and so were my DVDs.

I bypassed the long line of Ivy-approved comedies, and grabbed an action movie. Just as my best friend's secret vice was a hankering for light-hearted entertainment, Ali was a *Fast and Furious* fanatic.

Next, I detoured into the bedroom to change my shirt. The mirror that used to watch me and my dates from the ceiling now took up space in a small-as-a-box closet across the hall, as did the wrist cuffs that had once dangled from my headboard.

With much of my personality stowed away, my generously sized bedroom had never looked more drab. The satin sheets on my bed, never more dull. The thick carpet under my shoes, never more... beige.

Werewolves were a traditional bunch. Because of my link to Ali, any sex I'd have was expected to be with him, even though I'd never go there. I knew my life would change the moment I joined the pack, but I didn't expect it to change so drastically. Still, I wouldn't undo my choice if I could.

The werewolves knew how to have fun.

My sister could learn much from them if she just got over her prejudices for a second.

Despite the sister-shaped ticking time bomb downstairs, I sat on my queen-size bed. Perhaps the white, textured walls would reveal life's answers. Or at least something to get me out of the doghouse Julia had exiled me to.

"Where are you?" Ali's pitch rumbled inside my head, relayed by our magic bond with the clarity of spoken words.

What did it say about my life when hearing voices had become the norm? Getting his overflow of emotions was bad enough, but it was nothing compared to the speeches he sometimes transmitted.

"Florian. Are you ready?" Julia shouted up the stairs.

"Ali, I can't. I'll be there in about an hour." I got up off my bed and shuffled out into the hallway. "On my way, Sis. Stop yelling."

"Can you make it sooner?" No matter how much my *intended* insisted he was a laid-back guy, he couldn't hide his impatient streak. Not from me, anyway.

"I wouldn't need to yell if you'd do as you promised." Julia's real life voice, more of a squawk right now, grated in my ear.

If I ran across the street on Ali's say-so, my sister would have a coronary. The metaphorical kind, of course. But the prospect of listening to her yak for ten minutes about how her little brother was screwing up his life didn't make my feet move either.

"The situation's getting..." Ali.

"You said you'd..." Julia.

"...your input..." Ali.

"...today?" Julia.

On the way down, I gave the banister a good whack. If either Ali or my sister had an off switch, I had yet to discover it.

"Frère Jacques, frère Jacques..." My phone's ring tone, set by Rollo one drunken night, might save me. I retrieved the cell from my back

pocket and checked its display. Thank God. Ivy had impeccable timing.

I accepted the call and lowered my ass onto the bottom step. "Hey. Remember when you were hell bent on running away and getting a place elsewhere? I'm starting to come 'round to the idea."

"Florian." Julia stomped out into the hall, one hand on her waist. Her dark blue eyes held a gleam of evil, the kind only big sisters spawned. She built her average height up to tower over me and tapped her foot.

'*Sorry*,' I mouthed while pointing at my phone, and gave her a hurt kitten look.

"Hurry up." She stalked back into the kitchen, her long brown hair bobbing from left to right.

I slid forward to escape the step's sharp edge and stretched my legs out on the hardwood floor.

Julia didn't waste money on lighting, since we saw well enough in the dark, but every radiator in the house blasted at full power. The accumulated heat never failed to get my circulation in gear.

"Where are you?" Ivy's tone ran on DEFCON 1. "Two of the guys had the biggest blowout over the party preparations, and Parker's losing patience. When is the other pack coming over?"

"They're not."

"Excuse me?"

"They flat-out rejected our invitation. Oh, and they don't want to join our pack either."

Ivy whispered in the background. "You'd better come over and tell Parker in person."

"Thing is, this isn't the best time." *Understatement.* "I promised Julia yesterday I'd give her a ride to her friend's place, and I can't afford to piss her off again. And I thought, since the party is a bust, I should catch up on my caseload at work. If we don't start sending out bills, we might not make rent next month."

"Crap. Hang on." Ivy mumbled something away from her phone. "Still there? I'll take Julia on my way to the office, and you come over here. Mr. Tact says I should do fine at work without you by my side."

"Assuming Mr. Tact is Parker, he does have a point. The question is, if you can't drag me into danger for sixty minutes, will your life still have meaning?"

"Ha—wait for it—" She coughed. "Ha."

A mumble rattled through the line, followed by a deep chuckle by none other than Mr. Tact himself.

"What was that?" I asked.

"Someone thinks he's funny. So funny, he risks future kinky time with me." Ivy's dry tone stopped the background laughter in its tracks, presumably replaced by serious groveling. "Anyway, I'm on my way. See you in a sec."

I ended the call, took a deep breath, and stepped into the kitchen.

An intense coffee aroma hit me. Like Ivy, Julia lived on the stuff. While I was partial, I didn't feed it to myself mouth-enema-style.

The coffee maker was only one of several kitchen gadgets Julia, aka self-declared domestic goddess, hoarded. Any money we saved on general illumination flowed into keeping small operating lamps flashing on the off-chance some vegetables needed chopping.

My sharp olfactory sense caught a second scent. A pasta sauce— spicy, with a helping of herbs.

Julia hated tomatoes. When she asked me over last night, I'd assumed it was for another lecture, but had she cooked for me? Perhaps I shouldn't have avoided her again, but between her foul moods and the guys' non-stop banter... Hell, she never stood a chance.

"Hey." I slinked up to her and planted a peck on her cheek.

"There you are. I'd forgotten what you looked like." Although her voice mellowed, her scowl didn't.

I was such an asshole. She deserved more from her family than the drive-thru treatment.

"What was I thinking?" I gave her my brightest, most dazzling grin. "I didn't mean to deprive you of my handsome face, dear sister."

The gray, checked curtains over the sink moved, and a draft brushed across my face.

"I miss you." Julia's gaze scanned past me around the cabinets. "With both you and Eli gone, this house feels huge."

"I'll come 'round more, I promise." I should be able to swing that. Even two visits a month would be an improvement on the status quo.

Julia shoved the curtain to the side and closed the window.

"Anyway, now I'm late because of you." She smoothed her skirt and took her handbag off the counter. "You'd better drive fast."

No surprises. As usual, the smile count around here was lower than at a president's funeral.

I distorted my face into something I hoped was sheepishness. "Change of plans. Ivy's taking you. I have stuff to do."

"Ivy?"

I swung my hands out to shoulder level before dropping them back by my sides. "And what's wrong with Ivy?"

"Nothing." She frowned. "Although I'm wondering if your pressing matters involve werewolf politics. Again."

I shrugged. "I don't think you want the answer to that."

She gripped her forehead as if I'd given her a killer headache. "I don't get it, Florian. They're meant to be our enemies."

"That's bull." I leaned against the kitchen door and locked my arms in front of me. "A hundred, even forty years ago, sure, but times have changed. They're good people."

"You'll never truly be accepted as part of their pack." Her shoulders sagged. "Come home, back to your family. To your kin. I miss you, Flo."

Once again, my stomach lunged.

But she wasn't entirely fair either. When she was at home, she missed me. What about all those weeks my brother Eli and I held down the fort without her?

As a successful author of urban fantasy and everything paranormal, she often shut herself away in her home office, or even traveled the country to attend conferences and book tours.

The doorbell rang.

"That should be your ride." Without giving Julia the opportunity to voice her disapproval again, I rushed to answer the door and dragged Ivy inside.

Ivy raised her eyebrows, but didn't lose her smile.

"Tread carefully," I whispered. "Julia's swinging worse than the great Ali—Mohammed, not the werewolf."

"Hi to you too." She rose up on tiptoes to give me a hug, and with it came a hint of her citrusy shower gel.

She swept into the hall and waited for me to shut the door. Her faded jeans did her figure no favors. Not that there wasn't anything to be admired, notably the deepness of her top's vee, and the beauty spot right at her—

"Eyes up." She lifted my chin.

"Sorry." I dropped my voice again. "But seriously. Something's crawled up Julia's ass, and she isn't sharing. And with her fun-dial running at zero, I've become her punching bag of choice."

"Poor Flo." She patted my cheek in the most condescending way. "You're not feeling special? Don't worry. I think she's upset because she feels like she's losing you."

"I doubt it. Something else is bugging her." I hooked both my thumbs into my belt and narrowed my eyes. "And stop giving me a hard time. You don't know what a pain in the neck siblings are."

"No. But *you're* like a brother to me." Ivy smirked. "Especially in the pain-in-the-neck kind of way."

"Here we go. I knew you'd take her side." I gave her an evil look. "Women. Can't live with them. And too many laws to try living without them."

"Hey, I'm always on your side. I'm sorry. If you like, we can talk about your dire family life later. Now go. They're waiting." She winked. "*Ali's* waiting."

"Very funny." Even though my heart rate was particularly sluggish today, it didn't stop the heat from rising into my head.

Yes, being bound to a male werewolf had made my life more awkward, and Ivy loved rubbing it in. If Ali were a certain hot blonde, I'd be obscenely keen to see to her needs, no complaints, but Ali was the polar opposite, and I just didn't swing that way.

Ivy sauntered toward the kitchen. "Ready, Julia?"

"At least I can rely on you," my sister said. "My brother's the worst…"

I stepped out and closed the heavy door behind me. The women could nag and complain all they wanted as long as I didn't have to listen.

DVD in hand, I marched across the recently paved drive, past Ivy's small house and up to Parker's mansion.

Almost a copy of the one I'd just left, it was framed on both sides by towering trees that clustered into acres of woods. All owned by Parker. His computer software empire had served him and the pack, and now me, well.

Although not what I would call a mothering place, my new home had its perks. Ali did my tax returns. Rollo pimped up my ride. The guys always had a nod or a joke for me. Except for Parker, but he was grumpy without Ivy as a matter of course. I didn't take it personally.

"Ali?" I reached out with my mind. *"On my way now."*

I took the stairs up, two at a time, and strode along the corridor.

The doors to the left and right of me were shut, with the occasional telltale noise from a TV drifting out. The nametags on the doors were practical rather than decorative, and affixed at the same height. Just once, I'd like to shift one sideways to mess with Ali's head, but his revenge pranks were infamous, and I wasn't that brave.

Derek. Kevin, Malachi, Jim. The names on the doors said it all. Too many dudes, not enough chicks.

"Hey Flo." Rollo emerged from his room and blocked my path.

Although not quite as tall as me, his build made him appear larger. He looked better than when I'd last seen him. No longer the lost boy with a hangover, but back to full surfer-dude mode.

"How did it go?" His casual tone fooled no one.

"Let's say it's a work in progress."

He shrugged. "You tried."

Keely's suggested trade made sense, but what if Rollo didn't want to go? He was torn between his loyalty to Parker and his sister, and had never said he was willing to leave.

I shoved him. "Hey, I've barely started. Give a guy a chance."

Parker might reject the offer. I'd have to go back to Keely for another round, but at least I wouldn't have to say goodbye to Rollo.

He pushed his hands deep into his pockets. "Yeah. Anyway, I got you something. But don't make a big deal out of it."

"What is it?"

He moved past me and turned, sporting an enigmatic smile. "You'll see."

I took off my jacket and headed to my room. No doubt, he knew how to pique my curiosity. Ahead of me, a red light flickered.

I picked up the pace.

A flat LED display jazzed up my door. *Holy guacamole.* Rollo had built me a nameplate.

My name scrolled across it in digital letters.

And the letters didn't spell *Florian the Vampire*, or *Florian Dupree*.

It simply read *Florian*.

First names only. The werewolf way.

What's more, he hadn't fastened the sign with adhesive tape, but nailed it on so as to forever mark me as the inhabitant and owner of the room behind the door.

Good thing Rollo was gone. I could have hugged the dude right there.

"Rollo's work?" Ali stepped up behind me.

"Yeah."

"So much cooler than mine." He pointed at the simple black and white tag on his door.

"Where's Parker?"

"He was called away." He loosened his tie.

I lifted my shoulders. "So why did I risk my sister's wrath to race back here?"

"To brief *me*. Come on." With a nod, he invited me into his room and closed the door.

Its minimalist décor was typical Ali. A poster or two wouldn't have killed him, but he did own the biggest TV this side of the universe.

He removed the keys from his jacket pocket and placed them in the bowl on a shelf. "How did it go? I heard they're not coming to the party."

"She thought I was a werewolf."

"The alpha? Why wouldn't she?" He leaned against the door. For a change, his hair was tied at the back, individual strands falling into his face.

A double window spanned the side wall, letting in the early afternoon sun. His room was larger than mine, which wasn't surprising, since he was Parker's second, but it didn't seem fair for it to be too big for his few belongings. Not when I needed to keep half of my possessions at my old place.

I deposited the DVD on his nightstand and sat on his king-size bed. "I was told all kin recognized their kind by their aura. You know, fae recognize fae, demons recognize demons, and so on. *I* can spot my kind from miles away."

He chuckled. "Werewolves go by smell. You've spent so much time around here, even you smell like Parker."

"Like lemonade? Ivy smells just like him, you know. I didn't think I did."

"No, not the smell you get from shower gel or cologne. It goes deeper, a base note you can't scrub off. It lasts for years. Sometimes a lifetime. If Parker wasn't as strong as he's become, Rollo would still smell like his old pack." Ali tilted his head. "What's the face for?"

I intensified my grimace. "It's gross that I'll walk through the rest of my life smelling like my best friend's boyfriend."

"Scent is a form of communication for werewolves, and it would be odd if you smelled differently. It's like a club tattoo, or a membership card."

I pointed my thumb at my chest. "I earned my smell today. Their alpha is a pain in the ass."

"What's the problem?"

"First, they're all female wolves, but the alpha keeps a tight leash. Anyway, they're not joining our pack. Something about not trusting us because their old alpha was a perv. Her counter proposal is that she's prepared to leave if we give her Rollo. It's not the success I hoped for, but it's early."

Getting rid of her wouldn't be the worst thing that could happen. Being Ali's *intended* without a way out gave me enough headaches.

Resting his arm on the shelving unit, Ali crossed his legs. "The guys are going to be crushed that our guests aren't coming. Jim even shaved, can you believe that? The first time I've seen the dude's face, I swear."

"She just wouldn't budge. On the party or joining us." I squinted with one eye. "You made my assignment sound like a done deal."

"I thought it would be. Shame you can't use glamour to permanently change her mind. But you did well enough. You started negotiations, so we'll see where it goes from here. Parker will, no doubt, consider her proposal."

"It's a good compromise." I kicked off my shoes and shifted back onto his enormous bed.

"But?"

"Parker has the largest pack in the country. I don't get why she won't just join us. We're nice people."

"Maybe she's holding out for a better deal."

"What better deal?" I whacked my head against the headboard and touched the flourishing bump on my skull. "What else could she hope to gain?"

Ali lifted his dense eyebrows in a sort of facial shrug. "I don't know her motives, but what if she's simply reluctant to give up her position at the top? Maybe she's hoping to bond with our alpha to retain her status. Political matches aren't unusual."

A knot formed in my throat.

"That sucks. You know. I mean, well." I stammered.

What was wrong with me? What happened to my Florian charm? I coughed. "Ivy won't like that one bit." *Good save.*

"Nor Parker." Ali's gaze slid down my face, to my chest. "So if giving up Rollo will take care of the problem, Parker can't ignore this option."

I shifted further back against the headboard and pulled both knees up tight. "Right."

And once Keely got Rollo, she'd leave.

Ali crossed the creaking hardwood floor and sat next to me on the edge of the bed. "Okay. Something's on your mind, Flo. Let's talk."

Let's talk—two words that made my palms go clammy. "Talk about what?"

"Whatever's bugging you." His gaze softened as he leaned across the mattress. "Come on, out with it." He brushed a short strand of hair off my forehead before running his hand along my cheek.

Too close. I snapped my head to the side. "Ali. What—"

"I didn't mean…" He scuttled to the foot of the bed.

Shit. I thought I'd made my sexual preferences clear.

His features crumpled, and he touched his nose, covering his mouth. "I'm sorry. I don't know why I did that."

Jesus. Where was my diplomacy when I needed it the most?

I stretched out my legs. "You're a great dude and hanging with you is fun, but…"

He waved me off. "Don't you think I know? I shouldn't have tried. It's just, you were upset."

Keely had that effect on guys. Or at least on me. "You know I would if I could, right?"

And it was true. If I could make myself feel for him a quarter of what I felt in Keely's presence, I'd seal the deal and never look back. But my heart and body balked at the idea. The best, the *only*, thing I could offer him was my honesty.

His gaze grew dark and distanced.

"Sure." He gave my shin a slap. "At least you're not stringing me along."

I rolled my eyes. "Yeah, I'm a fucking hero."

"Let's drop it, okay?" His lips pressed together. "But you've got to tell me what's wrong. We talked about this. We can't maintain a peaceful pack life if some of us keep secrets."

I glanced at the nightstand, catching a whiff of the cinnamon candle standing next to his alarm clock. "Not the kind of thing you want to hear about."

"Why not?" His eyes widened. "Ah."

I dropped my chin, but continued to peer up at him.

"A woman." His Adam's apple jumped. "One of the wolf ladies?"

The temperature inside my head jumped a few notches. Did I really need to have a girl talk with *him?*

"It's not like I haven't expected it." He brushed aside any objection. "Not with them, of course, but it doesn't take a genius to know we're not meant to be."

"Guess not." I laughed. "But don't worry about her. She confused me, that's all."

He tugged his loose tie over his head and threw it across the room. "Are you lying to me or to yourself?"

Ali was a neat freak, so the fact he didn't hang his tie in its usual place was a big deal. His werewolf genes equipped him to literally sniff out the smallest fib, but for once, he didn't push me.

He got up, and his gaze drifted to the towering trees outside his window. The blue sky created visible warmth that didn't penetrate his room.

Deep breath. You can say it. "You want me to go?"

He dropped his hands by his sides. "No. But I've got to work, and you should go break the guys' hearts about the females."

I interlaced my fingers. "Won't they shoot the messenger?"

"Probably." He headed to the door. "Are you thinking of asking her out?"

Dammit. I massaged my icy fingertips. "She's interesting. That's all. Maybe she turns me on because it's been a while. But mainly, she's annoying."

"Or maybe she's your one true mate. I read up on vampires. That's what you call it when you meet your fated lover, right?"

"Ridiculous." I swung my legs out of bed and stepped into my right shoe, which slid sideways across the floor.

Keely, my one true mate? Please. I'd met and dismissed better candidates than her. Not only was I not a *forever* kind of man, but she was too obstinate and stuck up to even be in the running.

I chased my footwear all the way to the opposite wall, where I managed to ram my toes inside. "Definitely not."

A sly grin spread across Ali's face. "Oh yeah? Why?"

"First of all, we don't have predestined mates. We date, we like, and if we like enough, we make them our one true mate. Like a human marriage." I crossed back to the bed to nudge my left shoe into surrendering. "But I'm not the sort of guy to just fall for someone."

"Yes. Florian, *Man of Mystery.*" His eyebrows practically flipped me off.

Sure, I wouldn't kick Keely out of bed. She had appeal, I'd give her that. For one, her lips weren't just made for kissing. With the right guidance, they would do amazing things to my cock. Her tits held promise too, and I'd pay half my sister's fortune to see them bare. I'd make her nipples stiff and proud, like two buttons. Hell, it would take a lifetime to work through the list of activities she was perfect for.

But that didn't mean I was interested in her.

"None of this matters." My tone was intended to dampen any residual doubt, and with luck, our link did not tattle on me.

"Good. Keep your head in the game. Besides, at the moment, their pack has no standing." He fumbled with the door handle. Like me, he guarded his thoughts and feelings.

Werewolf etiquette and a pack's reputation were a huge deal, I was told, but I didn't need the reminder.

I went for a casual smile. "If Parker agrees to her offer, she'll be moving her pack once she gets Rollo."

"Hang on. You're talking about the alpha?" Ali gave a bitter laugh. "Oh man. You must have been a naughty boy in your former life. Alphas are bossy by nature, and that's just the men. You really wanna throw down with that?"

She was trouble, all right, but I'd know how to handle her. If anything, she needed a bit of taming.

But I had a plan. Prove my worth to Parker, somehow lose my link to Ali, and everyone would be happy. Especially me.

A relationship didn't fit into my schedule for the next century or so.

Ali opened the door and stepped out. "All I'm saying is, if you fall in love with her, it could become a problem. So be careful."

I followed him into the corridor and lowered my voice. "She's hot. No big deal. Love doesn't come into it."

I was pretty sure. Relatively speaking.

He turned to me, and a dark shadow fell over his face. "Right. Let's wait for Parker's word, and if he won't give up Rollo, make sure they submit to him. If you still want her then, we'll see what happens."

I pushed my way past Ali, unable to bear his gaze any longer. "I said a second ago I don't want her. And don't worry. I know how to do my job."

At least I had until he went and put confusing thoughts into my head.

CHAPTER FOUR

WHILE PARKER TOOK THE NIGHT to consider Keely's proposal, I spent mine tossing and turning in my bed, reliving my failure over and over. Not the failure of my mission, because the battle was far from lost, but my inability to convert a strong start into an easy win.

I closed my eyes, retrieving Keely's curves from memory. Her tatty clothes hadn't shown off her figure the way no clothes would have, and maybe it was this mystery that had caused me to take my eye off the prize.

By morning, I had a plan of action. Next time I faced her, I'd be prepared. Parker's decision would be delivered with a neutral tone. If I didn't piss her off, she wouldn't resort to her alpha power, which she'd proven could snap my resolve like dry wood.

If Parker agreed to give up Rollo, I'd just take the kid with me and drop him off. Job done.

However, if Parker rejected her suggestion, I'd need an *or else*.

The list of advantages of joining us was my carrot. Problem was, I couldn't think of a stick, in case she kept up her resistance.

My alarm clock sounded at eight a.m. By nine, I'd lured a comatose Ivy into my car with the promise of strong coffee, which I delivered as soon as we got to work. An hour later, I closed two case files, and Ivy was just about awake.

I filed the folders away in the wooden cabinets and picked up the newspaper to see if I could rustle up new clients. The P.I. business was a slow one, but Ivy and I had plans to become Northern California's go-to detective agency.

Ivy gave a lion's yawn and refilled her coffee.

And she wondered why I doubted her commitment.

I sat back at my desk and opened the local section.

The only downside to having an office in an apartment complex was the constant dog-barking. That, and the occasional loud stereo. Otherwise, I liked the setting. The neighbors were friendly enough, without any curiosity about how our boss got his agency to be located amid soccer mums and retirees.

In a way, the office had become my second home since I'd joined Fred Abner's P.I. agency. Plants in the windows now livened up the view, and I'd replaced the unreliable UFO-shaped lamps on our desks with sleek modern ones that worked.

Fred rarely joined us. A shame, not only because he was an okay guy, but mainly because Ivy figured his absence somehow made her my boss.

Ivy's dark red curls had a bounce today, more due to the half a liter of caffeine in her system than fancy styling products.

"So?" She peered at me over the rim of her mug.

I stretched out my legs. "So what?"

"I heard you spent last night in Ali's room."

"Not that it's any of your business, but we watched a movie until midnight, and then I went to bed alone."

Last year, Ivy discovered she had Guardian genes, which gave her the ability to transform metal plates into weapons and the responsibility to police the behavior of fae, demons, and other kin.

Ivy's physical powers were one thing, but her new training had also honed her investigative skills. Trouble was, where once she was driven by curiosity alone, she had since developed a keen instinct she liked to direct at me.

"Ali's crazy about you." Her soft words felt more like a slap. "Have you come clean with him yet?"

"More than once. And as soon as we dissolve our link, no more emotional baggage." I glanced up from the headlines of the day and turned the page. "Has Parker heard from the Elders?"

Part of me looked forward to having my feelings to myself again, even though I dreaded the price I'd have to pay. As long as I was Ali's significant other, I was someone to be called upon in times of trouble, or for a laugh. Someone to be reckoned with. But yesterday showed, once again, that the link hurt both me and him.

No, this charade had to stop.

Ivy shook her head, dashing my hopes-slash-concern with a flop of her curls.

"No dice. The Elders believe you have the soul of a werewolf." She grimaced. "Sorry."

"Yeah right," I mumbled.

Not that I didn't get a kick out of the comparison, but sharing emotions with a dude really sucked the fun out of life. Yet as long as these Elders failed to understand the realities, Ali and I would stay linked. Perhaps it was time they met a certain British chick haunting my thoughts, no matter how much I wished she didn't.

I pushed the paper and keyboard aside to make room for my legs. Feet up, I rested against the chair's back. "Let's talk about something else."

Ivy moved around her desk to sit on it, her jean-clad legs drooping over the edge. "Talk about what?"

"About the female alpha." I peered across the room to check if she'd caught my hesitation.

"Did Parker agree to her terms?" She picked up a stapler and fiddled with it. "He won't discuss werewolf policy with me, but I know he's thinking about giving her what she wants."

Maybe her investigative skills weren't that sharpened yet.

I sipped my cold coffee and swirled it inside my mouth.

"Allowing Rollo to join the other pack would be the best for everyone. We'll see. Parker will announce his decision this afternoon." I yanked my feet off the desk and smacked my hands on the newspaper in front of me. "Hey. Turns out, werewolves recognize each other by smell, not aura."

She scrunched her nose. "Seriously?"

"Guess Waylon got that wrong."

Under the coaching of her Guardian mentor, Waylon, Ivy had thrown herself into her new life, exiling kin baddies to the realm of Alethia, an offshoot of Earth that lay in permanent twilight. Nowadays though, Parker sat front and center in her life, forcing Waylon into the nosebleed section.

Ivy clicked her tongue in her *oh well* manner. "Give Waylon a break. He's new to this too. Of course, kin would be less afraid of us Guardians if they knew we were winging it, so we don't spread that detail around. Oh. And speaking of Guardian stuff, check out this new beauty." She waved a thin metal plate in the air, smaller than the display on my cell, but less techy.

Lines snaked across its surface without apparent pattern or regularity, yet capable of shaping energy into magic on her command. This one appeared to be aluminum, Ivy's metal of choice for experimentation because it was cheap, although she preferred copper or iron.

She raised her eyebrows.

I pointed at the object in her hands. "What is it?"

Being her sidekick involved certain duties. One was to play along with her games.

She grinned. "A guard."

I rolled my eyes. "I know it's a guard. I mean, what have you invented now?"

"Check it out." She closed her eyes and spoke an incantation. "It protects against glamour."

I squinted. "Aren't Guardians immune to glamour anyway?"

"Even though it doesn't affect me, I can feel when magic tries to influence my brain. But this." She waved the guard. "This won't let you near me. At least, I'm hoping it won't. Wanna give it a go?"

I reached into the power well deep under my skin, like a muscle to be flexed, and squeezed.

My vampire magic sprang to life. Waves of warmth spread through my flesh, radiating out toward Ivy, to hook my mind into hers. It didn't. The rays of my glamour bounced back, as if hitting a wall.

I laughed. "Damn. It works. Although as someone who relies on glamour to get courtside seats and the best deals at the mall, I disapprove."

She threw the guard in the air and caught it in her palm. "I could make you one."

"I'm immune to glamour too."

"I didn't know." She pouted. "We never talk anymore."

Jeez. "Our sires imprint on our brains, so only their glamour works on us. It's how they protect their families against outside influence."

Ivy pushed the guard deep into her jeans pocket. "I'm hoping the guard will also protect against the djinn's mental powers but haven't had the chance to try it."

Guardians like Ivy relied on their unique ability to identify all kin. Only djinn remained undetected. That landed her in trouble last year when Greg, her ex, pinged as human on her kin radar, but turned out to be host to a djinn, with the associated badassery. Unlike my own glamour, djinn's mental powers were so painful, they brought burly demons to their knees. Greg nearly killed Ivy before she dispatched him to Alethia.

"It's about time you found a weapon against the djinn. They've been getting away with their crap for far too long. I mean, I'm no stranger to violence, but the stuff they pull..." I snapped my fingers. "You could ask Waylon to do a test run."

"I will, next time he's in town. Whenever that is. But hey. No biggie."

As if she could fool me. Underneath her cheerleader tone, frustration lurked. It showed in her eyes, her posture, and her face.

Waylon was up to his ears in dispatching bad dudes, not just djinn, but also members of The Circle, who had the inter-realm trade locked up tight. If they didn't smuggle drugs into our world, they were moving defenseless humans into Alethia. Having Ivy sit at home playing house with Parker seemed a waste of her talent.

"No word from Waylon on lesson two?" I asked.

She shrugged. "Ironically, there are too many djinn around. That means it's too dangerous for newbie me. There's no way to kill them, and we can't get near because by the time you've taken care of their kin slaves, they go underground. So he's benched me. And it's not like Waylon is eager to have another discussion with Parker about dragging me back into harm's way."

I jerked my head to the heart-shaped picture frame on her desk of her and our alpha. "You could join Waylon and take Parker with you, even if it's only for a weekend."

"Being a Guardian with Waylon by day and spending time with Parker at night would be awesome, but now with this rival pack drama, it's not the best time to suggest it to Parker. That's why you *have to* get that blasted woman on board."

"I'm sure Parker asked me to handle the situation just so you two could sex-scape for a naughty weekend."

"Dumbass. You know what I mean." She tilted forward, granting me a more breathtaking view of two of the things that made Parker one lucky dude. "Was there anything else you wanted to talk about?"

So I'd misjudged her perceptiveness. "I don't know how to convince the alpha to budge. She's not...susceptible to my charm."

"Not as susceptible as you are to hers?"

Uncomfortable warmth rushed to my face. "What are you talking about?"

"Oh, come on. She's a woman."

I scratched my jaw with my middle finger.

Ivy twitched and whipped her hand to her mouth. "Oh, I get it. She's special?"

Fucking hell, how did she do that?

Once again, I picked up today's paper. "No. Yes. Listen, I just need to get this done, and she's a stubborn one."

She nodded. "I hate to shut down a fling before it begins, but she's not on the approved list, and stuff like this is important to Parker and the pack. Our pack."

"You're not getting it. I'm not interested in her."

"Good. In that case, persist. Women appreciate logic, so talk it through with her. She'll come 'round eventually." Ivy crossed her legs. "Now that's settled, back to the boring business of our jobs. Who's going to stake out the Bankside Hotel tonight? And in case you're wondering, it's not going to be me."

There she went again, perpetuating the illusion she was somehow my superior.

The thin paper of the Silverton Gazette rustled under my rough treatment. My focus zoomed to a black and white photo near my right thumb.

"Holy shit." I straightened.

My naturally slow pulse missiled through my veins.

"What is it?" Ivy slid off the desk and sidled up behind me.

Underneath the picture of a familiar-looking man, the caption read *'Gino De'Lorenzo Replaces Disgraced Councilman.'*

I placed the paper on the desk and tapped the photo. "This man. He..."

No. If I said it, it might be true.

"Are you okay?" Ivy placed a hand on my shoulder.

Her warm touch soaked into my mental blackout.

I brushed my fingers through my hair. Collecting my breath, I stared at Ivy. "This isn't possible. How can he be in Silverton?"

"What are you talking about, Flo?"

I gulped, unsure she'd comprehend the weight of my revelation. "My sire."

Shit, when had I started shaking?

After all this time, he'd come back to us. Julia and Eli would flip when I told them. His escape seemed impossible.

Ivy's voice knocked against my skull. "Flo? Are you still with me?"

I withdrew my arms from the desk. "I haven't seen him in a long time."

The paper had made a mistake. They could have found his picture in the archives. No other explanation made sense.

Ivy tapped the paper, tickling my neck with her breath. "But if he's your sire, shouldn't he be a Dupree, like you?"

"De'Lorenzo was his human name. His grand-grand-sire was a Dupree, and so are we."

Dupree—a name once spoken with reverence and whispered with fear.

"And how come I haven't met him?" She leaned in with a playful glint in her eyes. "Am I not good enough to bring home to Daddy?"

"Gino had to move away."

He was exiled by Guardians, and not without justification. But that was family business, not Ivy's.

"Well, good news for you. I can confirm he's back in town." Ivy pointed at my sire's picture. "I saw him yesterday."

My head snapped up. "What?"

"This is the friend Julia visited. He came out of his house and hugged her. Figured he was her boy toy." She shifted closer to the photo. "He's a handsome devil, isn't he? And he does look younger than her. No older than thirty." Her hand flew to her mouth. "Don't tell her I said that."

For a moment, I sat still. My chest filled with rocks, too heavy to let enough oxygen in. *It's confirmed. He's back.*

But what did that mean? Would we be a family again? We'd all changed so much over the last decades. The world was a different place.

I rubbed my breastbone, zoning out the crazy up and down of my stomach. "This is wrong. Julia wouldn't hide his return from me."

Ivy wiggled her hand. "Remember, your sister asked *you* to drive her, so maybe he was meant to be a surprise."

Something was... Fuck. I *had* to know what was going on.

"I need to talk to her." I surged to my feet. "Sorry about flaking out on you. Especially because..." I touched my chest. "I would have loved doing the stakeout."

"Of course you would." She squinted, as if she didn't believe me. "Don't worry. Family comes first."

There it was, the sadness in her voice. She hooked her arms around my neck and inhaled. No doubt, she'd just spared a thought for her late parents.

For a moment, her hug melted away my nausea. Her warm blood, so close to the surface, toyed with my instincts, but I'd never feed off my friend. Especially because she'd kick my ass if I tried.

"Are you nervous about seeing your sire again?" She tightened her embrace.

"Yeah." Seeing him, hearing his voice... My stomach didn't just somersault, but carried out a whole gymnastics routine.

"Or should I say *Dad*? Is that how you think of him?"

"Kind of. He's our boss, but he's also a father figure. Vampire women can't carry babies to term, but if you wanted to hear the pitter-patter of vampire feet, there's a way. An exchange of blood. Of course, turning a person is forbidden now, but it used to happen back in the day."

"So where's your mother?"

I pressed my forehead against her shoulder. Ivy was Ivy. No way would she drop this matter until I'd given her a rundown of my family tree.

"Gino staked his Claim on a human woman named Zoe. Staking a Claim means invoking magic to bind yourself to someone for eternity. Like a human wedding or a werewolf bonding ceremony.

Then Zoe died. Gino said losing her just about broke him, and that Julia, Eli, and I saved him. That's why he made us. You know, turned us into vampires."

"How come you never told me about this?"

"You never asked." I extricated myself from her arms and placed my palm against her cheek. "I should go. See you later."

"Good luck."

"Thanks." I waved and left the office.

The things I didn't tell Ivy about my past could fill libraries, and destiny willing, she'd never find out.

But despite my misdeeds, Eli, Julia and I had tamed Gino.

He'd earned quite a reputation under the guidance of his own sire. Once his sire was exiled, Gino continued his wild ways. After Zoe, he changed for the better. Then he found us, and he gentled even more. But the reputation stuck. For the most part, the four of us blended in with human society, but it was the rest of the time that was the problem. Even when we tried not to stick out of the crowd, too much feeding or killing in one town attracted attention. After four bloody months in Paris, we were forced to leave Europe for the brave new world.

Now in the twenty-first century, technology made hiding what we are even tougher. Whether Gino had the capacity to dial down his thirst for violence once more was anyone's guess.

How had he found his way out of Alethia anyway? Why hadn't he contacted me? And why the hell hadn't Julia told me?

More importantly, what if he couldn't adjust? One misstep, and Ivy would have him for breakfast.

Or he her.

The elevator door slid open to a girl in her early twenties. She was shorter than me and wore a tailored skirt-suit and reflective stockings. Not unattractive, but no match for Keely.

If I was to confront my sister, I should do so on a full stomach.

My taste buds pulsed and released saliva. The tight ring at the base of my skull that confined my magic loosened. My nostrils flared.

Her eyes widened.

Strands of my glamour coiled around her like snakes. *Too late to run, my girl.*

Her face morphed into a dumb smile, and any human awareness fell into a deep sleep.

The elevator coughed and came to a stop.

Shit. With a swift motion I positioned her near the buttons and pushed the one that kept the doors shut.

"This won't hurt," I whispered and flashed my teeth.

The lure of her blood twisted my stomach and my mind. Anticipation was as delicious as the main event. With my free arm, I yanked the chick toward me. Kinked her head. And bit her neck.

Sweet Jesus.

The hot and thick nectar poured into my mouth, as delectable as the first time I'd tasted it centuries ago. I massaged her vein with my tongue to keep her life force flowing, while her warmth coated my throat and my stomach.

The woman moaned, as unintended a reaction as my boner pressing into her leg.

Sex and blood were like a five-course menu and fine wine, my sister always said, which was why I picked the drabbest meals. They made for tasty, yet predictable snacks.

If I ever sank my fangs into Keely's neck, who knows what would happen. She had a hell of a fire burning inside of her. A single sip from her was sure to warm my heat-starved body. Not to mention what it would do to my dick.

No danger of that with my current meal. Still, each drop brought me closer to life. My pulse throbbed louder, my muscles flexed with energy. I drank until her body went liquid, until my natural strength returned to full power.

My saliva coagulated the girl's blood, and a final lick sealed her wound.

I stepped back and retrieved the tendrils of my glamour.

The young woman's face, paler now, shaped itself into an expression. Bliss, perhaps. Confusion, definitely.

Once I was sure she could stand unaided, I let go of the button. The doors opened, and I stepped aside.

She stumbled out into the empty hallway without glancing back.

The doors closed, and the elevator continued down into the parking garage.

My reflection in the shiny cabin walls showed a version of me that could pass for human, with rosy cheeks and a healthy complexion. Like fairground mirrors, they lied, but every day, I let them deceive me.

The elevator jerked to a halt, and I left the building. The urgency in my steps matched the frantic reeling of my thoughts.

A few minutes later, I climbed into my Benz, which roared to life at the click of a button. Wheels shot up the ramp and out onto the street toward Custer Fields, the in-the-sticks neighborhood the pack called home.

I turned on the local radio rock station, about the only thing I knew how to operate on my complicated new stereo system.

What was going on? First the intrusion of Keely's pack and now the return of my sire. I had a feeling my happy pack life was going to come to a screeching halt.

Gino, for all his good sides, hated werewolves. Shit. I couldn't stand trouble.

For once, I parked crooked in the driveway. If Eli were here, he'd have blown a fuse, but I'd have gladly taken his grumbles in return for his support in confronting Julia.

I slammed the door of my Benz shut, followed seconds later by the door to my former home, and headed straight into the kitchen.

Empty.

"Julia?" I bellowed.

Perhaps she was in the living room. I stormed around the corner and collided with her.

"Were you looking for me?" The straight line of her mouth described neither a smile nor disapproval.

"You didn't tell me Gino's back." I gripped her shoulders and snarled, my face inches from hers. "Why didn't you tell me?"

She stumbled away from me, her forehead wrinkled.

"What?" She gave a nervous chuckle. "Florian, I don't know—"

"Don't worry." A voice that called to me like my blood addiction entered the hall, followed by the suited figure of my sire. "He knows, child. And it's about time too. I am tired of hiding."

CHAPTER FIVE

Gino's smile greeted me. His purposeful walk, the glint in his eyes—my sire hadn't changed a lick.

"Aren't you going to say hello, *Cucciolo*?"

I charged past my sister and stopped short of falling into his open embrace.

"It's really you?" I forced my hands to stay by my sides.

His arms gathered me close with the strength that had once kept us safe, while his scent conjured powerful memories.

"It's really me. Now." He stepped back without relinquishing my shoulders. "Let me look at you, son."

The dark corridor didn't hide his youthful face. My sharp eyes soaked up his familiar traits, from the dimple on his cheek, to his straight nose. Not even his haircut had changed. His black blazer and gray slacks were tailored to fit him like a model.

For a brief moment, I was a young vampire again, finding certainty in the man who made me. The first drop of his blood had called forth my hopes, my dreams, and sure, my neuroses.

"How are you back?" My voice nearly broke, but I kept my shit together. Nothing upset Gino more than signs of weakness. "We were told even someone as powerful as you would never escape Alethia."

"Come. I'll tell you." He let go of me and stepped into the living room, which had been his favorite room once upon a time.

From its thick rugs to the satiny furniture, all items carried the Gino stamp of approval. The decor might be old-fashioned in today's terms, but it appeared much less so with Gino's tall frame inside. With his polished shoes and tailored suit, he smacked of the stereotypical Italian gigolo, a young man who'd never be stuck for a date. Guess we had that much in common.

Julia and I followed. He tugged on his pant legs and sat in his high-backed armchair. Grinning from ear to ear, Julia prostrated herself at his feet.

Although once I'd have done the same, I'd grown into a male of my own standing. Perhaps not as powerful as my sire, whose ability to glamour would remain beyond my reach for many more centuries, but now, I was pretty much on my way to making him proud.

I bowed before no one.

Instead I pulled up a chair, thin and old, but not so fragile as to collapse under my weight. A dusty staleness clung to this room, despite Julia's attempts to regularly clean and air out all the rooms, and with two fingers on my nose, I waited out the urge to sneeze.

"After the Guardians banished me to Alethia, I fought my way across the land to the Vampire Kinlord's palace." He crossed his legs. "As you may know, the kinlord is Mehmet Dupree, your grand-sire. A number of my brothers and sisters, the ones that hadn't been killed outright by Guardians, had returned to him over the years, but I soon had the chance to remind him why I was his favorite. You should have been there." His eyes widened, alight with memories. "My stay at his court was a joy. Familiar faces. No sun to kill you. And a stable full of human slaves to drink from."

I shifted in my seat and folded my hands in front of my stomach.

Alethia wasn't like our own Oldword. It was a place populated with ancient beings and teeming with ancient blood sports. Fun, exhilarating, and life affirming.

If you liked that sort of thing.

Gino fixated his gaze on me. "But as thankful as I was to be at Mehmet's side, I was unhappy without my children. I missed you. Six months ago, I came upon a traveler who, in return for future cooperation, told me of a way to escape Alethia. It took preparation, but here I am."

"I'm glad." I smiled.

"Me too, *Cucciolo*, me too." He narrowed his eyes and bared his teeth. "I have great plans."

I peered at Julia, who kept her gaze low. Her green skirt wrapped around her folded legs like a mermaid's tail. At any other time, I wouldn't let the opportunity to tease her pass me by.

"I don't know how much she's told you." I cocked my head at my sister. "The world's moved on since you left. Your picture is in the newspaper, read by thousands. And with advances in technology, keeping our identity hidden is more difficult than it used to be."

"So you cower to the humans?" He uncrossed his legs and slanted forward until his breath touched my cheek.

I flinched. Now he was being unfair. We merely found a way to live with them.

"But yes." He waved me off. "I have been back for six weeks

and observed this new technology. The changes run on the surface. Underneath, things remain the same."

"True." Julia nodded.

Once again my gaze drifted to her face. She was awfully quick to agree.

"No, they don't." I scratched my neck. "Humans outnumber us. If they knew we existed, they'd wipe us out. They have the weapons."

My sister frowned, and ever so slightly shook her head.

It wasn't wise to disagree with Gino. The old vampire traditions, like a vampire's respect for his sire, were paramount, but keeping him in the dark about the new world wouldn't help him fit in.

"Human superiority. Yes, that seems to be the general consensus among all kin." Gino pressed his lips together and glanced at the wall behind me.

The thick curtains in front of the windows were half closed, and most light came from oil lamps soiled with soot after years of neglect.

My mind wandered to the building across the road. My werewolf friends. Ivy. Ali. And located beyond them, in a clearing in the woods, Keely.

The new world had its advantages.

I peered at Julia. "We've carved out a pretty good existence for ourselves."

Her expression didn't change. She was usually first in line to remind me how good we had it.

"So I have heard, my son." Gino leaned back again and unbuttoned his black blazer, revealing a white shirt. "Although there are developments of which I do not approve."

His quiet tone crept the few inches to my ear, yet echoed loudly inside my gut.

The air turned syrupy, making each breath a struggle. The tendrils of his glamour cradled me, but did not pierce my mind.

I flexed my shoulders. "I mean it. We've made friends. I think you'll like the new Silverton."

"Pah, friends." Gino surged to his feet.

His voice, normally as calm as stagnant water, sprayed up in a whirl that froze my chest. "We did well without friends, my boy. What more do we need than family, servants, and food?"

His glamour knocked on my skull, but still didn't intrude.

"Friends can become family. Right?" Once again, I turned my focus on my sister.

"Julia. Leave us, please." Gino's brows formed a deep scowl.

My independent sister, who loved to control and command, got up without complaint, kissed his cheek, and left.

I got why Julia made nice. Vampire children did not confront their sires. Arguing with them could have painful consequences, but sugarcoating the world for Gino would confuse him. She and I would have to have a quiet conversation about her behavior. Reining him in shouldn't just fall to me. If anything, it should be a family endeavor.

I stood. Despite my taller than average height, Gino towered over me by at least half a head. His smile, benign on the surface, did not soften the hard sheen in his black eyes.

Even though he had been gone for decades, my Gino 101 returned in an instant. If I were a human, now would be a good time to run, but he'd never directed such a steely stare at me.

"Julia has told me much, but omitted more." His expression remained non-committal. "She loves you and seeks to protect you, but you are a man now and should not hide behind a woman."

"I don't hide." I squared my shoulders and fortified my mind against the continued probing by his glamour.

"Good. Good. Then tell me, my son." The last two words held little fondness. "Why are you distancing yourself from me? My glamour fails to reach you. If I cannot read you, I cannot help you."

So that's what bugged him. Despite his unparalleled mental powers, he'd lost the ability to penetrate my head. I wasn't old enough to have reached Master level, and even if I were, it would take Gino's approval—or death—before I could shake my connection to him. Yet something had interrupted, maybe even severed, his access to my brain.

My link with Ali perhaps?

"I've grown and learned." I pulled back my shoulders. "Perhaps I'm immune to your glamour now."

Gino shook his head, his dark hair catching the light from the oil lamp burning in the corner.

"A young vampire like you cannot shake his sire's glamour, unless—" He clicked his tongue. "You have staked your Claim on your one true mate? Without my permission?"

Another big vampire no-no. Only Masters controlled their own lives. Of course I hadn't staked my Claim on anyone, thank God, but my connection to a werewolf would seem so much worse to Gino.

"I haven't. I told you. I've simply grown up." Despite my muscles tensing harder than diamonds, I met his gaze with a smile. The sooner he understood I wasn't disrespecting him, the sooner he'd stop this nonsense.

"Then why can I not reach you?" His large hand gripped my shoulder, and the pressure sent me to my knees.

My kneecaps struck the hard floor. I absorbed the pain without a sound of weakness.

"If you refuse to tell me, there are other ways to discover the truth." He feathered the fingers of his other hand through my hair and yanked a clump back, jerking my head to the side.

The edge of the hard rug dug into my knees. I shoved against his chest, but didn't dare let my strength top his. As strong as his mental abilities were, he was touchy about being inferior to me on a physical level.

His breath collected against my ear, and his sharp, pointed teeth broke my skin. Holy mother of all—

The pull on my hair intensified. He scraped a trench into my neck with a single fang. Sharp slashes of pain shot into my brain as the line he carved singed into my tissue.

I punched his stomach to make him stop. Bad angle. My fist bounced off his side without inflicting damage.

He tightened his grip.

My thighs trembled and my knees ached.

His saliva took some of the pain from his first bite, but it couldn't cancel out his ferocity.

I swung back for another punch when he released me.

"Julia may not have given you up, but I know all about you, the Guardian, and the werewolves." His voice sounded pressed, as if spoken through clenched teeth.

"I was going to tell you." A white lie.

Without letting go of my hair, he slapped my cheek.

My throat and face now burned as much as my scalp. Okay, maybe I deserved that. Other sires would have already killed me for speaking up.

"How many times have I told you werewolves are an abomination? To keep your distance, or better yet, to kill them?"

"Gino—"

"As if that is not bad enough, you thought you could stake your Claim without my approval? And now you lie? God, I hardly recognize you." His eyes dilated and turned an even darker black. "I am your sire. *Your father.* Releasing you from our bond is my right and my prerogative. I will not allow you to take that right from me, even if I have to make you again."

He'd gone insane. He couldn't re-vampire a vampire. Could he?

In one swift move, his teeth sank back into my neck.

Blistering pain radiated into my chest, paralyzing my arms.

Without his glamour to absorb the sting, my bones and flesh ached as if immersed in a vat of acid. Any second now, my walls would fall, and I'd allow him into my mind. The pain would subside, and so would my self.

Yet I resisted. He gave me no choice but to block him and endure the torture. As long as he still hated werewolves, he would not control my thoughts.

He clamped his jaws shut and tore my flesh.

My words of protest came as a gurgle. Yet I didn't raise a hand to defend myself. My whimpers grew into pleas, each punished by another yank, another cut.

Maybe I should have been upfront with him. I'd been living as an almost-human for so long, I'd forgotten vampire etiquette. Hell, I hadn't just forgotten it. I'd thrown it in his face and slapped him with it.

But to try and remake me? So fucked up. Even without the bond between us, I was still his son.

My head spun. Spots troubled my vision. The pain…

"Florian? What's—" Ali's voice grew faint.

Gino released my neck.

"Mine," he whispered. "Be mine again."

He shoved me to the floor and once again, I didn't lift my arms for protection. My head slammed into the ground, tears stinging my eyes.

But I was stronger than this. Pain was in my mind. If I replaced the throbbing in my neck with something good, something like… Keely, I could withstand this. She would soothe me, cradle me in her arms.

Gino picked up where he'd left off. His saliva numbed the outer layers of my skin, but the damage was done. He prodded my wounds with his tongue, each touch causing a new flood of pain.

Why did I always make things so difficult for myself? I wasn't a Master, so why act like one? Giving in would be so easy. I was done hurting. Done denying the inevitable.

My limbs seized, and my consciousness retreated to make way for Gino's glamour. It settled on my brain like molasses, sweet and filling, suffocating my thoughts.

"That is better," he mumbled.

I pushed up against his teeth.

Drink from me, Master. Empty me at your will.

The room blurred, and I closed my eyes, letting his magic stain my every fiber.

He removed his fangs from my neck.

I gave a contented sigh.

"Tell me about the werewolves," he said. "What are they to you?"

My heart worked overtime, beating by his command.

"They're my pack. I'm linked to them through a wolf named Ali. He's my *intended*."

"A male?" Gino shook me. "Look at me."

I opened my eyes.

My blood stained his lips and painted his cheeks a dusty pink. Crouching by my side, he cut his arm with his upper fangs and held the wound over my face. It hovered too far for me to drink freely, but the drops striking my thirsty tongue did their work.

Even though my pulse now beat a steady rhythm and calmed my mind, the nausea crawling through my stomach prevented my trance from being complete.

"Who is this Ali? Speak!" He clutched my face in his hand.

I gagged and spluttered in his face.

His mouth twisted, and he slapped me.

I'd displeased my Master.

My cheek burned, and the pain drowned out my inner tranquility.

No. Not my Master. My sire.

Big difference.

I shook my head and pushed out his glamour by dragging the threads of my life back into my consciousness. Ivy's crazy laughter. Keely's rare smile. Rollo's drunken antics. Like letters dropping into a mailbox, the things that mattered returned to me.

I took two deep breaths and shoved him. "Don't do that again."

Gino fell back on his ass and laughed. "Manners, my dear boy."

He traced his tongue across his wrist to close his wound.

Had my first making, witnessed through the giddying haze of his glamour, been as vicious?

With the ceiling spinning above me, I spat out his taste. Even that took effort. My body was a mess of floppy appendages without the muscles to shift. But I'd done it. I'd pushed him out of my mind. Did that mean I was free now?

Gino shot to his feet. "Get up."

He turned his back to me and stared through a gap in the curtains.

I tightened my jaw, scrambled up, and had to lean on the armchair. No strength. Lack of blood. Total head rush.

"You are not to see your friends again, is that understood?" The sharpness of his voice didn't ease the thudding in my head.

I hitched my shoulders to restart my suffering circulation.

"Ali?" I called with my mind.

My *intended* would give me strength.

"Ali?"

Nothing. My knees trembled. The hollow Ali had carved out and filled with his bothersome emotions lay empty.

Memories of when we first met streamed into the void. We'd laughed, and we'd argued, and gotten piss-drunk at the local bar more than twice, but we'd always, always been like brothers inside that hollow.

I touched my pockets, felt my jacket for…for what? This was crazy.

He could be busy, or he simply hadn't heard me.

"Ali? Where are you?"

"Florian." Gino's pitch tightened. "I need you to listen."

I'd ejected Gino from my mind too late. Ali was gone. My sire's *remaking* of me had snapped our link like a brittle twig.

"I heard you." Sweat formed on my forehead, and I briefly shut my eyes.

"You have become weak. Weak like werewolves. Bah. You, my own blood. If my sire knew about this…" He wheeled around. "I hope you have learned your lesson, because I do not take pleasure in hurting you. If you had allowed my glamour in from the start…" One side of his mouth tilted up to reveal his teeth.

Human teeth now, but no less feral, even with as innocent a face as his.

I took a deep breath, the oxygen dousing my mind in ice. "I should thank you. You've reminded me what it is to be a vampire."

And the mess and violence that came with it.

"It was necessary." He nodded.

Gino may have won in the end, may have succeeded to impose his will on me, but cowering before him wasn't in my DNA anymore.

My glare held all the acid I could muster. "But if I want to see my friends, that's my decision."

"Is that so?" A note of challenge lurked in his otherwise blank words.

Once more, Gino's glamour probed my body, seeking an inlet into my mind.

Not again. Not ever again. I built bricks to keep him out, focusing on who I was, who I'd become. A P.I. with a ninety-five per cent solve rate. A vital member of the local werewolf pack.

This time, my mental wall remained strong. My grip on the armchair tightened. *Holy bananas.* I was actually doing it.

Continued resistance wasn't my healthiest option, but this had become a matter of pride. I would never allow him to look into my thoughts again. I was my own man.

I was a Master.

Energy swept through the pain, through my pounding head and my limp legs. Energy not supplied by my battered body, but by the conviction that I'd somehow won a victory.

Boo-yah.

A Master in my own right.

"Don't make me choose between you and them." I unrolled my spine. "You might not like the result."

He approached, one foot before the other.

"Interesting." He lowered his voice. "And who gave you permission to have free will?"

Buoyed by the changes in me, I lifted my chin. "You left us to fend for ourselves. To construct new lives that gave us a sense of meaning in a changing world. Our world, by the way. Not yours. It seems your long absence made me a Master without your consent, so you no longer get to dictate your terms."

He struck me with the speed of a rattlesnake, the pain he inflicted like a freight train against my cheekbone.

My skull rang, and colors shifted in front of my eyes.

I punched back. My fist tore a weak crunch from his jaw. His attack had not just drained my blood, but also my strength. *Bastard.*

He moved to the side, touching his mouth, and bared his teeth. "*I* decide when you become a Master. You need to learn your place again."

My body filled with cement that would not whither under his stare… Because I did know my place, and it was not as an underling. I was his equal now.

He hit me again.

I gripped the armchair to keep from falling. My temporary weakness didn't make this a fair fight, but at least my reflexes were still sharp—sharp enough to return the blow in the next breath.

My fist slid off his jaw without taking him down. At best, I dented his ego.

His punch landed on my nose. The force spun me back onto my heels.

"You shouldn't have provoked me." He thumped my jaw, landed a cross in my eye.

My legs gave way. I crumpled face first to the ground, and rolled onto my back. "Isn't that what you taught me? That I'm better than everyone else? Now I'm better than you."

I spat out my blood-laced saliva and moved my shoulders up off the ground.

"Nature might have made you a Master. I have not."

The tread of his shoe grew in size and slammed into my face, ripping the breath from my throat.

A second later, he fumbled with my belt and tore on it.

"You'll get this back when you earn it. My decision." He held up my guard buckle, the magical object that allowed me to face the sun without shriveling up, and pocketed it.

Gino's steps faded, and the door slammed shut on my broken form.

I tasted my blood, inhaled its tar-like tang. My sight reduced to whatever shapes my right eye recorded, framing the room in a new, dimmer perspective. But I grinned. Grinned wider than a kid on a space hopper.

Maybe I was teetering on the edge of sanity, but I'd fucking earned this pain, and I was going to soak every last ache into my memory.

CHAPTER SIX

I PULLED IN MY TOES, LIFTED my legs, prodded my waist, and continued my physical inventory until I came to the slick mess that was my face. As long as I kept my movements to a minimum, the pain was bearable.

Why hadn't I stood up for myself? I've never been prone to power displays, but today would have been an excellent day to start. Gino's time in Alethia had slowed him. The win had been mine for the taking, yet sentimental hesitation had robbed me of it.

Worse yet, the bastard had taken my belt buckle. The guard on it was more than a lifesaver. It was a status symbol for any self-respecting vampire. I'd be a poor version of a Master if I couldn't go out during the day. Besides, it had been given to me as an heirloom the day I slaughtered ten hunters and freed Gino from the Spanish catacombs. Was history undone because I challenged his authority?

A gnawing pressure rose in me.

In his mind, Gino had done nothing wrong. Hell, no vampire worth his salt would blame my sire for his attack.

I did, though. Why couldn't he just accept my freedom? He was still my father. My sire.

Fucking, stupid, motherfucking bastard.

My cell's distinctive tune sounded. I needed to ditch that kid's ring tone. I had been meaning to for a while, but each play triggered a blurred memory of my human family... *Frère Jacques, frère Jacques, Dormez-vous? Dormez-vous?*

My mother used to sing to us in her native French.

Us. There were four of us boys, crowded into two beds. Claude and me in one, and in the other Michel and... I'd forgotten my younger brother's name.

Who cared? That was a long time ago.

I tilted my face to the side to read the display. Ivy's name appeared in backlit letters. I let it ring, more fascinated by the puddle of blood and spit next to me. Even if I could lift the phone to my ear, I wasn't ready to speak to her. Or anyone.

I touched my neck. The blood had dried, but the lightest pressure smarted.

Of course Ali would—

I took a jagged breath.

Think, dipshit.

My *intended* was gone.

Heavy air squeezed my diaphragm. I closed my eyes, trying to recall his feel, his telepathic voice. How was it possible to miss something I'd never wanted in the first place?

I pushed up onto wobbly feet and made my way upstairs to Julia's quarters. Normally I wore my wounds with pride, but not today.

Vampire life wasn't as ordered as pack life. It was messy and violent, no matter how much I put into pretending it wasn't. Ivy had freak-outs every time I killed a guy, as if my victims didn't have it coming. Her sensitivities were as delicate as a human's, and her questions about my bruises might lead to answers I wasn't ready to give. Like why I'd let Gino hurt me.

Once I'd washed the blood off my face, only the black eye, a small cut on my lip, and my neck injuries remained. After a brief investigation into Julia's potions and lotions, I decided on two containers that looked like they might be useful.

If my sister ever found out what I was about to do, she'd either die laughing, or I'd have to kill her.

I fumbled with the lid of the first pot, but the beast wouldn't open. My teeth scraped the plastic.

No luck.

I used both hands, and the flat box clicked. The contents looked like watercolors, except soft to the touch. I dabbed the paste around my eye and my lip. Dark yellow patches now covered my bruises. I opened another box and stuck my finger into the beige circle. It was hard and left traces on my hand. The lid came with a handy brush, which I took as my cue to roll its fine hairs in the hard powder until they were coated. I shut my eyes and wiped the laden brush tip across the affected areas in even strokes, the way I'd seen Julia do it.

At least that was the plan. Fine particles spread out with a mind of their own, thickening the air and tickling my nostrils.

I scrunched my nose to combat the itch and placed the brush inside the container. Time to examine the results.

The same powdery substance that hid my bruises also covered my black eyelashes and brows, but did little to bring out my eyes.

On the plus side, the slight crook in my nose had disappeared. The crook was the result of an altercation with Julia, who had more fire inside her than her immaculate skirts suggested. Even she might be horrified by what happened today, or at least concerned. Not just that Gino used violence on me, but that I'd dared to stand up to him. I had provoked the fight.

Ivy, Parker or Ali would not see it that way. They would be appalled by this insight into what it means to be a vampire.

I was more than a vampire, but to get them to see that, some layers of me had to remain hidden. Under tons of makeup, if need be.

I angled my head. Right at the corner of my forehead, a pink blob clumped my hair, a mix of blood and powder. I washed the gunk out to retrieve my natural brown hair and stepped back.

My skin was matte and clear, no hint of stubble. Forget Victor Victoria, welcome Florian Floriana. Julia's makeup had obliterated any sign of masculinity.

Christ. What's next, a handbag and a tutu?

Fine flakes still stained my fingers, and it took two rounds with the soap to get me clean.

No wonder Julia spent hours in the bathroom.

I changed into a new shirt with a stiff collar. This would've been a great time for longer hair, but I had it cut when I'd moved across the road. Ivy wanted me to get a crew cut like Parker, but Ali suggested keeping it just long enough so the barber didn't have to shave.

Which way would Keely like it better?

For fuck's sake, Flo. The female alpha doesn't give a shit what you look like.

I grabbed my jacket and inspected myself one last time.

Gender insecurity aside, the dude in the mirror could just about pass for me.

I stalked back downstairs, suffering a heavier than normal walk. With a pained groan, I retrieved my phone from the floor and checked for messages. Ali had sent about a hundred of them. Worried about the way I'd *pushed him out*. If our link were still intact, I'd feel his concern like my own.

I couldn't ignore him, but I could deflect his questions for now.

Living with breathing lie detectors in the form of werewolves had enhanced my natural ability to bullshit without fibbing. Parker wasn't interested in emotions anyway, just cold facts, so he'd appreciate it if I kept the Gino mess to myself.

I headed for the door and stopped.

Holy balls of fire. I nearly accidentally killed myself. Without the guard on my belt, I'd be toast after a few minutes in the sun. Good thing I had connections in high places.

I dialed, and Ivy didn't leave me hanging.

"Flo? I've been trying to get a hold of you."

"I have a problem. I lost the guard on my belt buckle, and I'm stuck at home. Didn't you mention you'd made a new one a while back?"

To Ivy, making guards was like knitting for old ladies. Totally addictive.

"Still got it." Her words rushed out. "You're gonna love it. I'll bring it over right now."

The line went dead.

Forty minutes later, she rang the doorbell.

I pulled the door open, using its thick mass to shield me against the sun.

Dressed in a white blouse and high boots over black slacks, Ivy squeezed past me and lifted her arms.

"So?" She did a twirl.

I gave the door a shove, and it fell into its lock. "You look... different."

She dropped her hands by her sides. "It's something I'm trying out. Ali says as Parker's *intended*, I'm supposed to exude a certain image."

"And equestrian fashion was your goal?"

"High-powered businesswoman." She crossed her arms.

"Of course." I tapped my forehead, glad my body no longer zinged with every movement. "That was my second guess."

Her bottom lip pushed forward. "What am I doing wrong?"

I was such an ass. This unexpected foray into fashion must be important to her.

"You can wear just about anything and still look professional with a nice jacket. In this case, I'd go for the short, black one you wore to your mother's funeral. Just..." I bent over and fixed her pant legs. "Wear the boots underneath."

With my hands on Ivy's waist, I pulled myself straight without showing the pain in my head. Since I knew her too well to think of her as anything other than a friend, I only copped a small feel.

She still narrowed her eyes at me.

I stepped back and tapped my foot. Something was still off.

"Don't hit me." I opened the top button of her blouse, and then the second. "Better already."

"Not too slutty?"

"No such thing." Sexy as hell was more like it.

"Thanks." She reached into her pocket. "Here." She retrieved a belt buckle with tons of zigzag lines. "It's steel, so it should last a long time. Perhaps it will become your own heirloom one day."

"Unlikely, but as long as it will keep me safe, I'm good."

"That's what I'm saying. You kept complaining that with the old one, you slowed down around noon. But this should keep you fully SPF'd under the hottest sun."

"Should?"

"It's not an exact science."

I stared.

She laughed. "Kidding. You think I'd take any chances with your life? You'll be fine, I promise."

I attached the buckle to my belt. From an esthetic point of view, I had no complaints.

"Guess I should try it out." I shifted back, deeper into the hall.

"Well ahead of you." She opened the door.

A rectangle of sunshine fell into the dark hallway, and I approached it, inch by inch.

"What are you waiting for?" she asked.

Clueless Ivy had no idea how we vampire men prioritized risk.

"If I move my legs into this…" I flapped my hand. "Portal of death, and badness happens, my prized possessions will shrivel first. And women across the globe will hold *you* responsible."

"Try an arm."

"Actually, I've grown fond of those too."

She blew out a sigh. "You have to start somewhere."

"I sense there's wisdom in your words, but—"

She grabbed my hand and yanked it into the sunlight.

"Hey!" But I was in no pain. "Look at that. It works."

"Told ya."

I inched out into the driveway and glanced around, as if seeing everything for the first time.

"Don't stall." Ivy gave me a push. "Parker's made a decision. You're needed."

We crossed the road and strode up the pavement toward home.

I angled my face away from her. Makeup shrouded the damage to my face, but my mask might not withstand scrutiny in the bright light. If Ivy caught even the slightest wind of my raid on Julia's beautifying supplies, she'd never let me live it down.

We stepped inside to a quieter hall than last time. Parker and Ali sat at one end of the large table, flanked by another ten or so empty chairs. The four lights right above them were on, leaving the far side of the room in shadows.

"Hi." I stayed back from Ali and kept my gaze peeled on Parker. "What's the verdict? Are you going to give up Rollo?"

If he said yes, I'd lose a buddy, but at least my work was done.

"No." Parker shook his head. "I'm worried about precedent." His chair scratched on the tiled floor as he moved back to let Ivy sit on his lap. "When I accepted Rollo into the pack, I promised to keep him safe, the way I do with everyone who joins us."

My jaw twitched, and I swallowed hard. This hadn't gone the way I wanted. Or had it?

"I intend to keep my promise." Parker's hand slid across Ivy's waist, perhaps as a reminder that he'd pledged her safety too. "There's something else you should know. Nick's laid up with a fractured leg."

"And how did Nick's leg get that way?" I kicked the floor and stared down to hide my smile.

As if I needed an answer.

If limbs got broken around here, it more often than not had to do with alcohol, or one of the guys challenging Parker for leadership. Several displays of strength occurred each year, usually over ranking. The higher your ranking, the less your name would appear on the cleaning schedule.

Or the better your chances of moving out from under Parker's feet and into your own pad were.

Last month, Rollo invited me to watch a challenge between Malachi and Jeff in the basement gym. There was even a referee and a timer. The guys were so drunk, they barely got in any hits, and yet both needed stitches. Rollo brought popcorn and beer. We all had a great time.

I never figured out what Jeff's beef was, but he lost.

I think.

When vampires fought, it often ended in death, because there were no referees to call for a time-out. There was no scheduling either, rarely ever a reason, and definitely no popcorn.

"We've spotted six or seven rogues near the Lost Pines Inn, and they're baiting us." Ali tapped the tabletop. "Nick and Malachi were worried about the females and that Parker wasn't doing everything he could to protect them. Parker convinced them otherwise." Ali's tone was pure ice.

"He and Malachi know better now, but others might try their luck too." Parker's focus wasn't on me, but on something in Ivy's eyes. Puppies and kittens, judging by his adoring expression. "They're eager to see the females safe, and if I don't get it done, they might think of joining the female pack."

I grimaced. Thank God for their quick healing powers. Still, that kind of behavior would play right into Keely's hands. It might even be what she was banking on.

Time to collect my overdue win. Perhaps showing her who's boss would let me get a good night's sleep without her traipsing around in my head.

"Tell the alpha she's out of time." Parker's gaze landed square on my face. "Join us, or get out. This town is too small for this shit."

My lungs tightened. No more excuses. Keely had to see she was better off with us.

"I can work with that." I gave a grim smile.

Parker sipped from a glass of water. "I don't see any reason for her to continue to hold out, so get the negotiation wrapped up today. Considering their situation, don't make any concessions like, I don't know, an unlimited line of credit or expensive sports cars for all of them."

"Right. I have my orders, so I'd better be off." I turned and headed toward the door without looking back.

"See you later." Ivy's voice saw me out.

Ali said nothing.

These ridiculous feelings I'd shown yesterday around Keely were a smokescreen, hiding a subconscious hankering for a good lay. Simple as that.

Today I'd prove to her it was my way or... Nope. My way was pretty much the only option. Lips, hips or tits—none of them would mess with my concentration this time.

CHAPTER SEVEN

I APPROACHED THE BRIDGE TO THE clearing. The giggles of two children chasing two werewolf cubs between the tents set a peaceful scene, while a small group of women with huge stomachs sat around the fireplace, reading books.

Shifting into animal form was easiest for children. They just slipped in and out. Once they were grown, it would take them a few minutes. Ali said the change wasn't painful, just uncomfortable. Pregnant females, on the other hand, couldn't handle the stress of a shift. If they did, the babies might not survive.

These women's postures were relaxed, their faces free of frowns. Keely seemed to look after them well.

A tent flap fluttered, and Keely's head popped out. Despite her height, she didn't have to bow or hunch to exit. Blonde hair framed her flawless face and contrasted with the pink of her lips.

She stepped into the camp's center, and her head swiveled in my direction. Her checkered shirt with rolled-up sleeves hung loose, offering a glimpse of green bra lace that highlighted the golden shimmer of her skin.

"We don't bite." Smiling, she waved me over.

"Shame," I mumbled, stepping over a plastic toy on the grassy ground.

Before she opened her sinful lips again, I should kiss her deep and kiss her hard. Kiss her until no other kiss could live up to its thrill.

This train of thought was headed to Crazyville. There'd be no kissing. Nor would I want to feel her mouth on mine. Not why I was here.

This latest fantasy was her fault. What kind of game was she playing? I'd pumped myself up for a confrontation, an opportunity to show her she couldn't just commandeer my thoughts.

So where was the scowling, angry Keely that acted like she was too good for me?

Her blue eyes guided me the last steps toward her.

"Hi again." Her tone was light.

"Hi." Good. My sharp exhalation almost sounded like a word.

"What did Parker say?"

Go on, Florian. Dash her hopes. Give her the ultimatum. You've done worse in your life.

I looked at the wall of trees framing the camp and sent an evil glance to the courting birds singing in its branches.

"Parker says Rollo is a no-go." I let my attention wander back to the hollow between her breasts and leaned forward, unable to stop myself. "You must join us."

"I see."

I peered up. Instead of a scary-ass alpha face, incensed at my gratuitous gawking, I found a grim smile.

"Perhaps it's time to lay my cards on the table." She stepped next to me and gestured at her pack. "Come meet my people. I should have introduced you yesterday. I was a little rude."

A little? Yet her cute accent once again softened my response, and I waved her off.

"Not at all."

"This is Annabelle." Keely pointed at a blonde whose hand clutched her bulging stomach. "Rollo's sister. And Madeleine, Emma, Kirsty and Kirsty." Keely counted them off with her finger. "The others are in town, getting supplies."

Up close, their bellies were bus-sized.

I whipped out the famous Florian charm. "Hello, ladies."

They gave polite nods.

"See?" Keely crossed her arms, giving extra volume to the contents of her bra. "We're normal, not at all scary, and don't mean to cause trouble."

Trouble? She was causing absolute havoc in my pants right now. My balls were on fire.

"I'm not sure..." I cleared my throat to stop my voice from coming out squeaky. "Parker sees it that way."

"That's his problem more than mine."

"Okay. Answer me this. If you're not here for us, why did you leave..."

"Chicago?" She whipped up her arm, the gesture as violent as her tone. "We need males. Plus, Chicago's crawling with vampires." She nearly spat the word.

"You're not a fan?" My heart throbbed twice in my neck.

Her answer could win her the keys to my last defenses.

"Let's talk over here." She grabbed my shoulder and steered me aside, away from the sitting women, toward the far corner of her camp.

My pulse chased around my veins like a fucking Porsche, when only blood and physical exertion should coax it to life.

She gestured to a couple of logs that had been carved into makeshift seats. Not at all like a loveseat. Nope.

Scents of wood and grass mingled with the fruity base note from her skin.

Keely sat beside me. "Vampires are bad enough, but the Chicago lot? They're the worst."

Here we go. The second she found out what I was, she'd gut me and feed me to the crows.

"How are the Chicago vampires the worst?" I wiped my hand across my forehead.

"Well for starters, they nearly killed me. I take that personally."

"I would. What happened?" I interlaced my fingers in my lap, so I wouldn't do anything silly, like touch her.

"An organization called The Circle traffics females from all over the world to new owners. Less than a year ago, a bunch of werewolves belonging to The Circle kidnapped me from my Oxford home in England and shipped me to Chicago, USA."

"Are you serious?"

"Yes, it's in America. I checked." Her uncertain grin did a bad job of hiding her pain.

I rewarded her joke with the chuckle it deserved, even though my insides ached.

Who would do such a thing? Stick Keely into a small crate, stifling her natural werewolf craving to run free? With her shaking, her wide eyes pleading for mercy?

Fuck no.

I drank in her calm, feeling my nerves settle.

Her skin held the smoothness of velvet. Her smell was invigorating and soothing.

At what point would I stop fighting her lure? In fairness, south of my belt, the struggle was long lost. If she dragged me off into the woods now, I'd be on her, and in her, within seconds.

Perhaps the moment had arrived for me to at least consider that my feelings for her went beyond a liking for her tits and face.

"Tell me they didn't hurt you." I made a conscious effort to unclench my fists.

"They didn't get the chance." She placed a hand on her throat. "Anyway, there I was, sitting in this tiny cage with Kirsty, who was taken around the same time, when a bunch of vampires hijacked our shipment. Ironically, they were another faction of The Circle. While the werewolves and the vamps were waging Armageddon on each other, Kirsty and I slipped away and sought help from Garland, the Chicago pack leader."

"And?"

"Not the savior I thought he was. Turns out, he was the guy who'd ordered the kidnappings to make us part of his harem. But I didn't, *couldn't*, do that." She blew a couple of stray hairs out of her face. "I killed him." Her voice cracked.

"Good." With luck, she made him suffer first.

I flexed my jaw. Why did her story invoke such anger in me? Garland was dead. The Circle... Waylon would make sure they got what they had coming. But no, that wouldn't be enough. If anyone was going to end the bastards' lives, it should be me. I'd tear out their lungs by their asses and make them swallow them.

"Yeah. At least he isn't going to hurt anyone again." She plucked a small flower from the grass and tore off its petals, one by one.

She loves me. She loves me not.

No prize for guessing which side she'd come down on. Right now would be a good time to convince her of vampire virtues. If only I remembered what they were.

"So vampire or werewolf didn't matter in the end. All kin have their black sheep."

"That's one way of looking at it."

Her reply wasn't the enthusiastic embrace of my kind I'd hoped for.

She wrinkled her nose. "Still, I'd rather not run into the bloodsuckers again. Touch wood."

Oh, please do. My cock was nearly there as it was.

"Anyway, news of Garland's death spread, and rogues started to show, trying to take over." She straightened, the movement lifted her tits, highlighting their fullness. "If I had one or two legitimate males under my lead to bolster our ranks, rogues would approach us with courtesy and caution—as they would your pack."

Every word of hers was geared toward making a better life for her females. As if she alone had to make up for the degradation they'd suffered.

I shifted in my seat, rearranging myself, and moved my face closer to hers. Casually, as if it were no big deal.

"Why come to Silverton?" I nudged her shoulder. "Was it just to meet me?"

She smirked and glanced down so her hair covered the rising blush on her cheeks. "What other reason could there be?"

"I figured." I flashed a grin. "But seriously. Any other reasons?"

"Parker Reeves is known for being reasonable. Not just that. If your pack is large enough for the vampire faction of The Circle to feel threatened, you can afford to lose a few males to us."

I frowned. "Why would The Circle even care about us?"

She breathed through her nose. "While the bloodsuckers held me, they weren't careful about their conversations. They're setting up shop in Silverton. Sorry. Maybe I should have said so earlier."

I jerked back. "Not that I don't admire their entrepreneurial spirit, but moving to Silverton might not be as easy for vampires as they imagine."

Not with Gino around. He'd dispatch them before they caught sight of our fair town.

Her lips twitched into a half smile.

The minute shift in her expression brought heat to my body. She thought I was funny, and nothing attracted women like a good sense of humor.

I licked my lips. "That's assuming they find the place. Male vampires are no better at asking for directions than their human counterparts."

She placed her hand over her mouth and giggled.

The heat rose to my head, and I stared at my feet. Huge compared to hers, yet ready to walk to the ends of the Earth to hear the sound of her laughter again.

Maybe if she said something stupid or something unkind, maybe then I'd be able to tear my thoughts from her. Even a tendency to burp like a sailor would do the trick.

Unless my messed up heart found even that adorable.

Shit.

Okay. She was perfect. I couldn't get around that fact. Now I had to make her mine. Get to know her better, then make her fall for me.

Somehow.

"Did you want to know anything else?" She nudged me gently.

Yes. Does she like a guy to touch her gently or rough? How much foreplay is too much? Will she guide me, or assume I know what gets her off?

"Many things." I took a measured breath. "But I can't stop thinking that Silverton isn't a safe choice to call home. Sure, Parker's a reasonable guy and yes, we're a large pack, but if the vampires are on their way, things could get nasty for you and your pack."

"That's why I picked this spot on Parker's estate to make camp, rather than a place outside town." She gestured at the trees surrounding us. "We're okay here."

"You'd be even safer as part of our pack." I winked.

"Don't spoil a nice conversation, Florian."

No one had ever said my name the way she did.

"You're taking advantage of Parker's reputation as a good guy. Clever." I stretched my legs. "But poach our males? If what you say is true, this isn't the time for us to be weak."

"Not poaching. Asking." She dropped her gaze.

Four cubs ran up to us, tongues hanging out of their snouts. Their gold-flecked fur reflected the sun, giving them a satiny look.

Keely swept the smallest cub into her arms, while the other three coiled up into little balls by her feet.

She nose-rubbed with the lucky puppy then cuddled it tight. "I didn't come here to make demands, but with the wish to rebuild my pack and give them a safe future."

The cub licked her arm, and she gave the lightest of giggles.

My skin itched, but I suppressed the urge to give the little one the evil eye. He didn't know how important it was to be her sole focus right now.

Keely peered at me.

I nodded. "Family. I get it."

My human ties had long faded from memory, and the distance between Julia, Eli, and me had grown. The pack had become my real family, from goofy Rollo, all the way to Ali. Their support came without ties.

Parker didn't tolerate blatant disrespect, but he'd never strike me down for standing up to him. He'd pat me on the back.

Ali had mixed feelings about my wish to sever our link, but he never stood in my way. He was a better man than me.

All Keely had to do was join us, and she could be a part of this perfect arrangement. If she didn't agree...

Her lips parted.

Her mouth held power over me, whispering promises of the thousands of dirty things it would do if I gave it permission. Kiss me, nibble my earlobe, pluck the skin on my chest. It would move down, clamp around my dick, moisten and massage it with its tongue.

"I think you do understand the meaning of family, yes?" She gave me an approving nod.

The head of my family had given me a task—a task that had seemed well within my capabilities a few days ago. A task that now came with the power to dangle carrots, but also to wield a stick.

One way or another, she would join us.

"Thing is..."

My approval rating fell in just two words.

"Thing is, if I can't convince you to throw in with us, I'm supposed to ask you to leave. Our guys have also spotted rogue werewolves in town. Parker's hard pressed to allow you into his territory, and now he has them to worry about."

"We can't go anywhere. Emily has thrown a wrench in the gears for both of us. She's having complications." Keely pointed toward the camp. "The stress of another move could kill her and the baby. I refuse to put anyone in my pack at risk. And unless Parker's a complete wanker, he'll let us stay. Six months should be enough."

Sexy accent aside, her words were futile. Six months? Parker would have a fit.

"But you said if we gave you Rollo, you'd leave."

"That was the plan." She shrugged. "Plans change. Births are difficult to predict."

"Okay. Fine." I sucked in air. Why didn't she just give in? "So how are you going to survive in a camp with pregnant females until late fall or even early winter?"

"We just acquired twenty camping generators that should provide us with all the comfort we need."

"Twenty." I shook my head. "That sounds permanent. But it doesn't matter. If you're done with Parker, he's done with you. And if you're not Parker's responsibility…"

"He won't lift a finger should the rogues attack us, you mean? Don't worry. We can take care of the rogues. I told you. We're not weak, just not as strong as we want to be."

"You have it all figured out, don't you?" I muttered.

"Yes." She sounded awfully proud of herself.

While her independence was admirable, she wasn't only doing her pack a disservice, she was also chopping my hope into tiny, useless pieces. Not that I expected her to care for me. I was under no illusions.

But they weren't safe. She had to see that.

"Will you at least promise not to approach our guys about joining you?"

"But ignoring them would just be rude, right?" She beamed. "We're a friendly bunch."

"Christ, you're difficult. Okay, I'll talk to Parker." I exhaled loudly. There was zero chance of Parker not losing his temper. "I'll pass your message along, even though I think it's idiotic."

Her eyes flashed. "Idiotic, you say?"

"Not at all. You misunderstood." I lifted my hand and smirked. "I meant ill-advised. A solution not worthy of your intellect."

"Better." She nodded.

My smile wilted. "But let's be serious. I hope you're thinking this through properly. It's your females' lives you're playing with."

She dropped the wolf cub on the ground, and watched it and its friends scuttle away.

"I sound ungrateful, Florian, I know. Throwing your doors open to welcome me and my girls is generous. But these women have been through hell." Her voice cracked while her glance drifted to the camp. "Their ability to trust is all but destroyed, and they won't submit to a male alpha again."

"Keely."

"I'll be glad if their experience doesn't turn them off men forever." She tightened her jaw. "But to align themselves with a male alpha is too much to ask. I can't do it. I won't do it."

Okay, so she wasn't just being stubborn. Maybe there was another way to keep her safe while appeasing Parker. *Think, dammit.*

My cell beeped, and I fished it from my pocket. The message was from my sister.

"Gino is so sorry for what happened," Julia wrote. *"He asks your forgiveness. Will you see him?"* Followed by an address and a heart emoticon.

I rolled my shoulder and grimaced. The bitter aftertaste from my beating at Gino's hands was a mountain not easily overcome.

"Bad news?" Keely's soft voice wrapped around me like a comforting blanket.

"It's complicated."

"Does it have to do with the bruise around your eye?"

"You spotted that, huh?" I shifted my head, without losing sight of her. "It's a fashion statement."

"Bollocks." Her nose crinkled. "Living with Garland, we learned to see through the concealer down to the ugly truth. And that..." She lifted her hand to almost touch my skin. "Packed quite a punch. Did you break up with your *intended*?"

This girl had me down pat. "Yes. But hey, it was never meant to be. I'm not cut out to be gay. It's hard to believe, but I don't usually wear makeup either."

"What a shame. I have this killer eye shadow that's so your color."

I grinned. "It makes life easier if the others don't find out. About the beating, not the makeup."

She touched my arm. "I get it. But this isn't right. Your *intended* shouldn't have done this."

Her fingers were so warm.

I shook my head. "Ali's a good guy."

She placed her hands in her lap, taking the heat with her. "I thought you two split up."

"Two separate incidents. First I got punched by someone, and then the breakup came." Except, of course, Ali hadn't yet been clued in on this change of relationship status. "And the first hurt more than the second."

She gave a quiet laugh. "I can imagine. Why did you separate?"

"The *intention* ceremony was just to strengthen Parker's power when he needed it. Our relationship was never meant to last. We were waiting for the Elders to give the okay to split."

I, at least, was waiting for it. Once or twice, I might have been willing to murder for it.

Gino was still a complete bastard, but at least through his action, I was free for Keely—if she wanted me.

But she didn't want me.

If she did, she'd give signs, right?

She flicked her hair. "So. What changed? The Elders approved?"

I shrugged. "They were dragging their feet. Hey, it was a relationship based on practicalities, not, you know…" I waved my hand in the air. "The other thing. Anyway, it's done now."

"The other thing?" She gave me a playful shove. "God, you're such a guy. You know, your crown jewels won't fall off if you say the word *love*."

I smirked. "Why risk it?"

She clicked her tongue. "Go on. Say it. *Love*. You can do it. *Love*."

I held her gaze with mine. If I was going to put my *crown jewels*— not to mention my future sex life—on the line, I'd make it count. "Love."

She wet her lips. "Again."

"Love," I whispered.

She exhaled a jagged puff of air and pressed her knees together. "Good."

I leaned in.

She cleared her throat and turned away. "Right. Um. Well done. Anyway."

I rubbed my neck and gave it a quick squeeze to loosen it. If I had kissed her, I'd have parachuted myself into a world of trouble. Jeez.

She placed her small hand in partial overlap with mine. Her fingers were straight and smooth. A little dirty in places, with a day-old cut on her knuckle. She was an alpha who wasn't afraid to get in the trenches.

Her smile returned, as did her mellow voice. "Do you trust Parker? Is he as good and steadfast as they say?"

I stared at our hands, willing myself not to startle her through movement. "Parker's cool."

"Maybe confiding in him about you getting hurt wouldn't be bad then." She licked her lips. "Your alpha deserves the right to protect you."

"Maybe." I intertwined our fingers.

Holy beetroot, was I out of my mind? *Stop this, dickhead.* I wasn't supposed to consort with the enemy. Parker was pretty clear about that rule. Why did she have to be the right amount of pretty, the right amount of stubborn, and the right amount of kind, all wrapped into one?

She withdrew her hand. Pink spread over her high cheekbones, and it was torture not to stroke them.

I raked my fingers through my hair.

As a teenager, she'd probably dreamt of her ideal mate as a broad-shouldered, muscle-packed werewolf with testosterone oozing from every pore.

Vampires weren't built like that. *I* wasn't built like that.

I got up. "I should go and tell Parker. If I explain that you can't leave but are willing to work with us on issues of safety, maybe he'll go for that. As you said, he's a reasonable guy."

If he wanted to be, and today, I needed him to want to be.

"Thank you, Florian. Truly. Not everyone would be so understanding."

Yeah, right.

Despite my best intentions to lower expectations, I smiled. "You're welcome."

I tucked my right hand into my pocket and focused on her eyes. They were impossibly light, yet deep blue, which almost ran into turquoise. The lines radiating from her pupils were faint.

How did those eyes see me? As someone she could imagine being with one day? Or was I just the negotiator?

I blinked and shifted, even though I didn't feel any rush to discuss a compromise with my alpha.

But that was what I'd have to do. For her. She might not realize it, but she needed our protection. Large packs provide more than a sense of belonging. They give a feeling of safety that is underpinned by actual security measures.

Keely cared about her females. If Parker agreed to let her stay another six months while keeping her safe, I would think of something. If necessary, I would breed a rabbit that I could then pull out of my hat. *Face it, idiot.* If necessary, there was little I wouldn't do to get her what she needed.

There had been moments between us today. Keely had walked us to this alone place, held my hand. Laughed at my fucking jokes. Hell, I wasn't even that funny.

She stood, her long arms now hugging her slim frame, pushing her tits up enough to ensure I'd prance out of here with dirty thoughts.

"Will you be back tomorrow?" She tilted her head.

How did relationships work anyway? Real relationships that went deeper than a one-night stand? Talking wasn't for me, and flowers would get old after a while. *Christ.* Maybe sex was all I was good at. Would it be enough?

"Sure," I said. Assuming Parker didn't kill me first.

"Promise?"

A strange warmth took over my body and exploded a grin onto my face. "Promise."

CHAPTER EIGHT

A FEW SECONDS LATER, I PRACTICALLY danced over the bridge and into the woods between Keely's camp and Parker's house.

Forget about her full breasts, her perfect mouth, the constant curiosity, or the sparkle in her eyes. No, it was the thousand other things she poorly hid behind her tough-nut exterior that slew my defenses.

Every shift of her head, each twitch of her nose begged me to make a move. Perhaps to one day stake my Claim.

The likelihood of that happening was tiny, of course. I was sensible enough to know that. Too many things worked against us.

What a rollercoaster day. My knock out with Gino had been a shitty start. Having to avoid Ali had been awkward.

And somehow, Keely had turned it around.

But now it was time to face Parker. My insides knotted high in my chest. I'd arrived at Keely's camp with best intentions to ensure a smooth union between the two packs, but I crawled back to mine with nothing but compromises.

The trail widened into a pathway, and I kicked a stone. I'd do my best to spin the situation, but would my efforts be enough to buy Keely her six months?

The forest thinned, and the uneven terrain smoothed. I rounded the corner of our building, and the tension faded.

I waved to the figure a few yards away on the driveway. "Ivy, wait up."

She turned, still wearing her businesswoman's outfit, except this time, with the jacket I recommended.

"Hey, you. How did it go? Are we getting new blood or did you have to pack the pack away?"

For a moment I searched for mental strength in the paved ground. Finding none, I raised my eyebrows. "You mean, sent them packing?"

"Damn, that's better than mine. And yes, did you?"

"Not quite. But I'm working on an idea."

She wrinkled her mouth. "The last idea you took to him wasn't a resounding success."

Not for lack of trying. "All I can do is line them up. It's Parker's choice to knock 'em down. Where are you off to?"

She sent a quick glance at the mansion, and then dragged me with her further down the drive. "Remember what Parker said about the rogues? I want to know how they heard about the female pack."

"Isn't that how grapevines work?"

"If you're a rogue hoping to take over a pack, would you tell your rivals where to find it? Uh-uh. And Parker's people would never spill the beans to outsiders. No. The intruders' presence here should be the best kept secret around, and yet a group of rogues just happens to vacation here in Silverton?" She leaned in for a whisper. "I think they're here for a different reason."

Damn. Her moments of insight might be hit-and-miss, but when they struck gold, they were spectacular.

I rocked forward onto the balls of my feet. "Parker said we can find them at the Lost Pines Inn. Like, all of them. Do rogues group together?"

"I doubt it," she said. "Parker told me most rogues like playing lone wolf and hate teamwork. They're no use to the community as a whole. That's why they get kicked out of their old packs."

That much I'd learned. In a functioning pack, everyone had a job. I just sucked at mine.

I flicked my hand toward the road. "If they didn't come for the female pack, maybe we should find out why they're really here."

"That's what I was thinking. I don't want to speak to them, of course, but listen in on their conversations."

"Listen in on half a dozen rogue, dangerous werewolves? Well, that sounds perfectly safe and reasonable to me." Smirking, I patted her arm. "Should I pick your coffin, or have you pre-selected?"

She stuck out her tongue.

"Respect is hard to come by these days." I gave her a nudge to resume walking. "I'm coming with you. Can't let you have all the fun."

And who knows? I might get the chance to pick up a quick snack. Gino's attack had robbed me of precious reserves.

"Shouldn't you be reporting back to Parker?" Ivy glanced over my shoulder toward the house.

"Yes, I should." *Tell her. Tell her why you can't yet go in and lay your failure on the table.* "But he wouldn't mind if he knew I was chaperoning you." *Coward.*

"Good enough." She hooked her arm with mine, and we strode down the long drive. Outside her house, she slowed her pace.

I eyed her car, an old Mustang that spent more time in the shop than most mechanics did. *Yeah. Not happening.*

I dragged her with me across the road to my Benz. "I have news too. About The Circle."

Her eyes lit up, every inch the adventure junkie. "What is it?"

I climbed in and waited for her to belt up. "Nothing definitive. Keely, the other pack's leader, told me The Circle is operating in factions. Her old alpha was part of one faction of werewolves, and a bunch of vampires made up the other. Now those vampires are looking to make Silverton their stronghold."

Her expression dimmed. "That doesn't sound good."

"It's not." I reversed out of the drive and took off along the endless road toward downtown Silverton.

I flared my nostrils, trying to catch Ivy's *other* scent, but I still didn't detect the base note Ali insisted we both had. One more way in which my magic was inferior to the pack's.

"Like werewolves, vampires are territorial." I clicked the button on my steering wheel to change the music to something less rock. "There's only so much blood walking around, and we need to be careful, or risk discovery. Other vampires coming here is going to cause a pissing match."

"That sucks. What is your sire going to say? How did it go with him anyway?" Ivy rolled down her window and stuck her hand into the airflow passing across the car's exterior. "Sorry. Should have asked earlier."

"Fine. It's going fine." I kept my expression blank.

The spaces between the buildings became greener, the houses flatter.

"How is he settling in?" she asked.

Before we entered the town's center, I took a left out toward the 'burbs again.

"Fine."

"Good. It's always good to have another ally. Still, we should think about defenses. I'll get started on weaving protective guards."

"Yeah, all right."

Because at the moment, Gino was anything but my ally.

She patted my shoulder. "Don't worry, Flo. If need be, *I'll* protect you from the big, bad vampires."

I touched my hand to my chest. "That's a feather's weight off my mind, thank you."

Among the well-kept residential buildings lining the road, a narrow path led to a play area on which a dozen or so kids had gathered, surrounded by groups of parents.

Ivy blew her bangs out of her face and rolled the window back up. "Park here."

I pulled up behind a delivery truck outside a single-family home.

"Okay." She shifted around to face me. "I've had enough. Tell me what's wrong."

Not that old song again.

I averted her gaze. "Nothing's wrong. Let's go."

She placed her hand on my arm. "Flo?"

I squeezed my lips tight. "You said we should spy, so let's go spy."

"Look. It's just us."

"As if." I shot her a bruising glare. "Come on. It's never just us anymore."

"Don't you like being part of the pack?"

"Of course I do. That's not the issue."

"Then—"

"You're Waylon's protégé, fine, but you're also Parker's girlfriend, and that doesn't make you easy to talk to." I took a fortifying breath. "Things are weird for me sometimes."

Her encouraging smile vanished.

I did it again. These outbursts of mine always ended badly for me.

"I didn't know you felt that way." Her bottom lip quivered. "It's not like I'm going to run to Parker every time you confide in me. You're my best friend. Not for lack of choice, but because…because of who you are."

I shook my head. "I shouldn't have said anything. I'm sorry."

"Not good enough. I need to know you trust me, too."

I waved her off. "Of course I do."

"Prove it."

"What?"

"Tell me what's really bothering you. Is it the alpha female?"

A test. Fan-fucking-tastic.

"Her name's Keely. Yes and no." I rubbed my palm up and down my face, massaging life into it. "Everything's messed up. You were right, I should forget about her. Fulfill my duty to the pack."

She chuckled. "Yes, great advice. Parker's-girlfriend-advice, right?"

I rolled my head to the side. "Yeah, a little bit."

"I'm sorry." She turned in her seat and pulled her left knee up. "Tell me about her. Seriously, this time."

"She's perfect. Blonde, tall. Her scent…" The mere memory

rattled my nerves. "But I'm not an idiot. I'm the guy trying to make her submit to another alpha. She's bound to hate me. Maybe it's healthier to look at this as a test."

"Not everyone is trying to trip you up, Flo. Life isn't one long line of tests."

Her naivety should be endearing. Not two minutes ago, she asked me to prove my trust in her. I'd call that a test.

"Do you think she likes you?" Ivy bit her lip. "Just knowing that might help you figure out what to do next."

I sent my gaze across her button nose and the freckles she refused to acknowledge.

"I have no clue." I pressed the heels of my hands into my eyes. "God, I used to have all the grace of my species before I met her—could talk the moon off the sky—but the moment I'm in her company, I freeze. Fantasize."

"Oh yeah?" She clicked her tongue in a suggestive manner.

"Shut up. Not like that."

Exactly like that.

Ivy both raised her eyebrows and narrowed her eyes, but her facial acrobatics wouldn't make me admit to anything.

I nudged my folded-down sun shield straight. "It gets worse. She doesn't know I'm a vampire. And oh yeah, she hates my kind."

"Ouch."

I stabbed at the shield to shove it back up.

"She's not going to join us. That's bad enough. But I can't even make her leave. Many of her girls are pregnant, and one is having complications. The stress of having to move might be too much and kill the female and her baby."

"That's terrible."

"Yeah."

Ivy's gaze darted down to the gear stick. "But."

I nodded. "But."

We didn't need to say it. Parker would be pissed. Oh, I'd witnessed his protective side. His *heart of gold*, Ivy called it. Seen it. Benefited from it.

But that didn't always translate to what I considered logical or reasonable.

He always had reasons. I just didn't know them.

"What are you going to do?" Ivy asked.

"Right now, I'm going to engage in a little breaking and entering with my best friend."

She smiled. "As long as we're okay."

"We are. Don't worry. Everything's fine."

And for the first time on this godforsaken day, I believed it.

CHAPTER NINE

N OW FOR THE NEXT OBSTACLE to our mission.

I pulled at the car door handle, but didn't open it. "If Parker knows about the rogues, he might have people surveilling them."

"Shoot. Good point." With a somewhat pained expression, Ivy rifled through her pocket. "Got us covered." She produced two guards with identical groove patterns and gave one to me. "What a great opportunity to try these out."

I traced the textures etched across one side of the small rectangular plate. Tiny grooves meandered under my fingers.

I held it up to her. "What is it?"

"A guard."

Jesus. "I mean, what does it do?"

"Once it's activated, your face should become unrecognizable."

I squinted into the mirror holding a finger over my upper lip. "As long as it doesn't give me a moustache. I don't have a moustache kind of face."

"That's not how it works. Remember when Alan tried to kidnap me, but I didn't know it was him, because each time I looked at him closely, his face was pixelated? And nobody else noticed, because their glances kinda slid off him?" She took a deep breath.

Alan, her mother's husband, had worked for the Demon Kinlord Lathan at the time, who was obsessed with Ivy. The betrayal from inside her family had hit her hard, and was made worse by Alan killing her mother.

"He used skin magic, you said." I scratched my arm. "The kind that sucks energy from your body, not the environment. But if that's what this is, count me out. One addiction in my life is enough. At least blood doesn't kill me."

She gave me a pitiful look. "Don't worry. I mimicked the effect, but safely. It won't last as long as if we used skin magic, but it should help us slip into the motel. Did you bring our gear?"

"In the trunk." I pointed my thumb over my shoulder. "Where it always is."

"Great. Let's go."

We loaded up a large gym bag with binoculars, a camera, and a shotgun microphone.

The afternoon sun cast long shadows, turning even short-ass Ivy into a giant.

This was a quiet area, with plenty of green and wide lanes. A couple of kids zoomed past us, tracked by a tired looking woman.

After a quarter of a mile, I pointed at a U-shaped arrangement of three yellow buildings in the distance, nestled between large trees, none of which were pines. "The Lost Pines Inn. Time to do your magic."

Ivy touched her guard and mumbled a few words in a different language before repeating the same with mine. The plate in my hand heated up, and a small electrical charge made my hand tingle.

"Is it working?" I stepped ahead and walked backward to study her. "You look normal. Normal for you, I mean."

"Charming." She twirled to take in our surroundings. "When my stepdad used his spell, my first glance bounced off him. I forced myself to look at his face, but I had nothing to go by, so it was blurry and pixelated. Weird. But if you know who the other person is from the start, your brain fills in the details. So I'm not worried yet. Let's say if we make it into the motel without being taken down by Parker's men, we're good."

At the entrance to the motel's grounds, we waited to let a flashy sports coupé pass, and then headed to the main building tucked between two longer ones. Small trees dotted the parking lot, and a central sculpture of some historical figure from Silverton's past greeted us with a permanent salute.

Our guards gave a soft hum, too quiet for Ivy's ears. I opened the tinted glass door for Ivy, who made a beeline for the reception desk.

Dressed in a suit worse than Ivy's, a woman sat on a high-backed office chair, glued to a soap opera on TV. A steaming cup by her side sent a warm coffee aroma our way.

Ivy rapped on the desk. "Can we have a room, please?"

The woman looked up, frowned, and stared at the computer in front of her.

"For how long?" Chewing gum mangled her voice.

"A couple of hours." Ivy held up two fingers.

The woman's face snapped up, but her gaze rippled off me and landed on a point over my shoulder.

So far, these guards were doing their business.

Still, a smile wouldn't be wasted here, so I flashed her a big one. "She's kidding, of course. We'll take two days."

Ivy gaped and slapped her pockets with lackluster effort.

"I got it." I opened my wallet and handed the concierge a few large bills.

She placed them in the register, wrote our room number on a key card, then handed us a leaflet informing us about amenities and Silverton's social life. Her focus zipped back to the TV.

Now dismissed, Ivy and I crossed the parking lot to the building that, according to a small map printed inside the leaflet, housed our room.

"Are you crazy?" Ivy whispered. "Did you have to pay for two nights?"

"For someone as wealthy as you, you're quite a tightwad. This isn't the kind of place where you stop off for an hour to wrinkle the bed sheets. That's not to say I'd reject you, if that's your intention. I'd never crush your ego."

"Thoughtful. Parker would kill you." She punched my arm.

We entered the large building that housed a number of rooms over several floors, more like a hotel than a motel, and Ivy spoke a few foreign words. The buzzing from our guards stopped. I dropped mine into my pocket and took the lead.

A man in his forties wearing jeans and an army-style parka came toward us in the corridor. He fumbled with his breast pocket to stuff a thin plastic card into it. With his arm at an angle, he took up most of the space, leaving us little choice but to press against the light-yellow wall to let him pass. He exited the building through the glass door and shot a glance back over his shoulder at us.

Or more likely at Ivy. When I was around her, men tended to ignore me.

Thirty seconds later, Ivy lifted our key card. "Here we are. Room eleven."

She unlocked the door, and we entered a rectangular room with an entrance-facing sofa. The place was spotless with a lingering odor of citrus and cleaning chemicals. A TV of a midmarket brand hugged the wall next to the door, while the comfy bed at the far end was the star attraction with its crisp sheets and leather headboard.

The kind of headboard that would punctuate each thrust into Keely's wetness for all the world to hear.

I closed my eyes, pushing down my rising heartbeat. Too many hoops stood between me and making this particular fantasy happen.

Ivy approached the curtains.

"Do you know where the rogues live?" I pulled the camera out from the bag and threw it in the air a few times to see if I could catch it one-handed.

She unpacked the directional microphone and bent over to adjust the stand's height, pointing her ass my way. Parker was a lucky, lucky guy.

"We've already passed one. There he is, see?" She waved her elbow. "He's entering the building on the other side. Now, why would he do that if he lives over in this wing?"

"Are you kidding? The average Joe was a rogue werewolf?"

Not that I doubted her. As a Guardian, she could tell a werewolf from a vampire, even without a wolfish nose.

Still in her folded position, with her unruly hair almost sweeping the floor, she moved her head to give me a wide-eyed glance. "What did you think rogues looked like?"

"Biker jackets. Biker leathers. Biker boots. Motorcycles. Kind of like Waylon, but hairier."

She laughed, the motion making her ass wiggle.

Jeez, I have the best job.

"No such luck, Flo. They have to fit in like the rest of us. Human to a T, at least on the outside." She stood up and wiped her forehead. "When you're done doing nothing, how about you give me a hand?"

Uh-oh. Busted. I dropped the camera on the bed and adjusted the microphone to the perfect height for her.

"And now?" I pointed at the padded earphones on her head.

She pressed her face to the window. "Three more werewolves have entered the building opposite us. Something's cooking." Her volume was louder than was necessary.

"Let's—"

"Shh-Shh." Ivy repositioned the microphone.

I mimed zipping my mouth shut.

"Found them. Ground floor, one of those windows over there." She bent her knees for a better vantage point. "See? There's movement."

I took her word for it.

Voices streamed through her headphones out into my ears. My superior hearing had no trouble making out the words.

"A female wolf?" a wispy man's voice asked.

"Yes, and a single male accompanying her. A weedy looking guy, too. We should poach her. She'd be our alliance's first female."

That bastard called me weedy? I was a hundred and seventy pounds of pure muscle, and could lay out several of his kind without breaking a sweat. It was tough to find a more efficient killer than a vampire.

"Draylac said not to make trouble. When our job's done, we'll have plenty

of females. Don't you worry." Wispy Voice sounded more like a dad of five than an evil rogue werewolf.

"When it's done. Does he ever say anything other than if and when? How can you be okay with that?"

"You know what he can do," a third voice said. *"Let's give him time to prove himself."*

"She was pretty hot, though."

"Stop thinking with your cock. This is serious shit."

The other guy mumbled something. *"He'd better deliver."*

Ivy glanced up. "How can they be rogue if they have an alpha? And what kind of a name is Draylac anyway? Parker's going to be pissed when he finds out they've formed a pack—and in his town too."

"Definitely." And I hadn't even found a way to get rid of Keely's yet. "But he said *alliance.* Think that's what the cool rogues are calling a pack today, or is he talking about a hobby club like the Boy Scouts, and Draylac is their Bagheera?"

"You mean Akela?"

"Sure."

"I don't know. But if you're quiet, we might find out."

"I'm quiet." I spoke the words with a minimum of sulk.

We stayed silent for about ten seconds. Then...

"Should we get room service?" Ivy held her stomach. "It might take a while until they talk about their plans."

"I assume you want me to go to the vending machine and get snacks?"

"Great. Bring chocolate. And potato chips. And soda." She tilted her head. "Do you think they have pretzels?"

"Is Parker still insisting on a healthy diet?"

"He's crazy. As if carrots could sustain me." She flapped her hand. "Go get food."

"Yes, ma'am."

I took the key card and retraced my steps to the building's entrance area. The machine was out of order, and if I crossed the yard without Ivy's guard a-buzzing, I might be seen. Instead, I took the stairs up into another corridor with even more doors.

Five minutes of aimless wandering through the building brought me to the promised land. Or at least to the device that should keep us fueled for a while.

Arms filled with goodies, I returned to our floor. After some admirable acrobatics, I retrieved the key card and approached room eleven. Hanging out with Ivy was always—

A thump shook the door from the inside, followed by a man's groan.

My pulse revved, my muscles tensed.

"Ivy? Are you okay?" I dropped the food, swiped the card and rattled the knob. "Ivy? Can you hear me?"

Why wasn't she saying anything? I shouldered the door, which opened a few inches.

"Just a second." She huffed, and the weight pushing against the other side lifted.

I charged into the room, blood pressure dialed up to the max. Arms crossed, Ivy stood over the werewolf that passed us earlier.

The guy's lids blinked slowly, as if to refocus. His moves were sluggish.

Served him right. The jerk had walked in here assuming she'd submit to him like a good werewolf female. Instead, she'd rained whoop-ass on him.

Atta girl.

"Is that any way to treat a visitor?" I collected the food from the corridor, and then stepped over the man's form to drop the goodies on the bed. "Manners, Ivy."

"He knocked, and I thought it was you." Her cheeks were flushed. "Oh my God. I forgot. Is this going to turn you into blood-crazed Dracula?"

I'd nearly killed Ivy months ago while under a blood frenzy's thrall, so her concern was justified. I tried not to be insulted.

"Not to worry. It takes a lot more—like a large amount of actual blood—to kick-start a blood frenzy." I picked up a button from the floor and handed it to her. "Often with a lot of violence."

"Oh, there was violence. The guy pounced and shoved me onto the bed, but Waylon's training paid off." She glanced down at her midriff showing through a gap in her blouse.

"You should bake Waylon a cake." I gave the rogue's side a swift kick to see how conscious he was.

He yelped.

"I'm glad you're okay, Ivy."

Her smile relaxed my shoulders.

Ivy was pure magic. Despite her occasional self-centeredness, she cared. Her hugs soothed my soul, her smiles lifted my mood, and her laughter made all the bad things in life better.

"What now?" She scratched her neck.

"Let's pack up before his friends come looking for him."

She lowered her eyebrows. "I was really hoping they'd spill their plans while we were here."

"That would have been useful. And convenient."

"Yeah." She turned and folded up the microphone. "We can't tell Parker about this. If he finds out I got mixed up with the rogues, he'll go ballistic."

"No problem."

Parker also wouldn't be happy with her getting attacked on my watch. Good thing I knew how to clean up.

I kneeled by the groggy werewolf and tilted his head. The prospect of a meal was enough to make my fangs pop out, so I sank my teeth into his neck. His skin grated with five o'clock stubble, but my hunger didn't care. I sucked greedily. No point wasting good saliva or glamour on him.

Damn. He was too groggy to be scared, and the fear-induced sweetness I'd banked on to overpower the acrid taste of his blood didn't materialize. Still, his magic blood loaded my veins with life, and his inner power replenished what Gino had taken.

My strength returned in sizeable lumps. If humans packed the same punch, we wouldn't need to feed so often. But then, humans tasted a lot better.

With each droplet, my cravings subsided. After a minute or two, I released the wolf and licked my lips.

Ivy was the only person I'd ever let watch me eat.

The wolf whimpered.

"Better?" Ivy asked.

"Better." I lifted the guy's shoulders and snapped his head hard to the left.

His spine cracked, and his glazed eyes ceased moving. I let his shoulders plop onto the carpet.

"Florian." Ivy's tone sharpened to a point. "Why did you do that?"

Guardian or not, she was still squeamish like a human. She didn't get that even for a well-adjusted guy like me, the lines were pretty clear. Innocent people lived. People who meant to do harm to my friends didn't.

"We can't let him go back to his people and tell them about the hot werewolf chick beating him up. That would be dangerous to you and our pack."

"Hang on." She froze. "The hot werewolf female he mentioned was me?"

I made a point of studying her ruffled pants and torn and tangled shirt. "I'm as puzzled as you."

She placed her hands on her waist, permitting another delicious glance at her toned stomach. "I'm not laughing."

I got up and slammed my foot into the dead man's hip. "So much for me being weedy, asshole."

She sighed. "Anyway. I'm all packed." The candy I'd bought had disappeared from the bed.

I pointed down. "I'm gonna have to carry him over my shoulder."

"You want to deposit him in another room?"

"His own, yes."

"Hang on." She nipped over to the ex-werewolf and went through his parka's pockets. "Here." She held up a swipe card with the handwritten number on it. "Room nineteen. Must be a few doors down from us."

"Go on. You're the lookout."

"Wait…" She activated our guards and opened the door. "The coast is clear."

I hoisted the dead weight onto my shoulders and followed Ivy along the corridor into another room identical to ours. Another headboard of possibilities.

Enough with the headboards.

Ivy flicked her chin to the far side of the sofa, where I dropped his body well out of sight.

I left the room, and Ivy used her sleeves to wipe across his key card, which she placed on the stand, and closed the door behind her.

With me in the lead, we headed back. No one passed us, and thanks to Ivy's magical skills, no one would ever put us in this location.

I stepped aside to let her enter our room first. "Let's grab our gear and go."

"Are you sure we have to? We haven't learned anything."

"I want us far away when they find that body."

"But we're keeping the key card. We paid for two nights, and I intend to get my money's worth, even if I'm not here."

I lifted the card from her fingers. "*My* money's worth."

"You're such a scrooge," she mumbled rather loudly.

We retrieved our spy equipment, guards buzzing away, and made our way to the car.

Ivy cranked up the music for the ride, which wasn't unexpected. She tended to go quiet after we had to kill someone. Waylon kept pushing her to be more accepting of that side of our world, but she clung to her human morals.

I appreciated her innocence. She was my watchdog, and with her around, I wouldn't fall into the darkness.

Once my Benz stood in its usual spot outside my former home, we crossed the road together.

Ivy's small house was located about halfway between my family's leaf-covered structure and its twin across the street, the werewolves' stately mansion. Her drive was separate from Parker's, which extended to its left, past her house and large backyard.

Ivy rarely stayed at her place anymore, although she insisted on keeping it as her proper address. Maybe the reason she and Parker hadn't undergone the bonding ritual wasn't because of his schedule, but more her commitment issues.

She hugged me just outside her door. "Remember. Not a word to Parker about the rogues. I'm going to get changed, but you can wait for me if you like."

I shot her a smile. "I'll be okay."

"Good luck." She waved goodbye.

Her figure disappeared inside, and the door fell shut.

The plant in her bedroom's windowsill resembled a brown stick. Was her fridge still full of ice cream? Her step-trashcan overflowing?

I should ask her. Perhaps now.

Because my brain somehow refused to order my feet to move. Or maybe it did, and my feet refused to listen.

Ivy was right. I needed luck, and lots of it.

Ivy beside me would boost my confidence, but this conversation with Parker and Ali was the kind of thing I'd have to face like a man.

CHAPTER TEN

Taking a shower with liquid nitrogen would be a more pleasant experience than the one awaiting me now.

Despite the mansion's perfect white wash, the dull sky gave it a forlorn atmosphere. I stalked up the drive and climbed the three steps to the door, in no hurry to admit my defeat to Parker.

He might be used to my teasing, but this repeat failure to succeed in what I had declared a simple mission came close to disrespect.

My keys jingled in the lock, and I pushed the door open.

Heidi, a young werewolf female who'd once harbored a mega-crush on Parker, waved. "You're back."

I grinned. "You're observant as ever. Well done."

"Shut up." She blew a raspberry then stomped away.

She was joking, of course.

It was as Ivy said. No one messed with Ali's *intended*. In the future, I might have to curb my bravado. Without his protection, other wolves could take offense at my jests. That could pose a serious problem, because once my heart got pumping, it demanded my opponent's blood.

I straightened my spine and rolled my head, but the tightness in my neck and shoulders remained.

Keely's refusal to submit or leave wasn't the message Parker wanted to hear. But worse lay at the end of the corridor. Ali deserved an explanation.

Only, was this the best time? Shouldn't we concentrate on figuring out the Keely mess first?

Music sounded from upstairs, and the smell of stew curled through the air. Home sweet home.

At the table in the large hall, Parker and Ali pored over a stack of documents. Both had offices in the upper section of the building, but sometimes the lure of the multi-purpose hall proved too strong. After all, werewolves were sociable creatures.

Compared to kickass Ivy and hardass me, they struck a pale shade of vanilla. Twice my bulk, they didn't use their muscles half as much, but instead, they spent far too long obsessing over multiplying their wealth.

"I'm back." I projected my voice.

Ali's head tilted up. "I didn't see you come in. Where have you been?"

I pointed at the table. "You were engrossed in work."

He shoved the papers aside. "Sit. Tell us how it went."

"It didn't." I lowered myself onto the chair and kept my hands in my lap. "But it's nothing to do with demands or not sweetening the deal enough. She won't join us because her females were traumatized by their former male alpha. So I told her she'd have to leave."

Just lay it on the table, Flo. I swallowed.

"But that's a problem. Several of her females are pregnant, and one is having complications. If you make them move, you're signing their death certificates." Nothing less than mild exaggeration would sway Parker. "In fact, most of Keely's women are fragile. Christ, they're still girls. Some look younger than Heidi."

"I can't worry about that." Parker's voice was gentle. Like a father telling his son his pet rabbit has gone to live on a farm. "I know my guys. If I can't keep the women safe, they will, and that means they'll leave. I can't let that happen."

So the sympathetic approach alone wasn't going to cut it.

"But that's just it. By sending them away, you're *not* keeping them safe. Not the pregnant and vulnerable ones. But I may have a solution." I bundled enthusiasm into my voice. "If you loaned a few males to her, Keely would get the rep she needs to attract werewolves from legitimate packs."

Parker's frown didn't ease. In fact, it deepened, casting a shadow over his face.

"You want me to trick others into believing her pack is legit? Get real." He glanced at Ali. "If they won't move, we have to go in and force them to join us."

I shook my head. "The women would never allow it. They'll fight you tooth and claw."

"You're not listening, Flo. They're not giving me any choice. I'm sorry if they get hurt, but the safety of my own pack comes first."

I hooked my feet around the chair legs. "Keely has offered her own pack's limited strength for as long as they're here. That's almost like them joining us, isn't it?"

Parker and Ali studied me as if trying to locate my marbles.

"Maybe this is my fault. I should have explained my expectations of you better." Parker pushed back his shoulders. "They don't want to be part of our pack? Fine. Then I want them out. Off my property, and out of my town. We've been over this."

"You have to compromise."

"Why? It's my property. My pack is my responsibility. One guy's already laid up. If the situation continues, others are going to join him."

"But compromise is how negotiations work. Besides, they're pregnant. My job was to prevent bloodshed. This solution does that. It works."

Parker slammed his fist on the table. "Your *job* was to make them join our pack." He lifted his hand and flexed it.

His words sank my heart. After he'd trusted me like one of his pack, I'd failed him like the vampire I was.

Parker stretched his torso and leaned toward me. "Once an alpha accepts a werewolf as part of the pack, we promise protection for life. This is why we only allow bondings between packs in good standing. They've been approved by a responsible alpha. That way, my wolves know they'll be well cared for and protected if they join another approved pack."

"But the guys know the female pack hasn't been approved. So isn't it their choice?"

"If they get hurt down the line, my reputation is shot. Suddenly I'm the guy who can't keep his wolves safe. And if I look weak, the whole pack will be in trouble."

Up until now, he'd been the grumpy guy who complained a lot. It seemed there was more to being an alpha than shouting.

I propped up my chin with my hand. "I didn't know."

"I'm not saying werewolf conventions are easy to relate to. But my guys are my children. They have good hearts and want to see all females safe. Hell, I do too. But their good intentions could lead them into an unsafe situation. What if the other alpha beats them without reason? What if she makes them do things they don't want to do?"

"Keely wouldn't do that."

"You've known her for two days, Flo. My responsibility to them is for life. And this isn't about this particular pack, but about werewolf laws. So I have to stop my wolves from getting attached to an unsafe pack."

"Right. And there's only one way to stop them from just running off."

"Yes. I have to put my foot down." Parker lifted his hands to highlight the inevitability of the situation. "If they challenge my authority, I will beat them down. So bring me a solution that works, Flo, or get rid of the females. I'm done."

My brain chugged as it grasped Parker's perspective. A challenge on an alpha ended one of two ways. Either the alpha made the challenger submit, or the challenger killed the alpha. Animalistic, but cut and dry, in typical werewolf order.

"Am I getting through to you?" Parker picked up his pen, clicked it like a maniac, and then threw it back down. "And now with the rogues around, the situation has become a ticking time bomb. The moment they go after the females, my guys will run them out of town or die trying."

Somehow I'd convinced myself I'd find a way out. Getting people to see my side, even without glamour, had saved my ass many times. I should have been able to cut through Keely's and Parker's objections like they were water. Turns out my delusions were greater than any so-called skill.

The only way to do right by Keely and her pack was to make her understand.

Parker softened his lips into a smile. "Can you get it done?"

I'd been flirting on borrowed time anyway.

I steeled my gaze. "Yes. I'll get it done."

"Parker." Ali glanced from me to his boss. "Maybe Flo isn't the best person for the job."

"Hey," I shouted.

Had he lost faith in me?

"Why's that?" Parker asked.

"The alpha..." Ali peered at me.

God, no. I shook my head. *Don't tell him. Don't you dare.*

"This girl might be to him what Ivy is to you."

Bam. He'd done it. He'd spilled my secret like it was milk. Of all the people to betray my trust.

Parker laughed. "Seriously?"

He studied me, probably saw my jaw twitch, my eyes go wide.

His face sobered. "Oh shit. Does that mean you're going to leave us when she goes?"

"No way." My words shot out like a bullet. "You're making too big a deal out of this."

Assuming I *was* ready to give up everything, Keely would never play house with a vampire.

"What about your connection?" Parker wagged his hand between Ali and me.

Ali shrugged. "He's shutting me out. And I can't figure out why."

Parker stood, palms flat on the table. He whispered a few words, powerful words that tugged on me. Tugged, but did not compel.

No way out. Trapped in the certainty my secret was about to be exposed, I firmed my spine and lifted my chin. "Listen, about that."

Ali went rigid, his limbs locked in place, his face blank.

Two seconds later, he shook out his muscles. "Next time some warning, Parker."

I could have pretended to feel the alpha's call on me, but what was the use?

"How long?" Parker tightened his jaw and narrowed his eyes. "How long has the link been gone?"

"Actually…" My mouth dried.

I could salvage this. All it took were the right words and vampire charm.

My bottom lip quivered like a boy's, and I had to clamp it between my teeth. *Don't look at Ali. Just don't.*

"Florian." Parker's voice rocked with impatience. He towered over me from across the table, his scowl drilled deep.

A chill swirled my stomach.

I rubbed my forehead. "It's a long story."

"And you didn't tell us?" The alpha crossed his arms, looming like a giant who could stomp me with his feet. "How often do we have to remind you of the rules? We're giving you and Ivy a pass on your work-related stuff, but you've got to tell us everything else. Packs run on trust."

The ball of boiling pressure inside exploded, and I shot to my feet. "It's a family matter. My vampire family, so it's not your business. And it's not like I planned this."

His eyes twitched. "How is your link to Ali not our business? That's a big one, isn't it?

"Shut up." I interlaced my fingers, my knuckles turned white as I pulled and stretched. "Who are you to treat me like a child?"

I was a freaking centuries-old vampire, a Master no less. I'd been around longer than this puppy had even been a sperm cell in his father's testicles.

Parker pressed his lips together. His face turned a deep red.

I took a long breath then shook my head. "You two should have told me the stakes from the start. Instead you sent me in blind. You practically set me up for failure."

"What the hell?" Parker looked stunned.

It was hardly my fault Keely was playing ping-pong with my hormones, or that Gino had ripped apart my link with Ali.

I raised my hands. "It's okay. I get it now. I know the consequences of the other pack's presence. I'll get it done."

Ali shook his head. "Right. All of a sudden it's no longer a problem?"

Fuck it. "I told you. Keely is history. She's nothing to me."

Who knew my words would hurt me more than sticks and stones?

"Let's put aside the fact that you're lying through your teeth." Parker's tone lost emotion. "I want to know why you didn't tell us about severing your link to Ali."

Admit my humiliation at Gino's hands? "Don't you think if that had been my doing, I would have talked to Ali about this? He's my friend."

"Well, who did it then?"

The air around me vibrated and clogged my airways. Parker's alpha power pulled no punches.

"Okay. Shit. Fine." I dragged my hand over my face. "My sire reconnected with me."

Violently.

"You chose him over the pack?" Ali shook his head. "I know you've been dying to get rid of this link between us, but I hoped you'd take the time to talk to us before it happened."

"I told you, I didn't plan for this."

They wouldn't understand why Gino acted the way he did, or why I hadn't defended myself. At best, I'd be the victim.

I tucked my thumbs into my belt. "Let's drop it."

"You're still not giving us the whole story." Parker placed a hand on Ali's shoulders. "This isn't working."

His words iced my skin.

"What isn't working?" I sought my former *intended's* gaze.

Ali looked away. His skin was draped in a gray hue, practically unaffected by the light from the ceiling's powerful lamps.

My jaw tensed so hard, my teeth ached from the pressure. "You always say it's all about the pack. Well, I'm pack, too."

Parker raised an eyebrow. "How can we trust you?"

"I messed up, but I can turn it around. Give me another chance, and Keely is gone for good." I sent another pleading look to Ali.

Ali rubbed his Adam's apple.

I'd done that to him. Trampled his feelings. I'd wished for our link to break, and Gino had made my wish come true. *Well, congratu-fucking-lations, Florian.*

"You're still not getting it." Parker's pitch was weary now.

"I do." I clamped my hands around the table's edge. "I'll go right now. Kick out Keely and her pregnant girls. What do I care if they die, right?"

Any moment, Ali would say something to bridge the conflict.

I waited. Stared. Willed him.

He moved his head to the right. Then the left.

The delicate spheres I'd balanced on top of my head for the past few months came crashing down. Leaving my home, curbing my appetites, and squeezing into a tiny room wasn't worth jack.

Julia was right. I would never be wolf enough for them.

The fire to fight extinguished. "You want me to go? Fine, I'll go."

"Maybe you should." Parker tightened his grip on his friend's shoulder.

Given a few hours or days, Ali would pick himself up. He always bounced back. Once they had time to think about the situation, they might change their minds.

As if. Had I thought my time here wasn't limited?

I pushed my chair back against the table and strutted, chin up, out of the room like I was John Fucking Travolta.

CHAPTER ELEVEN

HEAD SWIRLING WITH *WHAT-THE-FUCKS* AND *how-the-hells*, I left the hall at a quick pace.

Jim stopped mid-run on the stairs and stared at the wall. He wouldn't even grant me a pity nod.

Somehow the whole pack knew to stay away from the leper.

I dropped my house keys on the side table, opened the door, and strode across the drive past Ivy's house, out onto the street. Outside, a brisk wind whipped around my ears. My feet did their job like those of a robot. If only the rest of me were no more than a collection of wires and switches, without pain, anger, and sadness.

Instead of heading to my former home, I carried on walking. Maybe oxygen would clear my head or at least alleviate the painful spasms in my chest.

Had Keely been right? Should I have told Parker the true extent of my family reunion?

At best, Parker and Ali would have shot me pitying glances. *Poor, weak Florian.* Bad enough I had zero alpha tendencies in me when I was around the guys. That whiney move would have lost me all respect.

I was faster than them and stronger than most. My ears and eyes worked better. So what if I didn't feel like proving my superiority every fucking minute of every fucking day? I'd leave that to the Ginos and Parkers of the world.

What was so bad about wanting a quiet life anyway?

Be that as it may, that wouldn't have even been the worst-case scenario.

If Parker had confronted my sire, he'd have died at Gino's hands. No question.

Werewolves and ancient vampires... You don't mess with that.

I folded my right arm behind my neck and gave it a good stretch by nudging the elbow, then repeated the procedure on the other side. Little good it did me, because the true center of tension lay far too deep for me to reach.

I'd walked two miles or more when my phone beeped.

"Please, Florian. Forgive him." My sister's words, but Gino's outstretched hand. *"Come for dinner."*

I shoved the phone deep into my pocket, hands trembling. The late afternoon temperature drop didn't help. Forgive Gino? Had he not told her what happened?

The humiliation he'd dished out. The sheer brutality of his failed re-making. I clenched a fist so tight, the bones in my hand cracked.

I should have hit back harder.

The flames within wouldn't be doused by thoughts. Gino wanted dinner? Yes, I'd make sure he got his just deserts.

Back at my old family home, wind buffeted my Benz and shook the yellowish green leaves climbing the walls. I got behind the wheel and put my foot down. The car blasted off like it had a rocket attached to it. The address Julia texted led me to a grand building dating back at least a couple of centuries. It took up the space of three of its family-sized neighbors, with a short drive, a well-cared for front lawn and plenty of windows covered with dense curtains.

Once my finger pressed the brass doorbell, it wouldn't let go. Any second now, Gino's face would feel my fist. Julia had better not get in my way.

Twenty seconds later, my sire opened the door. His turtleneck sweater made his frame appear broader.

He raised his eyebrows and removed my finger from the doorbell. "I was not sure you were going to show."

I straightened and pulled back my shoulders. He was taller than me, had access to vampire magic I could only dream of, but he wasn't faster, more agile, or stronger than me. He should be the one fearing *me*.

"How could I not accept your invitation?" My voice took the cue from him and gave away nothing.

"Well, I am glad you did. Come in, *Cucciolo*." He stepped aside and made a sweeping gesture, as if nothing had happened between us.

Like he hadn't destroyed my trust.

It took immense willpower not to let my knuckles dance across his face. Not that I wanted him dead. Just hurt. A lot. I brushed past him, and his familiar scent sent me back a few hundred years. *Shit*. I'd been certain his cruelty had erased my fonder memories, but the flutter in my stomach told me otherwise.

Regardless, it was time someone stood up to him. Belated or not, that someone was going to be me.

He shut the door, and his gaze drifted to my belt buckle. "You had a spare guard."

I struck out, my fist connecting with the golden spot on the bridge of his nose. Jeez, that felt good.

He jerked back and his eyes grew wide.

My next blow cracked his chin.

He slanted to the side and chuckled before spitting blood onto the floor. "You want to play it—"

"This isn't a game, dammit." I pummeled his stomach and chest with my knuckles.

My attack drove him against a sideboard. I settled into a drumlike routine, aimed at inflicting maximum pain. Nothing less than Gino's utter humiliation would satisfy me.

His knuckles soared into my vision, but I was just as fast and blocked him. For the shortest of moments, we stood belly to belly, face to face. His dark eyes, almost black, were surrounded by a red fringe of spidery veins.

The next moment he catapulted me into the wall. The plaster crumbled, leaving a football-sized bare patch.

I spun, kicking him in the balls.

He doubled over, and I followed up with a hook under his chin.

He whirled into the coat rack.

Between the two of us, I wasn't just the better fighter, albeit out of practice, but I was also the superior survivor.

I aimed my next punch at his eye.

He sidestepped me, avoiding my assault with his forearm, and wrapped a rough jacket over my head.

Going by instinct, I lashed out while contorting myself to shrug off the veil.

A punch landed in my mouth, another in my stomach, both dampened by the thick fabric.

I yanked off the scratchy coat and inhaled through my nostrils. "You haven't lost your flair."

"Neither have you." He struck my neck.

Pain radiated into my chest and mouth, forcing my change. My fangs pierced through my gums, and my senses came alive.

I came alive.

This was getting fun.

Gino nursed his nose with his palm. "Had enough?"

Smug bastard. I hurled myself at his raised arm.

His free hand gripped my hair, but not before I sank my teeth into his skin. He whacked my skull, but I held tight.

I tasted his blood—powerful blood—and needed more.

He shook his arm. "Get off."

He kicked my right leg out from under my body.

I dropped onto my knees, ripping a chunk out of his flesh as I went down.

He shoved me off, but the smell of his life force woke the old Florian. The Florian I kept stowed in the back of a closet, next to my bondage gear.

Blood was a drug, but nothing compared to my sire's blood. It had birthed my vampire self, promised powers I could only dream of.

That promise burned as brightly today as it did then. My heart fired on all cylinders, and I was upright faster than his eyes could track.

The brunt of my shoe wrenched up his chin, making his eyes water.

Gino slammed into the coat stand.

In the same instant, I was on him, clawing at his neck and lapping up his blood. My greedy tongue rolled up to channel it straight into my mouth and throat, into my circulation, where it sparked warmth throughout, and strengthened me.

Winded, Gino slid to the ground, and the rack toppled onto us.

He laughed and knocked my head away from him.

"Enough. You have made your point." He blew air through tight lips.

Had I? I let go, and then freed myself from the heavy jackets blocking my view. A grim laughter rattled the air, and it took a second to recognize the voice as mine.

"What else do you have for me?" Gino's canines gleamed as white as they always had.

He hadn't become a vampire Master by giving up. From his seated position, he hooked his fingers into my belt and hurtled me into the opposite wall.

A big fucking ouch was imminent, and I spun midair to cushion the impact. The blood and adrenaline combined into one mighty head rush.

I tipped my head and let out a fortifying growl.

Gino surged to his feet.

I gathered momentum in my arm to—

"Gino. Help me." Julia's high-pitched voice from somewhere back in the building halted my motion.

Gino and I looked at each other. My grin fell, followed by his a split second later. He wiped his bloody mouth with his sleeve and darted down the hall.

"Come on then," he called over his shoulder.

I followed at his heels. If there was trouble down that corridor, I wanted my share.

The varnished wooden door to one of the rooms crashed open, and a lanky vampire soared across our path. His face turned toward us, fangs out, but as yet free from blood.

"This is how you repay my welcome?" Gino kicked the back of the guy's knees then pounced on top, his jacket end draped over his own shoulder. His teeth tore into the stranger's arms.

The man's screams invigorated my body.

Feeling quite the gooseberry, I leaped over them, headfirst into a brawl between my sister and three more vampires. *Nice.* My family sure knew how to lay on the entertainment.

I grabbed the collars of two of her opponents and yanked them off her. One tumbled onto the ground.

The other whirled around and snapped his elbow into my face.

Shit. That hurt, but the line of fire from my nose to my brain fizzled under the assault of his body odor. A good knock-out was one thing. I drew the line at a lack of hygiene.

I took hold of his bushy beard and shoved him against the filing cabinet.

He bared his fangs, snapping at air.

Mine were on target. A slash with their pointy ends tore up his throat.

He gurgled and wobbled.

His acrid blood held the flavor of oil and moldy lemons, all but making me gag. Humans were the only species that didn't taste vile in the absence of an emotional connection. I let the guy fall and coughed up the fibrous flesh I'd ripped from his neck.

A punch to my kidneys made me groan. *Bastard.*

I kicked back, and my foot hit the target before I twisted to plant my fist in my attacker's chest.

His gray-streaked brows sagged, and he puffed minty breath in my direction. Tired eyes advertised his intentions. He was about to make an all-or-nothing move. So typical vampire.

His arm shot out, leaving his neck undefended.

Amateur move, buddy. I let my flexed abs absorb the force of his attack and clamped my hands around his head.

One crack of his spine, and he dropped like a sack of shit. His skull smashed against a corner of a white desk, then struck the ground. Few sounds were as beguiling as that of an opponent's death.

My training with the werewolves had paid off. My attack was

more considered, my defense ordered. The stranger didn't know who he was messing with.

I retracted my fangs, wiped my face, and smoothed my jacket and shirt.

"You good?" Julia sat beside her slain adversary.

His lifeless face pointed toward Bushy Beard, whose legs were trapped under my latest victim's torso.

My sister's grin spoke volumes. Most of the time, our hearts could at best be described as taxidermy stuffing, but nothing got it pumping again like a good old fight.

"Hell, that was enjoyable." Gino leaned against the doorframe, bruises and blood on proud display. "So good to see my *Cucciolo* hasn't been tamed by his friends."

Despite his dig, I smiled.

"Hardly tame." I stepped over a limp leg to help Julia up from the floor. "May I ask what they were doing here?"

"They are part of an organization called The Circle." Gino shook his head. "They came to recruit us."

Are these the bastards that kidnapped Keely? I gave one of the corpses a hard kick. *Assholes.*

I gestured at them. "And you invited them in for a chat?"

"Of course. You expressed concern about my preference for the old ways, so I wanted to give your method a try." Gino shrugged. "I do not care for this talk-first mentality."

Well, he got me there.

My high faded fast, replaced by weariness dragging on my limbs. I'd come to fight, although not by Gino's side. Had anything changed between us?

I forced my gaze away from the dead. "What now?"

"I am hungry." Gino's eyes were alight with the fire of a good kill. "How about you two?"

Except for blood, no solid food had graced my temple of a body today—filthy vampire flesh notwithstanding. But breaking bread with my sire was a hell of a first step.

I touched my stomach. "I guess I could eat. Hope you have wine to cleanse my palate with."

"I can rustle something up." Julia nodded at Gino and frowned at me. "Let's get cleaned up first, okay?"

I tugged at my green shirt, now covered in specks of blood. "It's the latest fashion."

She clicked her tongue and dragged me away.

"Here." She pushed me into a tiled bathroom and walked off.

Two large bowls sat on top of a gray dresser and functioned as sinks. I wet some toilet paper and dabbed at the blood on my face.

Julia stepped in behind me, now wearing a blue top.

"Let me." She threw a fresh shirt onto the toilet seat and took over cleaning duty.

When the toilet paper proved useless, she held the corner of a towel under running water and continued. The light-brown towel concealed all traces of makeup.

I grinned at her.

"Stop moving." She tilted my chin up and rubbed the towel over my stubble.

"I'm not moving."

"Quiet." She stood back and frowned. "Take your shirt off."

"I'm not a child." I still slipped my shirt over my head and handed it to her. "Don't you usually pay guys and girls for that pleasure?"

She grabbed my shirt and whipped it at me, a button catching my cheek.

"That hurt." I rubbed my face. "I know you definitely pay people for that."

Her lips twitched. "You're one to talk."

"I don't have to pay people, dear sister. They all want me."

"Lord, give me strength," she mumbled and wiped the towel over my chest to remove even more blood. "One day, some nice woman is going to drive that smugness right out of you."

Keely had succeeded on several occasions already.

I grabbed my sister's hand to make her stop. "Do you really think that's going to happen?"

Her gaze softened, and she placed her palm against my cheek. "I know it will."

"Do you know..." I exhaled and stared at the assortment of personal grooming products lined up along a shelf in the shower. "About staking your Claim? Did Gino ever tell you how it works? I mean, how do you know when the time is right?"

"Oh." She tilted her head and stepped back. "Actually he did. Once. He said some enter the bond with deliberation. But for others, it happens on the first crush. That's how it was with Gino and Zoe. A whirlwind romance, and a month later, they were hitched."

My heart thumped in my chest. So this crazy urge that overcame me in Keely's presence wasn't unprecedented.

"It's like human relationships in a way. Sometimes love develops over time, sometimes you fall fast." She nodded. "Zoe wasn't Gino's first serious girlfriend, you know. He'd entered into a committed relationship with a demon before."

I gaped. "You're joking."

"Don't tell him I told you. But Zoe was different. When he saw her, he had no choice. He said she bewitched him." Julia picked up the folded shirt and shook it out. "What's this about? Is there someone special in your life?"

"Besides you? Don't be silly. And you were the one who started this conversation." I ripped the shirt out of her hand and made a point of getting my head lost in a sleeve so she wouldn't see just how red my face must have turned.

"Jeez, Flo." She fumbled the fabric down and hooked in the top buttons. "You'd think you could get dressed alone. Gino said you're a Master now."

"Yeah. Don't ask how." I undid the two buttons at the top to prevent asphyxiation.

"That's...good." Her dark blue eyes shifted, unfocused.

"You'll get there soon." I pulled her into a big hug. "Maybe Gino's planning it already."

"Oh, it's not that." She pressed her cheek against my neck and interlocked her arms behind my waist. "It's just, you're already so independent."

Independent was one word for it. When I joined the pack, I dropped my sister and brother faster than a lump of uranium. This was my bad. Not theirs. I let them down.

I kissed the top of her head. "I'm sorry I moved out. Would it help if I said I hated every minute I spent at the pack's house?"

She shrugged and pulled me tighter. "It might."

"Well, I hated it," I said with conviction. "Ali's meatballs suck. He claims he can cook, but he can't. And you'd think living with Ivy would be fun."

"Isn't it?"

It so was.

But not even a knot the size of Utah in my throat would stop me from lying to my sister.

"She's always around Parker, making kissing noises or googly eyes. You know, she pretends to have a conversation with you, then her gaze will drift and she'll say something like, "Doesn't he have the best ass?" Seriously, what am I supposed to say to that?"

Julia giggled. "Parker does have a pretty good ass."

"Shut up." I nudged her away from me by her shoulders. "To be honest, I've had *some* fun with them, but I've missed you. Eli too, but don't tell him. I know I haven't always shown it, and for that, I'm sorry."

She patted my cheek then slapped me. Hard.

"Crap." I nursed my face. "What was that for?"

"For leaving me." She lifted her chin and glared. "If you want to make it up to me, then forgive Gino."

"You don't know what he's done. He bit me and drank from me." I rubbed my neck. "Do you know how much that hurt?"

"I know everything. And if you'd let his glamour in, it wouldn't have hurt at all."

Touché. "He beat me up and took my buckle guard."

"Enough." She gripped her hips, her bottom lip quivering. "You were disrespectful. Plus, you turned your back on your family and moved in with the furballs. His sworn enemies. What do you expect? You once beat the crap out of Eli for totaling your car."

Dammit. Now she was throwing reason in my face.

"It was a good car."

She leaned forward. "I'm not saying Gino didn't overreact, but you pushed his buttons. He's sorry, but I need you to accept some blame in this mess."

She hooked up my buttons again and turned. I followed her out of the bathroom, along the white corridor. Old and new scenes of Silverton hung on the walls in the form of photos and watercolors.

"I'll get dinner ready. You speak to Gino." Julia pointed at a room, her tone firm. "I won't be long."

"You'd better not be," I mumbled and undid my collar button once more.

CHAPTER TWELVE

M Y MIND TRIED TO CONVINCE me I was entering hell. In reality, I walked into a sleek, modern room without sofas or TV, like a doctor's waiting room. Plastic-covered supersized chairs without armrests faced one another, and a tall palm tree added a hint of the exotic.

Gino sat at an angle on a chair, one knee pulled up onto its edge. He threw a magazine he'd been reading onto another chair. "Come. Join me."

I took a single step. Then another. My snail's pace was pointless, of course. He and I would have a conversation. I'd promised my sister.

Family was important to her. When Gino left, she became the head of the household. She continued to cook and clean for us for many years, and her writing was a mere hobby. Later, it became a career. Her books took her away from us, but it brought out a confidence and strength in Julia I came to admire. With her encouragement, Eli and I made new friends, entertained girls, and found other ways to occupy our time.

So if Julia asked me to make up with Gino, I owed her that much.

Gino tracked my path to my seat.

"So." I raised my eyebrows and stretched out my legs. "Here we are."

"I am glad you came, Florian." Gino exhaled loudly. "First things first. I should not have taken your protection guard. There is no excuse for my behavior. All I can do is explain and hope for your forgiveness." He shifted forward, one arm draped over his knee.

He wore a white shirt like me, his buttons open over a black T-shirt.

Wow. Gino had discovered modern wear.

My body ached, missing the adrenaline that had spiked my pulse. Our rematch had been a more balanced affair, and all sorts of fun, but the slate couldn't be wiped clean by a short-lived high.

"I know this is hard." He shook his head, his eyebrows furrowed. "Come. I want to show you around."

I got up and joined him as he walked out of the door and turned right into a sort of roofed veranda, overflowing with vases of flowers and dainty decorations that served no purpose that I could make out.

I held my face close to a bowl of blue chips that smelled like pineapple. "Julia must love this place. It's so…"

"Elegant?"

I chuckled. "I was going to say girly, but sure."

"Apologizing is not easy for me, but I will try." His large hand settled on my shoulder. "You must understand, I have dreamt of our reunion. If nothing else, I wished to resume our relationship as if no time had passed. Now you are a Master."

"I am."

He nodded. "There is still so much I have yet to teach you. I had the whole occasion planned out."

I frowned. "What occasion?"

"The day I was going to release you and make you a Master, of course." His eyes lost focus. "We would take in a show, have great food, and then I would give you this."

He fished a black stone from his pocket and turned it over in his hand.

The words scored into its surface read, *"Be strong. Be you. Be a vampire."*

"Mehmet gave this to me when he made me a Master, and his sire gave it to him. I added the inscription."

I swallowed. If I'd known there would be a ceremony… No, it wouldn't have made a difference. It wasn't like I chose to be a Master. It had just happened.

He dropped his arm. "I see now how foolish it was to assume our time apart would not have ruined everything."

I gave a wide-armed shrug. "It hasn't ruined anything. You're still my sire. We're family, Gino. Master or not, no one is going to take that away from us."

He lowered his eyelids. "You are right. We have changed and must be patient with each other. Here. It is yours." He handed me the stone.

My lungs opened up, and fresh, cleansing air streamed in. "Seriously?"

I balanced the object in my hand. Even though it wasn't a guard, it did possess magic—rumbling, vibrating magic.

"It does not matter how you became a Master. You earned it." He squeezed my arm.

"Thank you." The stone's blank surface was cold and smooth, its carved side rough. "What is it?"

"Protection." He smiled. "When the elves disappeared from our lands, they left some of their possessions behind, including the Rock of Wisdom. This piece was taken from it and is said to bring luck."

"And you're giving it to me?"

"Who else? You are the first of my children to become a Master. I will not deny that the manner in which it happened frustrates me, but I am still proud of you, Florian."

I closed my hand around the stone, letting its vibrations melt into my cells.

"Please, son." Gino tightened his grip. "Forgive me."

Did the honesty in his tone come from him, or was I projecting?

I was too tired to deal with this shit. Our start was a rough one, sure, but the real victim of our fight was my link with Ali. A link I'd been working hard to get rid of for six months.

"Of course." I briefly closed my eyes and let him gather me into a father's embrace.

Besides, what did it matter if I sought comfort in his arms? After all, there was no one left to judge me.

He exhaled. "Let us get to know each other again."

I soaked in his signature scent, a woodsy note that would outlast all the body sprays and colognes in the world.

I nodded. "We should work on our communication."

He chuckled and released me. "Agreed. Come. Let's talk."

For the first time since I left Ivy, my walk was unhurried and light. Gino was back, and despite my initial impression, without his trademark urge for violence. Otherwise The Circle's vampires would have been dead the moment they rang the doorbell.

We left the veranda, and with little regard for the bodies in the hall, followed another boxy corridor with a hundred and one doors left and right of us.

"What is this place?" I asked. "I mean, how did you get it? Did you buy it?"

"It's my new home. When I came to Silverton, this city job was thrust upon me, and this house…" He gestured around him, "is one of the perks. Do you like it?"

I made a show of studying the arty, black and white photographs on the wall.

"Nice digs." I glanced at him. "But you could come home. If you wanted to, I mean."

I could keep an eye on him there. He seemed to have chosen the right path and shed his old superiority, but he couldn't afford any relapses.

Gino lowered his head. "Thank you. For now, this is where I am needed. Did you know forty percent of Silverton's population are kin, and among those in power, that number is even higher? Yet their incomes are lower, their living standards too." He flailed his hands in wild animation. "Why? Because they're at odds. They don't trust humans, and they don't trust each other. This world relies on connections. Imagine what would happen if we all worked together."

"A better life?"

"A *vastly* better life, Florian."

"And you want to change that? I mean, are the other kin going to trust you? Before you left, you had a reputation."

Not a good one.

"I am willing to make up for my mistakes. The poor people used to trust Guardians, but Guardians are focused on protecting humans nowadays, when they're supposed to protect kin. Think about why I was exiled. One mistake. I never intended to kill that woman. No, my mission is clear. Someone has to stand up for our kind."

Ivy and Waylon had given me a different description of their jobs, even though Gino had a point. Alethia was established as a safe haven for kin who felt suppressed by the growing number of humans. Guardians policed those who stayed in Oldworld to ensure our existence remained a secret, and they did so by sending troublemakers to Alethia.

The original Alethians couldn't have been too happy to see the worst of the worst being shipped off into their backyards.

Gino's gaze drifted across my face, as if he could read my thoughts.

"It may not be easy, but I can be better. I must be better." He nodded. "Still, changing our fortune is not the kind of thing I can do alone."

Judging by this house and his new position, he understood aspects of the new world better than I'd hoped. Unless my memory deceived me, he even swore earlier. That alone would be worthy of an entry in a diary, if I kept one.

I rubbed my neck. "What's your plan?"

"Food's ready." Julia shouted from somewhere in an exuberant song. It was such a contrast to her recent gloominess.

"She is different too." Gino flicked his finger at an open door. "For one, she is more accommodating and patient than she used to be."

I grinned. "Don't be taken in by her act. She's become a fierce and shrewd businesswoman. Glad to see you, that's all. She'll have you clean up after yourself in no time."

"Your sister? She loves being the mother hen." Gino's deep laughter felt like home. "Come. Let's not test her."

We turned down another long corridor, Gino in front, sending repeated glances at me, as if to be sure I didn't run off.

A ceiling lamp swung low above our heads, and with the moving shadows, it paid to keep my gaze glued to tiles paving the way. At the far end of the corridor, the smooth brickwork gave way to a long room with a dark-wood table, on which bowls of food gave off steam. Six plates had been set, and three seats were already taken.

Two young women and one man sat in high-backed chairs. Light from a chandelier overhead bathed the room in a soft yellow.

"I didn't know you had guests." I lifted a hand as a general greeting.

Gino smirked. "They live here."

"You have a staff?"

"Perhaps you are not the only one who has friends." He gestured to the empty chair between the ladies.

The women, one brunette, the other blonde, were dressed in modern fashion of jeans and T-shirts. For all their lack of animation, they could be shop window mannequins.

My breathing slowed and then stalled. The blood slaves we'd kept across Europe, before the Great Vampire Hunt, used to look like this. Wide eyes, stiff posture.

Judging by their skin and the veins running invisible underneath, these three had not been fed off.

I was overreacting. If nothing else, Gino's show of faith in letting the vampires state their case proved he was capable of adapting. If I wasn't careful, my doubts would drive a wedge between us before we reconnected.

That couldn't happen. I had already lost one family today.

"Sit. Please." Gino sat next to the man and brushed the crook of his finger over his cheek. "Are we ready to have a good time?"

The guy's Adam's apple bobbed with more force than his head. Julia was a great cook, but this dude seemed way too excited about food.

Unless she'd made her casserole.

"How do you know each other?" I took my seat between the two women.

"I know what you're thinking, but they are here voluntarily, I assure you." He gestured at them.

I waved him off. "I wasn't thinking anything."

"Dig in." Julia handed a bowl of stewed tomatoes to the woman next to her.

The steam from meat and vegetables in double-walled bowls suffused the room with wonderful smells, and the generous use of spices brought heat to my cold body. A sense of déjà vu slipped through my mind. I almost expected Eli to tell an anecdote, but his absence was the one thing preventing our reunion from being complete.

My cell beeped, and I shot my sire an apologetic glance before retrieving it.

His right eye twitched, but Ivy's message won.

"Where are you?" she wrote. *"Parker said you're gone, but won't tell me what happened. Are you okay?"*

I punched the exit key and stuffed the phone back into my pants. Finding the right words to explain my dilemma could wait.

"Wasn't important." I looked at Gino.

He dipped a slice of French bread into the sauce on his plate. "What's this I hear about Eli starting a new career?"

I rubbed my still sore chin. "Yes, you'll hardly recognize him. He's working with the Interracial Enforcement Agency. Says he loves the action. Right now, he's hunting The Circle. And here's the crazy thing. He's coordinating with a Guardian on behalf of the IEA."

He lifted his eyebrows. "The IEA is working with a Guardian?"

"Yeah. His name is Waylon. Nothing like the Guardians you remember." My smile faltered. "A lot has changed."

Gino shook his head slowly. "Son, I take back what I said before. I'm glad you have found friends. Truly."

"Seriously?"

He tapped the table with his fork. "Of course. I merely wish they weren't furballs." He laughed.

The man to his left laughed with him, but it was fake laughter. The guy didn't register as a vampire, and I couldn't tell if he was human or fae, but he seemed to have no understanding of our relationship with werewolves.

Gino shrugged. "As long as your friends treat you well, I will not complain."

Hmm. What if they steamroll me?

Keely had turned me into her tool with a flutter of her eyelashes. And Parker used my skills when it suited him, but the second I messed up, he kicked me out.

"What's wrong?" Gino's gentle voice pulled me from my dark thoughts.

I lowered my gaze. "Nothing. Did you…did you want to meet my friends?"

"Yes. But as I mentioned, our fellow kin have put me in this position to do a job." His tone held gravitas. "Werewolves make them uncomfortable, and it is too early to antagonize them. You'll need to stay away from them for a while too, but afterward?" He spread his arms out. "I do, yes."

"Right." I gave a satisfied yawn and leaned back.

Vampires weren't the only kin the werewolves had problems with. Other kin gave the furballs a wide berth too.

Of course, introducing the pack to Gino was a moot issue anyway. To them, I'd always be a vampire. An outsider. My rules, my restraint. None of it mattered in the end.

At least my sire didn't expect me to be something I wasn't.

Gino slid his hand across the man's arm.

The guy's eyes widened. His first movement in a while. In fact, Gino's guests hadn't joined in the conversation. The women smiled politely, but they didn't belong. Why were they even here?

"Ready for dessert?" Gino's eyes held a predatory glint.

The guy opened his shirt's top button. The blonde next to me took my hand and pulled me close.

A knot balled high in my throat.

That's why the guests were here. They were sheep, people who rented themselves out to vampires in return for protection or wealth. Hadn't they gone out of style centuries ago? The long-term effects of constant feedings and glamours on sheep were well known, from hallucinations to a disregard for their own lives.

Usually I glamoured my meals, so I could slip my teeth in, drink, and make off without being detected. Like a ghost. The last time I'd had a willing snack… Hell, I couldn't even remember.

"Are you happy or would you want to swap?" Gino's arm draped over the other guy's shoulder, like they were best buds.

The blonde who held my hand looked just as eager.

I pulled my shoulders back. "I'm good."

Julia sank her teeth into the brunette between us, one hand on the girl's hair, the other on her left breast.

Her victim gave an ecstatic moan, and I shuddered.

Wide eyed, the blonde to my other side leaned in to me.

"Do you want me like this?" Her voice was weak and timid.

"Umm. Yeah, that's fine." Without hiding my erection, I moved closer and laid my glamour around her.

A gurgle sounded opposite me as Gino bit into the man's throat.

The guy flailed his fists, a natural reaction, but my sire's grip proved too strong.

A hole opened up in me, like white noise drowning out the world. The scent of blood from Gino and Julia's meals smelled so good. I briefly closed my eyes and suppressed another shudder. So fucking good.

The man with Gino grunted.

I swept back the blonde's hair and looked across the table. The guy's eyes had lost their dreamy expression and gone to WTF mode. Gino had dropped his glamour. Nothing to soothe the man's pain. Later, he'd erase the guy's memory, but fear was a great flavor enhancer. A vampire's MSG.

The hollow inside me filled with unbearable hunger, and my gums pulsed and tingled as my fangs pushed through.

I plunged my teeth into the blonde's throat. Her blood poured into my mouth and kicked my synapses into action, its richness a sublime treat. The routine of life couldn't compete with the thrill of tapping a vein.

Each swallow replenished my energy. I drank deep. My stomach lurched toward the velvety treat, my senses came alive. Her virgin neck was fragranced with rose water, which gave her a sweetness that just about scattered my thoughts.

Gino made a noise.

I repositioned the blonde and peered past the bowl of carrots.

Gino lapped greedily, clawing at the man in his arms. My sire probably wasn't even aware we were here, so powerful a drug was the guy's fear.

The man would never remember. Never have nightmares. Not if this was a *one and done.*

I had denied myself even the tiniest sip of real terror for a long time. The flavor of thick, tangy panic was so utterly satisfying. My heart twinged. *To drink it one more time...*

Fuck it. I retrieved my glamour and let reality crash down on the blonde who'd molded herself against me.

She stiffened in my arms for a moment, then writhed and kicked out. Her small hands stretched and balled up, swiping at me like I was a fly. Her vulnerability was an aphrodisiac, her taste so encompassing I lost myself in it.

Her smell, mixed with the florals from her skin, pushed my restraint. Every feed should taste like that—so fulfilling, revitalizing, and completely rejuvenating.

Her thin frame trembled, and I drank in the scent of fear

streaming from her pores. I moved my tongue in, prodding circles, increasing her yield.

We used to dine like this a lot. In candle-lit rooms, surrounded by orchestras, we'd hold women in puffy dresses in our arms. We only ever fed off the rich, the fat cats who oppressed their servants.

I would sit to Gino's right, getting the pick of the spoils. Eli, the quiet one, dug in with more hunger than his lanky figure suggested. And fiery Julia, trying so hard to prove she could keep up with the boys.

My thoughts blurred, light with pleasure. When was the last time I drank? Really drank? Surrounded by Gino and Julia, no less?

This was as close to family time as we'd had in decades.

I poked the girl's vein, massaged her body to improve the flow. The restorative powers of her life force took effect in hesitant steps at first, then in leaps and bounds. A minute later, my heartbeat trotted, then galloped in time with the violins playing in my mind.

We didn't kill the musicians. Gino loved the arts. Over the centuries, he'd introduced us to countless famous painters and sculptors, and to celebrated actors. Humans never knew our true nature. Gino was careful.

The brunette to my left slid down the chair and onto the ground with a giggle, still high from my sister's glamour.

Julia retracted her teeth and patted her mouth with a napkin.

I also released the woman in my arms, my brain swirling and floating inside my skull. *What a rush.*

She slammed into the floor, and her eyes rolled back in her head.

I sucked in oxygen, which doused my blood-induced high.

A pang in my chest halted my breath. *Fuck.* I looked to the side, listened for my victim's heartbeat. Weak. Very weak.

This wasn't good. Not good at all.

I gripped the edge of the table, too shaken to speak.

The woman *had* to be okay. Maybe I should call an ambulance. But if I moved, I'd draw attention to my lack of control. What would Julia say to my carelessness?

No. The blonde was going to be okay. She had to be.

Gino smacked his lips as he let go of the man's throat. The guy's head lolled to the side, and his eyes glazed over.

Christ. The man looked in a worse state than my girl. I ground my teeth, fumbling for the words to explain the mess we'd made.

But did Gino share my qualms?

The rules I'd designed to mimic compassion, my abstinence from killing innocents... At one time, all this was supposed to be a façade. The face I put on so the world would not see the monster.

Somehow my friends had returned some form of humanity to me. Had they made me weak, as Gino had suspected? Or was it okay to feel like shit after nearly killing a human?

"I feel so much more like me." Gino carefully deposited his meal on the floor and accepted the napkin Julia handed him. "I hope everything was to your satisfaction, Florian. Your sister did an excellent job overseeing the cooking and procuring dessert." He tapped her cheek. "What a lovely surprise."

My mouth went dry. The sheep were Julia's idea? I stared at her, straining to keep my mouth closed.

Julia waved him off. "You'd be amazed how easy these things have become. Young men and women, forgotten by society, attend dark clubs and pretend to be like us. They wear black clothes and false fangs and sleep in coffins. Adorable, really. A few of them want more. They want to feel our teeth and experience our glamour."

Since when did my sister take advantage of people on the fringe of society? She'd integrated into human life more than me. She and her friends danced in nightclubs, her books set trends, and her parties were legendary in California. Hell, she was friends with Ivy before I was, and vocal about her dislike of blood slavery. The perfect human.

"You did well, my girl." Gino looked at me with a frown. "Didn't she?"

"She did." *Slow, steady breaths. Focus on the words, not the meaning.* "Take the compliment, Sis."

She beamed at us. "Stop it, you two."

Gino laughed. "This is how I imagined our reunion. If Eli were here, it would have been perfect, but this... This is good." He rubbed circles over his stomach. "I have work to do. You two will clean up."

We nodded.

"Of course," Julia said.

Gino stepped over the man sprawled motionless on the far side of the table, kissed my head then Julia's, and left.

Julia got to her feet. "Come on then."

Gino's guy lay on the floor. His ribcage didn't move. His skin was ashen, almost white.

A sound, almost a grunt, escaped me. "He's dead."

"Hang on." Julia rounded the table and poked him. "You're right. Oh, damn."

"Gino didn't even notice."

She fell back into her chair. "Well, maybe Gino's out of practice. In Alethia, he didn't have to be careful."

"Are you making excuses?"

"No, but I'm not turning it into a huge deal either." Her

overplucked eyebrows arched. "And before you feel all superior, what about your own meal?"

Shit. I checked the blonde's pulse. It was gone.

I'd killed. My vision went black for a second and then returned, blurry. *Fuck, fuck, fuck, fuck, fuck.*

I swallowed and made my face go blank. "She's dead too."

"There you go."

Where was the sermon? The telling off? Gino might be out of practice, but I wasn't. Had I been so engrossed in my memories that I overlooked the signs of imminent death on the blonde's face? I hadn't lost control like this in decades.

The blonde. Shit, I didn't even know her name.

Okay. Deep breath. These people must have been aware of the risks when they offered to give themselves to us. Everyone knew vampires could be dangerous. *Right?* My sister's successful series of vampire novels, TV shows and movies had done their part in revealing our nature to the masses.

So it wasn't like I'd killed an innocent. Well, maybe an innocent, but not someone I had to force. She had come voluntarily, even smiled and encouraged me.

"Okay. Right. Where do we put them?" I raked my hand through my hair. "And what about the vampires in the hall?"

Julia frowned. "Eli says the IEA uses incinerators. His bosses don't care about bodies, as long as people don't ask questions, so we should get them to do the cleaning up."

"Simple as that?" Sarcasm shook my voice.

"What the hell do you want from me?" Her small hand crushed the napkin she was holding.

Julia was right. This was my mess. Mine and Gino's.

"In that case, let's drop them in the warehouse district." I rubbed my neck. "We could place an anonymous call to the IEA, so they can pick them up."

"Sounds good." She led her own confused girl to a room next door and turned the key to lock her in.

The second Julia returned, she collected the dirty plates into a pile.

"Are you keeping the girl?" I asked. "Can't you erase her mind and send her home?"

Julia stopped mid-motion.

"I don't know what to do. We can ask Gino about her later." She used her fingernail to scratch a sauce stain off the table, and continued working on it after it was gone. "I mean, they asked to be here. Practically pleaded me to take them. Stop making this into something it isn't."

Her hand shook worse than an old motel's vibrating bed.

Of course it did, fuckwit. What made me think she was okay with this? She hadn't even done anything wrong.

Some kids had asked her to feed from them, and she probably never anticipated Gino and I would kill them.

"It'll be okay." I kissed her hair. "I'm sorry."

As if *sorry* would make up for it. This wasn't like killing rogue werewolves or demon drug dealers. No, this was different. We both felt it.

"I'm so sorry," I said again.

"Yeah." Julia didn't look at me. "I know."

I heaved Gino's victim onto my shoulder, and stepped into the corridor. While the man's neck no longer dripped blood, his clothes were slick with it.

I returned to the dining room and lugged the blonde corpse to add her to the heap. The scene at my feet would have made Quentin Tarantino proud.

Christ, what a clusterfuck of badness.

I slumped against the wall. A young life destroyed by me, not out of self-defense or to protect my friend, but just because. When had I deluded myself into thinking I wasn't dangerous?

My breaths came as wheezes, and I crouched, unable to stand. The girl looked peaceful at least. Her hair showed no dark roots, her blonde tresses fairer than Keely's.

Christ.

Keely. She wouldn't understand. Neither would Ali, Parker, or Ivy. They must never find out.

Keely's lips would never smile for me again, her cheeks never blush in my presence if she did. Yet tomorrow, she'd be expecting me to come by, with my friendly guy face on display, and the vampire locked away.

I could blow her off. She might not even notice my absence, especially if Parker sent a replacement. Someone more…wolf-like.

"So this is how it is?" Julia's voice startled me. "While I'm slaving away, you're taking a break."

I matched her fake levity with a fake grin and stood. "Not taking a break. Wondering if it's dark enough to carry them outside."

"With the trunk popped, no one will see you." Her gaze fell onto the carnage, and her shoulders stiffened.

"What are we going to do about Gino?" I bit my lip. "Should we tell him what happened?"

"And say what?" Her expression withered. "He's trying so hard to do everything right. Let's not tell him he failed. And for God's sake, don't visit the pack. You can't see Ivy either. I miss her too, but this councilman position is important to him. We're not going to mess this up by bringing in furballs, you hear me?"

"We won't." I took a step back.

"It's hard enough on him, having to be cautious around humans and such. He knows he can't drop bodies."

I pointed at the floor. "You have noticed this pile of deadness, right?"

She nudged my arm. "I don't mean the vampires. They had it coming. But the man's death was an accident. What counts is we reconnected. It was a nice occasion, a nice family meal. Don't ruin it."

The man's death was an accident. And my kill wasn't?

"You'll see." She bobbed her head. "He'll be more careful. Honest."

So this was the story she told herself to ease her conscience.

That didn't mean it wasn't true. Besides, what could I say? In light of my own accident, I could hardly berate my sire for being negligent.

Julia and I wrapped the corpses into sheets to prevent blood leakage, and heaved them into the trunk of my Benz. She handed me the door keys, and I drove out to the warehouse district.

The car's suspension came into its own in the bumpy streets on this side of town. I picked a secluded spot between two deserted buildings, where the street lights were dead, and I got out. Unlike lizards, my kind didn't seek out the warmth during the day. We tolerated it, sure, but the darkness was our friend. Weird how I'd all but forgotten my fondness for the night.

A dry, dusty smell tinged the air. The last time I'd been to this part of Silverton, Ivy and I were hot on the trail of a mysterious statue and a handful of organized demons. Now my detective days might be over, depending on how much influence Parker would wield over her. He might ask her to stop hanging with me altogether.

Would she side with me or him?

I deposited the bodies inside a trash container. Whatever life I hoped to carve out had disintegrated. No more pack. By some miracle, I wasn't alone. My real family was back together, the people who always had my back if I fucked up. In time, this whole mess could turn out to be a blessing.

I sat back inside the Benz and adjusted the heating. My sire was in a tough spot, getting the hang of things in this new era. Time to step up and give him a break. As for me, well, I had to shed my hang-ups and be the supportive son he wanted me to be. Without the killing.

I revved the engine and sped off.

Back at Gino's new home, I parked up the drive.

Julia opened the door and greeted me with a hug. "Come on. I'll show you your room. But don't assume you can have parties or come and go as you please. You need to act like a grown up now."

"A few hours ago, you were convinced I couldn't wipe my face without your help."

"Hush. It's so good to have you back, Flo."

She released me and flicked my nose. "But I know you. Two days, and you'll fall back into your old ways. 'Julia, get me this. Get me that. Rub my belly.'"

"What, now I'm a cat?"

Her chatty mood should have made me happy. And if I hadn't just dumped the bodies of our innocent victims, I'd have faked a smile.

She tilted her head. "You look tired."

"It's been a long day."

"I know. But hey." She gave me another hug. "Everything else aside, he's back. We are a family again."

"Yeah."

She guided me into a guest room, which held less personality than my de-Florianed quarters at home.

Once she left, I closed the door and studied the walls.

We are a family again.

Vampires weren't made for solitude. That much we had in common with werewolves. But could our family unit be so easily repaired?

My sister had eased my mind, even if she didn't know it. If our family could recapture our sense of belonging, Parker and Ali wouldn't matter anymore.

I took off my clothes and climbed into bed like an old man with arthritis. My mind raced between Keely's face and the features belonging to the poor woman who had died at my fangs. If I'd stopped drinking sooner... If I'd not allowed myself to be tempted by the taste of fear... If. If. If.

A faint tune sounded through the open window and faded before I'd identified it.

Slim fan blades whirred overhead, just as they did in my old room at Julia's. That room had been perfect for my...predilections. A huge mirror on the ceiling, thick insulated walls, and a bed equipped with two height-adjustable leather straps that ended in wrist and ankle cuffs. I licked my lips. Those puppies had seen plenty of use.

The height would have been perfect for Keely. She'd have sufficient space to ride me hard, her mouth agape, her breasts bopping up and down, and her concentration melting as she climaxed in a composition of screams.

Would she be into bondage? We could start light—straight sex. Maybe I'd introduce fun along the way. Whatever she felt comfortable with, as long as I got to hold her relaxed body afterward. Feel her skin against mine. Surrounded by her cherry scent.

I rolled onto my back. My dick might as well settle down, because I wouldn't give in to its demands in my sire's house. Way too weird.

I *had* to go visit Keely tomorrow. I'd made her a promise. If I didn't turn up, she'd be wondering where I was.

Of course Parker would chew me out if I started meddling without his permission. He didn't understand the give and take of mediation. A rapport with fellow negotiators was important, so the fact that I was off the case was something she should hear from me. For his pack's sake alone, I had no choice but to see her.

I placed my hands behind my head and conjured sheep in my mind. One by one, they hopped over hurdles, bah-bah-bah-ing.

Had Ali and Parker been fair? Or worse, had I overreacted?

Either way, with Gino's anti-furball policy, I might never find out if my friendship with the pack was salvageable.

I tossed back and forth on the firm mattress, gaze locked in a visual tug-of-war with the digital alarm clock, until one thought brought a sliver of light to the dark room.

Tomorrow I'd see Keely.

CHAPTER THIRTEEN

For a few seconds, a distant clatter of dishes and the weight of a blanket filled my consciousness. My body felt barely there as long as I stayed still, but the smallest motion lit it on fire. My stomach, knees and shins ached like mush. Even my neck wound that had healed thanks to Gino's saliva was still raw underneath the closed skin.

When my eyes refused to open, I remained under the covers. The day from hell was behind me, but what would this one bring?

Ten minutes later, my growling stomach won out. I had a shower in the en suite, put on yesterday's clothes, and plodded into the kitchen to demand my bacon and eggs. My bruises had vanished, but inside, I felt broken.

"Morning," Julia said, smiling.

"Humpf," might have been my reply.

Patches of red and green on the wall screamed at my poor head. I grimaced and, when that had little effect, whimpered, until Julia took pity on me.

She served up a heaping plate of warming goodness, a glass of orange juice, coffee and cereal.

"I guess it's too much to ask you to wash up when you're done, but please place your dishes in the sink. Did you want me to wash your shirt from yesterday?"

I shook my head. "I'll pop home later to pick up some clothes."

"Okay. But let Gino know if you have to leave."

Her gaze surveyed the space behind her, as if indexing the state of the toaster, coffee maker, stove and refrigerator, and she stalked out, mumbling.

Last week she was a successful businesswoman with a personal assistant and publisher jumping through hoops to accommodate her. Now she was more interested in white goods and clean clothes.

Unlike the guest room, which had black-out curtains, the bare kitchen windows let in plenty of light. A mistake, in my humble opinion, because it illuminated the garish tiles behind the stove.

Still, the bacon was crisp and salty. The eggs, the right kind of runny. My ailing stomach even found room for the cereal without complaint. Julia was right. I could get used to this level of service.

"There you are." Gino marched in and mussed my hair.

"Yup." As always, my conversation sparkled.

"Some things don't change, do they, Mr. Grouch?" He poured himself an orange juice and sat opposite me. "What are your plans for this weekend?"

I shrugged.

Maybe he was going to beat me up again?

"I read about a delightful new play they're performing at the local theater." His gaze drilled into me. "A crime mystery. I thought we should go see it."

I frowned. "Really?"

"Unless you don't want to."

"No." I sat up. "I want to."

"Great. Then it's a date. We could visit a local bar afterward. Much has changed since I left."

No kidding. "They now have karaoke."

"Poor boy." He shook his head. "I'm talking about women. Have you noticed how they dress?" He licked his lips. "Julia assures me it's the fashion, not a comment on their willingness to spend the night, but I so want to test her theory." He raised his eyebrows.

I'd made him pay for his sins long enough. We messed up our first reunion, but we were both guys trying to live a good life in a world that wasn't made for a vampire's base instincts.

After all our mistakes, wasn't it time to bury the stake?

"Humans do frown on killing." I grinned. "But yeah, a bar sounds great. You can't use glamour, although plying them with alcohol? Well, that's fair game."

"Have I taught you nothing, my boy?" He shook his head. "With our looks, we only need charm." He chuckled and got up. "Sorry. Wish that I could stay, but my job calls. You have no idea how much work goes into planning anything nowadays."

He waved and left the kitchen.

I grinned. How I'd missed our "us" time. Even if my mind wasn't on chatting up chicks, I could still be his wingman. Most people who saw us together thought us brothers or pals anyway, not father and son.

When no more food fit into my body, I slid the chair back and stood.

Of course my sister didn't really expect me to clean up after myself. She would wither and crumble if she didn't have anything to grumble about, so I left my plate and silverware on the table and trudged back up to my room.

An hour later and bored out of my brain, I returned downstairs. Going by the muffled voices, Gino took meetings behind closed doors, while my sister continued her cleaning bonanza in the washroom. A glimpse of the ironing board was enough to make me head the other way to the living room.

Something had to be done about Julia. She was so afraid of losing me and Gino again that she neglected her own interests. Writing. Getting lost in the worlds she created while showing confidence in ours. Maybe I should speak to Gino about getting her an office. His encouragement might be all that's needed to get her back to being who she was.

This was what I learned from my earlier mistakes. We could still be a family without sacrificing who we were.

I sat on the sofa. Now what? An existence of lying around waiting for Gino to call upon my help might suit some, but not me.

Long before we became civilized Americans, Eli, Julia, and I caused trouble in Europe. Our sire encouraged us. Times were different then, and among vampires, a kill wasn't the end of the world. And usually, our victims had it coming.

Not that the Guardians shared our opinion.

But it wasn't just violence Gino schooled us in. He had an appreciation for the arts, which he took pains to instill in us.

His interest in teaching me knocked me out. Eli and Julia had been around longer, but it was me he nurtured and guided most. Soon I dressed like him, adopted his mannerisms, his language, especially his ease around ladies from all levels of society.

Some time in the early 1800s, he invited me to the Drury Lane Theater in London. God, it was cold that winter, but Gino insisted it would be worth it. The play was Shakespeare's *The Merchant of Venice*.

Gino was proven right.

It was the first time since I'd been made a vampire that I felt like a person again. The great Edmund Kean in the role of Shylock had me gripped from the moment he stepped onstage. Afterward, Gino and I became regulars at theaters in every town we visited.

Nowadays, television streamed pre-packaged plays onto our home screens. I enjoyed kicking back in front of the DVR as much as the next vampire, but it lacked the live intimacy of the theater.

Yes, despite the changes in technology, I'd never known boredom like twenty-first-century boredom.

There was *one* thing I had on today's schedule. I'd made Keely a promise. Of course Gino would have a fit if he knew I was about to go outside. His new love affair with kin did not encompass the werewolves.

Yet he may as well be shaking his fists at a wall, for all I cared.

My life sucked, and something told me it would suck less if I talked to Keely again. Ten minutes in her company, and I'd either be utterly addicted, or we'd argue to the point where I'd never want to see her again.

Probably both.

I listened for Gino's mumbled voice in the back of the house. The rattle of dishes proved that my present for Julia had its desired effect. I grinned. Before she could find me and yell at me for my inconsiderate, lazy ways, I sneaked out of the house, closed the door behind me, and took a deep breath.

The temperature was rising, judging by the almost cloudless sky and the sun's rays warming my flesh. I got behind the wheel of my Benz and rolled down the sloped driveway. Once the front wheels touched the road's surface, I started the engine and drove home. The *old* Dupree family home.

Back in my quarters, I changed into a white shirt with sleeves rolled up and flexed my upper arms in front of the mirror. Not too shabby. Not even the werewolf at the motel would have called those guns weedy. No jacket for me today.

The constant bustle in Parker's mansion made the Dupree family home look cavernous. With Eli gone, and Julia and Gino in their new digs, I could have the run of the place. But three people, let alone onc, did not need twenty bedrooms.

Not unless I suffered from sleepwalking or split personality disorder.

In the woods, dense foliage shaded the path and kept my skin from warming up to human or werewolf levels. Once again in my guise as a were-elephant, I approached the camp and came to a stop on the outskirts.

The tents' former white had grayed somewhat, and stone plates formed smooth walkways around the minivillage. Two werewolf ladies hammered wooden planks together into signs, another built a structure from bricks, and the pregnant women sat on loungers in the center of camp, mending children's clothes and knitting blankets.

Yeah, they weren't planning on leaving any time soon.

Parker would be so pissed.

I grinned.

A blonde mop of hair popped through the flap of a tent, and Keely's face lifted.

At once, my body brimmed with energy. The sun's heat was no match for the warmth spreading in my chest.

With lips rosier than ever, Keely smiled. And for a moment, she seemed alone. Her darkly framed eyes drew me in, and I took my first step toward her. Her skin's luster defined her neck and the early swell of her breasts, like a bronze statue, but with all the warmth and softness a man needs. A gray skirt fell in ruffles to Keely's knees, underneath which her shins' smooth sheen continued the flawlessness.

The crowning glory was a pair of red shoes moving toward me. Not as high-heeled as Julia's favorite pair, but enough to get my pulse racing. The luscious red was as alluring and fraught with danger as the apple offered to Snow White.

As Keely approached, her legs crossed without touching, the curves of her hips swayed with each step. Not the most practical footwear considering the location, but you wouldn't know it from the way she held herself. By the time my gaze returned to her small nose and plump lips, she stood before me.

"Hi." Her voice was breathy, even though she hadn't been running. Her cherry scent tied around me and kept me motionless.

Be a man and say something, idiot. "Hi."

Great, my talent to wow the ladies with fascinating conversation had never shone brighter.

She rested her hand on her forehead to shield against the sun. "You're here."

"As promised."

A twitch of her lips drew my focus. Would they taste like cherries too? Would her tongue be soft and gentle with hesitant nudges, or would she take first and give later?

"Do you like what we've done with our camp?" Keely stepped aside to reveal a view of her home. "See that spot?" She pointed. "That's where we'll be building a learning center for our women."

"It looks great. And permanent." My stomach lurched as if to high-five me. Permanent was good.

Her shoulders fell by half an inch. "It should be. We're staying for a while. Or have you forgotten?"

I shook my head and filled my voice with intent. "I haven't forgotten."

"Good." She ran her hand through her hair.

This was where she'd ask about Parker and the future. Her pack's future. Not hers and mine.

If she discovered that Parker would be keeping me out of the loop from now on…

"You look..." *Yummy. Delicious.* I cleared my throat. "You look nice."

A shade of pink tinged her face. She smoothed out her skirt. "Oh this? I was in town and with the sun out, I don't know, it fit the mood. Perhaps I should get chang—"

I reached out, nearly touching her arm. "You look nice. Don't change."

An even deeper flush spread across her cheeks. "Okay. I won't."

I smiled, my chest swelling. "Good then."

She twisted on her heels. "I was about to set up a playground for the kids. Want to help?"

I raised my eyebrows. No questions about Parker. Did she already know I'd been sacked?

"Sure." I nodded.

She led me around the side of the camp to an area where ropes, wooden blocks, and tires lay strewn in the grass. Despite her heels sinking into the uneven ground, she kept her poise.

"We want to set up a few swings." She pointed to the grassy surface.

I took a quick count of the materials. "There's enough here for two swings, a seesaw and maybe a fort."

"A fort?" She gave a laugh, light and carefree.

I stood taller. "You have boys here, right? You gotta have a fort."

"If you say so. Come on then." She kicked off her shoes and strode barefoot toward a wooden beam.

"We need to dig a deep hole to set the post securely." I picked up a shovel. "Hang on. Do you have cement?

She bit her lip. "No. Is that a problem?"

"Not at all. How about a saw?"

She gestured to my right. "Will that do?"

"Yes." I picked up the saw. "Come on, give me a hand."

Together, we cut the ends of four sturdy posts at roughly twenty-degree angles. Sawing wasn't a hobby of mine, but it seemed appropriately manly. The kind of work a male werewolf might perform.

"We'll use four boards, two short and two long, as braces." I placed one of the planks on a wooden block. "That way, we won't need cement."

She used her weight to hold down the long end, exposing more cleavage than a man holding dangerous tools should see.

"Have you done this before?" she asked.

"No. But I've read about it." I placed the saw and moved it back and forth until the corner dropped into the grass. "It didn't seem difficult."

"You read about building a swing set?" She exchanged one board for another, which got the same treatment. "That must have been a riveting read. You should join us for book club and tell us about it."

I chuckled. "My memory has a thing for remembering weird information. Like how to build the frame, but not where I read it. Sorry. Am I still invited?"

"Sure. We'll be discussing the complexities and metaphors of *Little Women*. You can bring the snacks."

"There is no book club, is there?"

"No. Maybe next month." She straightened and ran the back of her hand over her glistening forehead. "What now?"

"We'll use the braces to form two large Vs with those." I angled my chin at the long posts. "The short ends should leave enough room to slot the crossbar in."

She turned her back to me and bent over to pull the first post into position. *Holy balls of fire.* Her ass was glorious. Yesterday, tits had been my thing. There had been nothing hotter than chaining a woman's hands behind her head and letting her breasts dance while she rode me. Still an enticing scenario, but right now, those ripe ass cheeks made the blood pump into my dick. If I slid up her skirt, pulled down her—

"Can you bring the other one?" Keely peered over her shoulder. "I'll get the crossbar."

She bounced off to the side, taking her swaying ass with her, and retrieved the piece of wood.

I reached for a plank and stood it upright, hiding my erection.

She returned, beaming.

Keely's curves held my body to ransom. The old emptiness inside my chest filled with heat, at once blistering like wildfire and calming like a candle.

She twisted a strand of her hair between her fingers.

"And now?" Her voice skipped across my skin, giving me goosebumps.

She took the saw from my hand and threw it onto the ground.

"Let's battle on." I turned my face to the side and breathed deep.

Being in her presence was tearing me apart.

If I were a werewolf with an alpha's support, bonding with me would give Keely and her pack legitimacy. But she'd never allow herself to fall for a vampire. Yet looking without touching her was torture. Working beside her when I envied the tools in her hand? Pure agony.

I was unraveling. This had been a mistake. I never should have come here. Parker's new spokesperson would succeed in integrating her, or more likely, seeing her off, and my life would go back to normal. Time to make a clean break.

"Keely." I rolled my shoulder.

"Hmm?" She dropped her piece of wood next to the saw and stepped closer, leaving mere inches between us.

If there were a way to not be a vampire, I'd seize the chance, but not even Ivy with her guards could make that happen.

"Ready?" Keely's gaze traveled to my chin, my mouth.

"I—"

She placed her hands, rough from dirt, against my cheeks. My heart throbbed, spurring me to run but also urging me to lean in to her. She lifted her face, and the softness of her lips cradled mine.

The first touch was feather light, like being kissed by the wind. We parted once, twice, then the tips of our tongues met.

Sweet Jesus.

I dropped the plank and wrapped one arm around her waist, pressing her against me. I roamed my other hand through her hair, drawing her closer to let our breaths mingle. She moaned, and my mouth swallowed the sound.

Keely *did* taste like cherries. And summer. And honey and bubblegum.

She raked my shoulders with her fingers, chasing tingles through my nervous system.

I found her ass, that perfect ass, and cupped my hands around it, driving her against my dick. Her body molded against me, following my lines as if chiseled to a precise blueprint.

Hell, she was perfect. My nerves reached out to her, instructing my muscles to tighten their hold.

Why wasn't this enough? Why did I still crave her as if she were miles away? I deepened our kiss, tearing another moan from her.

She lifted her leg and hooked it around mine, opening herself to me.

"Keely?" A distant voice.

I wouldn't let her answer. She was mine now.

Keely had used the short time in my arms wisely. Once she discovered how sensitive my neck was, she let her fingers take full advantage. Christ Almighty. Each touch ramped up my pulse, every flick nudged me toward losing my sanity.

"Stay," I whispered and trapped her between my body and a tree.

"Mmhmm."

Her vague sound was enough for now.

I pressed against her as if our clothes weren't in the way, and reveled in her sigh.

Whatever Parker's plans, I'd think of something, anything, to stop him from taking her away.

"Keely?" the voice shouted again, closer now.

Keely tilted her head out of my grasp.

I nuzzled her earlobe, then her neck, and moved my hand up to clutch her firm breast. A perfect handful. And my hands weren't small.

"Keely. Where are you?" The woman's voice made me hate her on sound.

Keely giggled. "Stop it, Florian."

"Never."

She grabbed my head and unglued my mouth from her silky skin. "That's Kirsty. I have to go."

And yet she resumed our earlier kiss as if she hadn't said anything.

I didn't remind her, just pulled her closer.

"Keely."

Keely mumbled something and nudged me aside. As we dissolved our embrace, our arms slid along each other, across my skin, until her hand lay inside mine.

It found a home there. If it stayed, I'd wrap my fingers around it and keep it warm and safe.

"That was…" Keely shook her head. "Wow."

I stole one more kiss from her lips then nodded. "I was going to say that."

"I should go." Her eyes pleaded for me to tell her to stay.

"Stay."

"Keely!"

I glared past Keely's shoulder at the figure walking up the clearing. *That female werewolf deserved to be muzzled.*

"It's not her fault." Keely got onto her toes to steal back her kiss.

"No, it's yours." I grinned. "I expect you to make up for it."

"I'll think of something." She gazed at me for an eternal second then inhaled sharply. "Okay. Going now."

Ever so slowly, she separated our touch and walked off.

I wasn't quite ready to follow her. *Dammit.* I breathed in, breathed out, and then punched the trunk of the tree. My focus didn't waver from her body. Those swinging hips. Her firm ass.

Jeez, that woman turned me into a puppet.

She threw a wide-eyed glance over her shoulder, mocking yet tender. Damn, she knew too well what she'd done to me.

She strode from the line of trees, where we'd somehow migrated to mid-kiss, across the playground, and picked up her shoes before disappearing with the female behind the tents.

Responsibility and duty were important to her. Sharing her with eleven women would be tough.

A breeze brushed across my bare arms. It was nearly noon, and Ivy's guard buckle did its magic. Instead of the usual twelve o'clock slump, my veins thrummed with energy.

I returned to the abandoned planks and posts, found a hammer and nails, and set to building the perfect frame. Nothing less would do. Once the two Vs were braced and sturdy, I affixed the ropes to the crossbar then tied their ends around a tire.

The makeshift swing-set held my weight, so those cubs should be safe. Since Keely hadn't yet returned, I set up a second tire swing, then the seesaw. Although I somewhat curbed my natural speed, I didn't hang about either. The fort proved trickier than anticipated, but the tools were no match for my determination to impress. After picking up the stray nails and boards, I stepped back to survey my handiwork.

"That looks great." Keely said from behind me.

I turned and smiled. "I'll say."

"One of my girls isn't doing well." She placed her hand against my cheek.

"Anything I can do?" I gathered her against my chest.

"You've already done enough. You built the whole playground. The kids will be excited." After too brief a time in my arms, she extricated herself. "I'm sorry. I have to go."

I kissed her once more, seared her scent, her taste, her feel onto my soul. When our lips parted, her eyes shone big and blue, dotted with little flecks of brown.

"Will you be back tomorrow?" A twitch of her cute nose threw loops around my mind, and she grinned. "Don't make me miss those hands of yours for too long."

"My hands?" I brushed my knuckles down her arm to her fingers and lifted them to my mouth. "What about my tight ass? My dreamy brown eyes?"

"All of those. And let's not forget your rock hard stomach." She play-punched my ribs.

My heart skidded.

I peppered her mouth with kisses before giving a frustrated groan. "Okay. I'll wait until tomorrow."

She pressed her thumb against my lips. "I'm not going anywhere."

"You'd better not."

Werewolf or not, she was going to be my future. I only needed to find a way to clue her in on it.

CHAPTER FOURTEEN

I HADN'T WHISTLED IN YEARS, WASN'T sure I remembered how, but I returned to our old family house in Custer Fields with a tune on my lips.

My attempt to push Keely from my mind never stood a chance. I'd fallen hard. By rights, I should have a concussion from the impact.

I ran up the stairs and stopped in front of the mirror. My bruises were gone. A big huzzah for supernatural healing.

I studied my face, inch by inch. Not bad. Not bad at all. At least I never had complaints from the ladies. Somewhere in there hid a clue to what attracted Keely to me. Not that she was so superficial as to be into someone for their looks alone, but if I knew what she liked, I could highlight it.

I'd seen Waylon make the girls giggle with a single eyebrow wiggle.

I gave it a go. Two anorexic caterpillars moved in unison. Try as I might, I couldn't separate one eyebrow from the other.

I squished my nose. Without the makeup, the slight crook had returned. An easy fix. I'd just break every other guy's sniffer then mine wouldn't look so bad.

My eyes' brown was darker than Parker's, yet without those flecks of color Ivy swooned over. Dull, but contact lenses seemed excessive. Just another flaw I had to live with.

Jeez. Was it this kind of insecurity that drove women to put makeup on their faces and silicone in their tits?

I marched to my closet and pulled out a new shirt that didn't look like it had been involved in construction work.

Keely was stunning, sure, but a subconscious part of me also recognized something kindred in her. Her thoughts about family, her sense of humor. Christ, even her obstinacy.

Could she like me for who I was, or who I tried to be?

My stomach flopped. One day soon I'd have to come clean with her about what I was.

A few minutes after I'd changed into new clothes, Ivy stood in my hall. She sported an incredibly cute face when she scowled. But then, Keely had kissed me, and nothing would spoil my mood today.

That wouldn't stop Ivy from trying, of course.

"What the hell is going on between you and Parker?" She gripped her hips, digging her fingers into her flesh. "And between you and Ali?"

I turned away and ambled into the kitchen. "Ask them."

"I'm asking you." Ivy followed, like I knew she would, and yanked out a chair. "Everyone was getting on so well but now..." She sniffed and pointed at the coffee maker. "I need caffeine."

Subtle.

"Flo, I need you to make this work." Her jawline tightened. "For the past six months, too many aspects of my life have gone from bad to miserable, and the only way I got through it was with your help. All of you. You, Parker, and Waylon. And now..." Her chin snapped up. "Hang on. Is this because of Keely?"

"No." A stern look accompanied my quick denial.

"Okay. Sorry. Then is it because your sire is back in town?"

Ah, another insight, although not one I wanted her to pursue.

"Sometimes people don't get along. It happens, Ivy."

With the coffee loaded into the coffee maker, I got out two cups before turning sideways to look at her.

"No, it doesn't happen to me." She shook her head enough to make her curls bounce.

I hmm-ed under my breath. "This may come as a shock to you, but not everything is about you."

"But—"

"But nothing." I punched the button on the coffee maker.

Why did she always have to prod, prod, prod?

She wrinkled her nose. "Cut the crap, Flo. It's bad enough Parker excludes me from pack stuff. You and I, we have a different kind of relationship. Remember how we talked about trust?"

I gave a suffering sigh. "Okay. Okay. Don't get your panties in a wad. My sire… Gino and I got off to a rough start. I didn't meet his expectations, so he tried to renew our sire-child bond. That's what cut my connection to Ali."

Ivy's cheeks paled. "Oh my God. I'm so sorry, Flo."

"It's okay." I crossed my arms and leaned back, my ass bumping against a drawer handle.

"No, it's not. Granted, my connection to Parker is different than yours, but losing the emotional link would be hard. I mean, I don't like the mind meld any more than you did, but I kind of do, you know? Sometimes it's nice not to be alone."

I swallowed. "Yeah."

Ivy tapped the table.

"What?" I followed her outstretched finger to the counter behind me. "Oh, you want coffee?"

"Duh."

I added the sugar—two for me, two for Ivy—to the cups and stirred.

"So you argued with Parker because you're no longer linked to Ali?"

"Yes." I threw the spoons into the sink and turned back to her. "Kind of. Since I'm no longer linked to the pack and failed Parker's stupid mission to get rid of Keely, he has no use for me anymore."

"Don't be silly. Do me a favor and at least think about making it work with Parker."

"Okay. Fine." Only the thought police would know my lie.

Ivy chewed on her bottom lip.

"You know," she said. "Kicking you out? That doesn't sound like Parker."

I handed her the drink, and she all but ripped the mug from my hand.

I joined her at the table.

"My *real* family is back, so I don't care anymore." The venom in my tone came out of nowhere.

"Ouch." Ivy's jaw tightened. "That bad, huh?"

"No. Ignore me. I'm just grouchy." I took a small sip of my drink, but shrunk back from the heat.

"How's the reunion going, anyway?"

"Hard to say." I rubbed a painful spot on my breast bone. "I think it's going well. Gino takes his new job very seriously, so we haven't spent a lot of time together yet. But we're going out this weekend, which should give us a chance to catch up."

"It's certainly a good start." Ivy took a large gulp of steaming coffee.

Years of coffee abuse had transformed her tongue into pure Teflon.

"Yeah. Oh, speaking of Gino." I leaned in and switched my tone to office mode. "Remember the vampire faction working for The Circle?"

She peered up from under her bangs. "What about them?"

"They tried to recruit Gino."

"You're kidding." She leaned in and gripped her mug. "What did he say?"

I wrinkled my nose. "He said no."

"Maybe we should spy on them a little." Ivy raised her eyebrows and nodded repeatedly. "Do you have an address for the vamps that approached him?"

And there was the grin. *Jeez.* She was such an adrenaline junkie.

"Some incinerator at the IEA." My voice hitched, and I cleared my throat. "They're dead."

"Of course they are." She sat back in her chair, sighing.

"Hey. It's not like Miss Super-Guardian was there to send them to Alethia to join that son of a human, Greg. So we did what we had to."

She glanced at me over the rim of her cup. "I thought we weren't going to mention Greg."

"Oh yeah." I grinned. "I forgot."

Again.

"I'm so glad that bastard is in Alethia." She shook herself as if from a shudder.

"It wasn't like Greg was Greg when you were making out with him. He was ridden by a djinn."

"Who Greg invited in to gain power. That's what I don't get. Djinn are power-hungry megalomaniacs looking for profit and control. Who in their right mind would want to share their body with one? No. I'm okay with werewolves, vampires, fae, and satyrs. But djinn creep me out." She planted her chin on her propped up hand.

"Because you can't kill them?"

"And because that mind control thing they have going on is creepy. But mainly because I can't detect them. I like knowing what type of kin people are. Everyone should have that ability. Life would be simpler."

I shot her a rueful smile. "At least Keely would know I'm not a werewolf."

"She'll be okay once you confide in her."

"Hmm."

"Anyway. How is Keely?" She drew out the sentence and slapped on a dumb expression.

As if she could get a rise out of me.

"Good. She's...good." Despite myself, my smile widened into a full-blown grin.

Dammit. There went my air of casual indifference.

"Is she still *perfect*?" Ivy fluttered her eyelids.

I shifted. "Even more so."

"What better motivation for you to make peace between the packs, right? Make up with Parker, then figure out a way to get the two sides to play nice. Any ideas yet?"

I tipped back my head and groaned. "Not a damn clue. And now it's not my place anymore."

Ivy brought up a good point, though. No one else would try as hard as me to arrange a ceasefire. Perhaps I could move Keely to Redwood, not far from Silverton. She'd be close enough in case she needed help, but out of Parker's territory. That's assuming Parker's territory only covered Silverton. Or was it all of California?

Ivy emptied her cup and rose. "I don't like you being at odds with the pack."

"I said I'll think about it." *Yeah, right.* I got to my feet and arm around her shoulder, led her out into the hall.

"You'd better, and soon." She hugged me. "I miss you."

She'd hardly had any time to miss me.

I held on to her warmth as if I could soak in her spirit and optimism, and make them mine. "I miss you too."

Ivy left, and my optimism went with her.

Last night, I was lured into my old vampire ways, but that wasn't me anymore. I didn't kill innocents. No way. Keely hadn't kissed a monster. She'd kissed the me who knew right from wrong. *That* was the true Florian.

CHAPTER FIFTEEN

S LIGHTLY MORE OPTIMISTIC THAN JOAN of Arc tied to the stake, I
drove my Benz back to Gino's place and slid my key in the lock.

Julia opened the door before I turned the key, her expression
dark. "You went to see the furballs, didn't you?"

"No, I didn't." Not exactly, although that hardly mattered, since
Julia didn't have Ali's accurate bullshit detector.

"Then what were you doing?"

"I told you I needed to get changed. And let's not forget, I have
a job. Don't you think it would be weird if I no longer showed up?
Don't spaz out."

Again, not a single lie. Ali would be proud.

"Florian." Julia stepped outside and pulled the door ajar behind
her. "I understand, just don't tell Gino. This council position is
important to him. He's working hard at it, harder than I've ever seen
him work before. He takes meetings, visits kin leaders, and all despite
the fact that modern society isn't the life he's accustomed to." Her
gaze darted over her shoulder. "Don't be the reason he fails."

"I won't. Lighten up."

She rubbed her arms, as if the mild temperatures carried the
breath of winter with them.

"What's up?" I gave her toes a playful kick.

"Gino's so serious about this new job, isn't he? When he thinks
you're not watching, he looks sad. Almost grim."

"Maybe. But we don't know what kind of spin he put on his stay
in Alethia. Perhaps the experience wasn't as great as he made it out
to be."

Julia bit her lip.

"Out with it." I bent my knees to be level with her eyes.

"He's doing well with kin though. In fact, he's…friendly. Very
friendly."

I covered my mouth with my hand. "Oh no. Call the IEA
immediately. We can't have friendliness going on. That's just taking
things too far."

Nothing. My comedy routine deserved a standing ovation, and my sister didn't even crack a smile.

"I'm serious," Julia said. "The humans treat him like any other, and the kin… He's got fae sending in donations. Trolls are doing his accounts and, on his instruction, helping out other kin with their finances. Gino even has demons working for him."

I frowned. "Demons? As in more than one? Demons don't work for anyone, let alone in groups."

"I saw them with my own eyes."

"Even if that's true, how is that a bad thing? Maybe he'll even come 'round to working with werewolves and the Guardians too. He's already proven he's willing to listen to other vampires, even if it didn't work."

"But what is he promising them for their faith? Since when do kin do anything for anyone but their own? It's just…" She shook her head. "I'm unreasonable. Ignore me. You usually do."

"I try."

Finally, she showed a hint of a smile. "He's doing good work. That's what counts, right?"

"Exactly."

Now she was going paranoid on Gino. What was he promising kin in return for believing in him? Free lollypops? Sexual favors? Or maybe exactly what he said: A better future.

Julia half turned to the door. "How do you think Eli will react to Gino 2.0?"

"He's going to be happy, isn't he?"

Julia scratched her nose. "He'll have to stop working with Waylon."

"That might be difficult, since his job depends on it. He's now liaison, remember?"

Once again, she cast a glance over her shoulder at the nearly closed door. "I wouldn't be surprised if the IEA stopped working with the Guardians soon."

I lifted my eyebrows. "You know something, don't you? What is it?"

"I overheard… Listen, when Gino wants us to know, he'll tell us."

Her eyes darkened, her lips set into a grim line. I knew this face, and it tolerated no more discussion.

I rolled my eyes toward the sky. "Fine. You're the one who brought it up."

She finally let me enter the house.

I was just getting over Gino's beating and our accidental double killing. Everything was settling. That was, until Julia kicked the dust back up with her conspiracy theories.

Dammit.

If it were up to her, Gino and I would spend day and night at home. But we both had jobs.

Gino's position dumped him straight in the public eye, with a duty to do his best for both the humans of this town and, of course, for the local kin. Perhaps Julia and I could pitch in. She was a great hostess, and putting together a party for Gino might raise his profile and get her out of the house.

The hall was empty. In a backroom, Gino gave a monologue about something, occasionally interrupted by a stranger's muffled voice.

What influence could Gino wield over the IEA? The Agency represented Alethia's seven kinlords in Oldworld and didn't take a piss without their say-so. Maybe the kinlords and the IEA liked Gino's work and urged their people to work *with* him to make his ideas happen.

"I have chores to do." Julia held her hand up to indicate stacks of clothes. "I'd forgotten how much ironing Gino's vanity demanded."

Still playing the dutiful daughter. Any day now, she'd run out of patience with us. Until then…

I grinned. "I'd help, but with stuff and everything else on my plate, I don't want to. But you knock yourself out."

Her smile faded. "Don't push it, little brother. I still know how to bite." She took a deep breath. "It's good to have you home."

"You already said that." I cleared my throat. "But thank you."

We didn't do mushy, so this influx of niceties was worse than sitting in a bath of scorpions.

Julia tilted her head. "Did I tell you about my special friend who does home visits? I know you've had to curb your needs around the furballs, but she'll be glad to serve you."

My skin went cold, even as my veins warmed. Was Julia really talking about sex with me?

I so needed therapy after this.

"I'll, umm, go to my room now." I eyed the stairs.

"Don't always run away." Julia palmed my cheek. "It's been a while, hasn't it? I didn't tell Gino, but those werewolves, they *have* tamed you. You've removed your gear, your whole personality from your old room." She stepped closer. "This girl, she won't need to be glamoured. She enjoys bedroom play and loves being submissive."

Her words vibrated inside me, but a stranger no longer excited me.

Keely would end my dry spell.

I rolled my shoulders, yet my blood flooded south until my dick nearly burst from heat.

One day soon, Keely would lie beneath my weight, her long legs wrapped around my waist. I would come hard inside her while she screamed my name. And if she was willing, we'd play. Christ, her perfect ass practically begged to be slapped. Her groans would be exquisite.

That day, if it ever came, was worth waiting for.

"I'll set it up." Julia patted my shoulder and made her way down the corridor.

"Don't." My voice croaked. "Thanks, Sis. But I'm not in the mood."

Julia cocked her head, then shrugged. "As you wish. If you change your mind, let me know."

Once she was out of sight, I flopped against the wall and took a deep breath. How long could a man go without sex? By denying myself the pleasures of the bedroom, the bondage—everything that made sex fun—was I toying with my other hungers too?

Perhaps my growing frustration was the reason I'd killed that woman.

But in the end, sex wasn't about violence. To me, it was about boundaries, and closeness, and trust. With a hint of voyeurism.

Not a distinction Julia made.

She was more adventurous than me. More adventurous than most women even, if her copies of Cosmo were anything to go by.

Of course, if she went too far for a date's liking, she'd make them forget. Her glamour packed an enormous punch, even more than Gino's. Both had the ability to delete memories.

Now I was a Master, I should be able to do the same. The only problem was I didn't know how. This was the kind of thing my sire should have taught me. Maybe Gino would, at some point. I was still his son, after all. That much hadn't changed.

A few feet up along the corridor, a door opened.

I retreated back up the stairs to get out of the way.

Gino led a man toward the exit.

"So we're clear?" The broad-shouldered dude, bearded with an earring, and dressed from head to toe in denim, held out his hand to Gino.

Had I met him before? Something about him pinged a memory I couldn't quite reach. Men like him, in eighties fashion they still thought cool, were staple guests at Julia's parties. Retro chic, they called it. *Douche wear* was more like it. But why would a friend of Julia's hang with Gino?

Gino and the man shook hands.

"Once we're done, they're yours for the taking." Gino beamed at him, using the business charm that complemented his ruthless streak.

The guy waved, then left.

Gino turned to me.

"Where were you?" He gave the door a shove, and it fell into the lock.

I came down the stairs. "Driving. Trying to clear my head."

"So you didn't meet with those fucking werewolves again?" His voice sounded pressed.

What the hell? Gino just swore *again*. Besides, didn't we have this conversation about being my own man already?

I shook out a leg and stood taller. "No, actually. I didn't. What's with the interrogation?"

Gino breathed through his nose. "I apologize. That was uncalled for. We have big plans for this town, and I am on edge."

I raised my eyebrows. "Yeah? Feel like filling me in?"

He placed his hands on my shoulders. "Life in Oldworld is hard for us. We must hide and pretend to be something we aren't. I understand we cannot reveal ourselves to the humans, at least not yet. They would destroy us from fear alone. But it's not always easy."

The passion with which he spoke connected with me.

I tilted my head. "Not yet, you said. Interesting choice of words."

"For kin to gain true equality, some believe it's time we came out. Revealed our presence among the humans. For that, we must show strength in our unity."

Would life be easier if we no longer needed to hide? If we could be who we were? I'd always enjoyed anonymity and slipping by in the shadows, but some kin had a hard time with it. How did you explain to little girl and boy fae why laying a curse on their human classmates, even for fun, wasn't permitted?

I nodded. "Kin must work with other kin, you mean?"

"Yes. Kin must work with other kin. That is my priority now." He pulled me closer, not quite into a hug, but near enough for his cologne to swirl up my nose and settle on my taste buds. "I'm trying for you, *Cucciolo*. I'm trying for you."

But he had already messed up. We both messed up when we lost control.

I snapped up my gaze, only to avert it again. "Last night, you killed a man."

"Yes." He exhaled. "I know. Julia told me. And you killed a woman."

"Yeah. And I... I just can't absorb the guilt as I used to. What I'm saying is I'm all for uniting kin, but I won't kill humans. I'm not weak, but I'm also no longer the vampire you knew." I brushed my hand through my hair. "To be honest, I don't know what I am, but I've changed."

There. I did it. I laid out the rules.

He kinked his head. "Of course you are different. Time does that to us. Look at you, a Master without the training. I have failed you."

"Your exile wasn't your fault."

Not entirely.

"Be that as it may, I want to make it up to you, but I also have new responsibilities." He gestured to encompass his house. "Like you, I see possibilities in this new world. To take advantage, I will have to change. Perhaps taking on human attributes is the way to survive."

"I don't know." Would Keely like me if I were human?

"Listen. We will figure it out. We have weathered darker storms."

The words, the tone, the unwavering grip. Gino was a man on a mission.

"That would be good." A knot in my throat muffled my voice.

"And you are still a vampire. Just closer to your human roots than I am."

I chuckled. "So the law of averages says you and I together make the perfect modern vampire."

"As long as you understand I am working on myself." He patted my shoulders. "Now. Please tell me the next time you go out. Not everyone is happy with the changes we are making. Some are not yet ready to enter into interspecies dialogue. The old days tend to stick to us like tar, and it takes willpower to turn in a new direction. A direction that shines the spotlight on them and the way they treat each other. It might be dangerous for you out there."

I squinted. "I can handle myself."

"I know, I know. You proved it yesterday. But we are trying to avoid bloodshed. I am not saying you cannot go out. Just let me know where you will be."

What was I? A hundred and twelve?

I kept my bottom lip from pushing forward and nodded. "I can do that. For a while."

"Good."

"Speaking of humans, we shouldn't keep the sheep." I lifted my chin. "If we're serious about changing."

He shrugged, a jerky movement devoid of his usual grace. "We need blood, and I don't have time to go out and pick up strays like you."

Yes, Gino was definitely stressed.

I took a step back. "Still."

"We shouldn't have killed anyone, that's true." Gino touched the bridge of his nose. "But the other one is here now. Cutting her loose might expose us."

"You could make her forget."

"Like Julia did when you thwarted the smuggling operation last year with your Guardian friend?" He narrowed his eyes. "Your sister told me all about it. What a victory." He bared his teeth.

"Yes, we did good that day." Or rather Ivy did.

I'd been a bystander. A bystander with snazzy clothes and snappy comebacks, but Ivy and Julia carried most of the weight.

"Once someone is broken, they'll remain broken. Even if you excise their nightmares. Last night, the sheep saw her friends die." Gino shook his head. "She is better off with us, where our glamour can lie to her."

I rubbed my arms. I should have taken the time to put on a jacket, especially because no one here cared about my well-developed biceps.

"We will talk later. I should go back to work." He turned on his heels and disappeared into his office.

Gino had few scruples, but he never used to be quite so ill-tempered. Guess I'd underestimated the effort it took him to play nice. And as long as he let the humans be and focused on engaging kin in conversation about a peaceful—

A shutter in my brain lifted. The stranger from earlier. It was his wispy voice that had made him seem so familiar. He was the werewolf on the mic at the Lost Pines Inn. I'd bet my right foot on it.

CHAPTER SIXTEEN

T HIS PUZZLE WAS A REAL mindbender. I sat in a blue armchair in my room under the halo from my night lamp, playing over the last few days in my mind.

Led by someone called Draylac, a group of rogues had come to Silverton. A clear violation of territory etiquette. Then, one of the werewolves had visited Gino. Why?

Gino couldn't have known the guy was a werewolf. He couldn't 'sniff' them out like Ali could, or recognize them on sight like Ivy. However, if Gino had known, would he have talked to him?

What about the rogue? Did he know who Gino was? Not to sound immodest, but we Duprees were royalty, or at least infamous, among kin.

Most likely, the furball had no idea. My sire had only been back in Oldworld for a few weeks.

Still, I'd sure like to know what they talked about. It would give me an idea as to why the rogues were in Silverton.

I listened out into the corridor to ensure no one was eavesdropping, then activated my phone. A tone sounded, and I leaned back in my leather chair.

"Miss me already?" Ivy asked in a cheerful tone.

"Always. We need to talk." I swallowed. Normally she was the one taking the lead on investigations, and I was the quiet sidekick. "It's important."

"Shoot."

I splayed against the chair's upholstery and stretched my legs.

"Just now, Gino met with a rogue werewolf. I recognized the guy's voice. He and Gino made some sort of arrangement. First the group of vampires, and now the rogues are trying to get into his good graces. Something's cooking in Silverton."

"What could the rogues have in common with the vampires? The vampires were part of The Circle, right? Unless you think the rogues are the other faction. You know, the one your girl talked about.

Because that would suck, but totally explain why they're working together as a pack, or rather as an alliance."

Important conversation, sure, but I took a moment to let my lungs widen. Keely was my girl. Mine.

I missed her. Not just my cock, but every inch of my skin yearned for her touch.

One more big sigh.

Moment over.

"Our pack—" I took a sharp breath. "Parker's pack might be at greater risk than we thought. Keely and her pregnant girls even more so."

"Can you find out what your sire and the rogue talked about?"

"I'll try to get into Gino's office later to have a snoop, but I can't guarantee it."

Ivy shouldn't have mentioned Keely, because her face in my mind made it tough to concentrate.

"Do you need any protective guards? You know, just in case?"

I rubbed my neck. "Have you made any?"

She gave a wry laugh. "Tons. Parker's busy with business, and you with, you know, your own stuff, which leaves me plenty of time to tinker."

"You could always go to the office and, oh I don't know, do that thing where you shuffle folders from one side of the desk to the other, hoping I assume you're working."

"I'm scratching myself with both middle fingers, just so you know." A scraping noise traveled through the phone into my ear. "Anyway, how many guards do you need?"

Keely's camp was still a priority. The total area of their minivillage took up a sizeable amount of real estate.

"How many would it take to protect an area the size of my house?" I asked.

"Thirty should do it. Should I bring them by? I'd love to meet your sire." She smacked her lips. "Can't wait to see him up close. So yummy. I mean, if I didn't have Parker..."

"Oh Christ." I shook my head. "Stop. And no, you can't meet him. I mean, I'd rather you didn't."

Of course he'd also prefer I stay clear of the werewolves, but he wouldn't find out about that. It wasn't as if I had any intentions of bringing Keely home to meet Daddy. Not until his kin-loving attitude extended to the werewolves.

"Oh." Ivy's voice flagged.

"He's just ultra-aware of how some kin don't like Guardians, and he doesn't want to offend anyone."

"Except me. But hey, no biggie." Her tone said otherwise. "Where do you want me to leave the guards?"

I checked the clock. Five-thirty.

"Can you meet me at my place in Custer Fields in, say, half an hour?"

"Sure." She gave a little 'oh.' "I'd better write down the user manual for you too."

"Are you listening? Thirty minutes. If you're late, I'm leaving."

"Hey, I said I'll be there."

Well, in thirty minutes I was about to find out if miracles happened.

I tapped the top of the phone against my mouth, then got up and went downstairs to knock on Gino's door.

"Yes?" He stepped out, his frame blocking his office from view.

"Just wondering if you'd like a cup of coffee."

He smiled. "No, but thank you for asking."

"Okay." Time for some Ivy-style investigating. Blurt first, deal with the fallout later. "By the way, the guy you spoke to. Was he another councilman? Because he didn't look like one."

Gino gripped the door's edge between pale-knuckled fingers. "Not a councilman. Just someone who wants permission to build something new in Silverton."

A human issue. Good.

"Like a Casino?"

We could definitely do with a casino.

Focus, jackass.

Gino chuckled. "Something like a casino, yes."

"Shouldn't building contracts go to locals?"

His mouth lost its smile. "How do you know he's not from here?"

"His accent, I guess." Score one for the quick thinking vampire.

"No. He's not local, just settling in Silverton."

Shit. That excuse must have sounded plausible to him. "The more the merrier, I say."

"True." His lips pressed together repeatedly, halfway between smacking and squeezing an invisible pencil.

Awkward.

I shrugged. "Okay. I'll let you get back to work. Call me if you change your mind about coffee."

He nodded and retreated back into his office.

Yeah, Gino was in the dark. If he knew the guy was a werewolf, he'd be throwing a hissy fit right now. Especially with the mood he was in. Maybe he was working too hard? I was all for being passionate about your job, but not if it made you cranky.

Maybe I should have told him I was going to step out. But then, why should I? Both Gino and Julia seemed intent on babying me. I was a grown male. A fucking Master. I could go when I liked and see who I liked.

I checked the rooms to make sure no one saw me and slipped out of the house.

The coffee ruse was a tried and tested method for starting a conversation, but Gino was smart. Next time, I'd better come up with a more inventive excuse.

My drive home took fourteen minutes, even though I stopped on the way for a blood snack. The standard kind. Plenty of glamour and saliva. No killing.

The sun hung low in the sky, the wind not strong enough to ruffle the leaves covering our building's facade.

I glanced over my shoulder to the road and scoffed. Of course Ivy wasn't here yet. If she made it on time, it would be a first. As for her being early? Never going to happen.

I got changed into a long-sleeved Tee and jeans to prepare for the night temperatures. Ivy thought it was vanity that drove my constant wardrobe changes. It was better she thought me vain, because she'd never understand what it was like to live in a cold body. Maybe that's why we vampires liked fighting, feeding and fucking so much. Whatever got our blood going also warmed us.

Back in the kitchen, I spooned coffee into the coffee maker and had a solid snack when a forceful double rap on the door alerted me to Ivy's arrival.

"Half an hour." I ripped the door open and held my watch to Ivy's eyes. "Thirty minutes. Three-O. That was ten minutes ago."

"Way to be a drama queen."

In jeans and sneakers, she looked more like herself.

"Drama queen aside, do you have any other roles in your repertoire?" She held up an overnight bag. "Your guards, good sir. As ordered."

I grinned and took her offering. "Thank you, kind lady. Will you accept dark liquid gold as payment?"

"Absolutely. And know my wares are extremely expensive."

I closed one eye and studied her. "You mean you want a strong cup, right?"

"The cup should be able to hold the liquid, yes, but what I'm really after is *strong coffee*."

I let her in and waited until she passed me before I shook my head.

"She thinks she's so funny," I mumbled aloud.

Ivy followed the coffee aroma into the kitchen. The sight of the pot put a spring in her step and within two minutes, we headed upstairs, cups in hands, to my quarters. My private living room was where Ivy and I hung out when we needed or wanted to be alone. Her place, although protected by guards from ground to ceiling, was not a Parker-free zone.

"What do you want to do about the rogues?" Ivy retrieved a tube of potato chips from my not-so-secret stash in the cabinet under the television.

"Have you researched what we've found out so far? The rogues' alpha is called Draylac. That's a start, right? We should try the Internet, call Waylon, or talk to local kin. You know, the ones that don't pee their panties when they see you." I deposited my cup on the knee-high coffee table and fell onto the couch.

As half-satyr, Ivy suffered from a sex drive that was higher than most men's, but worse, she attracted guys like blood attracted vampires.

Ivy giggled and joined me. "I don't mind the ones that scare easy. At least they don't want to hump me." She punched my arm. "I say we go back to the motel. Slip into the room where the rogues met, and see if we can find out what their plan is."

I swallowed my last piece of BBQ-flavored goodness. "Risky. If they catch us, we'll be dog food."

"What about the anonymizers?" She lifted her arm and let the charms on her wristband dangle.

Each charm was a powerful guard. She might be useless in choosing outfits, but she sure knew how to accessorize.

"At most, they'd make sure the rogues won't recognize us when they beat us to pulp."

"Sheesh. You're fussy today." She bit one side of her bottom lip. "Okay, then how about this? We could use my invisibility guards."

"I don't think so." I held my hands up, palms facing her. "You know I love your toys. Block the djinn from controlling my mind, or make me unrecognizable if you want. But those invisibility guards use skin magic, and I'm not going near that stuff. Let's not forget, it turned your stepdad into a demon's lackey just so he could get another fix."

She shrugged. "They make you woozy, but it's not like you get addicted after a single use."

"*You* might not. I'd rather risk a beating from an alliance of werewolves."

"Suit yourself. We'll make sure no one is at home. I'm sure it'll work out."

"Fine." I gave a limp shrug. "It's a plan."

In a manner of speaking.

I got off the sofa and dragged her up with me by her short sleeve.

"Hang on." She tipped her head back and attached the snack tube to her face, letting the crumbs flow into her mouth. She removed the container, righted her head, and smiled. "Now I'm ready."

I wiped a few orange particles from her cheeks. "In that case, let's go."

Ivy's conversation inside the car was lively, and she didn't mention Parker or Ali once. Who said she didn't have tact?

We parked about a ten-minute walk from the motel and got out. Ivy slipped into a jacket she'd brought along. I should have brought mine.

Darkness was settling in, but the night would not protect us from curious werewolf eyes, should they be watching.

Ivy handed me the guard that would anonymize us to anyone we passed, and activated it.

By now, the trademark buzz had a reassuring effect.

We walked to the motel and opened the door to the entrance area of the front building. A long corridor stretched in front of us.

"Looks empty." I pointed at the first glossy white door.

"Let's hope. Judging by where I had to aim the microphone last time, we know they met in one of those two rooms, I'd say." She jerked her chin toward two doors.

I scratched my head. "Guess we should go and listen on doors."

"Good thing you're a vampire."

"Yes, I have my uses." Bitterness tinged my voice.

Why couldn't I convince Parker or Keely of that?

Focusing my superior hearing on the rooms, I checked both for sound. "No one seems to be at home. What now?"

"Break in?"

"Nice to see there are crimes you're less concerned about than killing scumbags."

She reached deep into her pocket and got out a lock-picking kit our boss had bequeathed us.

"Speaking of dead guy, do you think they've found him?" She made short work of the first lock, glanced inside, and closed the door. "Pretty sure nobody is staying in this one."

"His buddies should have noticed his untimely demise, yeah. Dumped him in the woods or a lake. That's what our fellow criminals do."

Ivy worked on the lock to the next room. It clicked, and the door slid open.

"Yes, we criminals are callous." She checked, then stepped aside to let me pass. "This must be it."

Ivy was a Guardian with powers that could take out ten of me. But after an intervention featuring Parker, Waylon, Ali and me, we'd convinced her I'd be the first one to risk my neck on investigations. It seemed the gentlemanly thing to offer.

Looking back, my so-called friends had been awfully quick to support my argument.

I used a small LED flashlight to help Ivy see. Stale man smell aside, the motel room resembled the one in the building opposite this one, where Ivy and I had originally set ourselves up to spy on the rogues. Except this was a lived-in space, with clothes tossed on the floor, six used glasses with remnants of whisky on the table, and leaflets, receipts, and other printed material scattered across every surface.

Ivy switched on a desk lamp, picked up a pile of papers and sat on the edge of a chair.

I stuffed my flashlight back into my pocket, then got onto the ground.

"They get around." Ivy held up a brochure. "This is for a museum in Redwood. The voucher is still attached, so they didn't visit it, but it does suggest they travel the area. Hang on." She dropped the leaflet and picked up a white sheet. "They're looking for homes. They're settling here."

I fished a driver's license from the pocket of a pair of jeans. "According to Gino, the rogue who spoke with him said he's looking to build here. Like he's an architect or a property developer."

Ivy leaned forward, eyes narrowed. "If this stuff belongs to the wolves and they want to live here, they must be prepared to go up against the pack. But five or six of them wouldn't stand a chance. I simply don't understand their motivation."

I let my hands fall into my lap. "How many rogues do you think there are?"

Her face paled. "Parker says there are about two hundred and sixty in America alone."

"Hell." I stared at the wall. A werewolf war would not be pretty. "Let's not go crazy with speculation. There's only six glasses in this room. Hang on." I angled the driver's license into the sparse light. "That's the guy who visited Gino."

"Shazam. Let me see." She shifted over to have a look.

I held the card against my chest. "Shazam? Really?"

"Oh shut up. I'm working on expanding my vocabulary. You should try it. Now, let me see."

I handed her the flat piece of plastic.

"Daniel Furtek," she said. "Nice beard." Followed by a gagging noise.

I pulled a stack of crumpled business cards from another pocket. "These say he works or worked as a mechanic. Why would he need to talk to Gino about building permits?"

"It was a trick. Probably heard about the local vampire Master from the kin gossip line and thought he'd feel him out."

"That makes sense. In a suicidal kind of way." No point in hiding sarcasm between friends. "A werewolf voluntarily visiting a vampire? No, if he knew who Gino was, he wouldn't have just turned up on his doorstep."

"True. But here's a thought." She snapped her fingers. "What if the werewolves are planning an attack on you vampires, not on Parker? Or what if you were right all along, and they're the rival faction of The Circle?"

I kinked my head. "They heard the vampire faction was in town, so they popped in at Gino's under some ruse to check where he stands."

"Yeah. That totally sounds reasonable." Ivy raised her eyebrows. "Is this Furtek from the same place as the vampires?"

I waved the ID around. "It says Tennessee, but his drawl sounded more Midwestern to me. There's another reason the wolves might be here. Julia thought..."

Was it fair to drag my sister into this?

"She thought..." Ivy gestured for me to finish my brainwave.

"You can't tell her I mentioned this. Gino's working hard to improve cooperation between kin. I mean, he's working *hard*. Anyway, Julia indicated Gino is getting the IEA to help him. So maybe the rogue werewolves want a piece of the action?"

Ivy chewed her lip. "So now that kin are starting to work together, the rogues feel left out. Being treated like crap by the recognized werewolf packs is bad enough, so it would make sense for them to band together and finally get a group to belong to. And old feud or not, Gino's the go-to guy?"

"That's it. There you go. Mystery solved." I beamed. "We're good."

"Of course we are."

"Can we go now?" I reached for my toes and stretched my tight back. "I don't want to be here when the rogues come back."

"Yeah, okay." Ivy lifted a piece of paper, which showed a ring with two snakes coiled around it. "Crap. This is the symbol for The Circle."

"Dang it." I shook my head. "I was about to get excited about daffodils and everlasting peace between the furballs and the rest of us."

Voices sounded from the hall.

I cocked my chin at the door. "That's them."

Ivy got to her feet and frowned. "Who's what?"

A Guardian's hearing sucked.

"The sound. Furtek's coming. I recognize his voice." I surged to my feet and skimmed the layout. "Let's hide in the bathroom."

I turned off the lamp.

"Too risky." Ivy ripped a charm guard off her bracelet and pressed it into my hand.

Her incantation came quietly, and she disappeared from view. Popped out of existence. Became one with the dark.

Shit.

"Did you just do what I think you did?" Skin magic. The guard in my palm hummed, the vibrations ran down into my toes. "Does that mean I'm invisible too?"

She slapped around for me, grabbed my sleeve, and then dragged me to the window. "Well, I can't see you. Of course it's dark, so that doesn't help. Shush."

The door opened.

CHAPTER SEVENTEEN

C EILING LIGHTS CAME ON, AND two men entered.
One was Furtek.

I stood stiffly by the long drapes, shoulder to shoulder with Ivy, my gaze locked on the etched metal plate in my palm. The tiny guard's cool surface pressed against my skin, drilling an invisible hole that sucked out my energy and my mind. My life force flickered. Weakened. Faded.

Shit.

"... would possibly come in here." A white-haired man picked up the conversation I had missed. He gestured around the room. "There's nothing to steal."

Right. Panic over Ivy's dangerous accessory later. We had more immediate problems.

"Something smells off." Furtek pointed at his bed. "Like another wolf."

"How can you tell? It's a pigsty in here. Besides, everything in this shitty place smells like the local pack."

Both men had broad, athletic builds, like most werewolves.

"Got it." Furtek swished a piece of paper through the air, the one with the symbol for The Circle. "That should convince a few people to take us seriously. No one messes with The Circle."

"I'm still not sure why we get to do Draylac's dirty work." The other guy fumbled with the drawstring of his blue windbreaker.

"Draylac's a badass, but a badass with power. He trusts us. That's a good thing."

"Yeah, but working with other kin? We always said we'd wipe out the other factions to keep The Circle's resources to ourselves."

My muscles flexed and then loosened, strained from the waves of magic flooding through them. The fact that my legs still held me was a miracle.

Furtek put on a sweater, stuffed the paper into his back pocket, and headed back to the entrance. "We'll work with other kin for now."

"Even with a vampire?"

Furtek's gaze solidified into a determined look. "If that's what it takes. He has already taken steps to make things better. I'm tired of being a second-class citizen. Those packs, they think they're better than us. Soon, our alliance will be at the top. The females will be ours. We can be parents and keep our cubs safe."

"If you say it like that, it makes sense."

For fuck's sake, go already.

Furtek turned off the lights and stepped into the hall. "If I have to get in bed with a vampire to get what's mine, then that's what I'll do."

The other guy followed him out and mumbled something before closing the door behind him.

I dropped the guard like a glowing piece of coal and fell back against the curtains. *Holy Guacamole.* My insides were on fire. What the hell?

"Are you okay?" Ivy materialized next to me, a deep frown on her face. She inched toward the desk, bumped into it, and finally found the lamp's switch. "You're pale, Flo. Paler than usual, I mean."

I closed my eyes to ride out the whirring inside my mind and stomach. My neck was too weak to support the craziness in my brain, and if it hadn't been for the solid glass at my back, my head would be lolling to the side.

My shoulders swayed. My body swayed. I peered out from under my eyelids. The whole damn room swayed.

"Flo, you're scaring me."

A chuckle frothed in my throat and then erupted.

"Okay. A rollercoaster high is a normal effect of skin magic." Ivy's hand folded over my shoulder. "The disorientation will be gone in a sec."

Nothing about this was normal. My exhalations came as snorts tickling my nostrils. I blew through my nose again, and little bubbles formed inside.

"That's enough. Try to come back down." Ivy's hand pressed harder against my collarbone. "We should get out of here."

I opened my eyes fully. The room fell into place, pixel by pixel. The more order that returned to my surroundings, the more my legs shook. My arms. My whole fucking body. The guard had just about drained my life force.

"Blood." I slapped for support and found it in the wall next to the window.

Ivy shrunk back. "Uh, what?"

"I need to feed. Now."

She held her hand against her throat. "From me? I don't know."

Never. Never from Ivy.

Shit.

"Meet you at the car." I headed for the door, wobbly legs doing their best to keep me upright.

"Are you sure?" Ivy called after me.

I staggered from the building. *Fuck it.* Where had all the people gone? Hell, even some old guy would do.

I left the Inn's grounds, a strong wind plucking at my hair. Sweat pooled under my collar, under my armpits.

My run slowed to a jog down the dark road, back toward civilization. A house came into view. Outside, a brunette in her early forties locked her car and headed inside through her wide open door.

Blood. I growled.

My glamour zinged in her direction and entangled her mind in sweet promises. I stalked up behind her.

She turned to me, flashing a seductive smile.

I slammed into her, my fangs already out, and took her neck between my jaws. *Fuck yes.* The liquid swirled around my mouth. I gulped, too thirsty to even taste her.

I moved us inside, shut the door with a bump from my ass, and trapped her against a wall. Her blood warmed my tongue, cooled my throat. My heart beat fast, distributing nutrients to my starved cells.

More. I needed more.

I placed my hand around her neck, squeezed the nectar out of her. The iron tang of her blood nudged my taste buds. Then came the floral flavor, with a hint of spice. I dragged the goodness from her, let her platelets fill my stomach and my veins, the taste scattering my thoughts.

More.

I dropped my glamour.

She pushed against me with the strength of a fly.

I chuckled and shook her between my jaws, stoking her fear. Sweetness flowed into her blood, that delicate note I'd been waiting for.

I groaned and slid us onto the floor where her blood ran more easily. Each delicious drop of her life force plumped my muscles, each molecule strengthened my mind.

The subtle hints of grape and vanilla rounded off the saccharine aroma like a layer of cream to smooth the way.

A cry pierced my ear canal, shrill like a child's.

With a growl, I tore myself away from my meal.

"Mommy," a voice squeaked.

The word slammed into me, ripping me from my trance.

Shit. The sound *was* a child, about three years old. The boy tore on the woman's leg, tears streaking his face.

The woman's lids were closed, her mouth parted. Her arms hung limp on the floor. When had she stopped whimpering? When had she stopped fighting?

My heartbeat throbbed against my ribcage, my shoulders tensed, my whole fucking world crashed down on me. I'd done it again. Killed.

I fell forward onto my hands, crouching, snapping for air.

"Mommy, wake up." The boy, a light-blond kid with a round face and quite a set of lungs, threw himself onto her body, his shoulders hitching with sobs.

"*Shit.*" I checked her pulse.

It moved, barely noticeable, like a fine thread under my finger, but she wasn't dead.

I blew air out between my lips, and the pain in my neck subsided. Not dead. Thank God for that.

"Come on. Let go." I lifted the boy off his mother and draped her over my shoulder.

"Mommy." His crying got worse.

I raced past the toddler into a messy living room and dropped his mother on the sofa.

"No more crying, please." I waved at the still wailing child. "She's fine."

The boy stopped, widened his eyes, and then began anew at a higher octave.

"Quiet, boy." I lifted him into my arms and rocked him. "There, there. Mommy's going to be okay."

But he wasn't so easily convinced. Once again, I whipped out my glamour, this time to wrap him in hope and lullabies, then placed him into his mother's arms.

Her pulse beat stronger now.

Once her body had time to repair, she'd be fine. Healthy and alive.

No fucking thanks to me.

I shook out my shoulders and arms, and took a long breath. Her fate could have tilted the other way. *If her son hadn't stopped me...* That boy deserved a medal.

His breathing smoothed into long, deep movements. He was asleep, like his mother.

I leaned over her and licked her neck to seal the wound with my saliva, then covered both with a blanket I found in a corner of the room.

They looked at peace now. Once I was gone, they'd be safe again. If I had the power, I'd make both forget today. But I was a poor excuse for a Master. If they were lucky, they'd think of me as no more than a nightmare.

Using the walls for support, I left their house.

Outside, the wind blustered around my ears, knocking reality back into me. I walked a few steps before sinking onto the curb. The nausea was gone. My skin temperature had returned to a healthy cool-to-the-touch.

This lack of control, this losing myself in hunger... Without the weakness the skin magic had induced, I never would have lost control. Not like this. People became addicted to that? Masochists perhaps, but not me. Christ. Skin magic was definitely off my list of things to try again.

Or was I kidding myself? First I kill an innocent woman who trusted me enough to offer her blood willingly, now I'd nearly done it again. Was I so depraved? The scary thing was, for a while, the woman's life had meant nothing to me. Zilch.

I balled my hands into fists and struck the pavement. And again, letting the pain in my knuckles eat the ache inside.

No. Dressing up like a human wasn't a game. I wasn't evil. And that I knew for sure, because right now, the woman's life meant *everything* to me.

That knowledge would have to do me for now.

I wandered back to my car, making sure my face showed no sign of the monster lurking inside.

"You're looking better." Ivy beamed.

Get a grip. This wasn't her fault.

"Handsome, with a casual charm you might only find among the Hollywood elite?" I fake-grinned back. "Why would you expect anything less?"

"And humble." She pointed at me. "It's what I admire most about you."

We got into the car, and I fumbled with my mirror, in part to overplay my unsteady hands.

"Can you give me a lift to the office?" She fluttered her eyelids. "I left my car there."

"Oh yeah? If you're in our spot, where am I supposed to park?" I started the engine and peeled off the curb.

She adjusted the air to cold. "Across the road."

I sighed. "Still playing the boss."

I parked outside a cake shop, and we stepped out. Neon lights from closed stores mingled with streetlights and headlights, swallowing every morsel of darkness. A smattering of people were on their way home or out to meet friends in one of the area's many restaurants.

Silverton wasn't like other towns. Apartment complexes stood next to a shopping mall, which was in turn surrounded by smaller, independent shops. Trees dotted the spaces between the buildings. As if the city planners had designed our town after a night with a free bar and a bong.

What better place for a vampire who stumbled far too often, but tried to walk upright with all his might?

I nudged Ivy. "Are you going to tell Parker about what we learned?"

She shoved me back. "That would mean telling him I'm messing in werewolf affairs."

"That's not quite true, though."

We crossed the street through a smelly line of cars waiting for the lights to turn green.

"If the rogues are part of The Circle, it's Guardian business," I said.

"Yes, but I wouldn't know it's Guardian business if I hadn't snooped into werewolf affairs."

"Florian?" Another voice called out.

I turned.

Keely stood a heartbeat away from me, one hand touching the elbow of her other arm. A cone of light fell into her face and was reflected in her smiling eyes.

"Hi." I lurched forward, but halted.

Keep your cool. Be a man, goddammit.

"What are you doing here?" Her gaze fell to the left of me.

Christ. The last thing Keely needed was to meet Ivy, who had the tact of an elephant in a house of mirrors. Who knew what Ivy would blurt out? She'd embarrass me for sure, possibly even tell Keely I wasn't a werewolf in a misguided attempt to 'help.'

"Work. It's a late night." My smile somehow refused to stay in place. "The office is over there." I pointed.

"I'm getting takeout. By the way, you never gave me your phone number." Keely moved her hand toward the pocket of her jeans.

"I..." My gaze trailed to her bright red shoes before pinging back up. "I'll come by later. We're already late. I'm sorry."

"Don't you want to introduce us?" Ivy squared her shoulders.

Nope. No way. Not today.

"Sure. But we have stuff to do, remember?" I shot her a pleading stare.

Her lips twitched. Finally, she nodded. "Of course. Sorry. I won't keep him long."

Keely's arm dropped by her side. "Oh no. Not at all. Keep him for as long as you need." She turned and stalked off, her small hands forming even tinier fists.

"I'll talk to you later," I shouted after her.

The noise of running engines must have swallowed my words, because she didn't react.

Back at the office, I busied myself with a folder without paying attention to the document inside, while Ivy popped into our unused storage room to check in with Waylon.

Keely's words ran riot in my mind. Her tone had been cold at the end. Maybe something I said had upset her. There was also a chance she was jealous. I suppressed a grin. Jealousy could be such an attractive feature.

"So, was she an ex?" Ivy shut the door on her way back in. "You wanted to get away from her pretty damn fast."

I sniffed. "Let's not talk about my lady friends and instead, concentrate on the case, yeah?"

The recessed ceiling lamps were so bright, the windows had become pitch-black plates.

Ivy sank into her chair and crossed her arms behind her head. "Waylon says he's heard of Draylac—a guy who walks over corpses to get ahead. He killed about fifty people somewhere in Florida about two years ago, but last year, he just kind of disappeared." She sat straight. "Actually, it's weird because Waylon didn't know that Draylac is a werewolf."

"What did he think he was?"

She shrugged. "A demon."

"A demon isn't going to unite a bunch of werewolves into one unholy alliance."

She cocked her finger at me. "That's what I said. But you know Waylon. He always has to be right."

Must be a Guardian trait.

I rubbed my chin. "I still think we, I mean you, should tell Parker. It seems like something he should know."

"I guess." Her bottom lip pushed forward.

"What's the problem?"

"I don't want him to be mad at me for investigating the rogues." She beat an unnerving rhythm with her feet behind the desk panel obscuring her legs. "Couldn't *you* tell him about our investigation?"

"This is Guardian and werewolf business. Not mine." My tone was pure ice.

She let her head drop onto the desk. "I know. I know."

I stepped over to the cabinet to pick up the mail we'd collected on our way up. The stack was quite large, in its own way a reminder that neither Ivy nor I had been as diligent about work as we were supposed to be. I sat back down and rifled through the leaflets. Among them, I found two checks and one posh envelope.

I waved the letter through the air. "It's for you. From someone who knows you well."

She squinted. "Who?"

"Dunno. But it carries all thirty of your first names."

"I have three." She got up and ripped it out of my hands. "Felicity. Jocinda. Ivy."

"Hang on." I snapped my fingers to catch her attention. "What about the sender's address?"

She stepped away from me and turned the envelope over in her hand. Her usually peachy skin paled, making her freckles more pronounced.

"Ivy? What's wrong?"

She pointed at a symbol of triangles in the upper right corner.

I was up from my chair in a second.

"Oh God. I'm sorry." I made a grab for the letter and failed. "Don't read it. It's from Lathan."

As if she didn't know. The stuff the Demon Kinlord of Alethia had done to her made it impossible to forget him. In fact, I was convinced there wasn't a day when she didn't think of him or his cruelty.

She twisted to the side and took a jittery breath. "That's why I *should* read it. I'll be okay."

She opened the envelope and unfolded the sheet of paper. The tremble of her lips gave way to a deep frown.

"Ivy?"

She glanced up. "You gotta see this."

My beloved Felicity,

You are in danger. A dark force is about to flee Alethia to do you harm.

An ancient vampire has placed the kinlords under his command with his promises of power. Once in Oldworld, he will act with their blessing. Their kin will do his bidding, even work together to help him achieve his goal, and I cannot stop the IEA from supporting the kinlords' majority vote. Trust no one. Only my demons and your Aunt's satyrs have instructions not to join his scheme.

Be safe, my darling.

Yours truly,
Lathan

"Crap," I mumbled and slumped against the edge of my desk.

The only vampire I knew of who'd come from Alethia was Gino. And he was supposed to have the kinlords in his pocket? That didn't even make sense. Mehmet Dupree was a kinlord. And Master or not, Gino would never put himself above his own sire.

I was a selfish ass.

Bent over as if suffering a stomach ache, Ivy breathed loudly through her mouth. Despite the torments she was undoubtedly reliving, she didn't freak out.

"You okay?" I asked.

She straightened and nodded.

"What do you think this means?" She waved the sheet of paper through the air.

"First there's something I should have mentioned before." I sat up and rubbed my neck. "Gino wasn't just gone. He was in Alethia."

She frowned. "What? Why?"

"He lost control and killed a woman, and a Guardian exiled him."

"Christ, Flo." She stepped toward me. "Guardians don't exile people for a single kill. There are so few of us, we have to focus on the worst of the worst."

"I'm not saying Gino didn't have a reputation in the old days, especially under his sire's guidance. But he settled down once he had us three. Yes, now and again he killed someone, mostly because they pissed him off or by accident." I closed my eyes, the memory of the frail blonde still fresh. "And accidents happen, no matter how much we fight it."

"Well, they shouldn't."

Hard to argue with her when she made sense.

"How did he get back?" she asked.

"He said he had help. I mean, it happens, right? There are portals for trade and all sorts of things."

"Yeah, I guess. But why didn't you tell me?" She punctuated her words with swishes of her fist.

"Why do you think, Ivy? You're a Guardian. How comfortable are you knowing Gino escaped Alethia?"

She massaged her arm. "It's not like I would have sent him back, you know."

"Are you sure?"

She kicked the leg of my desk. "Yeah, I'm sure. You're my friend. Hang on. He's not still dangerous, is he? I mean, you said he was doing good, but here Lathan calls him a dark force."

"We don't know if Lathan's talking about Gino." I rounded my desk and fell into my chair, which rolled back a few feet from the impact. "Besides, Gino is active in the kin community, helping people."

She took my hand and then pulled me up. "You're cold. Even for you. You should look after yourself better. Drop and give me a hundred."

I glared.

"Drop." She wagged her hand at me. "Parker isn't here to say it, so I will. You must get your blood going. Go on."

The reminder of my time with the pack tinged my mood, but I crouched and rested my palms on the floor.

Forty push-ups in, and my circulation got moving. Once I got to a hundred, I went to get up.

She pointed down. "No, do another hundred, just in case."

She enjoyed bossing me around a little too much. No doubt it was my punishment.

"Tell me about your sire." She hopped to sit on the edge of my desk.

I got up off the ground and rubbed my hands together to remove bits of grit they'd picked up. My fingers were no longer icicles.

"Okay. Let's start with the worst. Gino once told us that somewhere in Eastern Europe, the father of all vampires went to sleep one cold night in a dank castle and never woke up. Some believe global warming will one day rouse him, and at that time, he will make the world run red with blood."

"That's a terrible bedtime story. What's that got to do with anything anyhow?"

I exhaled sharply. "Gino also said he would beat him to it."

"Oh." Ivy gaped.

"It was a joke, but it shows how dark my sire's mind can go. And yes, when Gino returned from Alethia, we had a fight. You know, the one that cut my link to Ali." I sat back down. "But since then, he's been great. He's doing good work. Helping kin work together. Making up for lost time with me and Julia."

Ivy twirled her hair around her index finger. "How does she feel about his return?"

"She's over the moon."

"You know this good work Gino is doing? That's exactly what Lathan said was going on." Ivy bit her bottom lip. "Right? He said this vampire is getting kin to work together."

"Yes, but he also said the demons wouldn't, and Gino's working with them too. So Lathan's lying." I gave a nod. "Told ya."

"Has your sire ever threatened me?"

"God no. Gino's not keen on werewolves, and he asked me not to speak to you, but no hate propaganda."

"Okay. Good." She stretched out her legs and wiggled her feet. "Then what I want to know is what Lathan hopes to achieve with this warning."

I pointed at the letter. "Since when is Lathan's word reliable? The guy kidnapped you, tortured you, tried to kidnap you again and killed your mother, all while proclaiming his love for you."

"Wow. Thanks for the update."

I breathed through my nose. "What I'm saying is Lathan always has an agenda."

"Another ploy to get me to investigate his claims, maybe get me away from Parker, so he can send another minion to kidnap me?"

"He wouldn't dare. Would he?" I frowned, pressing my palm against my tightening chest.

"Maybe he's trying to drive a wedge between us two."

"As if that would ever happen." I blew a raspberry. "Still, we should investigate. You give Lathan some thought, while I go speak to Gino."

Ivy's face relaxed. "I guess. Hey, should I tell Waylon?"

"Don't." I snapped my chin to the side. "Not Waylon."

"But—"

"Please." My voice hovered somewhere around whiny, but I didn't care.

Keeping the Guardian away from my sire was what mattered. At least until I came up with a great answer for Lathan's lies.

Because they were lies. Weren't they?

Fuck. This paranoia of mine was going to be the death of my relationship with Gino.

Ivy cocked her head. "Other than Lathan and Gino, are you good? I didn't mean to butt in with your friend earlier. You know, the blonde?"

I waved her off. "You didn't. Anyway, I should get back. You too.

It's getting late." I rolled my chair under the desk and dropped the glossy leaflets in the trashcan. "And Ivy?"

"Hmm?"

"I'm not always going to be around. So you be careful. Something about this whole thing stinks."

"You too."

I snorted. "Excuse me?"

Her shoulders heaved, and she made dying pig noises. "I mean, you be careful too."

No one had a less graceful or more infectious laugh than her.

My muscles unknotted. I shuffled over and leaned in for my hug. Since a person's touch soothed her hormones, she kept the high sex drive under control by snagging frequent cuddles from me. Not that I was one to ever turn down a hug from a pretty girl.

She clung to my shoulders for a minute before she sent me on my way with a peck on my cheek.

I didn't head home, and I didn't head to Gino's. Keely's tone from earlier haunted me, and no amount of intrigue trumped my need to set things right. Whatever I did wrong, I had to fix it.

CHAPTER EIGHTEEN

THE CAMP, NOW LARGER THAN on my first visit, was shrouded in darkness. The long tents were lit from inside and seemed to float like Chinese lanterns. A low hum settled in the air, most likely from the new generators. It was like a fucking town in here. Even the fireplace at the center had been replaced by a brick furnace with large pots and pans hanging off the sides.

Two werewolf ladies stepped off the paved path, faces tinted a deep yellow from the tents' lights, and shot me looks set on stun. Sometimes the fairer sex was hard to read, but this time, their message was clear: I wasn't welcome.

I never figured out if their emotions spread by way of gossip, or if their magical connection to the alpha filtered dislike down the ranks.

No one stopped or challenged me. If they believed me to be a werewolf, perhaps they were scared of me. Or they too considered me a rather weedy specimen, too weedy to bother with.

Scents of cooked food tickled my taste buds, but nothing could steer me away from my destination.

Keely's tent made knocking impractical, so I tugged on the fabric panel that wasn't buttoned up. "Keely? You in?"

"What do you want?" Her voice, despite its icy pitch, warmed my chest.

I flicked open the door and stepped onto the tarpaulin sheet that made up the floor. "Can I come in?"

The tent seemed too large for just one person. Keely, still dressed in jeans with her fuck-me red heels, was folding clothes and stowing them in a plastic tote suitcase. Her bed—a folding camp bed with a thick mattress large enough for two—stood at the far end, with black sheets that reflected the light from a shaded lamp on a nightstand.

Nightstand might be too impressive a word for the flimsy table, but I guess when you're camping, practicality was the key word.

In a corner of the tent, an oil-burning heater pumped toasty air into the room.

One thing was clear. This setup was for keeps. Keely had no plans to move her pack away.

I was good with that.

"Are you okay?" I entered and since I got no reaction, buttoned up the tent flap for at least the illusion of privacy.

"Why wouldn't I be?"

"You seem distant. Don't I get a kiss?"

"You are joking, right?" She spun around. "Just because your pack has a hard-won reputation, and we have no social standing, doesn't mean you can treat me like a cheap fling."

"What? Oh. No, honey. You got that all wrong."

Honey? I'd never called anyone 'honey' before.

Focus.

So she was jealous, but something told me a triumphant grin would not win me any points.

A smile would have to do. "That was Ivy."

"Mm-hmm." She pushed the lid closed on the tote, but it stuck. "Crap." She yanked out a slim, brown belt, then latched it shut.

"Ivy? You know. Parker's *intended*."

Keely glanced up. Her eyes clear now.

Phew. "She's my best friend, a great person, but devoted to Parker."

"What's your point?"

"I didn't think you two were ready to meet." I peered to the side and tilted my head. "Or maybe I wasn't yet ready for you two to meet."

She dropped the belt onto her bed and inched closer.

My breathing intensified, as if my inhalations could suck her into my arms.

She bit her lower lip, a task I was so much better suited for. "Did you think Parker would attack if she told him my pack's without supervision?"

That would make the perfect excuse, but as a werewolf, Keely would catch every little fib.

"No, although let's not take any chances. You should stick around the camp, just in case. I didn't introduce you to Ivy because she has the social skills of a mosquito, and I didn't want to make the situation awkward."

She raised an eyebrow.

Yeah. She got me there. "I admit, it could have gone better."

She set another foot in my direction. The heat from her oil-burning contraption carried her scent my way, and I needed no more convincing. I took two steps, and Keely was in my arms, her head tilted back, gaze drifting between my eyes and my mouth.

"Am I forgiven?" I hovered my lips over hers.

"You are. Next time, bring flowers." Her brows fell. "Hang on. Isn't Parker's *intended* a Guardian?"

"Hmm." My head moved in for the touchdown.

Keely turned her face. "Was that a yes?"

Since when did Ivy get in the way of my love life? Not a development I wanted to encourage.

"Yes." My deprived lips found a new home on Keely's warm, soft neck.

She slid a palm between my forehead and her skin, and nudged me away.

"Seriously?" I pouted.

I stepped away while holding on to her hands, and gave an amped up sigh.

Keely guided me across the tent's interior, closer to the heat source. "So you're friends with the Guardian?"

I dropped my shoulders. "Yes."

"What about the other Guardian? Do you know him?"

"Yes." I slid my fingers up her sleeves, to her shoulder, and stroked her neck.

"Is he as hot as they say?"

Christ, she was killing me.

I squinted at her parted lips, her cheeks, and her glinting eyes. "Waylon? If you look beyond his lack of hygiene, girlish voice and buckled knees, he's no uglier than a troll."

She leaned against me. "Sorry. Are these questions weird?"

"Not at all. Let's also discuss the virtues of George Clooney and Brad Pitt."

She grabbed my face with both hands. "Oh. Could we?"

I snapped for her lip and caught it between my teeth, careful not to draw blood. "Gah head. Ah dn't cur."

She giggled, a sound that softened my legs and hardened the part between, yet she didn't pull away. If anything, she pressed more closely against me.

I loosened my vice hold over her lip and transitioned it into a kiss.

Her flavor zinged straight into my balls, and my stomach lunged, hungry for more. She circled her warm fingers, rough from hard work yet soft like velvet, from my cheeks to my neck.

I arched her back, deepening our kiss until my strength alone stopped her from falling.

With one arm against her ribs, I used the other to lift her up and walked to the bed, halting once to nudge her tongue with mine.

Her soft lips sent shivers through me. This treasure I held was mine, and mine alone. No one was going to touch her or hurt her.

I lowered her onto the mattress and blanketed her body with my own.

The kink of her knee folded around my hip, and the spike of her heel traced a feverish craving into my skin.

I groaned, releasing centuries of tension in one sound.

She fumbled open the buttons of my shirt and reached in. Her fingers warmed my chest, while her touch gave my heart new life. It beat strong and loud. When she pushed her hips up against me, the fire she caused inside me tore on my restraint.

How was a guy to concentrate under this deluge of sensations? The very tingles skittering across my skin also stole my focus from the one thing that mattered… Keely's pleasure.

She took off my shirt, raked her hands downward, and played with the zipper of my pants.

I seized her hands. "Stop right there."

Her flushed cheeks and lips only made her eyes appear bluer. The belt on her bed peeked out under her short hair.

I pulled at the leather, sliding its length out from underneath her. Was she going to call me a freak, or play along?

"Too fast?" Her hot breath fogged my mind.

"Never." I lifted her hands above her head and wound the thin belt around her wrists.

"What are you doing?" A chuckle punctuated her words.

"I can't concentrate on you while your hands drive me crazy." I pressed my mouth hard onto hers, plunging my tongue in, and demanded her focus.

The air she breathed had to be mine, her warmth had to come from my pumping heart.

I tightened the knot against her bed's metal crossbar. No longer distracted by her curious fingers, I spent precious seconds unwrapping her generously filled bra. Her tits lifted and fell fast, her gaze on me, lips parted.

I put my mouth to her breasts, still cradled by the lace that barely covered her pert nipples. The satin texture of her skin against mine encouraged both my lips and my nose to trace the line of her ribcage. The way she smelled was indescribably sensual, making me close my eyes for a second to inhale her deep into my lungs.

I unhooked the button of her jeans, unzipped the opening, and rested my face above the linking point between her legs. Her stomach was flat, except for the small mound that did more harm to my restraint than her scent.

Tiny pauses followed her sharp inhalations, and the release of air came like a whisper.

I grabbed her pants and tugged. "Up."

"Say please." Her voice was deeper than usual.

She was such a tease. "Up. Now."

"Make me."

I swept her up by her lower back, eliciting a giggle, and tore her jeans down to her knees.

I took off her shoes, slipped her legs out, and replaced the red-heeled wonders.

What had I done to deserve this goddess under me?

Her rosy cheeks, messy hair, and soft curves lay waiting for me, ready for my every desire.

She bucked toward me, her body warm and soft.

I glided my hands across the smooth surface of her waist, then up to release her tits.

"You're a miracle," I whispered and cast the bra aside.

Her breasts were firmer than I'd imagined, and rounder than I could have hoped for. They flattened and spread, without losing their apple-like shapes.

I pressed my mouth on the right tit, twirled my tongue around her hard nipple.

Her breaths turned to yips, while her left foot cut into the bed sheet, and her heel tore the fabric.

I sucked harder.

She shuddered and lifted her knee.

My stomach contracted, my balls tightened. This was fucking unreal.

I gripped her leg and pushed it flat onto the mattress.

Her panties, already moist and no match for my passion, ripped with ease. Underneath, her soft, naked curves marked the place I'd longed for.

Her body, restrained and yet wild, touched a place deep inside me. The warmth pooling between my legs bathed me in a light-headed bliss. *Fuck*. And my journey hadn't even started.

I lowered my face onto her skin and nibbled my way to her folds.

Her light and fragrant smell spurred me on, ramped up the pressure in my balls—not just to fuck her, but to soak her in.

After a sharp intake of oxygen, her breath fell still.

I shifted my mouth to hover a millimeter above her, positioned my hands under her ass and dug my fingers into her flesh.

"What—" Her hips twitched, and her delicate nub soared toward my lips.

I put them to work on her clit right away, massaging and nuzzling. I varied the pressure, shifted positions and forced her legs further apart, opening the most private of places to my exploration.

The intensity of her moans guided me.

I hardened my strokes, and she sucked in air, flexing her muscles along the length of her body.

Hallelujah. I'd found *the* spot.

I kept my motions even, directed at the one point that drove her wild.

Keely's breaths came faster, and I matched my speed.

She whispered something.

I gripped her ass without losing my position and massaged her cheeks. Nothing mattered more right now than turning her whispers into words.

I licked faster and took the lead, waiting for her breathing to catch up with me.

"Florian," she mumbled.

No greater aphrodisiac than a woman, *my* woman, whispering my name.

The delicate scent of her wetness blended with her fruity base note. The combination sent my nervous system thrumming. My long strokes alternated with short tweaks, then faster ones, concentrated on her clit.

Her breathing followed mine in perfect sync. Each intake of air mirrored my efforts.

Her knees tightened around my ears, her sounds became louder.

"Oh God." She wiggled her body, but the belt held fast. "Oh yes."

Not quite. Her tone still held restraint.

"Florian."

My dick stemmed against my jeans, the pain of unfulfilled need heightening my pleasure. I licked and flicked, my breaths shortening, drawing her into me.

"Yes." She half shouted.

Not enough. Not nearly enough.

My tongue led her from height to height. My hands tethered her to me. She'd sing my name. Yell it until the world knew she was mine.

I pinched her clit, hard.

My name slipped from her lips in a groan.

My mouth glued to her slit, I rolled onto my side and took her with me, opening up enough ass. I smacked her hard.

"Florian."

Almost there. My balls throbbed, my cock sore, while my tongue and lips moved like a piston. Another slap.

"Oh God."

Finally. Another squeeze with my lips.

"Yes."

I spanked her again, licked her clit, working fast and hard.

"Oh yes. Yes." Her shouts rang out. "Yes."

She squeezed her thighs tighter.

Another whack on her ass.

She groaned in pleasure, spurring me on. "Yes, Florian."

Her juices trickled, her muscles seized, her breathing stopped.

"Ye-es."

One word that spanned a glorious eternity.

The kills I'd made, the laughs I'd had, nothing compared to this. This span of time, as she rode her climax, would remain seared into my mind.

She released the pressure around my ears, and I nudged her legs down.

I shifted upward, past her navel and her heaving ribcage. Her tits lifted toward me. I stopped to kiss both rosy nipples, and then moved to her face. She had her eyes closed, her lips parted, arms limp above her head.

I pressed my mouth onto hers. She strained against my grip, but I held tight to let her partake in her glorious taste. I spread her flavor onto her tongue, coating the inside of her mouth in my triumph.

Her resistance lessened, and she returned my kiss.

Finally, I released her from the belt.

She smiled.

My turn. I reached down my pants and rubbed the length of my dick.

A replay of Keely's sounds in my mind got me revving within seconds. Her smell, a heady mix of sex and cherries, sent waves of bliss through me.

Keely took over. She curled her hand around my shaft and made even strokes.

I covered her fingers, tightened her grip, and placed my head against her chest.

Her skin was electric, her movements skilled and determined. My vision tunneled. My pulse skidded across my body, throbbing extra hard in my cock.

Keely made a ring with her fingers and varied the pressure, pumping pure bliss into my blood stream.

Perfect. So. Damn. Perfect.

My breaths came fast as I soaked air and her scent into my lungs. *Oh fuck.* I was nearly—

I came with a grunt.

Christ almighty. My release packed the force of a thousand orgasms, made better because I was spilling into her hand.

After a few more breaths, my brain stopped spinning.

Whoa, that was something.

Sweat-soaked but satisfied, I kissed the softness of her breasts and tilted her chin toward me.

Her lids opened. The dark pupils drifted for a split second, then settled on me. "Hey."

I kissed her nose. "Hey."

Her mouth twitched once, twice, then widened into a bright smile. "That was one heck of an apology."

"Keely?" A woman's voice sounded from the tent entrance. The woman coughed. "I'm sorry to... to interrupt, but we need you."

Keely lifted her head. "Oh God. Do you think they heard us?"

"If I did my job right—"

"Oh, you did your job right, no doubt about it."

I nodded. "Then yes, they heard."

"Bugger." She wiggled an inch away from me. "I need to go."

I traced my finger across her breast and flicked her nipple. She shivered.

I rolled on top of her and leaned in close to her ear. "You don't need to do anything."

"Florian. This is important."

"Will you come back to me?" I took her nipple hostage.

She sucked in air. "Yes. Of course I'll come back."

"Keely?" The woman called again. "Are you coming?"

I released her tit and buried my face between her breasts. "She's late to the party, isn't she?"

"Get off." Keely laughed. "I'll be quick. I promise."

With a heavy heart, I did as she asked.

She'll be back.

Sprawled out on my side, limbs heavy but with astonishing calm, I didn't let her body out of my sight.

With her back to me, she linked her bra clasps and yanked away her shredded panties that were stuck to her legs. The look she threw me over her shoulder, both accusative and pleased, warmed my insides. She stepped into her pants, moved them up to her knees, then got off the bed.

God. Her ass was a spectacle that conjured fantasies, no, opened possibilities, for later. Too quickly, her jeans were in place.

"Keely?" The woman punched the canvas flap of the tent.

"On my way," Keely shouted. She fumbled under the bed for a more practical pair of shoes and leaned in for a kiss. "Don't go anywhere."

As if. "I won't."

She ran her hand through my hair and kissed me again. Then she swayed, glided, floated to the exit and left.

I rolled onto my back and crossed my arms behind my head.

Would tonight be the night? First, I had to find the courage to tell her I wasn't as werewolf-ish as she believed.

She hated vampires, and who could blame her? If her experiences hadn't turned her against my kind, I could explain how good or different I was. Except she'd catch the lie right away, because not more than a few hours had passed since I'd nearly orphaned a boy. I didn't even want to remind myself of the blood slave I killed, or the one I let Gino and Julia keep. The minute I confronted her with the reality of me, my dream would be over. She'd run. Perhaps punch me.

If I could take my shame to my grave, I would. But sooner or later Keely would discover my secret. If she joined the pack, someone would tell. Ivy, for one. In fact, my best chance was to encourage her to leave Silverton, and for me to go with her.

Something to think about.

I swung my legs over the side and got up without zipping up my pants. The metal frame of her double camp bed creaked. Had it done so before? I must have blanked out sounds that were not made by Keely.

It couldn't be that cold, but I shivered nevertheless. The clunking oil burner no longer pumped out heat, so I squatted in front of it and used the oil can to refuel. Stench aside, the equipment did its job and quickly warmed my skin.

The camp outside grew with each day. A new path here, a playground there.

Inside this tent, in Keely's home, the decor remained bare. There was a night lamp, a vase with daisies—maybe picked by the little ones—and a book on the history of the Guardians.

Once she was mine, I'd buy her whatever she needed, spoil her with everything she wanted. Picture frames, candles, even potpourri if she insisted. Fluffy throw pillows. A rug. I'd give her everything.

I got up from my crouch. First, I had to give her the truth.

The tent flap fluttered, and Keely popped back in. With the

gentle glow from the other tents, darkness had yet to fully enveloped the camp. She buttoned the flap and turned.

"I'm back." She slung one arm across her body. Her gaze roamed to my open zipper.

"Good." I beckoned with my head.

People moved through the camp, whispering. The children had fallen silent.

Keely shifted closer, as if counting her steps.

Did she still doubt me? I held out my arms, and she strode fast.

"Come here." I pressed her face against my shoulder and placed my hands on the small of her back.

"You're bossy, you know?" She traced the lines of my abs with her soft fingers.

"As long as we're both clear." I positioned her next to the bed, slipped off her shoes and pants, then her top and bra.

Curves mellowed the tall frame of her body. Her hips wide, her tits generous, but the softness of her stomach was the show stealer.

She pressed her thighs together, placed her hands over her breast. As if the Venus de Milo pose could hide her beauty.

"Don't." I pushed her arms aside. "Don't ever do that. Not in front of me."

"In front of others then?" Her flirty smile punched me in the balls.

"Not the time to make jokes." My cock was back in action. "Get in."

I lifted the covers.

She sat and stuffed her legs under the blanket.

I kicked off my shoes, took off my pants, and joined her.

"You're not naked." She yanked on the waistband of my boxers.

"Call it protection."

She laughed. "Since when do we need protection?"

Werewolves didn't take the pill or any other precautions. Anything preventing the making of babies was frowned upon. That wasn't the kind of protection she needed around a sexed-up vampire anyway.

I wiggled closer to her. "I'm not sleeping with you tonight."

"Oh?" Her chin lifted to catch my gaze. Her knee prodded my pulsing dick. "Are you sure?"

I kissed her lips. "Don't worry. He'll get the message sooner or later."

"If you say so."

"I mean, we will. Just not today." I switched off the lamp on the side of the bed and slung my arms around her shoulder. "I didn't hurt you earlier, did I?"

She chuckled. "I can't say you didn't surprise me, but no."

"The spanking?"

She burrowed her face in my chest. "Never done that before."

"It didn't hurt?"

"There was pain, but it didn't hurt."

I closed my eyes. "Good pain?"

She relaxed further into my embrace. "Very good pain."

I rested my nose above her hair and stroked her shoulders. "Sleep, Keely."

"This is good," she mumbled. "It's nice to not be the alpha for once. To just be a girl."

"You'll never be just a girl to me."

She planted a kiss on my arm and settled back in. "Let me be just a girl for once."

"Okay."

A few minutes later, her breathing slowed. Her body lay soft and pliable against me, and the air from her mouth coated my chest in warmth. The quiet clicks from the oil burner marked the passing of time, and soon the shuffled steps outside the tent ceased. The generators feeding electricity to the camp continued whirring.

My heart pounded. It shouldn't. At least not without adrenaline or exercise to coax it, yet my shriveled up organ thumped a steady beat, heating my body.

I drew Keely closer, quietly, gently, to share this miracle with her.

CHAPTER NINETEEN

I N THE MORNING, CHIRPING BIRDS pierced my dreams. The tent kept out enough sun to stop me from burning up. I smiled.

Keely stirred, still cocooned in my arms.

I tangled my finger in her hair, nudged her chin up and woke her with a kiss.

She moved her lips as if mumbling, before granting access to my tongue. I rolled on top of her, trapped her under my weight, and let her hands roam across my back and ass.

"You're the best alarm clock I've ever had." Her lids were heavy with lingering sleep. "Better even than waking up to music. Of course if you combined the two…"

"You'd change your mind if you heard me sing."

She squeezed my ass cheeks. "Are you telling me this angelic face lacks the matching voice?"

I chuckled. "Angelic?" Not a word usually associated with me. "Of course. I mean I wouldn't want you to develop an inferiority complex when you hear my rendition of Space Oddity, or whatever the kids listen to nowadays."

She bunched her nose. "Have the kids ever listened to that?"

I placed my hand over her mouth. "Sacrilege. Do not dis Bowie."

Her lips parted in a sly smile as she shook off my hand. "And what if I do? Are you going to teach me a lesson? Although…" She pushed off and turned me onto my back. "That belt would make a lovely accessory on you too."

"Not gonna happen." I kept my voice firm. "You might be the alpha out there, but not in bed."

"Not even a little bit?"

I snatched another kiss. "Not even a little bit."

"Listen. There's something I need to talk to you about." Her gaze drifted to the side.

"Anything."

"My girls have strict instructions not to begin relationships with males from the local pack unless the male agrees to join us, or at least doesn't rule it out."

Heat rose into my cheeks. Was this the moment I would have to confess my sin of being a vampire?

She stroked my chest, lost for a second in tracing the lines. "I need to know if you would consider joining us. You know. If this… thing between us goes well."

Join her pack? My breath hitched. What a thing to ask a guy. I wasn't quite over leaving my old pack. Moving in with a woman? Not something I thought was on the cards for another three hundred years.

But then, Keely wasn't just any woman. Waking up beside her every morning, holding her in my arms at night…

I smiled. "I thought I made it clear. I'm always on your side. Have I given you any reason to doubt me?"

"No." She wiggled down to nuzzle my ribs. "I just need to hear it so I can, well, not plan exactly. But just so I know. For the future, I mean."

She wanted confirmation. I'd have to say the words.

Parker would be pissed. Gino would be livid.

Then there was that secret between us. But maybe Ivy was right. Keely would understand. If she felt strongly enough to think of a shared future, she might overlook my vampire-ness.

I dragged her back up across my body and kissed her, deeply and gently. When we broke, my gaze stayed on her. "Yes. I'd consider joining you. Plan ahead."

"Okay then. I will." Her eyes moved about, and her cheeks acquired the pink tinge I loved so much. "Sorry, but I'd better get up. Last night's emergency was a broken heater, which needs replacing." She rolled off me. "The girls had to double up in their tents. They're big enough to house them, but it's not a permanent solution. They need their own space."

"That sucks." I traced my finger down her spine. "Who's going to cuddle with me now?"

"No one." She reached for her top and slipped it on over her breasts. "I mean, it had better be no one."

"I love your accent."

She turned her head and raised her eyebrows. "Yeah? What parts?"

"All of them. The way you swallow half your Ts and linger on the rest. Your long A in 'ask.' Most of all the way you shout my name when you come."

She reached over to punch me. "Shut up."

"Can I come back tonight?" With heavy limbs, I dragged myself up from the warm covers and started the task of putting on my clothes.

She circled the bed and kissed me. "I insist. But remember. Outside of bed, I'm the boss."

My heart gave two thumps, as if to contradict her, but settled into a regular beat. She was the alpha. Nothing I could do about that.

I grabbed her by the top of her pants and closed the button before zipping her up. "Okay."

Her smile filled my head with a tingle. She strode back to her side of the bed and retrieved her sneakers.

"You should wear your red shoes." I pointed. "All the time."

"They're not comfortable or practical within the camp."

"Please?"

She rolled her eyes. "Later. I promise. Anything else, or am I good?"

"You're almost perfect." I gave a deep sigh. "Except for all the clothes, but I'll work on getting those off tonight."

"I do enjoy your fashion tips." She stepped to the tent's exit and blew me a kiss. "See you tonight."

I waved. "Tonight."

The tent was colder without her.

I finished dressing with vampire speed, ensured my belt buckle was in place, and left. Keely's wolves nodded at me. I suppressed a smile. For once, life was in kilter. Not perfect, but close.

At home, I showered and selected black jeans and a T-shirt. It had been a while since I'd worn a humble T-shirt, but the day was made for casualwear.

I'd missed three text messages from Julia.

Boy, my sister was pissed. What were the chances Gino wasn't? Normally I wouldn't mind, but we'd just started getting along.

In the afternoon, I got into my Benz and drove to face the music. A block from Gino's home, I pulled over and parked in front of a whitewashed cape cod.

My sire liked to know where we were. Always had, but with his new situation, he seemed more intent than ever to keep an eye on us. No doubt once he discovered cell-phone tracking, he'd be on that like a bloodhound.

But I needed my space. I was my own man.

It would take both of us time to come to terms with that.

I marched along the sidewalks, past leafy trees and detached houses. My cell pinged.

Ivy wrote, *"Talked to Gino yet?"*

I'd forgotten about that. Or maybe I'd wanted to forget.

I pocketed my phone and strode up the short drive to the entrance. The second I slid my key in the lock, the door opened.

"Florian." Gino's face was all thunder and brimstone. "We've been looking for you."

I stepped inside and waited for him to close the door. "I had a prior engagement."

Gino herded me against the wall and whacked his outstretched hands on either side of my head. "I don't care if you had sex with Cleopatra. I asked you not to leave."

A whiff of human blood from his breath woke my hunger.

But I wasn't going to let my vampire needs control me. Not again.

"I told you, I take care of myself. Silverton is my town. Those who know I'm a vampire stay away from me." I let my gaze drift past Gino's shoulder onto the opposite wall. "And those who think they can take me also know I'm friends with the Guardian."

He flinched.

Or had I imagined it?

He pushed off the wall and turned his back to me. "Why do you keep defying me? My son cannot be seen cavorting with furballs or Guardians. How am I going to keep the kin's trust?"

A wagging fist couldn't have been more dramatic than his tone.

Was he upset I went out without telling him, or because I'd mentioned Ivy?

"If the kin haven't done anything wrong, they have no reason to fear or hate Guardians." I crossed my arms and frowned. "And the werewolves? They stay out of everyone's way. If anyone has a problem with my friends, they should talk to me. I'm glad you're back, but I have my own life. I'm not going to let a bunch of narrow-minded kin destroy that. And you can't tell me who to see."

Whoa. Did I just do that? A grin bubbled up under the surface, but I wasn't going to push it.

"You idiot." His pitch went up. "You're ruining everything. My plans, the future. Do what I say for once."

I stretched my fingers until they cracked. I was not his property. "What plans?"

He paced from the staircase to the coat rack, underlining his points with jerky arm movements. "I told you. It's getting more difficult to keep our existence hidden from humans. But why should we? We want to step into the light, take part in shaping this world again, but our numbers are too small. No surprise, because half of us are imprisoned in Alethia."

Hell. I pressed my back against the wall. Was he saying what I thought he was saying?

He stopped and nodded. "Make no mistake, my son. Alethia is home to no one. It's a prison colony."

"No, it's not. It's a world where kin can do magic without worrying about consequences." I straightened to make myself appear taller. "And those exiled were sent there for a reason."

"Because they were deemed unfit for Oldworld. By whose standards? Guardians? Humans?" He spat the words.

I rubbed my forehead. "I don't understand. First you want to help kin get a better life. That's why you're on the council, right? And now you're looking to unify Oldworld with Alethia? That's not just a leap, that's a fucking teleport."

"Oldworld is our original home, and it belongs to us as much as humans." He waved me off. "We just want back what's ours." He shot me an icy smile. "The kin in this city, and beyond, smell the change in the air. They flock here to work with me. Fae men and women line up to become blood slaves in return for protection. Trolls and fairies spy for us. Even demons flex their muscles on our behest."

Fog drenched my mind and my back broke out in a sweat. The English language offered a million words to interrupt him, but not one came to me.

He raised his hands. "Look around, Florian. The spoils and riches on tap here are far superior to Alethia's. But we need to be free. All of us."

Had he gone insane?

He'd promised to fit in. This was not fitting in. This was... anarchy. Insanity.

I rolled my cold hands into fists and leaned back against the wall, glad for its support. "The humans would never allow that."

He flashed his white, straight teeth. "Don't worry. The transition will be peaceful. The humans won't see the shift coming."

I swallowed past a rock in my throat. His words didn't match his conquering tone. The story he told me was terrible enough. The subtext was worse.

His version of freedom was tyranny. His idea of friendship between kin was tantamount to slavery. And I had praised him for the strides he'd made in his work, had taken pride in his progress.

All the while, he'd played me like a toy soldier. And I had let him.

Christ, I was such a gullible fucker. From the beginning, I'd lied to myself. I'd thought he was capable of change. At every turn, I'd given him the benefit of the doubt while blinding myself to the truth.

I scratched my nose to hide the nausea rippling inside me. "And what's the real reason I have to stay indoors? Do you fear the werewolves' interference in your plans? Or a Guardian's?" My voice flapped like a torn rubber band.

"Quite honestly, you haven't given me reason to think you'll keep my plans from your friends. In time, they will agree to our terms, especially once we have the remaining kin on our side. Until then, I prefer to have you by my side. Don't worry. There will be plenty to do here."

Jeez. On the surface, his arguments were persuasive. What choice did my friends have but to follow majority rule? If Ivy refused to accept Gino's plan, she'd be hunted. The werewolves could take their chances with the humans or stand alone. Either way the outlook wasn't good for them, and that was even before the Alethians were free.

Once upon a time, I went along with Gino's plans, even the crazy ones. But this topped them all. I didn't want any part of it. Power had never been on my Christmas list. But how could I stop him?

Maybe I couldn't. If he had already amassed a following, perhaps it was too late.

Breathe. Breathe and listen. First I needed to know the details of his harebrained scheme.

"So you want my help?" My pitch held steady for now.

"Of course." He lifted his chin. "You are crucial. When the time comes, you will convince the werewolves and Guardians to join our cause. Besides, even for a vampire, you are strong. Stronger than I remembered." He sniffed me, Hannibal Lecter style. "My exile has done wonders for you. You are my legion."

I shuddered and reached for a grin from my arsenal of lies. "Okay. Sounds good."

"You'll stay?" He narrowed his eyes. "No arguments?"

I touched my belt buckle, the one Ivy made. The cool metal gave me strength, as if Ivy stood beside me. "No arguments."

"And you won't see your friends until I say you're ready?"

"Not if you don't want me to. But if I don't stay in touch with them, they won't be my friends for long. It's up to you."

He shook his head. "Don't worry. We're nearly at the final stage. Two weeks down the line, and you can begin bringing the furballs and Guardians into the fold. That is when all our hard work will pay off. Until then, I can't have you spilling our secrets."

"I wouldn't."

Yeah, I would. I would sell out this new, unhinged Gino for a piece of chewed bubblegum.

He tilted his head. "I wish I could believe you. First, I need you to prove yourself."

Right now, he probably trusted my enthusiasm for his plan as much as I trusted his reassurances, though his attitude still got to me.

"How could I prove myself?" I squared up to him. "I will prove that I'm staying by, well, staying."

"Why do you have to argue over every single point?" His voice boomed.

Gino looked sick with a fever that stemmed from deep-seated delusions. His skin, usually marked by an elegant paleness, held a clammy gray sheen. His eyes, darker still from the shadows underneath.

Had I been too occupied with Keely to notice his descent into madness? My throat went dry. "I told you, I won't see them if you don't want me to."

He sighed.

"You're my family, Gino. And I understand why you're doing this. Kin being second-class citizens is unfair. Living side by side, allowed to be who we are—why wouldn't I want this?"

His eyebrows lifted, and he nodded.

There you go. Gino wasn't the only fucking actor in this family.

"This is not how I wanted the conversation to play out." He sucked in air. "You don't understand what Alethia is like. You would think a world without a sun is wonderful for vampires, wouldn't you? But the air is thick because it lacks the richness of oxygen. Its beauty is monotonous. And no matter how many months you spend there, it never feels like home. What it did have, though, was freedom."

"Right."

"You must think me mad."

Duh. "No, I get it."

A smile changed his expression. It held a strength that cut through his weak pallor.

"I won't lie to you." He loosened his stance, softened his gestures. "In Alethia, fae got a hard deal in the Dupree's stronghold, as did the humans. We're vampires and have needs. But our kin fare just as badly in the demon court. True equality leads to a natural hierarchy, and the humans might not end up at the top. You and I were human once. Does that make us automatically more deserving than the rest?"

"No."

"Exactly." He placed his hand on my shoulder and guided me along the hall. "Our ancestors vacated the old world to let mankind grow, unchallenged by magic. And what have the humans done with the opportunity? They wage war against one another and kill more of their own than kin ever did. The air is as stale here as in Alethia. The seas so polluted, the merpeople are forced to inhabit a small patch in the Pacific Ocean."

Hard to argue with a madman when he was right. Maybe if the alternative didn't involve Alethians, I'd be on board. As it was, I'd take my chances with reality.

I stuck my fingers into my belt loops. "And you think we can do better?"

"Don't you?" He stopped in front of the stairs and turned to me. "Kin love order. Even your werewolves understand the need for both equality and a top-down hierarchy."

I was all for order, but his way involved total mayhem as everyone clambered to the top.

"That's true." I nodded.

Listen and learn. That's all I had to do for now.

"The kinlords and the IEA support me. So I'm asking you to pick your loyalties, my son. But choose wisely." Gino hung both hands around my shoulders. "The wrong decision could have dire consequences."

A shiver ran down my spine. Not too long ago, I warned him not to make me choose. Guess the lines were drawn. Just as I'd lost one family, I was set to lose the other.

"Yes. Of course I'll stay." I retrieved my house keys. "Here. I'll prove it. You can keep them. I won't leave."

He studied me for a moment then accepted them. Even though his face didn't brim with trust, he slid them into his pocket and rattled them a few times.

"I hoped you'd come around. I've tested your strengths and weaknesses, seen your personal abyss. I want you by my side. And you have my word. Do your part, and none of your friends need to die."

The shiver from earlier returned, skidding up the sweat on my back. As if his word still meant anything.

I rolled back my shoulders. "I'll do what I can. That's what family's for, right?"

The front door opened. Five men entered, carrying a gilded chair—not quite a throne—and stacks of books.

They walked toward us, keeping their heads low. Gino stepped aside and pointed to the bowels of his house. "Be quick about it."

One of the dudes dropped a couple of books, which thudded as they struck the floor.

The man bowed deep, his moustache trembling. "I'm so sorry, sir. So sorry."

The other men, dressed in grimy jeans and T-shirts that showed off bulging biceps, froze.

Sissies.

I'd seen scary Gino, and this wasn't him. Annoyed by their clumsiness, sure, but far from scary.

Gino let out a low rumble. "Get on with it."

One guy picked up the books, then all five scuttled along the corridor and disappeared through a door at the far back.

"The staff nowadays." Gino crowded into my line of sight. "At least you and I are on the same page now. So how about you run upstairs into your room, while I step out and attend to business?"

"Sounds good." The first cracks showed in my voice, and I gave a weak-ass smile.

He took a jacket from the rack. "I'll be back in a short while. And remember. Don't warn your friends. I trust you, *Cucciolo*."

"I'll be here."

For a moment after he left, I stood in the drafty hall between its modern chrome staircase and the polished hardwood floor, staring at a black-and-white photograph on the wall.

That first day of his return, Gino had given me a glimpse of his plans. Yet I'd dismissed my doubts, because he was so fucking convincing.

Lathan had been right all along.

I trudged into the living room, sat on the edge of the sofa, and retrieved my lucky stone from my pocket. The magic that flowed from it calmed me. Its shape had been carved from the Rock of Wisdom, Gino had told me. Maybe giving it to me had been a mistake, because his plans were anything but wise.

No, his ideas must have spawned much earlier. Perhaps even before he returned.

I would go a step further. There was every chance that uniting Alethia and Oldworld wasn't Gino's scheme in the first place. Maybe Lathan misunderstood. What if Gino was the kinlords' emissary, the guy to make their wishes happen? Gino was already out of Alethia. The kinlords weren't.

Most importantly, Mehmet wasn't. And he was just about crazy enough to set such a crazy plan in motion, with Gino eager to help.

Once the kinlords and other kin crossed over into Oldworld, not even the human militia could turn the tide. Who would they shoot at? We looked human too.

I tapped a finger against my cheek, making popping sounds to help me think. If Gino was just a pawn in their game of chess, maybe there was hope for him.

No. Gino was a Master, but his loyalty to his sire was absolute. As my loyalty to Gino should be.

Christ, I'd been so certain of myself. Thought I was all grown up, until *Daddy* came back. No wonder he lured me back into his arms. The bond we once shared seemed unbreakable. Our trust rock-hard.

Maybe he *was* right. Maybe his way was better. He'd been around longer, and back in the day, he never let us down.

And if I weren't so selfish, I wouldn't balk at the idea of falling in line. But in his world, the weak would be at the bottom. Preyed upon by those stronger than them, because their magic was not as aggressive or invasive as vampire or demon magic.

With a united kin front, there would be no equality with humans. Only kin rule.

Let's not forget many Alethians were dangerous and downright psychotic. Even with all their vampire powers, Gino and Mehmet couldn't hope to keep them under their control.

Ivy and Waylon wouldn't let this madness happen anyway.

Taking a stand would make them enemies numbers one and two. And fuck it, I was going to be number three. Where Ivy went, I went.

A chuckle bubbled up in my throat. *Christ.* Who would have guessed Lathan's warning held weight?

I pushed my 'lucky' stone back into my pocket. *Fat lot of good it had done.* A few days ago, my situation had been sweet. Spartan digs in the werewolf mansion, sure, but with front row seats to real life drama and friendships, and all the warmth a cold-blooded vampire could need. I'd been in the center of it. My presence at parties was welcome. My opinion considered. My advice sought.

Gino's return had changed that. Now my two remaining silver linings, Ivy and Keely, were at risk by this new world he proposed. If Gino knew me at all, he'd know I wouldn't follow him to world domination.

Gino had accepted my keys as a symbol of my allegiance. A symbol without true meaning. The fob to my car had never left my pocket, and I could leave here any time. And once I'd had a snoop, I would.

Ivy and Waylon, and Parker and Keely needed to be warned. If we wanted to stop him, we'd have to act soon.

Digging into my sire's plans, upsetting his machinations, would be dangerous. Going against him and my sister...

Fuck. What would I do about Julia?

I wasn't going to leave Gino without her. If anything, I could use her help.

With little input from my brain, my feet moved from the living room back into the long corridor that split the building in two.

Amid the silence, I was back in the camp, pressed against Keely's soft body. Her taste still covered my tongue. Her scent lingered in my nose.

"Florian?" A few inches from me, my sister stood in the doorframe of the laundry room. "Hello. Are you awake?"

"There you are." I squeezed my lips together. "I've been looking for you."

"Well, you found me."

Her long hair was tied high on her head with a plastic contraption that looked painful. Her makeup, less flamboyant today, gave her the air of a middle-aged woman.

"I've had an illuminating chat with Gino. Wait until you hear about his plans. He wants to free the Alethians."

"I know." She swallowed.

I felt my mouth gaping.

Julia laughed. "Don't look so shocked. I know stuff."

"Why didn't you say something?"

"I found out yesterday. Then you disappeared. He says that's what all of this council stuff has been about from the beginning, and he's not the only one. More and more kin are infiltrating high-level political positions, subsidized by kin money."

"Excuse me?" I blew air threw my nose.

"Yeah. That's quite something, isn't it?"

"What are we going to do?" I grabbed her shoulders.

"I'm not sure there's anything we should do. Think about it. True equality. Who doesn't want that?" Her voice trembled.

"You don't sound convinced."

"I trust him, Florian. As should you. He is our sire."

What a flimsy reason to trust a psychopath. Once I might have been swayed by his cheap arguments, but not anymore. Maybe becoming a Master had rid me of this blind trust.

If so, Julia would find it harder to see the truth. Especially because for some reason, she hadn't yet regained her old confidence.

I cocked my head. "The Circle's trade relies on keeping kin existence secret and won't take this lying down. Has Gino taken them into consideration?"

If nothing else, The Circle was vicious. Kin that made up the group had differing agendas, held together by their use of obscure trade routes across the globe and into Alethia. Theirs was an uneasy alliance, and as much as The Circle's factions fought one another, their defensive actions against any and all who threatened their profits were just as swift.

"Gino is on top of things. Don't worry." Julia blinked hard, as if emphasizing her point.

"What about Ivy?" I shook her shoulders. "She's your friend. Remember that."

"Ow." She pulled herself free. "What does this have to do with Ivy?"

Had Julia switched off half her brain cells, or did she deliberately not question Gino's plan and its consequences?

"Do you think she's going to stand by and watch dangerous Alethians return to Oldworld?" I slammed my fist into the wall. "They were sent there for a reason. Do you really want them to come here?"

"Gino said you would talk to her."

She glossed over the issue there.

I raked my fingers through my hair. "Think, Julia. How likely is it that Ivy will just go along with such a threat to all our lives? Or Waylon? Or the werewolves?"

"That's what this is really about, isn't it? Your precious furballs." She pressed her lips together.

Christ. What was wrong with her?

She rocked onto her heels. "Well, Gino doesn't want to kill the werewolves. In fact, he doesn't want to kill anyone."

"Yeah, that'll happen. Kin taking over the human world without bloodshed?" I leaned forward, my arms inches from her as if to grab her again.

"Stop it." She averted her gaze. "Gino knows what he's doing. And you said you'd help him. Yes, I overheard you. We're family, for Christ's sake. It's time you acted like it."

"Me?" I thumped my chest. "I'm the one looking out for you. This is going to tear us apart. Letting dangerous vampires into Oldworld, let alone demons, can't be a good thing. You think they're just going to leave us to our family bliss?"

"Shut up." Her voice shook, but she lifted her chin. "You're breaking us apart. I won't let that happen."

"Julia." I softened my tone. "I need your help. Do you want him to fall back into being the person he was when his sire still roamed the Earth? Violent. Uncaring. He said it himself. *We saved him.* We showed him the meaning of joy. And do you want Lathan free to come after Ivy, *your* friend? Gino is powerful, but not even he will be able to protect her against a Demon Kinlord."

Julia opened her mouth as if to shout something, but ended up shaking her head. "I know you have questions. So do I." Her frail frame trembled. "But I can't lose either of you again. Just trust him. For now. For me."

A knot grew in my throat. Was she so obsessed with her idea of family, she'd turn a blind eye to his scheme? Six months ago, moving in with the werewolves had seemed like a great idea.

"I'm sorry." I dragged her into my arms.

She buried her head in my neck, sniffing. Her skin was ice cold, so I shared what little body heat I had, and rubbed her shoulders.

"Shh," I whispered.

Julia clung to me like I was her last chance at life. Her mast in a storm. She felt slight in my arms, like a chick that had fallen from its nest. She and I, we'd been through so much. Gino's exile had drawn us even closer together. She had always been the sensible, reliable force in our family.

Our sire's return should have made her happier. Stronger. Instead, she'd never looked more terrified. Not terrified of Gino's mad ramblings, but of losing him and of losing me.

Now more than ever, it was my role to watch out for her. I would make it up to her. Regain her trust, somehow, and let her know she could rely on me. But I had to do it slowly.

If Gino continued to follow this path to destruction, he wasn't going to take my sister with him. I wouldn't allow it.

"Will you trust him?" Her words came as a plea.

I swallowed. She wouldn't settle for anything but a comforting lie.

"I will." My voice stayed firm.

Gino said the final stage, convincing Ivy and the pack, wasn't yet ready. That gave me a few precious days to win over Julia and alert Ivy.

Julia freed herself from my hug and blew her bangs from her face. "Do you have any wishes for dinner?"

"How about your famous tomato-less lasagna?" I gave her a gentle smile.

"We're having guests. They might not like it."

"Yes, they will." I placed a peck on her cheek. "They'd better."

"Thank you." She beamed through still glistening eyes. "I'm so glad you're okay with everything. I need you, and so does Gino."

"Sure."

"Between you and me, he's impressed with how you've changed."

A few days ago, pride would have swelled my chest. Now it just felt like I ate a rock for breakfast.

CHAPTER TWENTY

S LEUTH TIME.

After Julia disappeared through the door that led to the dining room, I strode along the corridor to Gino's office. Once I made sure I was alone, I pushed the door ajar. Two filing cabinets lined one wall, adjoined by south-facing windows, and a white desk bulged under mounds of paper in the center of the room. No computer. *Good.* Without Parker's hacking skills, I was limited to traditional snooping anyway.

I slipped inside and rifled through the documents, but couldn't connect them to Gino. He was a councilman now, entrusted with important tasks. But instead of contracts and reports, the stacks contained car repair quotes for a dozen different vehicles, warehouse receipts, and blank sheets.

I circled the desk and rolled the chair aside. The drawers held only pens and paperclips. Perhaps he kept more revealing blueprints and schematics in the filing cabinets.

I slid open the first level of the filing cabinet, thumbed through the thin folders, and found banal nothingness. Dealing with kin issues would take up most of his time, sure, but the council worked for the entire population, including humans. So where were the complaints, the building permit requests, the minutes of meetings with the other officials? I leaned against the desktop and crossed my arms. The walls were smooth and blank, no paintings to hide a safe or concealed alcoves. A total bust.

Everything about his new position was a façade. Gino was a councilman in name only. The bastard never even tried to keep his promise to me.

Shit. I swiped a pile of papers off the desk.

He sold his vision of a united kin front as a new discovery, sparked by the plight of his fellow kin here in Oldworld. But my suspicion was right. This was a plan long in the making. Freeing Alethia had been the endgame all along.

Asshole.

He deserved the beating I'd so far spared him. Better yet, Ivy should dispatch him straight back to Alethia, where he could cause no more harm, and where I wouldn't have to look at him anymore.

But the minute I involved Ivy, the number of options open to me would go down. My sister would never forgive me if I was the reason Gino abandoned her again. If I had been a better brother…

Maybe it wasn't too late. We'd be fine without him. That's what I would tell her. If she shared his plans with us, helped us take him down, the world as we knew it wouldn't change.

Even now the idea of a conflict with humans, just because Gino willed it so, didn't seem real. Wars happened in other places, and a war would be an optimistic vision of what could happen. Genocide might be a better term. What's more, it was a comfort to live in a world where I didn't constantly worry about who was going to blitz me into oblivion with their magic.

The click of the front door raced down the hall and into my superhuman ear canal. If Gino found me in here snooping, his trust in me would take a nosedive.

I gathered up the papers I'd shoved onto the ground, set them back on the desk, and slipped out of the office.

Gino was already inside the house. I did a one eighty and rapped on the door.

"Who are you looking for?" Gino shot me a grim smile.

Furtek, aka rogue werewolf, walked up behind him.

I met Gino's gaze. "Julia. But now that you're here, I want to talk to you about our plans. I have ideas about how I can help."

The hard glean left his eyes. He ruffled my hair. "Wish I could, but council business calls. Still, keep up your enthusiasm. We'll need it."

Council must be code for 'evil conglomerate of unhinged kin.'

"Let me introduce you to my new friend, Daniel Furtek. A werewolf." Gino beamed, so fucking proud of himself for mingling.

Furtek sniffed, making his grizzled beard quiver, then growled. "I know that smell."

I smiled.

He lunged in my direction.

I slipped past him.

He spun and struck with his fist.

I swayed out of his way, punched his gut, and used his bowed posture to slam the heel of my hand into his neck.

He hooked behind my knees and yanked.

The force nearly brought me down, but at the last second, I

shifted my mass forward. My weight bore down on his shoulders, and I beat my rolled fist into his kidney.

Gino tipped back his head and laughed, letting the sound reverberate through the air.

"Now now, kids. Get up, Florian." He dragged me up by my arm and patted my cheek. "You're not even fanged out. You trickster, you. You've been holding out on me. Your speed, your moves, your ruthlessness. You fight like a true Master. I'm pleased."

Despite his words' double-edged nature, my lips widened into a smile. "I told you."

"Yes you did. I just wish I'd been here to teach you everything you need to know, but we will make up for it soon. No one but you deserves to walk by my side." His glance skipped to the right. "Mr. Furtek. Daniel. Please say hello to my son, Florian."

The jeans-clad werewolf had pulled himself up and growled. "He smells like the local pack. The whole town does, but he's worse."

I shrugged. "I used to hang out with Parker Reeves's pack, yes."

None of my loathing made it into my voice. Drum roll for my Oscar-worthy performance, although it paled in comparison to Gino's acting.

He suppressed his hatred every day to further his goals. The sign of a true believer. Shame he believed in bringing evil into my world.

"Florian is *not* hanging with them anymore." Gino's posture straightened. "Daniel is part of The Circle. Working with him will open up vital trade routes."

One of Gino's final stages. Once my sire had control over the secret routes in and out of Alethia, there'd be no stopping him. His odd choice of a business partner finally made sense.

"*If* we can reach an agreement." Furtek lifted his chin. "We've been working our asses off, even brought the reclusive Order of White Ladies and the town's remaining dark fae to you, but you haven't convinced me yet it's worth it. My guys are getting antsy."

Pompous ass.

"Of course." Gino's eyes narrowed, but he did not blow his fuse. "That's what I would like to discuss with you today. My daughter is preparing a meal in your honor."

"Oh." Furtek mumbled something that could have included an apology.

I pointed my chin toward the rogue. "He's part of The Circle?"

"We call ourselves The Alliance." He pulled himself up into a slightly taller asshole than before.

"Can you trust them, Gino? Profit is all they care about."

"Which they will continue making." Gino gestured toward his office. "Daniel, please go inside. I'll be right with you."

With a squint, the rogue slinked past us, into the room.

"Don't question me in front of others." Gino pulled me all the way back to the stairs then sighed. "For now, I must work with the furballs. I don't like it any more than you."

"Sorry." I gave the expected head bow. "But what's the payoff? What does Furtek want in return for his help?"

Gino glanced past me at the wall.

"What is it?" I crossed my arms over my chest.

There was a chance I would not like the answer.

"This is where you come in, *Cucciolo*." Gino wet his lips. "Once my deal with Furtek is in place and you bring the local pack on board, they will help us with the other packs across America."

I frowned. "To do what?"

"Furtek and his creatures want equality with the organized packs. They demand access to ancient texts and spells the Werewolf Elders have been hoarding."

I knew it. Gino's plan for me sucked. Or it would, if I subscribed to any of his idiotic ideas.

I nodded. "I'm sure I can get the pack on board with it, if it's for the greater good of all kin."

Meanwhile, here on planet Earth, Parker would never agree to equality with the rogues. Just another sign that Gino still didn't understand werewolf mentality.

Weird. A policy of equality was supposed to be a good thing. Maybe it was, but in Gino's hands, a good intention had morphed into something ugly. Free Alethia. Unite all kin. Enslave humans.

Quite the game plan.

"I'm so glad you see my wisdom. We knew you would be an asset." Gino exhaled loudly.

"Sure." I switched my weight around on my feet, unable to stand still for another minute.

Gino hooked his hand around the back of my neck and touched my forehead with his. "Thank you, my son."

I cleared my throat. "Sure thing."

We parted, and his smile remained.

He may have convinced the furball of his kumbaya attitude, but how solid was their new partnership really?

"I don't trust this Furtek." I gave a deep sigh. "He'll betray you the moment he has a chance."

"No doubt. But it's worth it. To appreciate The Circle's importance in my plan, you must understand its culture. Its distribution venues change hands almost weekly. Its members kill each other faster than they can recruit new supporters. Their inner ranks are so fractured, they are close to collapsing. With my backing, Furtek and his people will clean up The Circle and create a streamlined organization that has direct and consistent access to Alethia."

The puzzle pieces started to come together just as I thought.

I raised my eyebrows. "Once that's done, you will take over The Circle, I assume."

"You know me well." He chuckled. "Until then, we will play the perfect partners."

"You shouldn't keep him waiting then." I returned his wink.

"No, I shouldn't." He gave my arm a friendly slap and brushed past me to disappear behind his office door.

I moved into the living room, and dark foreboding festered in my mind. My acting was pure method and sustainable for a while, but I had to get Julia to see reason and then out of harm's way. Because as soon as I had details, Ivy and Waylon would swoop in to rain whoop-ass on Gino's keister.

Odd. All those fuzzy feelings that ran through me when I heard of Gino's return were gone. His favorite pastime used to be the arts. Why didn't he take that up again? Or shuffle board? Why did he have to set his sights on fucking up the world?

I slumped onto the couch, mentally and physically fried.

Knowing his precise schedule would help us take Gino down. If I got Julia on my side, together, we could even work on destroying his pretend bromance with Furtek. And dinner would be the perfect occasion to chip away at their relationship. Without Furtek and The Circle's backchannels, my sire would stay cut off from Alethia.

I touched my knuckles to my mouth, silently cursing. As long as Julia remained under Gino's influence, I couldn't risk making a move. Without her help, there would be no plan.

I would need to talk to her right away. Convince her that *I* was the guy to trust, and not Gino.

A scratching, like from a cat, came from the window. Though the voile curtains let in plenty of light, they were thick enough to block my view. Did Gino have a cat? He wasn't a cat person, although Julia kind of had cat lady written all over her forehead.

I exited the living room and opened the front door. A warm gust swept over my face.

The step was empty.

"Psst. Florian."

I hung out of the doorframe and glanced to my right. Rollo waved, having a hard time hiding his size behind a leafy bush.

I checked over my shoulder and slid out of the house. "What are you doing here? This isn't a good place for you."

"I know. Ivy told me. But I need your help."

"*My* help?" I whispered. "What for?"

"It's the female pack."

My skin went cold, and I grabbed his arm. "Are they okay?"

"Not for long." Rollo squeezed his legs together as if he needed to piss. "I'm so gonna get in trouble for this."

Next to me, the living room curtain twitched. My lungs stopped moving.

No. Just my guilty conscience crying wolf. If Julia or Gino knew about my unannounced visitor, I'd be in trouble already.

"You don't understand." I pushed him further into the bushes bordering my sire's grounds. "You need to go. Now."

"Jeez. What's up with you?" Rollo rubbed his palm over his stubbled chin. "Never mind. Just listen, okay? Ali tried to negotiate with the female alpha earlier today, but he got nowhere."

I crossed my arms. If she didn't already, now she knew for sure I'd fallen out with the pack.

"This morning, Kev and Byron squared up to Parker. They were going to leave us to be with the female pack, even if it meant submitting to a woman alpha." He kneaded his neck muscles. "They've been secretly meeting with two of the girls, but the females told him they wouldn't consider the guys' advances unless they joined."

I raised my eyebrows. Parker had foreseen this situation all along.

"The boss tried to reason with them." Rollo's fingers mimicked a talking hand. "But they wouldn't listen. So he answered their challenge."

"You mean he fought them? Both of them? How badly injured are the guys?"

"Let's say, no one else will make the same mistake."

"Shit." I tapped my foot, eager for him to leave. "Or not. Think about it. That's a good thing. If everyone got Parker's message to stay away, Keely and her pack wouldn't need to move. You should tell him that."

"No, the boss has had enough. He's getting rid of the females once and for all." Rollo's voice dipped. "Ivy's not happy with the decision, but you know what he's like."

"His pack comes first." I nodded. "No surprise there."

"So, are you gonna talk to him?"

"To Parker?" *Yeah, because an irate Parker will listen to the exiled vampire.* "That wouldn't do much good. Did he say how long he's giving Keely?"

"You ain't hearing me, Florian. He's putting his squad together right now. The only reason I'm not in it is because he doesn't want me going up against my sister, but they're marching tonight. A few hours from now, tops."

I took a step back. "Jesus. What's his plan?"

"They're gonna steamroll the camp. Probably threaten to take the cubs and raise them within our pack. If the women still won't submit, they'll be chased out of town."

"That's brutal."

Rollo nodded. "Yeah. But Parker doesn't think the females alone are strong enough to protect their young in the long run."

"He doesn't know that."

Rollo kicked a stone on the ground. "He's not going to take the risk."

"This is going too far. Taking the cubs? Threatening the females?" I placed my fingertips on the bridge of my nose. "I know Parker sees himself as the protector of all the weak creatures out there, but that's insane."

"He's my alpha, so I can't call him out. But he's never even raised his voice at you."

Talk about skewing the facts.

Rollo's broad shoulders withdrew deep into his body. As the pack's enforcer, he must have traded his share of uppercuts, but the confidence had fled his eyes.

With Gino's plans coming to a head, this was not the time for internal fighting amongst the furballs. At any rate, I couldn't leave Keely to face bloodshed without me by her side.

I closed and opened my fists to warm my hands. "If he wants to fight the females, they won't be alone. I'll stand with them."

Of course, with my lack of control, I might end up killing someone. My jaw tightened.

"But we're your friends." Rollo yanked his eyes wide open. "Besides, even with the females, you're outnumbered. You have to do your diplomatic thing."

I crouched, one hand held to the ground to keep from tipping over.

First Parker charged me with talking to Keely. Next, Keely sent me to argue her case in front of Parker.

Both had been epic fails. Hadn't they figured out by now I was hopeless at negotiation?

In Rollo's defense, violence wasn't the appropriate response either. Murdering werewolves, members of my pack, wasn't an option. Gino might have severed my link to them, and Parker might have exiled me, but as far as I was concerned, the connection was still alive.

I pushed through my knees. Once upright, I stretched my arms. "I need to go home to grab supplies. Will I have safe passage to Keely's camp, or did Parker set up a watch?"

"No, you should be good. What are you going to do?"

I patted his back and then holding on to the collar of his T-shirt, dragged him with me, out of the drive and down the road.

How would Gino react when he found out I was gone? Maybe I could convince him my leaving was vital to maintain my rapport with the furballs.

I unlocked the Benz with my key fob. "Get in."

"Parker can't see me cruising with you. No offense."

I opened the door and placed one leg inside. "Hop out before we get home, but I'm not leaving you here. That house is home to two vampires who're cranky on a good day." I climbed in and put the key in the ignition. "And at least one of them is about to rain hell down on Silverton."

Rollo joined me and fastened his seat belt. "Your sister's a sweetie, not to mention a hottie, and everyone knows your sire's trying to make nice with kin."

"My sister's way too old for you. Or do you like older women?" I turned in my seat. "Hang on. What do you know about Gino?"

"He's the talk of the town. How do you think I found you?"

"Talk of the town meaning what?"

"They *talk* about him in bars and on the street all across *town*. Even at the shooting range. The powerful vampire who returned from Alethia a changed man to unite all kin."

Christ, they're hailing him a savior.

"Don't believe for a second that's a good thing." I started the engine and pulled out into the road.

It was five o'clock now. Rollo said a couple of hours tops, which gave me until about 6:15 p.m. I put my foot down, and the Benz screeched around a bend.

"What are you saying?" Rollo slapped for the car's oh-shit handle.

My Benz didn't have one.

He wasn't the only one being flung around without an ounce of control.

Why wasn't anyone telling me what to do right now? Normally that's all everyone wanted to do. Ivy pretended to be my boss, Parker *was* my boss, and Gino played the sire card. Even Julia couldn't help pushing me into being a good boy for Gino.

Only one person hadn't ordered me around, even though she'd

be the one whose word I'd take as gospel. That's why Keely came first. Now and always.

I shifted up a gear. "Gino eats werewolves for breakfast. He also doesn't like Guardians." I took a deep breath. "Stay away from him."

"I can handle myself." A sulk stretched through his voice.

How could I convince this man-child how seriously fucked up Gino was? "Do you know I'm no longer linked to Ali?"

"I heard. I liked it better when you were. Did you decide to separate or—"

"Not my decision. Gino half butchered me to break the link. That's how we vampires roll. Especially vampires as old as my sire. Trust me, if he caught you, you'd be dead. Anyway, let's deal with one drama at a time."

Two minutes later, I came to a screeching halt and kicked Rollo out of the car. My rapid acceleration cut off his goodbye. Once again, only one thing occupied my mind.

Keely.

CHAPTER TWENTY-ONE

With a bag of Ivy's guards in my arms and speed in my feet, I zipped over to Keely's camp. The trail through the woods lay in shadows, but the shades of gray that zoomed past me equaled the entirety of the color spectrum of human vision.

Rollo's warning gave me time to set up Ivy's guards.

Just.

Once Keely was safe, I'd turn my attention to convincing both her and Parker of the merits of my new plan. Parker had already made it clear he would not budge or compromise, but that was the beauty—he wouldn't have to.

The rippling surface under my feet flattened into something of a trail. A shadow moved beside me, a wolf with a black W framing its eyes. It wasn't Kev or Jim or any other of my friends, but Parker's pack was so numerous, I couldn't know them all by their shifted forms.

It didn't attack or stop me from proceeding, but its growl and bared teeth quickened my pace all the same. No way would the animal be able to keep up with a determined vampire.

I raced past tree trunks, down a slope and up again. When the wolf had disappeared from sight, I forced myself to slow, even though my nerves egged me on.

But vampire speed was too much of a giveaway of my real identity, and I needed Keely focused.

With my insides vibrating with urgency, I forced myself to stroll into camp at 5:35 p.m.

And by camp, I meant city.

The werewolf ladies had been industrious. They had extended their infrastructure, set up signposts to a kindergarten, and found time to lay the foundations for a wooden cabin. Parker would be so pissed. After all, their hard work cast doubt on their so-called inability to move at a moment's notice.

The females relaxing on their sun loungers nodded at me.

I returned their gestures while I zigzagged around a toy truck that stood abandoned on the path.

"Keely?" I brushed aside the flap to Keely's tent.

Empty.

"You're back." Coming from behind me, her voice bathed my mind in calm.

I dropped the overnight bag and took two steps toward her.

Her gaze darted to the females, whose faces turned in our direction, but I pressed my lips onto hers, reminding her whose attention mattered most.

Once more, she shaped herself against me in the special Keely way that left not a molecule of air between us. The tips of our tongues met, and a spark chased down my insides. This moment of breathlessness, this ball of lightness in my guts, would have to last me until she was safe.

We parted, and I tucked her hair behind her ears.

"I'm glad you're okay," I whispered.

The late rays of the sun reduced her pupils to tiny orbs.

"Of course I'm okay." She kissed me again.

This time she didn't check her friends' reactions.

Priorities, dude.

I put air between us without relinquishing our connection. "I don't have time to explain. We need to protect the camp."

"What's wrong?"

"Do you trust me?"

Her gaze shifted down and back up just as a blush worked itself onto her high cheekbones. "Of course."

"Good. We need to set up guards around this camp, right now."

She frowned. "What do we need guards for?"

"Protection." I picked up the bag. "Parker's about to do something stupid."

Her alpha power slammed into me, jolting my circulation almost as much as her naked curves had last night. The heat in my chest spread across my body, giving me goosebumps.

It was hard not to smile.

The females around me sat stiff, sharing their alpha's alarm.

"Bugger. Stupid how?" The softness had fled Keely's expression, replaced by hard, tight lines.

Christ, she needed a situation report now? "Parker is about to take your kids to force your hand, but he cannot do so if he can't get inside." I lifted the bag up. "So help me set up the guards. Now, Keely."

"If he wants to fight us, I'm not going to cower. Let him come."

For the first time, a werewolf's bluster struck me as endearing.

She dragged me to the side. "And don't order me around. Especially not in front of my pack."

"I'm not usurping your position, honey. Just telling you we need to get our asses in gear."

"Whose side will *you* be on?" Her voice faltered.

What a shitty time for her to feel insecure. And yet, those big blue eyes and parted lips melted my need for speed.

If only she didn't keep pushing me into saying words I've never said before. Coming to terms with my feelings in my head was already a huge step. Giving voice to them?

Dammit.

I gathered her against my chest and folded my arms around her. "Yours. Always. I'm here, aren't I?"

"Just checking." Her shoulders relaxed. "Are you going to tell me what happened? Did you tell him about the black eye?"

Christ. "Yes. It didn't go well. He said some things, I said some things. And we decided I should leave."

"As long as it's nothing to do with me. I don't want you to lose your friends."

I smiled. "I want to be here, Keely. That's what matters. And no doubt, you and I could do some damage to Parker's pack, but is that what you want?"

"He's the aggressor." The steel was back in her tone.

"And you have an obligation to your females and the little ones. You can't protect them if you're fighting the other pack."

She moved out of my grip and peered at my bag. "Are those guards from your Guardian friend?"

"Yes. Come on." I was about to commandeer her females, but stopped myself. "Can you spare one of the ladies to give us a hand?"

With a few eye and hand signs that would have zoomed past me had I not expected them, she called two women over. Neither was pregnant, which gave me cause for optimism. We might set up a defensive perimeter within my lifetime.

"Parker's pack is on the way." Her voice remained calm, and the young women before us showed no anxiety. "Florian is going to explain what to do."

Me explain magic? My experience with guards was limited to my belt buckle and a few other low-magic gizmos. Nothing like the powerful devices we were about to use.

Assuming Ivy had done her job, and the guards didn't fizz out on me.

I fished a metal plate out of the bag. "Okay, first step. Distribute these guards around the camp. Remember where you placed them, so you or your kids won't stray outside the zone."

With a military nod, they each took a handful of guards and set off.

I kissed Keely's lips, soaked in her taste. "Let's do this."

We separated and paced in opposite directions.

I placed the thin copper plates, no larger than the palm of my hand, into the ground near thick trees, boulders or dry patches of grass so they formed a smooth curve around my assigned quarter of the camp.

My cell beeped, and I retrieved it to check who it was.

"Where are you?" Julia wrote.

"I have something to do. Be back soon." I sent.

"Gino's going crazy. Thinks you're betraying him."

Fuck. *"I'm not."*

Not yet.

"I don't like seeing him like this again. And you promised you wouldn't leave."

I swallowed. *"Gino's gonna blow off steam, then he'll be fine. Keep your head down till I'm back."*

A glance at the clock ramped up the pressure inside me. If Rollo's information was correct, Parker's group would march in less than an hour. If the wolf I'd met on my way had snitched on me, maybe we wouldn't even have that.

"Must go. See you soon." I sent and pushed the phone back into my pocket.

One of the werewolf ladies paced in my direction, placing a guard every fifteen steps. Efficient, but without a sense of urgency.

"Do you have any left?" I asked once she was close enough.

"Two." She handed them over.

I quickly placed them, then returned to the spot outside Keely's tent.

The female joined me without making small talk.

I folded my arms in front of me and tapped my fingers. The tick tock of my watch came like hammer strikes, and I took a few steps toward the other side of the camp to see how Keely was getting on.

She didn't leave me hanging.

Keely swayed her hips, casting a trance over me the way a metronome might. She'd swapped her red shoes for her run-of-the-mill sneakers, which, all things considered, was for the best.

My mind should be on magic, not fantasizing of the things I'd do to her *after* I saved everyone's day.

Keely stood by my side. Our hands touched, as if by accident. I needed more contact than that, but now wasn't the time.

She might not be the alpha in our relationship, but she was top wolf out here. To prevent her small pack from panicking, I had to maintain that image at all times, even between us.

I handed her the printed sheet with the incantation. "Your camp. Your magic. And remind everyone to stay inside the circle. Once they leave, they'll need permission before they can come back in."

The two females gave me the same look Rollo and Jim reserved for Ivy's lengthy explanations.

Keely studied the piece of paper, then handed it back. "No problem."

She strode off and halted a few feet from me.

The dark sky frowned onto tall trees that hugged the clearing. Clouds had called for an early dusk, and night wasn't far away.

Keely lifted her hands and closed her eyes.

The kids stopped yelling, the females ceased talking, and the wind left the leaves in peace.

She mumbled the words, and magic sang.

Invisible waves of energy propelled from her body, sweeping over my hair and cheeks with comforting assurance.

I wasn't part of her pack, yet my senses reached out to get a taste, a whiff or a feel of her power.

For a few seconds, time stood still. A vast tranquility reigned over us.

The female to my right made a sound. The reversing tide of energy scrambled past me. The potent magic slapped and bruised through my nervous system, leaving an angry cry in my core. *Shit.* Its frequency made my skin burn and forced my hairs to stand up.

The flood ebbed back into Keely's body, carrying with it the magic transformed by the guards. She lurched.

And the wonder was gone.

A boy of around five years ran crying to his mother. She crouched to hug him tight. He pressed close to her and an instant later lay in her arms in the form of a wolf cub. Female voices reached my ears, quiet at first, then louder.

Hairs extended at odd angles from Keely's head, a remnant of the static that had tinged the air a mere moment ago.

She opened her eyes to connect with my hungry gaze, as if she'd kept my position stored in some onboard computer.

"It's done." She walked past her females who bowed their heads in reverence to the power her position as alpha granted her.

Compared to hers, my abilities were a whiter shade of snow. Sure, I slung a mean glamour, but as far as magic went, it was pretty weak-ass and transient.

Werewolves drew on nature to make things happen, while demons wielded amulets and weapons imbued with their brand of magic.

I could see well in the dark, sniff out a drop of blood from many yards, and kill people without making a fuss. Useless skills in most circumstances.

Nothing like the power of a werewolf.

She strode toward me and threw her hands around my neck.

Despite the tightened spot in my throat, I leaned in for a kiss, which she returned with fierce enthusiasm.

"I guess we should try out the guarding wall." I extricated myself and strode toward the bridge, hand stretched out.

My fingers tingled, then throbbed. Who knew those guards came with integrated proximity alerts? No doubt, a result of Ivy's tinkering. What other surprises did she have in store for us?

I dipped into the dense energy field and out the other end. A shudder gripped me, spanning from my head to my toes.

I turned and prodded the field. The invisible wall bit me.

"Shit." I snapped back my arm and shook it.

The werewolf girls by Keely's side giggled.

"You didn't see that coming?" Keely rolled her eyes.

"You three are hilarious. The last time I saw a guard-induced magic wall, it didn't attack me." That was six months ago, the day Ivy's mother died, and I'd nearly lost Ivy too.

"Did you not read the lines in the guards?"

"I *use* guards. I leave the weaving and the wielding, and the reading and interpreting to the Guardians. Like normal people. How come you can read them?"

"I learned from my parents. Guards are used in so many areas of our lives, it pays to know how they work. I'm not at Guardian level, but I've picked up a thing or two." Keely pointed at the woman to her left. "Sabine knows too. Want to enlighten him?"

The female narrowed her eyes. "Once we call upon the atmosphere's energy and guide it into a guard, the pattern of deep lines and ridges imprints on it. This pattern determines what effect the energy has once it leaves the guard. The effect is magic. The guards we used today had a jagged semicircle at one end, like a curved blade, so they cut, the way the shield cut you."

Keely nodded, and Sabine beamed.

"We use mnemonics to remember what shapes have which effect." Keely bunched her mouth. "Garland tried to keep them down, but my wolves are quick learners. Of course, we're not perfect. I myself still have lots to learn. Maybe one day I'll discover how to *make* guards."

I squinted at Keely, half agape. "Oh my God. You're a nerd. A fricking nerd. That explains your fangirling over Ivy and Waylon."

"Shut up." She peered at her females.

This time I wasn't going to back down. I'd been around Parker long enough to know how far alphas could be pushed.

I flicked my hand at her. "You'd better invite me back in, so you can make me shut up. Nerd."

A hint of a smile played around her lips. "Sure, if you say the right words."

"Open Sesame?"

"No. The password is '*Keely is smart, beautiful and altogether perfect.*'"

I grinned. "Keely is smart, beautiful and altogether—"

A pregnant woman scrambled from her lounger and pointed behind me. "They're coming."

CHAPTER TWENTY-TWO

M Y STOMACH CHURNED, BUT SECOND thoughts were for losers.
"Over here, Florian." Keely beckoned, her beautiful face marred by a deep frown.

I stepped to her side and pulled myself up to full height.

My heart pounded in my chest, threatening to drown out the noises Parker and the pack made.

"At least he isn't sneaking up." I took Keely's hand.

She squeezed, then let go. "Why does it matter?"

"If he wanted to harm your pack, surprise would have worked better."

The females who weren't pregnant took position behind us, with looks that could kill and taut bodies hunched, in case they needed to shift. Those expecting a child and the little ones retreated into their tents.

This wall had better work. Not to disparage Keely or her pack, but compared to Parker's trained squad, my backup was no more effective than a bunch of fae toddlers in a wrestling match with their hands tied behind their backs.

Keely's gaze darted from left to right, without settling on one point. "We're safe, but he could let us starve in here."

"Parker wouldn't do that. Besides. I have a plan."

"What plan?"

"You'll find out soon enough."

"Well, that's not going to bloody fly with me, mate." The threat in her voice jarred the air. "Tell me."

"You are the females' alpha, and I will have to live with that." I frowned. "But you aren't mine."

She gave a growl, punctuated with a nod. "Fine."

Wow. That was easy. I raised my eyebrows. "Okay then."

Parker and Ali crossed the bridge, and Ivy followed a few feet behind.

"Should I feel insulted there are only three of them?" Keely whispered.

I placed myself between the approaching alpha and Keely. "If I know Parker, he has us surrounded."

All around the camp, wolves stepped into the clearing from behind the trees. Their fur caught the dying light, contributing to the muscle play in their powerful shoulders.

Jim. Kev. Malachi. I knew them all. More than once, I'd run with Parker's enforcers through the woods, let them chase me and sniff out my secret hiding spots. Now, the full brunt of their threat collapsed over me. Their bared teeth and tight bodies seemed a wrong move away from cutting us down.

This was so fucked up. We shouldn't be on opposite sides.

"Are you okay?" Keely took a step to the left to stand beside me. "You look a tad peaky."

I shot her a bruising glance. I did not look peaky. Whatever *peaky* was.

She shrugged, practically flipping off me and my male ego.

I drew a sharp breath. "I'm good."

For now.

Ali and Ivy stopped, while Parker marched toward us with his chin held high.

Two steps later, the wall fizzed, and he jumped back as if stung by a wasp.

"Ivy." He turned to my friend and beckoned her with a flick of his head. "Tell me these aren't your guards."

Her expression switched from guilty to *how dare you*.

"I didn't tell her what the guards were for," I said. "Leave her alone."

Parker whipped around. "I see you've switched sides."

For a second, I thought he'd lay into me for disrespecting him. Then again, he'd always let me get away with more than the rest of his pack.

I shot him an assuring smile. "I have a solution that benefits both sides."

Ivy gave an almost imperceptible fist pump.

Parker frowned. "You know better than to suggest another compromise."

Plenty of feet behind me altered their position. The dude hadn't lost his fright factor. I usually attributed his manner to what I called *grump*, but his dark expression packed a powerful jab.

No wonder the ladies took notice.

I shifted my weight from my toes to my heels, and folded my arms in front. "Well, you can't come in, and since you're already here, why not hear me out?"

The rumble from his throat penetrated the energy field and vibrated the cells in my body. His alpha power hooked straight into the wolves around the camp, who took two steps in our direction. Intimidating, but pointless in light of the electric field protecting us.

"Stop throwing your weight around." Keely's alpha force flared up. "You're not the only alpha here."

Her and Parker's werewolf magic swirled the air, and judging by Ali's expression, churned stomachs on both sides of the wall.

The situation couldn't be more serious, yet a chuckle rose up inside me.

"Guys?" I coughed to suppress it. "The plan?"

I preferred taking the honey route in negotiations, but if needed, I'd bang their heads together to make them listen.

Ali sidestepped Parker and approached the invisible partition. The twilight left the whites of his eyes glowing.

Parker's growl subsided, and the camp fell quiet once more.

Ali's gaze lingered on my face, then swept aside to study Keely. *Awkward.* Annoying Parker was a personal pleasure of mine, but taunting Ali wasn't my style.

I shifted on my feet. "Listen."

He raised a hand, his attention back on me. "Tell us about your plan."

The hurt in his voice, whether real or in my mind, cut my insides to shreds. His pain was my fault.

He stared down for a second. When he faced me again, his expression softened.

"You said you'd think of a plan, and now you claim to have found one." His lips twitched. "I knew you would."

I smiled and took a step forward. "I could have used your confidence back at the mansion."

He shrugged. "I'm the silent type."

"I forgot."

"Are you two done?" Parker crossed his arms.

"Keep your tighty whities on, Parker. I'm getting to it." I pointed with my head. "Keely is the alpha of the female pack. Not one of her females will submit to your authority."

His eyelids shuddered. A bad sign.

I flicked my hand to stop him from erupting. "Just summarizing."

"I'm done with their shit." His lips pressed together. "I want them gone."

Jesus. Werewolves were so mulish.

"No, you don't. What you want is to see them safe." I exchanged a quick glance with Ivy.

She stood by her man's side, the way Keely stood by mine, but her encouraging nod refueled my flagging willpower. She still had faith in me. Whatever happened, she wouldn't allow this situation to get out of hand.

I let the tension out of my shoulders. "You said it yourself. Many times. Well, today's going to feel like your birthday, because you're going to get your wish."

Keely's gaze was on me, her stance stiff, but confident. *Good.*

I focused on Parker. "All you need to do is let Keely become a member of the pack."

"Florian." Keely touched my arm. "I told you, the girls—"

"No, not the girls. You."

She furrowed her brow. "I'm not leaving them."

"No. You will remain their alpha. In all aspects regarding the women's future and wellbeing, you make the decisions. Parker will continue to rule his pack, you will rule yours, and where the two intersect, you will run things past Parker."

Her eyes darkened. "He could force me to act against our interests."

"If he gives his word that you will remain in charge of your pack, not in name but for real, he will keep it. That's why you came here, remember? Because you know he's a good man."

Parker studied me, frowning, doing that thing where his tongue poked the inside of his cheek—his thinking face.

"Florian." Keely glanced at her pack. "Can I speak to you?"

I beamed at the females, so willing to protect her. "Could you give us some space?"

They didn't move.

Keely growled. "Don't order them around."

I sighed. "Would you ask them to leave for a minute?"

Keely nodded her okay, and the females retreated.

I turned Keely so she faced me, and only me.

"I admit I haven't always been supportive of your alpha status." I softened my voice.

She glowered. "No, you haven't."

"But I've watched Parker deal with the pack. He's autocratic, sometimes a bit of a tyrant. I've heard the word jerk used a lot. Usually by me."

A growl came from my right. Parker also had excellent hearing, even for a werewolf.

I rolled my eyes. "A pack is not a democracy. You're the one who decides what's best, and this is the best, if you ask me. But the final decision is yours."

With every word, my respect for Parker grew. What that dude had to carry on his broad shoulders wasn't something I could even imagine.

Keely crossed her arms, clearly not impressed with my pep talk so far.

I placed my hand on her neck, drew comfort from her warmth, her slowing pulse. "You can keep everyone together *and* become part of a pack in good standing, without relinquishing your position. You and Parker will butt heads on occasion, but isn't that better than guaranteed bloodshed?"

Who knew a vampire would shy away from that? Gino would be mortified.

"But if my plan isn't something you can get onboard with, say so. I'm behind you either way." I steeled myself against the rising pressure.

Parker and Keely glanced at each other, their alpha powers holstered for now.

As much as I wanted to sweep her up and tell her everything would be okay, this wasn't my decision.

I stepped aside and looked at her females. Their tight faces and tense postures spoke volumes. With luck, they'd relax once the uncertainty was over.

Keely's lips twitched then spread into a smile. "Bloody hell, Florian. No wonder they chose you to negotiate."

Did she just say what I think she did? I sucked in air, my lungs open wide. Did I—

"Come on." Keely marched past me and my ballooning ego, right to the edge of the invisible shield to where Parker stood.

I'd done it. I'd gained her trust and approval.

She nodded at Parker. "Do you give your word to acknowledge me as alpha of my females?"

Parker's jaw muscles tightened a few times. "I do. Do you give your word to acknowledge me as your alpha from now on?"

"I do."

No hesitation. Her voice remained strong.

My chest filled with pride.

Parker gave a curt nod. "Tomorrow evening, you will join my pack."

Keely raised her eyebrows.

Ivy moved in front of him and all but ignored his scowl. "What he means to say is we'll be glad to welcome you into our family."

While Ivy wasn't supposed to interfere in pack business, she'd become the *de facto* translator for those of us who didn't speak grump.

"Right." Keely's voice didn't sound any friendlier than Parker's.

I smiled. "What Keely means to say is it will be my pleasure, and thank you for your kind invitation."

Keely glared so hard, her cute nose wrinkled.

"Great." Ali pointed his thumbs over his shoulder. "We'll be going back then to prepare everything. The location of the ceremony, the time…"

The tension that had seized the clearing minutes ago had dissipated. And so had the heavy weight squeezing my chest.

"I'd better get back and tell my pack the ramifications of my decision." Keely bit her lip.

"Me too." Parker nodded.

I pointed at both of them. "See? You have much in common."

His stare all about killed the fun.

Keely took two steps, as if she wasn't sure what to do, then walked away with her chin up. Her females approached and closed a circle around her.

I forced my attention back to Parker, but he and the others, including the wolves that surrounded us, were already walking back. Back to their mansion. To their home.

Ivy gave a half twirl and waved before falling into stride beside Parker.

She belonged with him. Soon, Keely would as well. So where did that leave me?

CHAPTER TWENTY-THREE

WHILE KEELY TALKED TO HER pack, I commandeered the playground swing on the left as my thinking spot.

Six children busied themselves, carrying plants and other items to the fort. One girl, not the tallest of the bunch, but the one with the loudest voice, didn't stray far from the wooden structure.

Perhaps I was more of a chauvinist than I thought by building the fort *for the boys*. Hadn't Keely and Ivy taught me the era of men ruling the world was long over?

I swung back and forth, entranced by the kids' play. What did they care if it was almost dark? They were too engrossed in their narrative. Miss Bossyboots played the alpha, who instructed the others to fetch flowers so she could grow her treasure. The treasure, as far as I could make out, served no purpose.

A metaphor for their thought patterns if I ever saw one.

The kids were at the age where their slivers of life were in constant flux. Your friend kicked you in the shin, you hated him. Two minutes later, the two of you shared a bar of chocolate.

Events mattered. Consequences didn't.

Reality for adults wasn't like that. In my world, the tiniest act cast a long shadow. Shadows intersected, covered other shadows, and before you knew it, you were fumbling around in the dark.

Keely now had a safe home, one in which I, a vampire, would not be welcome. My future lay not with my sire, nor with Parker's pack.

For the first time, I was alone.

Shit. They should serve alcohol at these pity parties.

To my right, Keely crossed the grassy expanse toward me with determined steps. The top she'd changed into hugged her breasts, but concealed the softness of her stomach. Although the real stars in that outfit were her well-rounded thighs and legs. The bottom of her gray slacks gave a tantalizing glimpse of her tanned ankles.

I stopped the to and fro of my seat.

She had slipped into my favorite accessories—the red shoes, whose lines accentuated her graceful walk.

She gave a small wave, and her smile got my blood pumping.

I tightened my grip on the ropes that held the tire. "How'd it go?"

"Surprisingly well." She sat on the swing next to me. "Assuming Parker keeps his word, we can make this work."

"He treats his wolves well." If not his vampires.

"He'd better." She gave an exaggerated sigh. "Bloody hell. What a crazy couple of days."

"Yeah."

She looked into the dark gray sky. "It's getting cold. The crappy weather makes night come faster."

"You want to talk about the weather? Sometimes you're very, very British, you know?" I smiled.

"Yeah." She pushed off and swung. "Florian?"

"Hmm?"

She cleared her throat. "I thought you were okay with me being an alpha."

"I am." I twisted my head to follow her back and forth.

"You didn't seem to be earlier. And it wasn't the first time you've tried to take charge. We're already headed toward a pack with two alphas. I don't think there's room for one more."

"Very tactfully put." I scrunched one side of my mouth. "I'm pretty easy going usually. But this wasn't about your pack. I just... Hell, Keely, you have to allow me to protect you."

"I don't need protection."

"I'm not saying you do. This is about me, and what I bring to this relationship."

Her pink, full lips twitched, and she widened her smile. "Thank you."

I had sacrificed much for her, was ready to sacrifice even more, and a *thank you*, a single fucking *thank you* was all it took to make my mouth grin and my head buzz. "You're welcome."

She coughed. "I would like to, umm, *show* you my gratitude. If you have time."

I raised an eyebrow. "What did you have in mind?"

She stood and beckoned with her head. "Come on and find out."

She walked off without looking back, leaving the tire swinging beside me.

I surged to my feet and followed, unable to take my gaze off her ass. Perhaps I was reading into its sway and her words, but if she meant what I thought she meant, her females had better get their earplugs ready.

She reached into her back pocket and withdrew a shiny object she dangled by her index finger over her shoulder.

I squinted.

Fuck me. A pair of handcuffs.

I swallowed. Red shoes. Handcuffs. No, I hadn't misread her intent in the least.

She bunched the chained rings together and slipped them back into her pocket.

A metal tab peeked out, stealing my focus, and I stumbled and staggered across the uneven ground.

God, the things I'd do to her. The many ways I'd make her come.

I'd make her scream my name until she lost her voice, and with a whisper, begged me to start again.

Keely opened the flap of her tent, breaking my trance.

I stepped inside and arranged my back to her, half to hide the grin that remained chiseled on my face, and half to button up the tent. My fingers shook, but I got the job done without making an ass of myself.

I inhaled the smell of canvas and oil, and turned.

The lamp on the nightstand was on. Keely was bent in front of the heater, ass up, teasing me.

Blood flooded into my dick, which strained to see action.

Once she'd refilled the oil and adjusted the heat, she stood.

A Mona Lisa smile on her face, she circled the bed and sat at my end.

I swallowed. "About that gratitude."

"A little thank you." She leaned to the side and retrieved the cuffs from her pocket. "You're so difficult to shop for."

The metal chain looped over her outstretched finger, balancing the two rings. She'd gone for keyless toy cuffs, easy to place and remove by way of a latch.

Not too comfortable for her in the long run, but perfect for right now.

"It's what I've always wanted." I grinned. "Thank you."

She stretched back onto her arms and raised her eyebrows. "I suggest you try them soon, in case you don't like them and I have to take them back."

Our knees touched. I bent over, arms framing her on both sides, and kissed her. Deep. Hard. Filled with possessive intent. My mouth laid the path for the next few hours. She was mine, and she'd soon know it.

She cupped my neck with one hand and placed the other across my pecs. Her touch raised tingles on my skin.

My tongue dominated hers, our breaths mingled. I pressed her head onto the mattress, soaked in her taste.

Dammit, that Keely flavor held too much power over me.

I shifted my hand around to her front, and ripped open her button and zipper.

Her breaths came fast now, faster than mine, and she tightened her grip.

I reached inside, found the entrance of her panties and the smoothness behind, but couldn't move beyond. Her clothes were too tight.

With a few rough yanks, her pants slid down her thighs. I broke our kiss to remove them altogether. While I replaced her shoes, she lay with her arms angled by her side, one finger by her mouth, her gaze locked on my eyes.

Her sun-kissed face was flushed, her lips plump and ready.

I crouched back over her, submarined head first beneath her top, and pushed it up.

She laughed. "That tickles."

My lips traced the line of her stomach, between her breasts, up to her mouth.

While I claimed my next kiss, we freed her arms from the fabric. Next came her bra. Once she was naked, I pressed her back into the mattress, giving her tits a good squeeze.

Her lithe and rounded figure was infused with grace, her complexion with a natural glow. Her pose had the makings of a Playboy shot, except no one but I would ever get to see her wonders. Somehow, I'd make sure of that.

I lowered my weight onto her so my cock knocked against her slit, and angled her leg to hook around my waist. My feet used the ground's friction to press myself against her, careful not to penetrate yet.

She was fucking perfect. Soft where it counted, her skin like satin.

I slid my fingers from her butt cheek along her side, and used my tongue to make love to her the way my dick would in a second, with long strokes and total control.

She yipped.

I swallowed her sound, drank it down. I released her lips and nuzzled her neck. There was still so much of her to cover, and only eternity to do so.

I moved to her right nipple, proud and berry-red, and closed my lips around it, hard. Her moan was short and loud. I'd surprised her. My dick bucked against my jeans, demanding to be let loose.

She grabbed my head, controlled the movements of my mouth back up to her neck.

Had she not learned anything?

I removed her hand. "Shift up and over on the bed, Keely. Arms up."

"Like this?" She shot me a naughty grin.

The vixen. She knew what I'd do the second she took control.

"Shush." I took the handcuffs and placed them around the end of the bed frame, then clicked them shut around her wrists.

Her grin softened into a teasing smile. "Okay."

The top she'd discarded lay next to her. I picked it up and placed it, double-layered, over her eyes.

"Hey."

I squeezed her nipples.

She flinched.

When her mouth relaxed, I ran my hands along the sides of her full breasts down to her stomach. She'd be trained in bedroom etiquette soon enough, but for now, I wasn't going to push it.

A light rain beat a drum on the canvas ceiling. Everyone would be in their tents, settling in for the night. We were alone.

That meant I'd have to make her scream louder.

I got up, placed my phone on the nightstand, and took off my shirt and pants. My cock stood at attention, eager to stretch her walls. I kneeled onto the bed between her legs, and ripped open the sides of her panties.

She grinned. "If you carry on like that, I'll soon run out of clothes."

"Or better yet, walk naked."

I rubbed the fabric of her underwear between her legs to soak up her juices and stimulate more, then cast it aside.

The feel of her skin was exquisite. The muscles in her thighs flexed with my strokes, and she rocked her pelvis up as I approached her slit.

I pressed my nose onto the softness of her stomach, trailed the line between her ribs until my mouth closed around her tit.

She shifted under me, her motion stroking and teasing my shaft.

I pressed harder against her clit. The wetness between her legs and her nub stimulated my already bursting dick, and my balls vibrated with a need for release.

Her heavy breaths and the sudden pauses whirled around me, fogging my mind with only her moans as a guide.

She bucked up against me.

"What do you say, baby?" My voice came out hoarse, bulging under my primal hunger to fill her. "Do you want me?"

"Yes."

"Yes what?"

"Florian."

"Florian what?"

"Oh God. I want you inside me. Now."

I plunged my length inside, and her walls tightened around me. Clouds of white exploded in front of my eyes, and with a sharp inhalation, I withdrew.

Keely flexed her arms, straining against the cuffs.

I circled her entrance with my tip. "What do you say?"

"Please, Florian. Now."

I dove back in, squeezed into her taut space, and groaned. The warmth in her core tested my sanity. Fuck, she was snug. I retreated.

"Please." She bit her lip. Her tone made me smile.

I slipped back in and lowered my mouth onto her breasts.

"Oh God," she whispered.

I sucked hard, flicked and bit, never letting her settle.

She writhed under me, but couldn't escape.

I rocked my ass up and down, my nerve endings firing out of control. Too early. Way too early. *Distract yourself. Focus on her.* I lifted her knees, shifted my position inside her, and pinched her clit.

She moaned louder.

"Still with me, baby?"

She rolled her hands into fists. "Oh God, yes."

"More, baby. I want to hear you."

"Oh God. Yes. Yes."

I forced myself into her with all my might, striking her end, grunting with effort.

"Oh God. Please."

My strokes varied from light to hard, her noises a triumphant echo.

As much as I wanted to caress her, ride her into the morning hours, my balls were aching for release.

I shifted up and let my length massage her clit, gently this time.

"Oh God. Florian."

"That's it, baby. Talk to me."

"Yes. Florian. Please. Please."

Her pitch went up, higher and higher. Each syllable begged me to give what I was already primed to grant.

That such a strong, beautiful woman would let me be in her, fuck her the way I wanted, didn't make sense. Yet here I was, ready to explode inside her.

"Please. Please." Her breath warmed my ear.

My heart pumped in my chest, its beats filled my head. "Christ. Keely. You're killing me."

I sank my fangs into her neck and rode her toward my orgasm. Her blood flowed into me, its unexpected sweetness heightening the sensations. My cock shuddered under her pulsing walls.

"Oh God," she shouted.

Everything made sense. I was staking my Claim, and with it, I promised her my utter devotion. Keely was going to—

Keely flailed. Her hips bucked.

My inner peace shattered.

What was she doing? I wobbled, forced to release my grip on her throat.

"...go. Bloody hell. Don't." Her screams stabbed into my subconscious.

I shrunk back. Two thin lines of blood ran from the puncture wounds.

"Let me go. What did you do?" She threw her head around, and the makeshift blindfold slipped off.

Her blue eyes stared up, watering. Seeing my monster laid bare.

"I... Keely..." I retracted my fangs and wiped the blood off my mouth. My skin grew cold. My chest locked tight.

"Vampire." The single word teemed with disgust.

"I meant to tell you."

As if that made everything okay.

She twisted against the handcuffs. "Let me go. Or I swear, I'll scream so loud my pack is going to tear your limbs apart."

The chain connecting the rings tore, and the device disintegrated, its parts flinging onto the ground. She rubbed her wrists, now covered in red welts.

I reached out to her.

Her knee soared up into my stomach.

I folded over. "Keely." Pain stole whatever else I was going to say.

"Save it." She kicked my ribs.

I flew off the bed, and my head struck the corner of the night table, knocking over the lamp. The light went off. My skull filled with noise and pressure. I stayed still, waiting for the throbbing to subside.

A shadow blurred past me.

I nudged my head to the side.

Keely tore on the buttons of her tent, then disappeared out into the darkness.

"I'm sorry, Keely."

CHAPTER TWENTY-FOUR

I STAYED ON THE COLD, HARD floor for minutes.

Keely didn't return.

Once the pressure in my head had settled into a dull thumping, I pushed myself up.

What I'd done was unforgiveable.

My control had slipped from me more than once before, and I should have taken precautions. Instead, my little brain commandeered my big brain with little resistance. Now my inability to restrain myself had hurt Keely.

Staking your Claim on someone without warning was bad form, even among vampires. Keely probably had no idea what happened. She may have even thought I was going to kill her.

I should have talked to her first. Explained what I was.

I picked up my clothes and got dressed.

She was out there, scared of me and feeling betrayed. Even if I never touched her silken skin again or kissed those ripe lips, she needed to know I was sorry.

At least I knew where I stood now. Nothing about the most amazing sex I ever had was real. She didn't let *me* sleep with her, but some werewolf who looked and sounded like me.

To her, I was an imposter.

She was right. I was that and much worse.

I stepped out of the tent into the breezy night and sniffed. My nose wasn't as tuned as a wolf's, but good enough.

Keely's unique scent came from the playground. And where my nose failed, my superior eyesight stepped up. At the end of the paved patch, moist grass revealed the tread of her shoes, which I followed with increasing urgency.

Maybe she'd forgive me. This hatred between vampires and furballs was antiquated anyway. For a while, I'd been part of Parker's pack, so if I was good enough for him, maybe I'd be good enough for her.

I found a rock and kicked it. Hard. I wasn't a monster. I wasn't. She had to see that.

The treetops swayed up high, their leaves and needles rustled softly. The moonlight shone onto the empty playground, casting enough brightness onto muddy footprints. Heels. In her hurry to get away from me, Keely hadn't even thought of retrieving her sneakers.

I tracked her past the magic shield to the edge of the woods. Good. After a run in wolf form, once she'd let off steam, perhaps I could reason with her. If I loved her enough, treated her well, wouldn't that make up for what I was?

A red shoe peeked out from the grass. The other lay right beside it. She could have hurt herself running on the damp grass in heels.

I cradled the pair in my arms and checked the forest floor for the rest of her clothes.

A whiff of something familiar crawled into my nose.

I edged further into the woods to discover its origin. Only the trees and a couple of owls made noise.

Keely must have hidden her clothes, but why didn't she keep them with her shoes?

The scent intensified.

BOUND

On a veined rock below me, three drops of blood outlined the corners of a triangle. A chill skidded down my spine. Suppressing a shudder, I knelt and touched my finger to the still wet liquid.

I flared my nostrils, let the soft breeze carry the scent into my nose. Sweet, fragrant, with a touch of earth. Keely's blood.

This couldn't be right. I'd smothered her wound in so much saliva, her blood should have congealed within a minute or two.

A few feet further up, a clump of grass had been carved out of the soil. The long divot pointed toward the main road.

A drag mark.

The meaning was hard to miss for someone like me, who was once used to hunting human prey. I briefly closed my eyes.

Keep it together.

I hadn't hunted in years, so maybe I was wrong. Unless I found more clues, like broken branches or—

Further up the trail, an object glistened amid the grass.

Muscles taut, I sprinted to its spot and palmed the item.

My old belt buckle. The one Gino had taken from me and never returned.

Christ. My own sire had kidnapped Keely and left the buckle as an invitation. I'd invented this game, once upon a time. Take away something precious and leave a token, and your mark came after you, be he prey or enemy.

Then the trap would spring.

I took a rattling breath. Stood. Tightened my fists around my former heirloom until the metal's sharp edges drew blood.

If he hurt her... *Dammit.* I punched a tree. The skin around my knuckles tore, but the pain lingered on the surface. It didn't sink deep where it might have done some good.

I had every reason to be pissed off with Gino's megalomaniac ass, but why was he so quick to abandon centuries of loyalty and love? He was my sire, my Master, and my father. Did our former bond mean so little?

The moon hid behind a cloud, and the temperatures dropped. The grays of my environment sprang to life in infinite variety. I never would have known this world without Gino. The varied notes of blood, the power of my glamour, witnessing the deaths and rebirth of countless countries—none of these miracles would have been possible without him.

The Gino who'd made me once had principles and boundaries. You didn't mess with family. Where were his values now? Had Alethia driven him to madness, or was it his age?

No matter. I would kill him regardless. His hold over me was gone. I would fight for Keely until she, and only she, sent me away.

But first, she would see I wasn't just a goofball or a vampire. I was a warrior. A protector. A Master.

Fuck it. I was a man. *Her* man.

I punched the tree again, and dark bark came loose from its trunk. It fell onto the soft ground in small pieces. Broken, like me, but I was more than the sum of my parts because she made me more. She made me whole.

Nothing was lost yet. Assuming I acted fast and didn't die, I could have her back before morning. I opened and closed my fist to subdue the throbbing inside. The camp back in the clearing was safe. Keely would never forgive me if I left her pack undefended.

The moon broke free from the clouds, lighting a thin path out to the road.

I slid the buckle into my pocket. Walked. Ran. Trees blurred. At this speed, the breeze blew into my face, cutting me with its chill.

Within minutes, I'd reached my house, barely out of breath. Instead of hopping straight into my Benz, I shifted my gaze to Ivy's home across the road. She wouldn't be in, of course. She likely lay warm and loved in Parker's embrace.

I struck my car's window.

Cracks radiated out from the impact point.

Shit.

So far Gino had gotten the better of me. This time, I'd be the one left standing. Me and Julia. I just had to make my sister see Gino for the devil he'd become.

Of course, a Guardian by my side would even the odds. Even a Guardian in training would give me half a chance.

Except Parker wouldn't let Ivy go. As powerful as she was, he'd lock her up if he had to, and throw away the keys. For the first time I understood his burning determination to keep her from harm.

That was what I felt for Keely, and that was also why I had to rip Ivy from her safe shelter.

She was all I had left. With her powers, her guards, and her friendship, she would have my back while I took care of Gino.

I reached into my back pocket for my phone. It wasn't there. *Shit.* I'd left it in the tent. Looks like I was making a house call.

I raced across the road and up the drive to the place that had been my home until recently. I jiggled the front doorknob. Locked. *Idiot.* It was 2 a.m. Of course it was. I rapped on the door, then remembered the doorbell. I rang once, twice. *Dammit.* Wasn't anyone awake? I kicked the door.

Heidi opened. She was dressed in fluffy pajamas, her eyes sleepy, her blonde tresses a mess.

"What are you doing?" She shook her head. "You're gonna wake Parker up."

"Sorry," I mumbled and hurried up the stairs to Parker's and Ivy's room.

I knocked. "Ivy? It's me."

Ivy's slumber was unusually deep for someone who was on many a baddie's hit list, whereas Parker's hearing was excellent. By my guess, he was already awake.

I turned the handle and stepped into the room.

Parker was upright before I'd closed the door behind me.

Ivy glanced up, sleep in her eyes, blanket pressed against her chest and bare shoulders.

"Have you gone crazy?" Parker's alpha power blew into me, ruffled my nerves, and suffused my mind.

His powers exceeded Keely's, capable of making my guts jitter under the assault, but he lacked her unique style. Her flavor. Her Keely-ness.

"What are you doing here, Flo?" He checked the alarm clock and tousled his short hair. "Do you know what time it is?"

"I—"

He called me Flo. Like he'd done when we were still friends. When I was one of his pack.

I pushed two fingers against my chest to clear the airways. "I need Ivy's help."

"Are you okay?" Her groggy voice crawled across the room.

Since I'd just woken her, I swallowed the *duh* on my tongue.

"Gino took Keely." I marched to her side of the bed.

Her clothes lay across the back of a chair and on the floor. I handed them to her.

"Come on. Get up. Where's your guard bracelet?" The nightstand was empty. I checked the chair, even underneath. "Keely's going to die if we don't get moving now."

"What? Christ. Fine." Parker got into his jeans and tapped barefoot across the room to get a fresh T-shirt from his wardrobe. "Let's get Ivy some coffee, so she can register what you're saying."

Hand on my arm, he angled me toward the door.

I dropped Ivy's panties onto her blanket. "I can't stay. Keely—"

"It's okay." His tone soothed my frantic mind as he pushed me out into the corridor.

We walked down the stairs into the kitchen. If I were still linked to him, his calming aura would cut right through my confusion, get me focused on formulating a plan.

Instead, a thousand scenarios whirled through my head. In every one, I got there too late. Keely's skin was cold. Her lifeless eyes stared at me, filled with the certainty I wouldn't rescue her.

"Are you listening?" Parker's voice hadn't lost its patience.

I refocused my gaze.

On the counter behind him, black liquid dripped into the coffee pot. A crash sounded from upstairs, followed by clomping feet. The pack was on the move.

"I didn't mean to wake everyone." I paced. "I was going to pick up Ivy and..."

"And do what?"

I frowned at Parker, whose expression was free of grump for once.

My skull pounded, each thump another tick on my clock.

I swung up my arms. "Save Keely."

Parker pushed me back against the countertop. "How? What's your plan?"

Dead. She was already dead. No matter what I did, I'd be too late.

Ali crossed the kitchen to retrieve coffee cups from the cupboard.

My former *intended* was dressed as immaculately as always, in dark jeans and a crisp white shirt. No sign he'd even been to bed.

Parker stepped aside. "Tell me what happened, Florian."

My heart still pounded like a SWAT team on a raid. "There's no time. We need to go now. Where the hell is she?"

Parker rose to his full height and crossed his arms. "I say when Ivy leaves."

"But—"

"No, Florian. I don't know what kind of idiotic mission you think you're going on, but you're not dragging Ivy into it without a fool-proof plan." He pulled out a wicker-backed chair. "Now sit and calm the fuck down."

I slumped into the chair and let out a long stream of breath. If I wanted Ivy to help me, I'd have to play by his rules.

Soon sleepy-time princess plodded in, feet dragging across the hardwood floor. One hand on Parker's shoulder, she reached for the coffee pot.

"It's hot, sweetie." Parker took her arm and guided her to the chair next to mine. "I'll get it for you."

Ivy glanced up from under heavy lids. "So what do you need me to do?"

For a second, I sat cocooned in this familiar world. Parker, efficient as ever, ready to hear me out. Ali by his side. And Ivy… She didn't even ask. She was prepared to fling herself headfirst into danger on the strength of our friendship.

Once everyone had coffee and a seat, Parker nodded. "Tell us."

Despite my racing pulse, fatigue dragged down my body and mind. "Gino, my sire, took Keely."

Three faces stared at me, probably expecting me to be more specific.

"My sire returned from Alethia. He was never an angel, but he was family, and I was convinced that with Julia's help, I could acclimatize him to the twenty-first century."

"He was in Alethia? Voluntarily or exiled?" Parker sat up, his power barely contained.

"Exiled."

He let out air. "Okay. And?"

I shook my head, my foot tapping to the sound of *hurry the fuck up*. "When you kicked me out, I had nowhere to go but to Gino's. And suddenly, we were family again."

"I didn't kick you out," Parker said. "You left. But one way or another, you're still one of mine. Maybe no longer linked by magic, but I once made you a promise, and that promise stands."

I stared, breath hitched as if my brain pulled all my body's resources into making sense of his words. Parker told me his pack enjoyed his lifelong protection, but I never assumed that included me.

"And you're more than just a vampire." Ivy elbowed me. "You're *my* vampire."

"*Our* vampire." Ali grinned.

Shit, this was way too teary for me. I sucked in air.

Parker cleared his throat. "You should have told us you were no longer linked to Ali. And why."

Ali shook his head. "Getting Flo to open up is like breaking through a wall with a toothpick."

"Anyway." I picked up my cup and drank, let the coffee warm my throat and stomach. "Gino's working with the IEA to unite all kin and open the doors to Alethia." I leaned forward, elbows on the table. "I suspect the kinlords are behind this. It's unlikely he's working alone."

Ivy gaped, while Parker scratched his head.

"He wants me to get you and the two Guardians to sign up to the apocalypse." I scoffed. "He thinks with the rest of the kin behind him, neither werewolf nor Guardian would have the balls to oppose him."

"Shit." Parker's frown wrinkled his forehead. "Okay. Do you know any details?"

"Not really."

"What about the rogues?" Ivy warmed her cheek on her mug.

"The rogues are working with Gino." I pulled up my toes, my legs itching to get moving. "As part of The Circle, they have access to backchannels into Alethia that Gino needs. He has other help too. Fae are offering themselves as blood slaves in return for his favor, demons are rallying around him to offer muscle."

"Hang on." Ivy waved. "Demons go solo, and they don't work for anyone. Remember?"

"It's not unprecedented though. Now don't hit me." I held up my hands to ward off any retaliation. "But Greg had the local demons on his side too."

She pulled a face. "Yes, but Greg was a human with a djinn inside him. He controlled them through the djinn's mental ability to inflict pain. Glamour isn't painful, and you can't control demons with it. So what has Gino promised them?"

I touched my fingers to my lips, and then shrugged. "All I can think is that Lathan has changed his mind and is working with Gino."

Shit. I checked Parker's face. Lathan was a sore subject with him.

"Ivy?" Parker caressed Ivy's cheek with his thumb. "Are you okay?"

"I'm fine." Paler now, she swallowed. "No one knows Lathan better than me, and I can assure you that as much as he would love to get out of Alethia, he will never submit to a vampire, and he would never instruct his demons to do so either. No way. Not gonna happen."

I set my elbows on the table. "Perhaps—"

"*Not* gonna happen." Her words cut through me. "That much of his letter was true, and possibly all of it. Hey, I'm not saying you're wrong about the demons helping your sire. But Lathan has nothing to do with it."

I waved her off. "I don't care how he did it. God, this is so fucked up. And did I mention? Julia's so happy about having a family again, she's letting Gino brainwash her. We need to save her too."

Parker tapped on the table. "That brings us to Keely."

"When I found out about your attack on Keely, I raced over to her camp. Gino must have followed me." I scratched my temple. "I didn't pay attention on the drive home, and I would have spotted someone in the woods, so don't ask me how he found us. Did your scouts see anyone who shouldn't be there?"

Parker glanced at Ali. "What scouts?"

I balled a fist. Great time to play games. "You had at least one wolf running near the camp. I didn't recognize him, but I know what I saw."

"It wasn't one of mine."

"*Shit.* Maybe he sent Furtek after me." I shook my head.

"Furtek is a rogue." Ivy raised her eyebrows.

"And how do you know that, sweetie?" Parker's casual tone fooled no one.

"Okay. Don't be mad." She took in some air. "We kind of listened in on the rogues one time."

"Why would I be mad?" Parker's eyes had darkened to two pieces of coal. "I assume you were careful?"

"I can look after myself." Ivy leaned back in her chair and crossed her arms.

Parker chewed his knuckles. "Did your excursion at least yield information?"

"Not really." She shook her head. "Just that the leader's name is Draylac. They don't even call themselves a *pack* of rogues, but an alliance. Oh, and they're part of The Circle."

"Is that all? Hang on." Parker massaged his forehead. "Did you say Draylac?"

"You've heard of him?" She placed her hand on Parker's arm.

"Yes. I don't know. Remember the killing spree in the seventies, Ali? Eighty kin found dead in one small town down the road from Aidan's pack?"

Ali nodded. "In Texas? That was Draylac?"

"That's what he called himself, but I thought he was a human and long dead by now. If he was a werewolf, someone would have heard of him."

"Even if he was the child of another rogue?" Ivy asked.

"Maybe not then." Parker shook his head. "But those hardly ever survive without the protection of a strong pack."

"Great." I let my hand drop onto the tabletop. "Anyway, can we rescue Keely already?"

Ivy punched my leg under the table. "You said Furtek might have taken her?"

"Yes." I retrieved my guard buckle from my pocket and placed it on the table. "And Gino might have been around, because someone left my old belt buckle behind. He took it from me to punish me."

Silence fell over us as my words sank in.

"Keely's camp is protected, as Parker's nose remembers very well. How did he get inside?" Ali, ever practical, asked.

"He didn't. She got out. She and I, we…" I glanced away from him. "You know. And I bit her."

"You fed from her?" Ivy whipped around to scowl at me.

"No. God no." I rubbed my neck. "Things got away from me, and I was about to…you know…"

"What?" She shifted into my field of vision.

"Stake my Claim on her. Okay? I was about to stake my Claim on her."

"That's when a vampire bites his chosen." Ali stared at the table between us. "He excretes a chemical that enters her bloodstream, and through her blood, runs back into him. It creates a magical bond meant to last the rest of their lives."

"Okay. But why did she run?" She straightened. "Right. Gotcha."

I shot her a sheepish smile.

"What am I missing?" Parker asked.

"I may have forgotten to tell Keely I'm not a werewolf." I crumpled under his look.

If I'd been straight with her from the start, Keely would be safe now, because she never would have fallen for me in the first place. And Gino would have had no reason to take her from me.

Parker shot to his feet. "This damn secrecy, Flo." He banged his fist on the table. "If you still want to be part of this pack, it ends now."

I shrank in my seat. If I had even a quarter of a leg to stand on, I'd defend myself, but he was right. "We can't let Keely suffer for my idiocy."

He propped his hands on the table, his gaze full force on me. "You made this mess. What are you going to do to clean it up?"

CHAPTER TWENTY-FIVE

A DARK BLUE SKY, NEAR BLACK, shaded Gino's home and made it look like the Evil HQ it was. The night's gentle breeze had vanished, leaving an eerie stillness behind.

Keely was still alive.

Once my mind and guts had calmed and logic won through, my waking nightmares stopped. Gino loved drama and games. That hadn't changed. He was going to use Keely to force me back to his side.

Facing her was going to be a different form of anguish. Not only had I betrayed her trust, but I was also the reason the biggest, baddest vampire this side of the Rim had gotten his hands on her.

Parker and the pack had been at a loss to understand why overpowering Gino wasn't going to be a cinch.

Parker's young features didn't fool me. He had to be many decades old to have become an alpha, yet compared to me, he was a pup. None of the werewolves except the oldest and luckiest in their pack would have fought a vampire and lived to tell the tale.

We weren't dainty killers.

I placed my cold fingers to my neck. In a minute, adrenaline would be warming my muscles to prepare me for the fight of my life. More importantly, for the fight of Keely's.

I lifted my chin and walked to Gino's door, Keely's red shoes in my hand. No point sneaking up. He was expecting me. He had called me out, and what could I do except answer his challenge?

Furtek opened the door to a brightly lit corridor, a sneer on his face. I liked denim as much as the next guy, but this dude was a total fashion disaster.

He had a squat build, a tad shorter than me. His bald patch reflected the hall's ceiling lights, but his insecurities lay further south. Either he was pleased to see me, or he padded his crotch.

What a joke.

The rogue gave an exaggerated nod. "You're back."

Great. He wanted to play games.

"You're observant." If my smart mouth upset Heidi, it would make Furtek livid.

"What could you possibly want?" His eyes twitched.

"To see my sire." I raised my eyebrows, still in charge of my composure. "He has borrowed something of mine without asking, and I need it back."

Furtek growled and stepped aside to let me in.

As certain as I was that Gino wouldn't let this furball harm me, I didn't turn my back to the wolf.

Furtek stalked off along the corridor, through the bowels of Evil HQ, and into a part of the building I hadn't explored before. Voices and rough laughter streamed from the rooms we passed.

True to his plan, Gino seemed to have extended his welcome to our fellow kin. In addition to the demons who'd carried the books into the house, at least another ten people sat in chairs and on sofas, looking up as I walked past. How many of them were demons? How many weaker fae? And how many werewolves?

Having Ivy by my side as my kin-radar would have been helpful, but then I wouldn't have gotten as far as I did into the mansion. Parker had been right about that when he pooh-poohed my original Rambo plan of action.

The tunnel-like hall opened into a spacious room. Keely sat tied to a chair by a stone fireplace. The acrid smell of ash still hung in the air, although the fireplace hadn't been used in a while, judging by its relative cleanliness.

Scratches zigzagged Keely's bare feet. An adhesive bandage covered part of her temple, and a shadow formed around her right eye. At least her arms didn't dangle as if broken, and her veins were untapped.

Thank God.

Her gaze found me.

Something inside me died.

Her dulled eyes contained no tenderness, not even a hint of relief at my presence.

"Nice of you to join us." Gino sat on the gilded chair his minions had carried in yesterday, as if it were indeed a throne.

Two burly men, demon thugs I knew from around town, stood behind him. Their build might be impressive, but their faces expressed little hostility, at least not toward me. However, the guy on the right eyed my sire with a sneer.

Maybe I could use their dislike to my advantage.

"Of course I came." I smiled. "How could I refuse your kind invitation?"

A square rug with an oriental pattern spread beneath Gino's seat. Next to him stood an empty chair, as if he didn't rule alone.

"Your girl and I had a nice chat." He leered at Keely.

"What makes you think she's my girl?" If it weren't for the ache in my heart, my casual tone would have convinced even me of my indifference.

But not Gino.

"We followed you and saw you kiss. Touching. Can you imagine my dismay when she ran away from her secure camp? Of course we were concerned for her wellbeing, so we brought her here for her safety."

Seriously? This was his angle? Torture me with banalities? Still. While he was talking, he wouldn't be doing anything stupid like killing Keely.

"I'm grateful," I said, lifting the shoes in my hand. "I assume she's free to go?"

"Of course, *Cucciolo*. Of course. However, my conscience will not allow me to let her leave my house while you're running around free. Would you believe our Keely doesn't like vampires?" He gave a sad smile. "She's frightened of us." He tsk'd. "It's too bad for you, son."

He was not allowed to say her name. For that alone I was going to mulch his face.

Keely stared into the barren fireplace. No sign she had any fight left in her. Werewolves thought showing submission was safe in times of danger. It's how they acted to appease their superiors.

Vampires considered the weak prey. We loved to pick them off one by one, watching their struggles, and finally drinking the last drop of blood that extinguished their spark. Their blood and deaths made our hearts beat. Made us feel alive.

I placed my hands behind my back and assumed a relaxed stance. "Keely is a big girl and can look after herself."

"I'm glad you're not possessive, because Daniel here believes he'd make a better match than you. He is, after all, a werewolf too."

Even though my hands were hidden from sight, I wouldn't allow them to roll into fists. Gino was looking for my Achilles' heel.

This time, I was up to the task. "That would be between him and her. But if the big bad wolf needs help to score with the ladies, I can recommend a few excellent dating sites."

"Bastard." Furtek took two slow steps in my direction and pounced, surprisingly agile for his bulk.

I whirled on my heels, too fast for him.

Werewolf strength was slow. Inadequate. I lifted my arms and shrugged him off. After training side by side with Parker's pack for months, I'd learned how werewolves moved, understood their technique. Gino would be a worthier opponent.

Furtek, who'd fallen to the floor like a wet towel, got back up and combed his beard with his fingers.

"Leave him, Daniel." My sire shook his head. "Now, my son. Let's get to business. I must be mad, but I still want your help. This is your rightful place." He tapped the brown chair beside him.

Cool as a python at night, I picked Keely's heels off the floor. "To help you free Alethian psychos and overthrow humankind?"

"You make it sound so…Napoleonic."

I arched my eyebrows. "It kind of is."

Once upon a time, I'd worshipped this man. Our closeness had been the envy of others, including that of Eli and Julia. Not even a morsel of affection for him lingered inside me now.

Gino gave a wide, toothy smile. "In any event, I'm fond of you and understand your skills better than most. If you return to my side, you may keep the girl."

I expected trash talk and peacocking, but this concession hadn't featured in any of the scenarios I'd played out in my head. His willingness to work with other kin was odd enough, but to allow a vampire-werewolf relationship ran counter to his deepest beliefs.

I didn't like it. Not one bit.

"Keep her?" I kept my tone non-committal.

"Yes. With one minor change."

I moistened my lips. "What?"

"Turn her. Make her one of us."

I took a step back. "That would kill her."

"Not necessarily, although I would concede a splash of luck wouldn't go amiss."

I focused on Keely, her taut posture, her still flawless skin. Many times, I'd wished to be a werewolf. Never once had I considered making her into a vampire.

Gino tapped his foot. "Choose, *Cucciolo*. The enemy or your family?"

Put in those terms, the answer was easy.

I met his gaze head on. "Family."

Keely gave a quiet groan.

A series of clanks erupted from the front of the house. Thank the devil, because I was running out of material.

I grinned. "And that would be my family right there. You must excuse the noise. They are undisciplined werewolves after all."

Keely's head whipped around.

I ran over, but her growl rooted me to a spot a few feet from her.

Gino beckoned his demons to check out the noise. "You're trying to make me think your pack is coming to your rescue, but Keely told me they kicked you out. That's the thing with werewolves. They hate everything we are, hate our speed, our grace, our position among the kin. Jealousy, Florian. And you were too blinded to see."

It wasn't like I'd never questioned the differences between vampires and werewolves. But vampire superiority? Delusions of grandeur, more like.

Concentrate, dickhead. Until Keely was safe, I'd play my part.

I pushed a good amount of ridicule into my laugh. "Are you sure the werewolves wouldn't come for me? That's a lot of noise."

He pushed off his chair and stood in front of me in a flash, his breath hot on my face. "I'm sure. I bet you brought your Guardian friend, though. How nice. I've been meaning to settle a score with her."

Gino was an idiot for underestimating a Guardian, especially after his last encounter with one.

I lifted my chin and weathered the somewhat deranged look in his eyes. "Your two demon pets won't stand a chance."

"How about fifteen demons and sixteen werewolves?" He got off his throne, chuckling. "I have friends too."

That was an even greater number than I'd spotted on my way in. I sent a quick glance behind me.

"Ivy will be fine." My voice trembled.

He could read into that what he liked.

Gino waved me off. "Of course she will. I've given instructions not to kill her. That's something I want to do myself."

"Gino, you promised." Julia rushed into the room, her fingers interlinked. "Ivy is—"

He raised a hand. "Quiet."

Julia dropped her head. Her elegant split skirt and shimmering top were out of place in this theater that so expertly showcased Gino's madness.

"Seriously?" I glared at her. "That's how you stand up for Ivy? Hell, with friends like you, who needs suicide pills?"

My sister's shoulders jerked, and she lifted her face. "I'm just not taking sides. That's all. And the only side you should be taking is ours—your family's."

"Julia." I gentled my tone. "Think about what you're doing. His plan is crazy. I know you see that. Help me, so we can be a real family again. You, Eli, and me. We don't need him to make us whole."

Julia raised her head, her arms slung around her thin body. "He's my sire."

She was right. She wasn't a Master yet. His hold over her would be tough to break, but I owed her to not give up.

Another crash from the back ripped through the air, followed by shouts from many voices.

The commotion made my guts roil. I should be out there inflicting damage, but Parker was right. Some messes I had to clean up myself. And Gino was more than mere spillage.

"Can we settle this like men?" I widened my stance and pushed out my chest to take Gino's mind off the noise.

Gino's expression flickered between determination and uncertainty.

"I don't want to fight you." He leaned forward. "This is our moment of greatness."

"By doing the kinlords' bidding? Since when do you do other people's dirty work anyway?"

"That's where you're wrong." He shook his head. "The kinlords work for me." He punched his chest. "They take my orders."

I swallowed. "*L'arrogance précède la ruine, et l'orgueil précède la chute.*"

I hadn't spoken French in decades, but the moment seemed to call for it.

"Those were the first words you ever said to me." Gino tilted his head.

"I remember. You threatened to kill everyone in the tavern single-handedly."

He'd been the most handsome man any of us had seen. His white, straight teeth, his latte tan, his slim yet powerful figure—he had the women swooning and the men on edge before he'd uttered his first word.

"You stood up to me." He laughed. "Such a large personality in so small a village. You were full of potential, even if reckless. I soon showed you the falsity of the proverb, didn't I?"

"Did you? You didn't kill *me.*"

"How could I? You were my boy from the moment I saw you. And together, we rose to even greater heights. Remember the rush of being on top, *Cucciolo*, of having the world at your feet?" He took small steps toward me. "Prove yourself to me, and we can have it all. Turn your girl. Make her one of us."

My gaze darted to Keely.

He slapped my back. "But with the Guardian causing havoc among my ranks, I have to hurry you. Or if you prefer, your sister will do it for you." He shifted forward, close to my ear. "I think she would enjoy sinking her fangs into such a pretty neck, but that's between you and me."

Julia took a hesitant step past me toward Keely.

My stomach lurched. "Don't. Julia. Please."

My sister stopped and glanced at Gino, then at me. "Don't make me choose."

"You have ten seconds to get started, son." Gino didn't spare her another look and walked back to sit on his throne.

This wasn't the plan. I was supposed to save Keely, not kill her.

"Eight…seven…"

Julia strode to the fireplace and placed her hand on Keely's head. Keely kept her eyes low, still playing weak.

Fight, honey. Don't let them see your fear.

"I'm sorry, Flo." My sister scratched Keely's neck with her nail, and blood trickled from the wound.

"Don't." I leaped at Julia and shoved her out of the way.

She soared against the wall, but was on her feet in a second, her eyes wide. "You pick her over me?"

If Furtek wasn't a serious threat, my sister might be if I couldn't make her take my side. Or at least stay out of my way.

"I'm sorry, Julia." I lifted my arms and approached her. "I don't want to choose either, but hurting Keely means hurting me. I'm asking you not to hurt me."

Julia bit her lip. "I don't want to."

I smiled. "Good. Then let me deal with Gino my way, and then we'll talk. Okay?"

"You children are too sweet." Gino laughed and stretched out his legs. "But you see now why I need you, Florian. Your sister cannot be my right-hand man. She's not strong enough. Make the girl a vampire, *Cucciolo*. You're a Master now. Prove it, or I will."

"No." I took my position next to Keely. "I don't need your help."

"Don't touch me." She strained against her ties.

Finally, a flicker of fight in her. Bummer it was directed at me.

Thick leather reams encircled her body, reinforced with metal threads. The ends were chained to wide leather cuffs.

The bastard used my gear from home to secure Keely.

I pointed. "Nice touch."

"I figured you'd enjoy the irony. Where was I? Five…four."

Come on, Ivy.

The sounds had died down. The front of the house was quiet.

I raised my hand. "You win."

Hidden behind Keely so she wouldn't see my change, I located my magic. My teeth pushed through my gums, and my saliva flowed, stimulated by the scent of Keely's blood.

I took a few deep breaths. If only she didn't smell so tempting. Nothing about her lured my blood lust, but the urge to stake my Claim warred with my self-restraint.

"Three…" Gino was back on his feet and inched toward me.

A slow clap from behind sounded. Gino whirled around.

Ivy stood in the entrance to the room, a demon on either side of her. They didn't restrain her, simply waited by her side.

"You can count. Impressive." Ivy tilted to the side to glance past Gino. "And you said he was stupid."

Gino stepped to the side, his gaze darting from me to her.

I retracted my fangs. "I said he was pompous. Arrogant. Batshit crazy."

"And stupid. I'm sure you said stupid."

"Hmm. Perhaps I did say he's stupid. You're right. I'm sorry."

Gino growled. A terrifying sound, were I not used to Parker's grumpy outbursts.

"Shut up. Bring her here." He instructed his demons with a gesture.

They gripped Ivy's arms and helped her along until she stood in front of the rug.

Gino sat back on his throne and regarded her. "Where are my manners? Let me introduce myself."

"No need. You're Gino Dupree. Vampire, Florian's sire, and also a djinn."

Gino let out a hiss that seemed oddly comical.

Ivy rolled her eyes. "Yeah, we know what you are."

I nodded.

"How?" Gino shook his head. "You're lying."

"No, I'm not." Ivy licked her lips. "We had to wonder, who could make demons work for him, especially without Lathan's approval? Only a djinn."

I walked up to Gino, putting my body between him and Ivy. "Is Gino even still in there somewhere?"

He got up to place a hand on my shoulder, and shot me a tender smile. "I'm still me. Think of the djinn and me as a business partnership. I found him trapped in some idiot's dying body, and we struck a deal."

I flexed my jaw. "If that's true, why would the djinn even help you?"

"Your Guardian friends have exiled many djinn to Alethia over the years. They have allied themselves with the Alethians." Gino tilted his head. "The djinn's power helped me escape, but we both had to leave our friends behind. For now." He leaned in, his breath skimming my face. "Make no mistake, Florian. The rim will fall. Djinn and kin, we will be free."

The sincerity in his voice shook my confidence.

"Humans join with djinn for their magic, but you?" I stepped back. "You were already a powerful vampire."

"Not powerful enough to free Mehmet or the rest. The djinn are necessary." His brown eyes glistened with unshed tears. "Stand by my side, son. Let us change the world together. You are my blood."

"Never." My voice cracked.

My sire. My family. Our bond was meant to last forever. It was ash now, blown away by his delusions.

"Making these demons work for you against their will?" Ivy thumbed at the baddies flanking her. "Lathan's not going to like that."

"Lathan doesn't matter." Gino shouldered past me to stand before Ivy and chuckled. "If he'd supported me, I would have handed you over to him." He waved her off. "Still, this way is better. You two." He glanced at the demons. "Make her kneel."

The men looked at each other, then at Ivy.

"Now." Gino wagged his fist.

The demons studied their worn shoes.

Gino's face wrinkled.

"Why isn't she kneeling, Draylac?" Furtek stepped up. "You said you had them under control."

Draylac? Wow. Okay, that explained a few things.

Parker and Waylon suspected Draylac was a werewolf, a human, or a demon. As a djinn, he could have been all three.

"My powers aren't working." For the first time, Gino's voice lacked confidence.

The demons moved away from Ivy.

I made my way back to the fireplace, trusting Ivy to keep things interesting until I freed Keely, and got to work on Keely's restraints.

"I said my guards would keep you safe." Ivy pointed at the rubber bands around their wrists, to which guards were attached. "Run along now."

The demons glanced at each other, nodded, and got the hell out of there.

"Finally," I mumbled and pulled on the buckle of Keely's left cuff.

"Gino, Draylac. You're full of surprises." Ivy held up a crackling guard. "Are we gonna fight then?"

Sparks scattered to her left and right, followed by a jet of blue energy that struck Gino's chest.

He soared toward the wall and crumpled on the floor.

Ivy mumbled a few words to recharge her guard.

Gino rolled his head and got up, displaying his fangs. "You little…"

Shouts sounded from the corridor, accompanied by thuds.

"Hear that, Gino? That's the pack you said wouldn't lift a finger for me." I let the pride in my voice shine through.

"Yup, first we subdued the rogue werewolves, then we promised to free the demons." Ivy grinned at me. "Told you my guards would work."

I gave her a shaky thumb. "You said *might*."

Gino struck Ivy's chin with his fist.

"Ivy," I shouted.

The impact ripped her head to the side, and she fell. Her hissing guard skittered across the floor.

Gino lifted his foot for a kick, but Ivy rolled out of the way.

That's my girl. I pressed my lips together. It wasn't easy to beat a vampire's speed.

I left Keely to undo her leg restraints and raced toward Ivy.

Ivy closed her hand around her guard and held it up toward Gino. Sparks fizzed the air.

With a deep breath, I turned around. Ivy seemed to have things under control for now.

"Come on, honey, let's get you out of here." I took Keely's arm.

She snapped it back and nursed her wrists. "I'm not your honey."

Even though I'd expected it, her words cut deep enough to leave a scar.

"Julia." Gino's voice boomed. "Get your brother under control."

"Crap." Julia made short work of the distance between us, fangs out, ready for the takedown.

Without my canines prepped, I had little choice but to roll up tight and let Julia soar over my head. Keely gave her a push midflight, and Julia crashed into an armchair, toppling it.

Within a second, she was back up.

I yanked Keely out of the way, and stood ready to strike my sister.

A shadow warned me of a new danger from my left.

Furtek rammed me, head first. He hooked into the inside of my knees, and his impact took me down. With the elegance of an anvil, he fell on top of me.

His weight knocked the wind from my lungs. I checked on Ivy, who landed a punch in Gino's face.

Fuck. He was supposed to be mine.

I heaved Furtek off me and leaped up.

Furtek lay on the stone-tiled floor, rubbing his head. A second later, he got up, his heavy figure poised for a powerful punch.

This had escalated fast. Our plan was the textbook example of order. This… This was just messy.

But then, as a vampire, I was used to messy.

I jabbed Furtek's chin—two, three times.

His shape plummeted in front of Julia's legs, causing her to trip, which might have saved Keely's life.

Keely's lithe form whipped past me to take on Furtek.

I allowed myself a wry smile.

She was a smart cookie. It had taken her only a minute to understand Julia might be too fast and powerful for her, and she was ready to take on someone her own size.

"You okay?" I whispered.

Her flushed cheeks tightened into a determined stare, in perfect concentration. She booted Furtek's ass and flung him in my direction.

Disoriented, he sagged against me.

"I have no use for him either." I grinned and shoved him back in her direction.

Furtek raised his fist.

Keely lifted her elbow first and blocked his punch. Then she pushed him with her hip and rotated into a high roundhouse kick. As if nothing happened, she was back to dancing on her bare feet, light as Tinker Bell, waiting for her attacker's next move.

"Florian." Ivy planted the heel of her hand on Gino's face, and then ran to the other side of the room.

Shit.

As fun as it was watching Keely, I couldn't afford to be careless. Ivy was still a novice at hand-to-hand combat. Without guards, she became the underdog.

It didn't help that Parker's eight-man squad was delayed. The scraping and muffled groans from the corridor continued, and they'd get the upper hand sooner or later. Until then, I was supposed to give Ivy the space needed so she could activate her magic.

Ivy stood behind a bench, faking left, running right, chased by Gino.

I took off after Gino, but Julia clutched my arm.

"Please don't fight with him." Julia's bottom lip trembled. "You're making me choose. And *he's* never let me down."

"I'm making you choose right from wrong. There was a time

when that wouldn't have been too difficult for you. Look." I pointed at Ivy. "He's trying to hurt our friend."

"I love you, little brother. And I don't want to lose you." Julia squeezed my arm.

"You'll never lose me." I cupped her cheek and smiled.

"Good." Her fist came out of nowhere. The impact knocked me off my feet, and I landed on my ass.

I rubbed my face and glared at her.

She kicked my nose with the pointy toe of her shoe.

My skull whacked onto the ground. *Shit.*

Julia stood in front of me, fanged out, beckoning me to get up.

Was it too late for us? Had she already made her decision?

I blinked up at her. "Now my own sister's beating on me?"

She smiled grimly. "You asked for it."

Gino and Ivy circled each other warily.

"Why do you always cause me trouble, dear Ivy?" He made a half-hearted attempt to grab her.

Ivy ducked, still holding on to her guard. "Always? What are you talking about?"

"We met last year. Of course I wore a different suit back then. You didn't mind, and were eager to stick your tongue down my throat."

She paled and dropped her hand. "Greg?"

Oh shit. Draylac was Greg's djinn?

Gino laughed. "Oh, Greg's long dead, but his memories live on in me. He liked you, you know."

I scrambled up, catapulted my sister into the far corner behind me, and made my way toward Ivy. This revelation was going to take her mind off the ball. Against a vampire, that was fatal.

"Swap," I shouted at Ivy, who switched places with me.

Gino was finally mine.

CHAPTER TWENTY-SIX

I WAS ABOUT TO COME FIST to fist with my sire. The fact his djinn
tormented Ivy last year only fanned my need to kick the shit out
of him.

I gave a grim smile. "Here we are."

The hollow of Gino's right eye sported a shiner. *Way to go, Ivy.*

"You think *you* can take me on?" His genial voice scraped my
nerves. "You aren't even suitably attired."

I peered to my right, where Keely traded blows with Furtek.

My canines were powerful weapons that would help me get the
better of Gino. But first, I'd have to vamp out. Let Keely see the
monster again.

"You like her, don't you?" Gino's caring voice was back. As if we
weren't about to be locked in a fight that would kill one of us.

The hint of a black eye and a bloody lip hadn't taken Gino's stoic
elegance. His hair lay smooth against his head, his woodsy scent kept
the odor of his sweat at bay. The same charisma that surrounded him
when we first met in that tavern too many years ago.

My magic sprang to life, my fangs pushed through my gums. I
tipped my head back and smelled the air.

"There's my boy," Gino whispered.

I struck my fist at his bruised eye.

He spun to his left in time, showing only a red mark on his cheek.

"Florian. Think about what you're doing." He completed a one-
eighty and pushed the heel of his hand into my face.

The pain fueled my adrenaline, and I laughed.

Our fists flailed, connecting, missing, denting bones.

Memories flooded me, tearing at me. But that simmering heat I'd
ignored for the good of Parker's plan finally boiled over.

"You shouldn't have taken Keely." I kicked his leg.

He went down on it, shot back up.

"You shouldn't have sided against me." His arm overshot my
face.

I slammed my knee into his stomach, my breathing faster now. "You shouldn't have joined forces with the djinn."

He struck and missed. Sweat pearled on his forehead.

Djinn granted powers to their hosts, but also sapped their life force. Judging by Gino's flagging punches, the trade-off wasn't worth it.

But he was far from beaten.

His elbow connected with my nose, spinning my head.

I rammed him with my head and used my body weight to smack him into the wall.

"Julia still needs you. But threatening Keely..." My lungs pumped hard. I pummeled his chest with blows, my insides jolting with each punch. "You. Went. Too. Far." I hammered my rolled fist into his jaw.

He swayed.

"You're weak." My neck was hot, my words came like lava spewing from a volcano.

I kneed the asshole in his balls.

He groaned.

"A disgrace." I aimed an uppercut at his jaw.

Quick as a flash, he sidestepped and knocked my shoulder back. *Shit.* I widened my stance to stop the fall.

He leaped into the air, graceful and fast. His knees angled for the mother of all kicks.

Double shit.

I spun out of his path and kicked his legs out from under him as he landed. He fell onto his face and grunted.

"You're mine." I pounced onto his back.

He strained, flailed, struck out.

I thumped his head into the ground.

He moaned.

I wrapped my arms around him and sunk my fangs into his neck, letting his blood flow into my mouth.

"Fucking bastard," he mumbled. "Stop."

But his swear words didn't touch me. *He* was the weak one now.

I licked and prodded his neck, until his blood streamed freely. The thick drops spread out, kicking my synapses into gear. *Christ.*

He didn't taste like Keely had, sweet and real. He was more oaky and heavy, but oh so powerful. How easy it would be to get lost in his blood's thrall.

Gino's body blocked my sight, but my ears picked up enough— Ivy's pleas for Julia to remember their friendship came from my right, the crack of bones from behind, then Keely's calm breaths. And finally, Parker's calls to his men to transport the prisoners.

Gino twitched.

I locked his arms against his body, while keeping my teeth hooked deep inside his throat. The heat from my breath collected in the small hollow between my face and the ground.

The thick liquid settled in my stomach, its force stoking my greed. My heart beat with life, my pulse raced like it had places to be. *More.* Fuck, I wanted it all.

I gorged myself on his terror-soaked blood, kept my saliva back to let him suffer every ounce of pain. His life force drowned me in strength. It turned my head and stole my thoughts.

"Flo?" Ivy touched my shoulder. "Flo?"

I growled.

She walked off.

If she could feel the power that ran through my body, she wouldn't have bothered. The striking awareness of my surroundings, of every change and movement in the room, grew inside me like vines.

I squeezed Gino's body like a tube of toothpaste, so that not a drop would escape me. My nerves fired, and I fed until a bitter tang struck my tongue.

Countless times, I'd heard of the moment when a vampire took his last breath. A seminal moment in his killer's life.

Gino's powers rushed into me as his struggle ebbed.

A sharp pain, hot as a lump of coal, seared through my brain and stole my air. My vision turned black, my balance deserted me.

I released Gino to grip my skull, ready to bash it in with my fist.

His past. His dreams of the future. My race's darkest secrets. They all ran riot in my head.

Then came images from a world made of energy, where djinn's insubstantial bodies soared through vapors and mist, locked in an eternal war over resources. Their spells. And their plans.

Christ.

Their plans.

My head thudded, and the pictures went black. The pain stopped. I sat up, unable to see.

"Flo?" Ali's voice now.

Despite my attempts to spare him pain, I hadn't made it easy for him, yet here he was, his tone strained.

"Are you okay?" He kneeled beside me.

The darkness lifted and shades of gray filtered into my eyes, then yellows and reds, blues and greens, until the room fell into focus.

Keely.

She met my gaze, wiping blood from her mouth by her sleeve. Her blue eyes made my heart beat even faster.

Ali's hand rested on my shoulder. His temperature, the cinnamon on his skin, and his familiarity soothed me. My fangs retreated inside my gums.

I dropped my head out of Keely's line of sight. "I'm good."

But she'd already seen behind my mask.

I mopped the blood from my chin and stared at it.

Keely picked up her shoes I'd dropped earlier, and left.

Ali helped me up.

"Gino!" Julia tore from Ivy's grasp and threw herself on Gino's lifeless body.

Her tears should pain me. His lack of response should kill me.

He was dead.

Gone.

Killed by my hands and fangs.

Yet no tears came. No grief over his passing tightened my lungs.

A sizzle reached my ear, then a big flash.

Ivy stood with her legs apart, her eyes focused. Her right hand held a guard. A jet of energy crawled through the air, then widened into a kickass square of burning energy.

A portal.

"I wish I could do more than send the djinn to Alethia." The draft from the energy field made her curls flutter. "Is someone going to throw him in, or do I have to do that too?"

Ali dragged Julia off Gino's body. My sister's stoic gaze stayed locked on him, her tears dry now.

I would be there for her this time. She wouldn't have to go through the heartache alone.

At my nod, Ali guided her out of the room.

I stepped over and hooked into Gino's collar and belt to hoist him up.

"I've seen more dignified funerals." I gathered momentum and swung him into the portal.

Ivy let out a deep breath. "Me too."

The energy dissipated with a quiet *plop*.

"I'm sorry. Not a tasteful joke."

She shook her head. "I wasn't thinking of my mother's in particular." She placed her hand on my shoulder. "Are you okay?"

"I don't know."

On the day of his return, Gino had kicked me, savaged my neck, and tried to impose his will onto me. All of this, I'd forgiven. It was the vampire way.

Even when he revealed his crazy idea to me, I didn't want to see him dead.

Hurting Keely was his mistake.

"Yeah." I nodded. "My sire, the man who made and protected me, was lost a long time ago."

"When he entered a pact with the djinn?"

I cleared my throat. "Maybe. But it's not so much that he changed, you know. I think the problem was that *I* had."

She gathered me into a hug.

I savored her warmth, her firm embrace. "Keely hates me."

"Give her time."

I chuckled. "Time heals wounds, weakens memories, but I don't think time can fix trust. It's not something you can earn back."

"You always say trust is given. Maybe Keely will give it again."

"Maybe." I freed myself from Ivy's embrace.

Yet my stomach knew better. My lungs knew better. And my heart knew it for sure.

Keely would never aim her smile at me again, never let her laughter tickle my ear canal or allow her breath to warm my chest.

"Draylac's still alive." Ivy sucked on her bottom lip. "And he'll be back."

"No doubt. But we have your fancy guards now, and they work. It's a step in the right direction."

Plus, I knew his agenda. But this wasn't the moment to open that can of tuna. For now, the djinn was history.

My leather cuffs draped across the toppled chair. Once they seemed the perfect prop for fantasizing about Keely. Now they were tainted.

Ivy and I walked with our arms hooked together past a broken cup, a small pool of blood, and my last memory of Gino.

We joined Parker, Julia, and Keely by the entrance. Keely held my sister's wrist.

The open door let the fresh air in, but my body still popped with energy from my latest feeding.

"Come here." I pulled Julia close. "We'll be fine. I promise."

She stood stiff as a board, her breathing calm.

By tomorrow, she'd feel the full impact of her grief.

Ivy stepped into Parker's open arms. "Thank you," she said.

"What for?" His voice sounded muffled through her hair.

"For letting me do this."

Allowing Ivy to be a Guardian was the most heroic thing the dude could do. All of us knew it.

He tightened his hold on her. "Of course."

A few hours ago, they'd sat in the kitchen, Ivy flinging her hands in the air to convince him to let her take lead. She got her way.

She usually did.

Right now, the argument was forgotten.

I tried to catch Keely's gaze, but she looked away.

"You killed him." Julia finally spoke. "Gino believed in something for the first time. He wanted to give kin back their original home. Alethia is a horrible place, and no one should have to be there."

She pushed me away.

I peered at the floor, unable to meet my sister's glare. "Bringing Alethia's evil to Oldworld isn't the answer."

"He simply wanted freedom." Julia gave a grim smile, her eyes red. "You would think that's something even you could get behind."

"Julia, please. Let's go home and—"

"Save it." She shoved me into the open door. "You chose your friends over your family. Just remember. Karma's a bitch."

She shouldered past Parker and Ivy, and ran into the pink morning.

"Bugger." Keely took off after her.

I raised my hand. "Let her go."

"Don't." Ivy shouted at the same time.

Keely stopped three steps into her run and glanced back. "Why?"

"She's my friend," Ivy sounded from somewhere among Parker's arms. "We'll find her later."

"Okay." Keely nodded.

"What about the blood slaves?" Ivy asked.

"There was just one. Ali's taking care of her." Parker squeezed her closer into his shoulder.

Yeah, he wasn't going to release her any time this week. At this point, I was glad he gave her room to breathe.

We stepped outside, onto a quiet driveway. It was still too early for work, too early by far for school. Only the birds sang their songs, welcoming the day.

Parker shifted his arm over Ivy's shoulder and strode along the sidewalk with her tucked against his side.

Keely followed them, her red heels clicking. Even from behind she was a vision. The yellow cone from a street light spun a halo around her hair, while her posture was strong and confident. And why wouldn't it be? She'd beaten a male werewolf. She'd proven her status.

Keely was an alpha werewolf.

I was a vampire.

We didn't belong together, and that was the end of it.

Her hips swayed further away from me with each step, causing my mouth to dry.

"Keely." The name was out before I thought of anything to say.

She stopped.

My heart pumped at Mach ten, my hands locked in fists so tight I might break my bones.

She glanced over her shoulder and raised her eyebrows. "What? Are you hungry again? Did you want to finish your snack?"

The flame I'd kept inside flickered and extinguished. Snuffed out by her words. She was right. By drinking from her without her consent, I'd violated her trust.

Ivy extricated herself from Parker's arm and turned on her heels. "That's not how it went." She rolled her eyes toward me. "Tell her."

"You weren't even there, Ivy." Keely's voice was pure ice. "He drank my blood."

"Because he's crazy about you. Don't you get that?" Ivy shook her head. "Florian came to save you, so you owe it to him to hear him out." She glared at me. "And you'd better make it a good one."

Parker walked up behind her and placed his arms around her waist. "No more secrets, Florian. Remember?"

Keely glanced from the happy couple to me, and back.

I exhaled sharply. "Fine."

Ivy gave a smug grin and dragged Parker away with her.

Keely and I followed them silently.

Sure, I could talk to her.

What did it matter if I made an ass of myself? Keely hated me already.

CHAPTER TWENTY-SEVEN

Before Keely agreed to hear my sins, she insisted we went back to the camp to check on her females.

On our return, a relieved pack welcomed their leader back into their midst.

The minute Sabine had discovered her alpha was gone, all hell broke loose. Even the pregnant ones were ready to march on Silverton to find out who'd stolen Keely. The reason they didn't was that wise Parker had left Rollo behind to calm them.

We reassured the women and sent them back to their beds before heading to Keely's tent. It wasn't even six yet. Plenty of time to catch a few more Z's.

The oil burner toasted up the inside of Keely's tent quickly. Its regular clicks the only sounds in camp now.

"You wanted to talk. So let's talk." Keely sat on her bed, her knees pulled against her chest.

The tent's canvas was pervious enough to let us know it was day outside, but sufficiently thick to blanket us in twilight.

I interlaced my fingers behind my neck and breathed out. My body hurt from the fight. Gino must have gotten more punches in than I remembered.

I set one foot in front of the other, ready to stop the minute she told me to, but I made it to the bed's end intact. "Surprise. I'm a vampire."

What sounded like a charming opener came out deader than last week's beefsteak.

"So I hear." She rested her chin on her knees.

I hadn't expected anything but hope in talking with her, and now even that left me. How could she forgive me? My sire had kidnapped and hurt her because of me. She could have been killed.

But my real sin was much worse. I'd failed to give her what she needed. The one thing werewolves cherished more than life.

The truth.

"I should have told you." I cast a glance across the room.

Our fight had left its marks. I picked up the lamp and placed it on her nightstand. The torn pair of handcuffs lay scattered across the floor. I collected the pieces and threw them into a trash bag.

There, next to her tote, lay another pair. Two rings connected by a chain. Brand new. I swallowed.

She looked at me. "Yes, you should have."

"I'm sorry."

"I know." She shook her head. "I thought you were different. I thought you were someone real." She scoffed. "But nothing about you is real, is it? And a vampire, of all things."

I sucked in a dose of oxygen. Was this where I'd get the heave-ho?

Later today, she and her pack were going to pull up stakes and move into Ivy's childhood home and estate on the other side of town. It was large enough to house the females and children. Parker used it as an entertainment center for his wolves, with a decked out gym and a swimming pool. Yet the many rooms at the back had stayed empty since Ivy's mother passed. It would make the perfect home for them.

I, on the other hand, had nowhere to go.

I wasn't yet ready to move back into Parker's mansion, at least not without his express invitation. Going home to my old family house would be awkward, not just because it would mean facing Julia, but also because once my brother returned from his business trip, he'd have a word to say about killing Gino.

There was only one place I wanted to stay anyway.

Right here with Keely.

If standing awkwardly at the end of her bed was the closest I'd get to her, I was content.

"At first I didn't tell you because it made my job as Parker's spokesperson easier." I crossed my arms.

Too defensive.

I flopped my hands to my sides.

Too awkward.

I pushed my thumbs into my belt.

Definitely not the time to play cool and aloof.

"Sit down." She pointed. "You're making me dizzy."

"Sorry." I occupied the far corner of her bed and shot her a grateful smile.

The sun cast a pool of weak orange light through the canvas. Bad for reading her expression, but it gave me a sense of safety. I could guard my last secret in the shadows.

"You were explaining yourself, bloodsucker."

I winced, but took the verbal slap without complaint, because I deserved it.

"I figured you'd be more inclined to negotiate with me if you thought I was a werewolf." I made fists then stretched my fingers, trying to get the blood moving again.

"You figured right. But then we kissed. Everything changed."

"Yeah, but you told me how much you hated vampires, so telling you what I was became harder the more I got to know you."

"So you chose to tell me after biting me? God. If I hadn't kicked you off, would you have killed me?"

I leaned forward, touched her arm. "No, honey. Never. I was… staking my Claim on you."

She frowned, but didn't shake off my hand. "What's that?"

"I bite you during sex. Right at the moment you—"

"I got it."

"No, I don't think you do. It's more than that. To stake my Claim means to make you mine." I clamped a sweaty hand on the back of my neck. "It's kind of a forever deal. But don't worry. You hadn't come when I bit you, so you're fine."

"Oh." She cleared her throat. "So that's what Ivy was talking about." Her tone had thawed somewhat. A little. Perhaps a smidgen.

Or once again, I was kidding myself.

I dropped my gaze.

There was blood on my T-shirt. My sire's blood. Filthy vampire blood. I bunched up the fabric and looked at her to make sure she hadn't seen the reminder of what I was.

She lifted her head and swallowed. "So you bit me on purpose? It wasn't an accident?"

My grip on the fabric tightened. "Yes and no. I didn't plan it. It just happened."

"You're not hearing me. *Why* did it happen?"

My last secret. Once it was out, it could not be unspoken.

I took a long breath. "Because I love you."

Her expression didn't change.

Had I said the L word out loud or thought it? Perhaps I had mumbled.

"I love you." I checked her face for a flicker.

She wasn't even blinking.

"Keely?"

"Sorry. I wasn't listening. What did you say?"

I scowled. "I love you. What the hell is wrong with you?"

Her lips twitched, then a smile broke out on her face, bathing the whole room in its glow.

"You were playing with me?"

Smile firmly planted on her mouth, she took my hand. "No. Maybe a little. I wanted to hear it, Florian. For someone who talks so much, you say surprisingly little when it matters most."

"I'm shallow."

"No. You're not." She pulled my hand toward her face.

I scooted closer, so I wouldn't lose the connection.

"This is crazy. I thought you…" Her lids fell shut for a second. "But you didn't try to kill me."

"Of course not." I glared.

"Got it. In my world, that's usually why vampires bite you. To drink from you, or to kill you."

"Never."

"Okay. Wow." She shook her head, chuckling. "Blimey. You're full of surprises."

I squinted. "Does that mean… Does that mean we're good?"

She nodded and caressed my palm with her fingers. "Yes, we're good. But no more secrets. Deal?"

She wasn't the first alpha to tell me that. But this time, I was listening.

I opened my mouth, which she blocked with her free hand.

"Think about it first. This is important. If we want to make this work, you have to mean it."

I kissed her fingers. "Deal. No secrets. Not in front of you. Let me prove it to you."

"You don't have to prove yourself."

That would be a first. But then, this was the time for firsts.

She shifted her feet to the side and got onto her knees. The tightness under her eyes had gone, only the dark shadow from Gino's or Furtek's fist remained.

I placed my hand on the small of her back, as far as I dared go for now. "If you change your mind, I have a whole library of embarrassments to share."

She pulled herself onto my lap, her hands around my neck. "I'll keep that in mind."

"Okay."

I may have said something else, but she twirled my hair between her fingers, leaned in, and my thoughts, at least the coherent ones, went elsewhere.

"I'm going to kiss you now." She shifted closer against my cock, which strained toward her.

"Okay."

She pressed her lips onto mine. The heat from her mouth swirled into my chest, setting my heart on a fast trot. Those tiny shifts on my lap teased my dick more than her weight.

With my left hand prodded behind me, I sneaked my right under her top to trace the line of her spine.

Keely shuddered and laughed—a sound I greedily swallowed.

She flexed her thighs and pushed me onto the bed without relinquishing the contact with my erection or mouth.

I dug my fingers into her ass for a closer connection then slid her top up and over her head.

She didn't give me time to revel in her shape, because she resumed our kiss, her tongue more possessive than ever.

I unhooked her bra and slipped the straps down her arms before slinging the bra onto the ground. My free rein over her satin skin drove me close to insanity, yet I needed more. I hungered to feel her nakedness against mine, under me. Every time I was about to take charge, I got sidetracked by her roaming fingers.

But I couldn't stop her. If I tied her up and lost control, I'd only try to stake my Claim again. It was too early. I knew that now.

She ran her hands up my abs, to my chest, tracking the valleys and peaks like they spelled out a secret code word.

They did… Her name.

My body vibrated for her, the receptors in my hands scanned every inch of her skin. Nothing in life had prepared me for such helpless lust and passion for one woman.

Control be damned.

I gripped her legs and flipped her over.

She laughed and whisked the T-shirt off my back. The next minute, she made short work of my zipper.

I let her push my jeans and underwear past my ass. My cock was pumped enough to nearly touch my stomach, and I ripped on her pants to give my erection a nesting place.

There was nothing romantic about the way we tore on each other's clothes. Every inch won, we celebrated with a harder kiss until freedom fused our naked bodies.

Keely slapped along the bed to her nightstand. "I know I had another pair of handcuffs."

"They're by your suitcase." My lungs pumped like a piston from anticipation rather than exertion, but I wouldn't get the restraints. Couldn't get them.

"Don't you want them?" Keely's breathless voice sent shivers through my cock.

"I don't think that's a good idea given what happened the last time." I brushed away the hairs stuck to her forehead. "My control is jittery as it is."

"What's the worst that can happen?"

I kissed her. "I'd fang out and stake my Claim on you. And I'm not sure if you could fight me off this time."

"Suppose I don't want to fight you off?" Her eyes twinkled, although her tone was anything but light.

I ran my hand along the line of her waist and side, up to the swell of her breast, before cupping her cheek.

"We've only known each other a few days, and staking my Claim is a forever deal. Once the chemicals are released and the magic invoked, we'll be emotionally bonded. It's like having an eternal crush on each other." I tapped my temple to her shoulder and groaned. "And I don't have the power to stop myself. You already make my heart beat when it shouldn't."

I took her hand and held it against my chest, against the steady rhythm of my love for her.

"I can feel it." She smiled.

"You're making it do that." I put weight into my tone. "I have no choice in the way I feel, but you do. Don't rush into anything."

Say you choose me. Say it.

"I see." She lowered her arm.

I suppressed another groan. Not an outright rejection. I would be patient.

"Then I'm yours. Forever." She kissed me deep and long, holding my head still with her hands.

She parted us and ran her thumb over my moist lips. "Now, the cuffs?"

"Sure." I darted off the bed and got the cuffs, tightened them around her wrists, and slapped what I could of her ass.

Just to set the tone.

She laughed as I sprawled out on top of her, breathing in her scent. In my arms, she wasn't a kickass alpha. I had my private Keely, a Keely no one else saw.

Without the distractions from her hands, I focused on every cell of her skin. I nuzzled her neck, blew onto her collarbone, rolled her nipple with my tongue and fingers. The heat and wetness between her legs wrapped around my dick, which teased her slit.

Her breaths became shorter and louder than mine.

My need for her grew, coiling in my stomach, feeding pressure to my balls. I plunged into her without warning.

She lifted her head off the pillow and gave a moan from deep within her core. Even though I wanted to play with her, leave her waiting, I was running out of time. My body had its own agenda, and I was overcome by the urge to bury myself in her hot channel, up to my balls.

She widened her legs, yet tightened her walls around my shaft as if drinking me in. Each stroke got me closer to completion, but she wasn't shouting my name yet.

I kissed her, her teeth pressing against mine each time I went in. The world swirled before my eyes while my dick just about burst with need.

Keely was my everything. And she was about to let me prove it.

"Florian?" She yipped.

I growled. "What?"

"I love you."

Three words to describe my future. My dreams. Spoken at the right time.

A lightness rushed through my head. There would never be a *wrong* time.

I pushed back in, now groaning with her. "Say that again."

"I love you."

"Good."

"I—Oh God."

The road to her climax had begun. My senses heightened as if in the throes of a feeding. Her breathing, her moans, the feel of her skin—I wasn't going to miss a thing.

I wrapped her legs tight around my waist for a better angle, and plowed back in.

"Yes."

Smooth strokes down and up soon gave way to a frantic rocking. Her heat held tight, the smooth friction winding up the time bomb in my cock.

"Oh God. Florian." Her lids were down, her cheeks flushed.

Her tightness was killing me. Absolutely killing me. If she was going to change her mind about us, she'd better do it now.

I moved from my legs, swinging my ass hard enough to strike her end with my tip. "Are you okay?"

"Yes." She half chuckled, half gasped. "Christ. Yes."

I flexed my muscles, took my cues from her noises. Everything had to be perfect for her.

I changed the angle again and pumped, ready for my release. Just a few more seconds.

"Oh God. Yes." Her eyes rolled as if in REM sleep, her lips plump as they shouted my name. "Florian. Oh God. Florian."

Christ.

"Let me hear you, baby." I lifted up onto my arms to enter her deeper. "Come on, baby."

My body was alive, the sole purpose of each cell and muscle to make her come.

"Yes. Oh God."

Her words washed through me, priming my instincts. My fangs popped out, and I locked my gaze onto her throbbing pulse.

"Yes. Yes. Oh God. Florian. Yes. Y—"

My canines pierced her moist skin, and I let her blood flow into my mouth. She wriggled, but my hold on her neck was tight.

"Oh God. Yes." Her hesitant voice firmed.

She was so snug around my dick, her blood sweeter than any human's.

"Yes." Her mouth was so close to my ear. "Yes. Yes. Yesss."

She seized, and her red nectar flowed clear and unhindered. The magic seeped into my cells, feeding not my blood lust, but a different kind of hunger.

She was finally mine.

Sparks went off inside me, my balls tight. A pressure surged from my brain through my body, ready to squeeze my cum into her. The magic of our union unspooled. Our beings became one.

My release hit me like a jumbo jet, and I grunted.

My fibers reached out, my skin melted with hers. Never again would she look at anyone the way she looked at me. Never would she speak anyone's name with the reverence she held for mine.

The flood of bliss ebbed, and I opened my jaw, licked her wound shut, and fell on top of her.

The moment I made her mine had passed in seconds, but it had forever changed us. Keely's body felt more substantial, her skin softer and richer, her natural scent more enveloping than perfume.

Her chest's up and down slowed. "That was… Wow."

I chuckled. "I couldn't have said it better."

"You're mine now."

I lifted my face, still light-headed. "Ditto."

"Wow."

I rolled to the side and caressed her curves, making her shudder. "Did it hurt?"

"When you drank from me? It really, really didn't. It was…wow."

"Sex turns you into quite the wordsmith." I fake-bit her shoulder. "So. We should do that again someday?"

"Definitely. And, you know, the other thing too." She yanked on her cuffs.

I raised my eyebrows. "The other… Oh, the spanking?"

Could I be so lucky?

"Yes, that." She laughed.

I grinned. "Count on it."

We lay in silence for a few minutes.

"What do I taste like?" she asked.

"Iron and cherries. Sweet, slightly tart. It's difficult to describe." I placed my palm over her heart.

Yeah, okay. Who was I kidding? I placed it on her right breast. Then I squeezed.

"Stop that." She twisted away, but with the restraints holding her tight, all she did was make her tits jiggle.

"Why? If you're mine, then so are your breasts. I'm really only touching myself."

"I don't think that's how this works. Besides…" She arched her back and gave a big yawn.

I shook my head. "I'm an idiot. Are you tired?"

"After the night and morning we had?" Keely moved her face to look at me. "Yes, I'm knackered. Aren't you?"

"I don't need a lot of sleep."

She tore at the cuffs. "I'm not going to nod off like this."

I smirked. "And what are you going to do about it?"

"Please?"

"Good girl." I unlatched her restraints to free her arms and tucked her against me.

"So. Forever. Eh?" She rotated her wrists and then kissed my chest.

I placed my chin on top of her head and moved the rest of my body so close to hers, no one could tell us apart. "Forever."

She let out a long sigh. "Having children is overrated anyway."

"What are you talking about?" I frowned.

"Vampires are infertile, right?"

Wow. That question made me feel all manly.

I inched back my head and studied her. "You don't want kids?"

"Of course I want kids." Her expression softened, and she rolled a strand of my short hair between her fingers. "But I don't want them as much as I want you."

"In that case, I feel I should tell you that my swimmers are just fine." I kissed her. "Me infertile. As if."

"Oh. I didn't know." She rubbed her cheek against my skin. "Me not wanting kids. As if." She mocked my tone and somehow nailed it. "That's why female werewolves don't use condoms or take the pill."

I swallowed. No condoms. No contraception. I knew that, of course, but the reality just hit home. Females didn't conceive easily, but having sex with Keely may have brought us closer to a baby. *A baby.* Christ. That happened fast.

Bearing in mind I had just staked my Claim on her, second thoughts were a little late though. *Deep breath.*

"We'll work it out." Her tone was even, gentle, and so feminine. "If I get pregnant, I get pregnant. And there's always adoption."

"Adoption. Sure. Yeah." I unlocked my tight neck and forced my lips into a smile. "No hurry, though. We have forever, after all. Right?"

She laughed, her eyes becoming little slits. "Wow. That panic in your voice is priceless."

"Not panic." I coughed. "Let's say, I'm not ready to share you yet."

"Yeah, okay." Her laughter died down, but a smile remained.

"In fairness, I don't know if we'll have children." I combed my fingers through her hair. "Our sperm works with humans, but no vampire has ever mated with a...furball."

"Or a werewolf with a bloodsucker."

We both grinned. Keely and I were literally on the cusp of changing the future of werewolf-vampire relations.

She cuddled up close, pressing her nose against my collarbone.

I stroked her back, followed her breaths as they went from active to slow and steady. Thanks to her, and perhaps the oil burner, I carried sufficient heat to keep her warm.

As before, my heart beat strong. Even when the breakfast calls started up and day was in full swing, my pulse kept going.

Finally I closed my eyes but kept my hold on Keely strong, even in my dreams.

CHAPTER TWENTY-EIGHT

"K EELY." A VOICE YANKED ME out of the sweetest dream. I opened my eyes. *Thank God.* Keely was still in my arms.

"Keely." Sabine thudded against the tent flap.

"Yeah?" Keely hadn't gotten her awake voice yet, but was loud enough for her female to hear.

"Rollo is here. He's telling us to pack up. It's moving time."

I sat up.

"Hey." She pushed her bottom lip out. "No one said *you* could move."

"We're in bed. My rules, remember?" I leaned back down to kiss her.

Her arms slung around my neck to deepen our connection.

"Keely?" The voice shouted. "Did you hear me?"

"I'm coming already." She sounded pressed, mainly because we were still mid-kiss.

I shrugged. "Guess our honeymoon will have to wait."

She sat, lifting her blanket to her neck. "Our what?"

We really needed to talk about her nakedness, and my absolutely being in favor of it, at some point.

"Our honeymoon. In human terms, we did get married." I reached over the edge of the bed to collect our clothes.

More by touch than by sight, I found a top that was definitely hers. I threw it over my shoulder and dived back in to eventually come upon my jeans.

"Oh. Okay."

I grinned. "Oh honey. Was that a hint of panic I detected?"

"No panic." She sniffed. "Don't I get a party?"

"Do you want a party?"

"Yeah."

Of course she did. She was a werewolf. "I'll see what I can do."

We got dressed in record time. This honeymoon definitely sucked.

Keely headed to the exit, but I grabbed her hands and kissed her one more time. A languid kiss as a promise that I'd do my best to make her happy.

She slid her hand over my ass, then slapped it.

I released her lips. "Careful."

"Are you ready?" She caressed my mouth with her thumb.

Her touch latched on to the nerve endings spanning my body, giving me that drive-over-a-hump feel deep in my stomach.

I smiled. "Are you?"

"We'll cope." She dragged herself out of my arms and smoothed her blue top, which had somehow got tangled up.

The next few hours were manic. I added my muscle to that of Malachi and Rollo, and together, we lugged suitcases of clothes and furniture to van after van.

Keely didn't leave my sight.

The commotion seemed like a dream. While my head buzzed and my heart thumped, the rest of the world kept turning. As if only I understood the depth of the change it had undergone.

Keely and I stole secret glances, so our happiness was, for the moment, just ours.

The females escorted their pregnant friends to their rides. Somewhere around that time, I got separated from Keely.

I glanced around, spun on my heels, but couldn't see her.

"She's gone ahead." Ivy munched on a chocolate bar.

"Who?"

She rolled her eyes. "Keely. The object of your obsession."

"You should be nice to me, if you don't want me to tell Parker you're not sticking to the carrots."

She pushed out her bottom lip. "Now you're being mean."

We hooked our arms together and marched to the road to catch the next transit ride.

I nudged her. "You don't mind offering your estate to Keely's pack?"

"Nah. It's meant to be lived in. Not used as a bachelor pad when it suits Parker." She tucked the empty chocolate wrapper in my jeans pocket.

"Yeah." I pushed it in all the way.

If Parker knew how many candy wrappers and other evidence of secret snacking my clothes held, he'd hit the roof. He was all for fattening her up, especially because she'd lost weight since her mom's funeral, but he wanted to do it the healthy way.

Poor deluded Parker.

"What's wrong?" Ivy peered up at me in that oddly penetrating way of hers.

"Nothing. Just wondering where I'm going to live. Has anyone seen Julia?"

"No, she hasn't been back home. When's Eli back?"

We got in one of the vans that were parked near the path like cabs at an airport. Nathan, a timid and quiet wolf who lived in another of Parker's estates, nodded at us from behind the steering wheel.

"No clue. Maybe another week." I pulled the sliding door shut. "I don't think he'll like living with me."

The van drove off.

Ivy sighed. "If you don't want to move back into your old room, you could use my house. It's small, but close enough to the pack so you're not alone, and gives you privacy if Keely comes over. At least until you make an honest woman of her. Will you and her do the intention ritual?"

I coughed. "That won't be necessary."

She stared at me then slapped my arm. "You fox. You did it? You claimed your stake?"

I smirked. "I staked my Claim, yes."

"So you're what, married?"

"In a manner of speaking, yes."

She fell back against the seat. "Wow."

"Well said."

She swiveled her head to face me. "That's a vampire thing. You know you'll have to do a werewolf bonding ritual. And that's a doozy. The party takes almost a week."

"So I get to have another voice in my head?" I grimaced.

"Keely's voice."

"Oh yeah." I smiled. "I guess I can live with that. Have you and Parker talked about it?"

"Talked, yes. And Ali has kind of mapped out the whole event, I think, but we're not there yet."

I twisted my torso toward her. "Why? Do you have doubts?"

"Nothing like that. Emotionally we're there. But my Guardian training is hanging over me. Then there's The Circle. I might not get the human wedding I've always dreamed of, but my bonding ceremony should be perfect."

"It will be, even if the world outside isn't." I gave her arm a comforting squeeze.

"Hmm."

The van lurched to a stop, and we leaped outside. I thanked Nathan with a tap on the roof of the car, and he drove off to pick up more stuff. We stepped through the open door into the large house, and past the manic bustle of female and male werewolves.

"Watch out." Parker yanked me back.

In front of me, two small wolf cubs rested in the middle of the entrance to a side room.

I nodded my gratitude. "That's a great place for them to take a nap. Very Feng Shui."

Parker pulled Ivy into a tight embrace and kissed her hair. "Every time their mothers try to get them to move, they throw a tantrum. Way too much excitement going on for them to miss."

"So you have been selected to watch over them?"

"I've selected myself. It's a perk of the job."

"So does that make you lazy, or a softie?" I took a step back, in case he threw a punch in my direction.

"Both." Ivy said.

"Hush." Parker beamed. "And I hear you have news for us too?"

I frowned. "Do I?"

"Keely? Or have you already forgotten about this Claim thing you did?"

The werewolf grapevine had done its magic again.

My frown turned into a grin. "None of the things Keely and I did were forgettable. Songs will be written and movies made. Trust me."

Parker laughed.

"You're a pig," Ivy said.

"Quiet." Parker clamped his hand in front of her mouth. "Does that mean you're moving in with her right away, or will you be staying in your old room until the bonding ceremony?"

Ivy chomped gently on Parker's finger and used his pain to shake off his touch. "Ha. Bonding ceremony. I told you."

Why did that prospect leave me with an uncomfortable pressure?

"Things are still moving awfully fast." I stared at him. "Awfully fast."

He'd get the sudden panic. He was a guy.

"You were the one who couldn't keep it in your pants buddy, or rather in your mouth." He slapped my shoulder.

So much for sympathy.

"I should talk to Keely about that." I scratched my brow.

Parker's laugh startled the cubs into cuddling up closer together. "Whipped already. Before that, you must undergo the same ritual as Keely to officially join the pack. She's an alpha and should get bonded to a male from a pack in good standing."

My chest filled with gushiness, and I cleared my throat. "Umm, sure."

"Well, go on. She's out by the lake." He waved his hand toward the outside.

I rushed off, but not fast enough to miss the kissing sounds he and Ivy made behind my back. Damn my superhuman hearing.

I stepped onto the terrace.

Ali and Rollo walked past me, locked in conversation.

"Congratulations," Ali said.

I smiled at him. His face had lost the sadness I'd caused.

"Yeah. What he said." Rollo pointed his thumb at Ali.

"So you heard." I crossed my arms.

"Heard?" Ali waved me off. "We've scheduled your party for next weekend."

"Aren't we already having one today?"

"Yes, for the ritual." He gave me his version of a *duh* face, which came across professor-like. "Keely said you promised her one for your vampire Claim thing."

Claim thing was probably going to stick.

I gave a loud sigh. "One thing at a time."

"And we'll do your bonding ritual in three weeks. It's already scheduled." Ali's tone turned serious. "You'll have to be more cautious about being a smart mouth around the pack without my protection, you know."

"I'm always cautious about being a smart mouth." I faked a solemn expression. "You can't be a smart mouth on the fly. It takes preparation."

"Don't worry," Rollo said. "Now he'll have Keely's protection."

I raised my eyebrows. "Since when do I need anyone's protection?"

Rollo and Ali walked past me on either side, and both gave my shoulders a hard slap.

"Of course you do." Rollo chuckled. "You're hitched. You need all the protection you can get."

I stared after them. Way to ruin my happy day.

"Hey." Keely marched up toward me.

"Hey."

Her eyes widened, and her smiling lips parted for my kiss.

I made it long and passionate.

She clung to me as if I were her anchor, when in fact, she was mine. If the guys' banter had brought doubts, her touch blew them away.

A child's giggle separated us.

The little boy who'd cried yesterday after we raised the guard wall held his fist against his cheek. The tip of his index finger disappeared into his mouth.

"What's so funny, Joey?" Keely bent down.

"What'cha doing?" Joey asked.

Keely looked at me. "Help?"

I grinned. "We're canoodling."

Joey turned around and waddled in his mother's direction.

"Keely's noodling." His laughter was a sound so bright, it could heal diseases.

"How about we noodle some more?" I pulled Keely back up.

She grinned. "Are you upset they know about the Claim thing? They guessed part of it, and wheedled the rest out of me."

"Ah, the origin of the term *Claim thing* is finally revealed." I gathered her tight. "No, I'm not upset."

She freed herself and placed her hand in mine. We walked across the lawn, past a couple of long tables already half stacked with dishes and silverware in preparation for the festivities.

The lake before us glistened like the fur of a werewolf in the sun. The breeze carried the scent of fresh air, and I inhaled thoroughly. Gino had been wrong. The atmosphere in Oldworld wasn't as rotten as he claimed.

I slid his stone from my pocket and rolled it over in my hands.

"What's that?" Keely asked, her head pressed against my shoulder.

"Gino gave it to me. A family heirloom, passed down from generation to generation." I flipped it in the air and caught it. "It's meant to bring luck."

"Does it work?" Her blue eyes narrowed a fraction.

The magic inside tickled my palm. I shoved the memento back in my pocket and brushed my finger across her velvety cheek.

My days of sleeping with random beauties were over. My sire was dead. My sister pissed as all hell at me.

I kissed Keely with all the tenderness I possessed.

She responded to my tongue's demands with abandon, gave herself to me, as if I was her whole world.

We parted, and the noise and bustle from two hyped-up packs flooded back into my awareness.

"Yeah, it works." I smiled. "I'm the luckiest guy in the world."

Not a lie.

"I never said I'm sorry." Keely leaned back to look at me, her palms flat against my shoulders. "About your sire, you know, and about losing your family."

"I didn't lose anything worth keeping. As for my family." I cupped her face and swiveled it toward the activity behind us. "They're right here."

She placed my hand on her chest. "And here."

I gathered her tight, body against body, to share my heartbeat with her. "Damn right."

THE END

BOOKS BY CARMEN FOX

DIVIDE AND CONQUER – Champions of Elonia, Bk. 1
Urban Fantasy

Two women. One prophecy. Zero places to hide.

Flung from her mundane Seattle existence into a world of magic, scientist Lea struggles to make sense of a destiny she doesn't want. The moment she finds comfort in the arms of a man who appreciates her inner nerd, a new magic sweeps the realms.

Nieve, Lea's instructor, may be seasoned in the art of war, but she's clueless when it comes to romance. To save her world, she allies herself with her enemy, a kindred warrior soul, who leaves no doubt he's after more than her cooperation.

As each tick of the clock swallows another person's memory, Lea and Nieve will do anything to hang on to theirs, but betrayal drives a wedge in their friendship. Can they reconcile and rally the troops before the magic wipes out their pasts?

GUARDED – The Silverton Chronicles, Bk. 1
Sexy Urban Fantasy Mystery

When everyone's existence depends on the lies they tell, trust doesn't come easy.

Ivy's neighbors have a secret. They aren't human. But Ivy has a secret, too. She knows. As long as everyone keeps quiet, she's happy working as a P.I. by day and chillaxing with her BFF Florian, a vampire, by night. When a routine pickup drops her in the middle of a murder, her two worlds collide. While Florian knows how to throw a punch, deep down he's a softie. His idea of scary? Running out of hair product. It's time Ivy faced facts. Even with a vampire on stand-by, one gal can only kick so many asses.

Torn between these men, Ivy must tread carefully, because one wants her heart, one wants her body, and one wants her dead.

SHOW DON'T TELL – Immersive
Writing From The Roots Up
Writing Guide

3D Writing At Your Fingertips

Showing and telling are among the most powerful skills an author can acquire, yet incomplete and misleading information has caused much confusion. No more. Using easy-to-understand examples, this short guide demonstrates how to compel and immerse readers in 3D writing, without clogging scenes with unnecessary description.

Aimed at new and intermediate authors, 'Show Don't Tell – Immersive Writing From The Roots Up' will set you on your own path to excellence.

For help, she must put her faith in others. A human, who might just be the one. A demon, who will, for a price, open the doors to her heritage. And a werewolf, who wants to protect her from herself.

ALSO PUBLISHED BY SMART HEART PUBLISHING

THE MEDIATOR – Cupid Dating Agency
by Candace Laville
Erotic Paranormal Romance, Ménage Novella

That Kerry's birthday falls on the most romantic day of the year sucks. That she's set up on a date with both an angel and a demon sucks worse. But she's about to discover that being trapped between good and evil makes for one hell of a good time.

Mike and Cal, angel and demon, are reluctant business partners. To help them get along, Cupid sends a mediator called Kerry, but rather than working on a truce, the guys are soon locked in a different battle, this time over Kerry's smoking curves.

Novella length: ca. 22,500 words (Reading time: < 2h)
Explicit sex scenes, DP and strong language.

ACKNOWLEDGEMENTS

Bound was quite the undertaking. My goal was to make it as enjoyable a read as possible, and many people helped make this happen.

Let's start with the writing. Julie LaVoie, author of The Glass Ceiling, was my first port of call, as always. Without her, I might never get anything written.

When two of my characters needed names, I asked two lovely ladies to help me out. They did. Michelle Slagan provided Gino's name, and even a picture. I might not have done his yumminess any justice, but believe me, that girl has taste. Shari Chisholm gave me the name Draylac, which I loved instantly. It's ominous and just a little weird. Well done, you two!

Once the book was written, it entered the first of three content edits, carried out by Dylan Quinn. Part of me hates her. Seriously. She pulled no punches, called me out when I could have done better, but always, *always*, gave sound advice. With her support, I pinned down Flo's character and his relationships with friends and family. She's done awesome work, and should any of my readers write a book of their own, she's the torturer, I mean *editor*, to hire.

Then came the beta reading stage. Julie LaVoie made the leap from the relative comfort of YA into the sordid world of urban fantasy and added much needed common sense. Celia Breslin, author of the Tranquilli Series and contributing author to the Black Hills Wolves series, offered suggestions and improvements that made all the difference. You two rock!

Next, we enter the book cover stage. Ana Grigoriu once again knocked the ball out of the park. I love Bound's cover and want to hang it on my wall, put it on magnets, on book marks... Oh, hang on. I did. Thank you, Ana.

Let's turn our attention to copy editing and line editing. First Dylan had a go. How she wasn't sick of me by then I will never know. Then Monique Fischer received a relatively clean manuscript, and in addition to offering wisdom and proofreading, she caught two major problems in the manuscript. Not difficult to remedy, but a crucial spot nevertheless.

Think this is it? Far from it.

Proofreading. After I gave the manuscript another thorough once-over, I handed it to Sharon Gibson, who used eagle eyes and patience to polish it.

Next, my book went to a small number of early readers for a reader's perspective. Mary Blackhurst Hill answered my call with incredibly helpful suggestions. Thank you!

After some last minute panic and changes, the finished text was sent to the print formatters Streetlight Graphics, who also did excellent work on Guarded.

Smart Heart Publishing did the rest.

To all of you, my heartfelt thanks.

I also want to thank my family, and especially my mother for her unwavering support.

ABOUT THE AUTHOR

Carmen lives in the south of England with her beloved tea maker and a stuffed sheep called Fergus. An avid reader since childhood, she caught the writing bug when her Nana asked her to write a story. She also has a law degree, studied physics for a few years, dabbled in marketing and human resources, and speaks native-level German and fluent Geek. Her preferred niches of geekdom are tabletop games, comics, sci-fi and fantasy.

She writes about smart women with sassitude, about pretty cool guys too, and will chase that plot twist, no matter how elusive.

For two months, **Guarded** (The Silverton Chronicles – Bk. 1) was an Amazon no. 1 bestseller in the vampire and werewolf mystery categories.